Gods of Phenóx
The March on Phenóx

Book II The Gods Saga

A NOVEL
BY

Orlando Smart-Powell

CHAPTER 1

Jared opened his eyes. His head felt as though it was about to burst. That was the first sign that he knew something was horribly wrong. Since transforming from mortal to celestial almost five years ago, he had never been harmed, not even when he nicked a corner of a building he was flying past and knocked a chunk of stone out of it; such was the sturdiness of his angelic skin and bones. But something had rung his bell, and hard enough to knock him out.

He was on his back; his legs were askew. His bones ached from head to feet, and the muscles around them quivered with weakness. But feeling pain, or any discomfort for that matter was the problem, he reasoned, simply because, his celestial body was supposed to be immune to injury. He knew now—achingly so—that it wasn't true. Some power greater than his own had bested him; though try as he might, he could not remember what or *who* had done it.

He raised his head. His eyes slowly converged the double vision he was seeing back to a single one. Though still, all that he saw was covered in a haze of black smoke, some of which was coming from the flames on his skin and clothes. With quick slaps of his palms against his pants and t-shirt, he put out the flames.

He looked around. A circular wall of smoldering rock and rubble, much of it still on fire and glowing red-hot surrounded him. The air was thick with black smoke and steam. Looking up—peering through the black haze—he saw glimmers of a pale blue sky. He pushed down with his hands and raised his torso up; his palms and fingers sizzled as they touched the searing, hot ground. Still, all he could see was rock and fire and smoke, and an occasional hint of blue.

He swung his legs around and stood, and then looked down. He was at least two feet below the rim, he saw, realizing it was actually a crater he was in. Down where he had been on his back, the dirt, rock, and rubble had been fused into glass, leaving a mold of his body in the middle of it. Seeing the image of himself in glowing glass, he understood why parts of his memory were gone. He understood the *why* he didn't remember, though now it was figuring out the *how*—how he'd come to this place.

He turned around. In front of him, there was a pair of white, bare feet at the edge of the crater. He looked up into the face they belonged to; it was a woman's. She was wearing a brown sleeveless dress that seemed made from the cloth of a potato sack. It was frayed at the edges, even at the snug neckline, but it matched her well, for she, like the square cut dress, seemed but a pull away from coming undone. Her eyes were sunken and surrounded by swollen, purple lids; she looked as though she had not slept for days, or even eaten for twice that long. Her matted, blond tresses moved in clumps as she bent over and looked down at him.

"What happened to me?" Jared said, peering at her through the smoke.

She looked up, and then down at him. "You fell," she replied simply, as though it were just a matter of fact.

His brow furrowed. "I fell from the sky?"

She nodded. "Where else?"

The problem is, lady, is that I fell at all. I fell?...from where? And who in the hell threw me?

He began gathering his lifeforce—that energy that swirled in his chest and fueled his angelic body, giving him inhuman strength, speed, and skin as dense as metal—but he found it wanting. He barely felt his lifeforce at all. There were only whispers left of his God-given force, which allowed him to manipulate matter, which in turn gave him the ability to become lighter than air and to fly.

Flying out of the crater was out of the question now. As far as leaping out of it, he didn't think he could make it halfway up. He resorted to crawling up the smoldering hole. He slipped down a few times, as his quivering arms and legs refused his every other command. He made it to the jagged, rocky rim and swung his legs up and over it. He lay on his stomach for a moment, and then stood on his feet and wobbled for a moment. He bent over and put his hands on his knees, and looked up at the woman.

"Hey Ms.," he called. "Say that again…about me falling."

"There was a big bang, she said. "And then we all looked up and saw you falling. You looked like a meteor. Ya'know…on fire." She shrugged. "But then we could hear you yelling. And then the next thing, *bam* into the ground. And now you're here."

Jared tried thinking back to the last thing he could remember. In his mind's eye, he saw his friends, Henrì and Olivia; he remembered being with them at their home out in the bayou. And then there was an image of his mother, Dorthea; she looked tired, as though she had just woken. Phineas, his father, came whisking past as his mother's picture faded away. Though try as he might, he couldn't recall any memories after those.

He stood up straight and caught sight of a forest over the woman's shoulder. From one side of the horizon to the other, it seemed to go on for miles. However, the trees seemed all wrong to him. They looked as though they rose hundreds of feet in the air, soaring far higher than the sequoias and redwoods of California; and he was pretty certain that he was nowhere near California. "I might have slept through World Geography like everyone else," he said, and pointed over her shoulder to the forest, "but I know there's no way I could have missed that. That can't exist."

"Here it does," she said. "They say it's been that way for thousands of years. Probably even more than that."

"Thousands?"

"Ten? I don't know…fifty? You guess," she said. "It's not as though they tell us. Not like we need to know. We mean only one thing to them."

"You mean what to who?"

She walked over to the edge of the stone road; she beckoned him with a finger over her shoulder. Before him, a field of green rolling hills stretched out as far as his celestial eyes could see; they ended only where the monstrous forest began. He turned and looked across the other side of the stone road; it was the same…hills, hills, more hills, and then forest. He turned around. The woman had knelt and was plucking white flowers that had grown along the edge of the road. She stood up and presented them to him like a mini bouquet.

"Here," she said.

He took them. As the flowers passed from her hand to his, they began to change; their delicate white beauty grew dark. Half of a moment later, they turned to ash…black and grey, like the smoked end of a cigarette. No longer able to support their own weight, the ash-flowers fell apart and dusted his hand with their remains. He wiped the ash off on the side of his burnt jeans.

"Now look here," she said, pointing to the spot where she had plucked them.

He looked and saw the plant renewing itself; green stems were growing from where they had been torn away. The tips of the stems then grew buds. The buds swelled and bloomed tiny white flowers.

"What is this place?" he asked, looking about the field and spotting more of the white flowers scattered amongst an array of different varieties—red ones, blue ones, purple ones, orange ones, and more. Some were pastel; others were dark and rich. "Who are you?"

"I'm just Ellen," she said. She gathered the neckline of her dress into a ball, as though she were suddenly bashful. "This entire place is Orsha-Na —the Northlands."

"Orsha-Na," he whispered, trying to recall that name and coming up empty. Instead, the past that had been shadowed suddenly began to show in the light. He remembered flying with his father, Phineas, cradled in his arms like a child; they were going to meet someone. There was water below them—lots of it. And they had flown for hours, or at least that is how he was remembering it. But from there on, there was no more to be glimpsed.

"This whole realm is Orsha-Na," she said. "We're in Verancia, a province of it. It belongs to the lady of the forest. But the other way," she faced the other end of the road, "leads to Hedun, the capital, where the duke lives. He and the lady are mates."

"None of this is making sense."

"Exactly," she said, bobbing her head and widening her eyes. "This all looks so beautiful, doesn't it? But it's all a lie. The rocks we're standing on. The grass. The trees." She looked back at the forest and lingered there for a moment. She pointed up and behind Jared. "You tell me if that makes any sense."

Jared looked up at the light in the sky. He knew immediately that it wasn't the sun; it was far too close to the ground—miles close instead of millions of miles away. Though the orb gave off white light like the sun, it was not blinding. Protruding from its coronal edge, he counted six arms; each limb moved in an opposite, undulating wave of the one next to it. Inside the orb he saw a figure...a body...a nude one. It was curled up in a ball with its knees pulled to its chest. Its baldhead rested on its knees and was turned their way, as though watching them.

"That's Wormwood, the sun demon," Ellen remarked.

Jared gawked. "Demon?"

She cocked her head. "What else would it be?"

Anything but a demon, he thought. And as he pondered why there would be a demon in the sky, and why what was so beautiful—those flowers—once plucked, would turn to ash and then regenerate, more of the past that he had forgotten began to come back.

He and Phineas were going to do battle, not just to meet someone. *That's it! Yikan was there,* he remembered. *He brought others with him. We fought. And I killed someone.*

He tried to recall the man who had come with Yikan and caught glimpses of his face. He was middle aged. His hairline was receding; but that man was not the one he had killed; it was a woman. But the man was a killer; Yikan had bragged about that. He was a protected one of evil, just like his father, Phineas, was of light. Whereas a celestial protected Phineas, a demon guarded the man. As the past again went dark, he heard sounds coming from down the road that Ellen had said led to the capital.

"You're not a demon," she remarked, peering at him. "I told the others you weren't one, but they ran off anyway. I told them that demons don't fall out of the sky, because there's really nothing up there to fall from. It's all just an illusion, like everything else in this place. The only thing real here is pain."

The sound in the distance was growing louder—closer; he could now make out that it was the sound of hooves. There were one…two…there were three patterns of hooves striking stone that his keen, celestial hearing picked up on. Ellen was oblivious to it. But his expression and silence, he guessed, must have clued her in that something was amiss, for she tilted her head at him and gave him a quizzical look.

"What is it?" she asked softly, nearly whispering it, as though prying ears were suddenly about.

"Someone is coming," said Jared, "a few of them." He looked down the flat road, though could see nothing yet, but now heard the horse's huffing layered atop of their frantic galloping.

Ellen's face went pale as her lips parted and hung open. "They're sup-posed to ring the bell. They always ring the bell before they come for us. It puts more fear in our bones, and that gives them more power. But they're coming…and they didn't ring it. Wait a minute." She wrapped her arms across her chest and began backing away. "They're not coming for me. They're coming for *you!* I should've ran with the others."

"Me?" Jared blurted. What wisps of lifeforce that still swirled in his chest seemed to stop in mid-motion. "Ellen wait!" She was walking backwards, and had already crossed from the road over into the grass. "Who's coming? Where…what is this place?"

She stopped and looked down the road leading to the capital, and then turned back to him; her expression was of pity. "This is Hell—haven't you got that yet?"

"Hell?"

Her empathy was short lived. She smirked. "I know. Unlucky, huh?" she said, with a slow bob of her head. "But I'm here only because I've been falsely accused. They'll get it sorted out, I'm sure. Maybe some day, or month, or year, I'll get out of here and away from these creatures. But with Wormwood going back and forth, and that's all he does—he goes east and then west—, there's no telling how many days really pass by. But you…" she shook her head; her expression was grim, "I don't know how you got here. You're not a soul like the rest of us. And you're not a demon, but you look like they do…your skin and sparkly eyes," she pointed at him, "they give you away, because they look too perfect to be real." She continued walking backwards. "Whatever you are, they want you, and they're coming for you."

Jared was slack-jawed. He couldn't feel his lifeforce. In fact, at the moment, he couldn't feel anything at all. He simply felt hollow. "I'm in Hell?"

"You're in the realm of demons," she said. "And if they catch you, they're going to tear you apart. They feed on suffering so they can make more of this." She looked down at the thick grass and flowers at her feet. "You better run before they get here." She took her own advice and did just that; she turned and ran, and disappeared from sight as she descended a hill.

What had not made sense to Jared suddenly did. Ellen's mention of Hell pulled away that last veil of darkness that shrouded his memory. He and Phineas had gone to confront the immortal, Yikan, and to retrieve Lucifer's tome that was still in his possession. But Yikan also had his friend, Chris Knopfitter, whom he had taken prisoner after the battle in the Egyptian desert. And with his God-given powers—the might of an angel; a celestial of the heavens—he was going to rescue Chris and retrieve the tome, setting the world back into balance. However, something had gone wrong.

His thought back to the mortal Yikan had brought with him—that killer—the protected one of evil. The only thing was, the mortal had not remained mortal, but had changed. In the midst of the fight, the mortal had transformed from human to a….

Demon! Jared thought in a panic, as an image of long, black fingers reaching out for him suddenly passed by his mind's eye. *It grabbed me and tried to crush me. I pounded on it, but it wouldn't let go.*

He lifted his scorched t-shirt and looked down at his chest. Dark purple bruises marred his brown skin on both sets of ribs. Though on the left side there were four cuts; they were round in shape; and threads of new skin were already weaving across the holes, albeit very slowly. But then, he remembered, the demon began to leave and it still had a hold of him; it was transforming back into the mortal from whom it had sprung. It was returning to whence it had come and was taking him along with it.

The horses' snorts and pounding of their hooves grew louder and pulled him away from the past and back to the present. Ellen was gone and now he was alone. On either side of him, there was just grass-covered hills dotted with flowers, and not a single tree or shrub to hide behind or in. He turned to the forest and knew it was his only option. He knew he would be no match for whoever or whatever was coming for him, for he was weakened, drained of his lifeforce, and now virtually powerless in a realm where his adversaries were at their strongest.

Worse yet, he thought, was that he was trapped here and Yikan was still on the earth to do as he wished, which was, and had always been, to rule it as a god. Jared ran toward the forest as quick as his weary legs would move. He had to hide somewhere. He had to recover his strength.

I have to get out of this place. Dammit!—I should have listened to you, Henri. I really messed up this time. And I don't think I can fix it.

CHAPTER 2

"I'm not a celestial like you, obviously," Henrì said to Jared, "but that doesn't mean I don't know what I'm talking about."

"I hear you," Jared said. "I just don't agree."

They stared at one another for a moment. Henrì huffed, and then rose from his chair. He crossed in front of Jared and walked over to the bookcase; he turned around and leaned against it. Next to Henrì was a round table, and a lamp on it, which cast a dim light and created shadows on the floor and walls. It was near ten o'clock at night. There were many shadows in the room, though some Jared glimpsed were not true shadows and were moving about.

The shadows, as they were referred to, had lived in their life-after-death existence in the bayou mansion for more than a hundred years. Henrì's adopted mother, the witch—Aria, had brought them here with her magic; and he, as just a teen boy, was brought to her by Tamen, the Egyptian, who had rescued him from a life of abuse and degradation. Now, years later, other than the spirits lurking about, only Henrì and his wife, Olivia—they wed for just five years—occupied the old mansion set deep in the bayou away from prying eyes.

The columned, two story mansion had been renovated from top to bottom—inside and out. On the outside, six columns wrapped in ivy stood sentry. The lower and upper porch—open-slat railings across both —retained their old world, French design and southern charm, a combination of both, yet a contrast of each. But inside the mansion, over the course of their matrimonial five years, and under the meticulous orchestration of Olivia, Jared had witnessed the ornate, gilded French décor that Henrì had purchased, being replaced with one seeped in African culture, past and present, ancient and modern. Woodcarvings of ancient, African deities demanded, and were given their proper place on pedestals, for they were thousands of years old and priceless. Modern black art, bold and daring, and haunting too, hung in hallways, bedrooms, studies, and across the other many rooms of the secluded mansion, including the living room, which boasted a one-of-a-kind, frosted chandelier by the artist David Hammons, it no less than five million dollars; and they had three in total. Another of the chandeliers was upstairs in her sitting room off the bedroom, and the other was downstairs in Henrì's study. Still, the total of the chandeliers and wall art combined was but a pittance of the small treasure they possessed, courtesy of Tamen, the hybrid half-man and half-angel. Though for all of Tamen's god-like powers, the one thing Tamen could not give Henrì was time.

"Let me read the letter again," Henrì said. He walked over and took it from Jared and read it out loud. "'You have searched ceaselessly for me and for your friend, Christopher Knopfitter. He prays that you will rescue him. So now, it is, that I seek to end the feud between you and me, once and for all. I know you desire Lucifer's tome, and I shall bring it. I shall chant into the wind for you, Jared Tripkin, who is now Mizel— angel of God. I shall lead you to me. Know that the land of Egypt is all I have ever desired. Concede it to me and you may have Lucifer's tome… and the boy.'" Henrì shook his head and tapped the center of the letter. "It's called a trap, Jared. He might as well have written as much."

"He wants more than Egypt," Jared said.

"Obviously."

"You don't think I know that?"

"I don't know," Henrì said, staring at him. "Do you? I'm not being a smart ass about it, but do you? Really? This is not how it was supposed to happen, but it has, and we don't have Tamen here to help us." Henrì scratched his head and tussled his short brown hair; wayward sections now stood on end. "You're barely twenty-one. You're still basically just a kid. But you have the power of an angel. I mean…you're an angel with the power of a god."

"I'm not even close to being that," Jared said and smiled. But how true, he thought…how close Henrì really was to capturing how his angelic power made him feel. He could control nature. Easily, he could lift a car, if not two if he channeled his lifeforce into his arms. And most marvelous—wondrous of all—was that with focus, he could deconstruct and reform matter. To mortals, he knew he appeared godlike.

"Yikan wants one thing," Henrì said, holding up a fist and raising a finger from it, "to keep good and evil unbalanced. God and Lucifer's covenant is that man would be able to choose his own path freely, with good and evil on earth in balance. And then, once there is balance and the End Days come, there's salvation and redemption for the faithful. But like I've told you before during these little impromptu visits of yours, between you staying here and unbalancing good and evil, and Yikan with his hands on Lucifer's tome, the earth is screwed. It's bad enough that Yikan is out there, and with Chris, mind you, but you're out there doing exactly what you know you shouldn't be doing." Henrì smirked, as if daring him to deny the charge. "You just can't help yourself, can you?"

Jared hung his head. He felt as though he was a student of Henrì's again, when—with Tamen's illusion upon Henrì—he masqueraded as a teacher to keep an eye on him, until he was ready to become who he was born to be…*the Angel of Balance*—a mortal made into a celestial who would bring balance back to the earth. He knew exactly which incident Henrì was referring to. Cable news channels and newspapers were still covering it, and weeks had already passed by. Church attendance, they reported, had risen ten percent afterward.

"I won't next time," he said coyly.

"You can't go catching people in mid-air," Henrì admonished. "I thought that was just understood, but silly me." He glowered at Jared. "This is the technological age we're in, or has that passed by your six, vast immortal years of accumulated knowledge? Everyone has a camera now, Jared. CCTV caught it all. You can't do something like that in downtown Manhattan and think no one is going to catch it?"

Jared sighed. "I couldn't just let her fall."

"You could have and should have."

"Would you?" Jared cocked his head.

Henrì looked at the ceiling and closed his eyes. "That's what good and evil is," he said, and looked at Jared. "Good things happen all the time. But there's a whole lotta evil out there, too! In fact, as you know, there are three of them protected by demons, just like the three of good who are protected by the Heavenly Host—one them being your father. The rest of us...*well*...we just have to navigate between good and evil the best we can. That's what life is, kiddo! And in death, if you've been good, you get to go up. If not, well then, I hope you like it hot. But regardless," he handed the note back to Jared, "you can't interfere in mortal lives like that again. You have to maintain some kind of balance between good and evil, especially since you're the one unbalancing it."

"If I had just stayed in California, I wouldn't have even been near New York that day," he said, which was true. He had been on the hunt for the old temples of Shazadeh, Yikan's deceased acolyte, in hope of finding some clue to Yikan's present whereabouts. Though, as it had been for the past six years searching her temples, he found no clues to lead him to Yikan. With the force of mind, he had ignited the oxygen within the three temples he had found in the northern woods of the Golden State, and reduced them to ashes. And then on to New York he went, it being another bastion of Shazadeh's temples and worshippers. That's when he saw the woman step over the guardrail of the skyscraper next to him and jump.

"Maybe you could have let her fall, but I couldn't just let her go splat!"

"Yes, you could have," Henrì insisted.

"She could have fallen on someone and...." Jared stopped, as Henrì was already waving him off.

"I love ya...Olivia loves ya...but ya gotta go," Henrì panned.

"How is Olivia?" Jared said, piping up rather cheerfully, trying to change the subject.

"My wife is fine and she's not going to save your skinny ass this time," Henrì warned. "I don't care what a blessing she it was…you doing what you did." He rolled his eyes. "I'm not amused like she is watching you play Superman on TV. No-no," he wagged his finger at Jared, "I'm the one sitting right there on that sofa, looking at that TV," he pointed at the flat screen above the fireplace, "and watching some suicidal woman fall to her death, but then—miraculously, halfway down—she begins to float the rest of the way and lands on her feet. Hmm?" He stopped and raised a brow. "So I'm watching this and thinking to myself, wow!; I thought when I spoke to him a few weeks ago we agreed that he wouldn't interfere with mortals again. There were the floods down in Houston, which should have wiped out a good many suburbs. And what happens? The water just evaporates? Because flood water does that on its own, right?" Henrì went silent and stared at him. "Tornado alley is supposed to have tornadoes. But not when you're around, I guess. House fires…no problem if you're near. Gunshot wound?" He shrugged. "No big deal for you." His tone turned cold. "This isn't some game, Jared."

"I know that, Henrì," he retorted.

"Then start acting like you do." Henrì stood his ground for a moment, and then turned and sat on the sofa that was in the middle of the room. Jared was sitting in the chair to his left. "We have a chance to reset the balance. And by *we*, I mean the human race. We can't have you making rash decisions like you did in Manhattan. And not to mention…." He looked away for a moment. "Tamen gave his life so that you could live and bring God's salvation."

"He meant something to me, too," said Jared, rather defensively, but more out of hurt that Henrì felt he thought so little of Tamen's sacrifice.

"Good then," Henrì said, wiping at his eyes and wet nose. "The only way this turns out right is if you get that tome out of Yikan's hands, and then kill him. That means you get the tome, even if you have to leave Chris behind, just like you should have let that woman fall." He got up and walked to the glass doors leading out to the patio and looked out into the moonless, dark of night "This world was almost under Shazadeh's rule, remember? My father is the one that stopped that…with his life. Tamen died so that you could balance Shazadeh's evil in the world, but she's gone and you're not, and the world is unbalanced again, only this time, it's an angel, not a demon doing it. But you have to do what needs to done, no matter what...no matter who is sacrificed in the process. That's what Tamen had to do, and he did it without hesitation."

"Do it in spite of Chris?"

"Despite Chris," Henrì corrected. He turned around. "Get that damned tome of Lucifer's, and the one you have buried out in my back-yard," he jabbed his thumb behind him, toward the patio, "and take them to Heaven where they can be kept out of mortal's hands. Then we won't have a problem with half-breeds like Yikan trying to rule over us as gods."

"The demons *were* those old gods," Jared commented.

"Yeah," Henrì said, "with Astaroth being one of the worst and most powerful, of course. We can thank him for giving the world Shazadeh." He took a seat in a long-back chair next to Jared's; a wood table with books upon it separated them. But it seemed Henrì found the chair an ill fit, as he changed positions several times before eventually sliding to the edge of it.

"I wonder sometimes," Henrì continued, "that if you and the other celestials are this powerful, then how great is God who created all of you?"

Jared thought back to a moment of reflection he had had about God not long ago. He was perched upon a mountaintop in the Blue Ridge Mountains of Virginia. He had just freed twenty men, women, and chil-dren from one of Shazadeh's temples, who were being held prisoner by zealots who refused to believe their goddess was dead; he had torched the place afterwards, sterilizing it with blue, celestial fire. And after the deed was done, and he finding a mountain peak with an unimpeded view of the sky, he flew down to it, and then lay down and gazed up. It was a cloudless night; it looked like diamonds sprinkled upon black velvet. The dark of space teased the question of whether or not it was indeed in-finite, which had made him begin pondering about who God was, or better yet, what God was.

The more he focused on God, the larger space seemed to become. The stars seemed as though they were fading away; the darkness grew darker.

And as his focus on God deepened, the heavens began to part; it split open, as though it were a curtain and giant hands were pulling it apart. Light poured out of the split in the sky and bathed him and the mountain in its white glory, which made him lightheaded and giddy, and at peace, and full of want for the one who was shining it on him. He could hear his name being called from deep within that light.

'*Mizel,*' a voice beckoned. '*Come to thy home.*'

Opening that portal to Heaven was just as easy as closing it, he discovered. When he turned his thoughts away from God, the fissure in the sky began to close. He knew eventually he would have to go there for the sake of the earth and all upon it, for Henrì was right, he was the one who unbalancing good and evil on earth. He was the one who was preventing the End Days from coming. But he couldn't leave yet. Chris was still out there, as was Yikan, who still had possession of Lucifer's golden tome. And while he had it, no one on earth was safe.

"God is Alpha and Omega," Jared finally responded. "He has no beginning or end. There's no other power like that." He picked up a book from the table and held it up to Henrì's face. "I can turn this into gold. It's nothing but a bunch of quarks that I can rearrange at the quantum level, where something can be *something* and *nothing*, or *everything* at the same time. But I can't create something from nothing. Only He can." Jared stood. He clasped his hands behind him. "I know saving Chris is not the primary goal. Killing Yikan and getting the tome back is."

"That damn tome," Henrì grumbled.

Jared turned sharply toward the door. A presence was nearing, though it was not a shadow that he felt. He probed for the approaching mind and found it, and read its thoughts, and then smiled at Henrì. "Olivia's coming."

The door opened.

Olivia pushed the door open wide with her shoulder. She was carrying a silver tray with a porcelain teapot and two dainty cups on it; the sugar bowl and creamer were on the side; they were decorated with pink and purple flowers around their rims. She passed by Jared with not even a glance his way. She set the tray down on the table next to Henrì and began filling the cups. "I thought you might like some tea, seeing that you and Jared are in for another long strategy session." She poured milk into both cups and added a cube of sugar to one, and three to the other, which she gave to Henrì. "Hello, Jared. I didn't bring a cup for you, for obvious reasons." She smiled. "But you can enjoy the aroma can't you? It's Valerian. It's very calming. Can you smell the hint of bitterness in it?"

"How do you always know when I'm here?" Jared asked, bemused by her skill. "Even Henrì can't sense me."

"You know better than me," she replied. "Tamen's gift of magic to his African people still remains. I guess I got a heaping dose of it like your mother's people did." She sat on the sofa and crossed her legs, and adjusted the skirt of her loose, light blue flower dress over her knees. She took a sip of tea. Her hair was short, nearly to scalp. Her skin was black as coal. Her eyes were dark brown and glinted when she smiled, as she did now at Henrì, turning toward him, and he turning toward her and returning her sentiment of love with a toothy smile. "Am I interrupting?"

"There are no secrets here," Henrì said. "I can't stub my toe without a shadow running off to tell you how and when."

"Jackson Lovell is quite the busybody," she admitted. "No sooner than I felt you were here," she looked at Jared, "and came down to put on some tea, but here comes Jackson out of the corner to tell me all about it. He looked more real tonight than he ever has before."

"He's one of the strongest shadows," Henrì said, offhandedly. "Jackson is in this phase where he wants to appear alive. And he's pretty good at it. Just like he is at eavesdropping."

At the mention of his secret deed come to light, the shadow, Jackson, oozed out of from behind the bookcase to Jared's right. But it did something Jared had never seen a shadow do before. As it came closer, its black, smoke-like form began to thicken and took on the shape of a man. His shadow lightened to a chestnut brown, and then took on the appearance of skin. He manifested clothes next—a black and tan checkered vest, a white shirt, a red bowtie, and dark brown khakis. He had gray at his temples and his beard was salted. He was quite handsome, though alive he was not.

"Thank you, Jackson," Olivia said, and then grinned at him.

Jackson replied with a nod and bowed at the waist. He rose upright and smiled at Henrì. His faux human form began to blur and turned back into a shadow. He fled to the corner of the room and melded with the real shadows that were there.

"You better run, Jackson," Henrì called after him lightly.

"So?" she asked, looking from one to the other with suspicion keen in her eyes.

"Yikan left Jared a note at one of Shazadeh's old temples," Henrì said. "He wants to meet with him to settle this feud."

"He's tired of running," she proposed.

"Looks like it," Henrì said.

"And Tamen did it for how long?" she inquired.

"A few thousand years, give or take," Henrì added proudly, as though the exact number did not matter, but that what did, was that Tamen had been up to the task and Yikan wasn't.

"We know it's a trap, Olivia," said Jared.

"I'd be worried if you didn't think so," she said. "Did he mention Christopher?"

"Yikan said he would bring him," Jared replied.

"What do you think Yikan is really up to?" Olivia posed.

Henrì looked at Jared. "That's what we were just talking about."

Olivia looked from one to the other. "We all knew that this might come up," she said. "He's using that poor child as bait."

"To throw you off your game," Henrì added. "That's what he wants. Just when you think you've looked at every possible angle Yikan is working, you end up missing that one little piece, because your head isn't all the way in the game; and then he has you—that's what he's betting on."

"He's going to make you choose between Christopher and the tome," she said.

"But there's more to it than just that, Olivia," Henrì proposed. "Jared is the added weight offsetting the balance. Yikan has the power to rule earth, but Jared is standing in his way." He nodded at Jared. "You're his monkey wrench. He's not strong enough to get rid of you, but you can get rid of him and he knows it. That's why he's been on the run for so long, and why he's still holding on to Chris. He knows how much you care for him...how he's like a brother to you."

"He is my brother," Jared insisted.

"And that's a big problem for us," Henrì warned. "Yikan is not going to fight you without a chance of winning, at least in his own mind. One thing we all know that he's not, is a fool. "

"You're right, mon amour," Olivia said, transitioning to French and speaking it as though it was her native tongue. "He's using your love for Christopher to blind you to what he's really up to. He's survived the centuries where others have not. Don't think he hasn't already thought of everything."

"Twice," Henrì added. He suddenly became somber; his eyes swept back and forth across the rug at his feet, as though searching its patterns for answers. "Chris might have to be sacrificed to save mankind. I'm sorry, Jared—I really am." He reached for Olivia's hand and held it tight. "I'm sorry, kiddo. I know what it feels like to have someone close to you put in mortal danger. Tamen told me for years that to protect you, and to give you the chance to become the Angel of Balance, he would have to sacrifice himself, and he did. But me knowing that didn't make it any easier when he was killed. It doesn't make it any better now." He sighed and looked up. His bottom lip began trembling.

Olivia squeezed his hand. "It's a horrible choice you've been given, Jared."

"I never asked for any of this," Jared bemoaned. "This was put on my back before I was even born. I was shoved into this war of angels and demons when I was just a kid—a teenager. Now I'm an angel and stuck in the middle of it."

"We know, mon cher."

Do you? he thought. Neither of them knew what it was like to bear responsibility for mankind's salvation. And in truth, neither did he. He was made into a celestial, not born one; no one had handed him a celestial playbook to follow. As an immortal soldier of God, he was no longer a part of the mortal world of suffering and joy, birth and death, happiness and despair, hope and despondency—a menagerie of good and evil.

Yet, he yearned to be like them once more, though always felt like a stranger when moving amongst them.

Now, with Chris's life teetering on the edge, he felt drawn back to that mortal part of himself that looked upon Chris as a brother, which fueled his desire to protect him at all costs. That human emotion—love—pulled at him to save his friend. Yet, for all of his power, he felt helpless in doing it without damning billions of others in the process. *One life for billions or billions of lives for one; and you get to decide*. He knew what choice had to be made. He just didn't like it…at all.

Jared stood. "Let's got outside for some air," he said, *insisting*, allowing his skin to return to its natural angelic state, which was of glow. A soft white radiance shone through his skin, and even his t-shirt and jeans, and brightened the room. The shadows moaned and groaned as their dark hiding spaces were cast in light. They fled behind and under furniture; others oozed up the wall and across the floor, and then squeezed through the seams of the windows and walls and where crown molding met ceiling.

"If you're trying to enchant us," Henrì said and stood; his light brown eyes were a'twinkle, "it's working." Olivia took his arm—her eyes were equally glassy, and her smile was just as wide as his. They walked over to the patio doors.

Jared opened the patio doors by the force of his mind, just as he was doing with Henrì and Olivia's consciousness. He pushed all thoughts going through their minds out and away, leaving only their love for one another as their sole focus. It was exactly how he had introduced them, though it was they who had found each other first, so to speak, he recalled.

He and Henrì were at a museum; Olivia was there with her doctoral art students. She was there to see the new African art exhibit; Henrì and him were there to discuss where to look for Yikan next. Though too, in addition to getting Henrì's advice on hunting Yikan down, he had wanted to get Henrì out of the mansion, where he had become a hermit since Tamen's death. They had passed by Olivia and her students several times; Jared made sure that they did, after having seen Henrì take more than a passing notice of her when he first saw her on the main floor. By superb, angelic timing on Jared's part, they all just happened, once again, to find themselves on the third floor at the same time; and that's when he shot them with his arrow of love; and all that they saw at that moment was each other, which was all it took to let them fall in love, and be in love, and stay in love, like they were now, strolling dreamily arm-in-arm out onto the patio.

Jared seized the particles of water in the air and pushed them out of the garden, cooling the humid summer air for Olivia and Henrì. He walked ahead of them and passed under a shrub that had been shaped into an arched doorway, and came out into a flower garden. Tamen's headstone—a replica of an Ancient Egyptian pylon—was to the right in an alcove made of shrubs shaped like a horseshoe. In front of the grave marker was a marble bench, where he often found Henrì when he came to check on him and chat, and to get advice, whether he wanted it or not. Tonight, he didn't want the advice Henrì was offering, for that meant Chris's doom.

The moment Jared had read Yikan's note, he knew how Henrì would respond...*Get the tome...Chris is expendable.* And that was exactly what Henrì had advised. Jared didn't fault him, for he would advise Henrì similarly if their roles were reversed and it was Olivia's life versus billions on the line.

Henrì and Olivia sat on the bench looking at Tamen's marble pylon. She laid her head on his shoulder and moved her hand up his back and twirled the ends of his hair at the nape of his neck. Their love was real, Jared felt, for his glow grew brighter in the presence of their truth and acceptance they had for one another; his celestial body was feeding off of it, just as it fed off the ambient energy that surrounded him.

Jared wasn't sure what that energy was, though had named it the God-force. Though he couldn't see it or touch it, he felt it all around him. It even passed through him as though he were not there. Though when he needed it to fuel his lifeforce to manipulate matter, it was always there. That force would rush into every part of his body, and then gather in his chest, where he could feel it whirling and waiting to be used. And no matter how much he drew in, there was always more to be had.

Jared reached up to the sky and felt for that power. It responded at the quick and poured into him, and through him, and all over him—from fingers to arms, toes to head—, and then it rushed into his chest where it spun around and around. No matter how much of that energy he absorbed, more and more came. It was like riding a growing wave. The power seemed infinite—all-powerful.

The dark skies began expanding. The stars appeared to fly away from each other, leaving only the blackness of space before him. The garden was suddenly gone and Olivia and Henrì along with it; nothing existed to him except the darkness, which he felt all around him, for its power was limitless; it was the power of a god, indeed.

Realizing what was happening again, he quickly pushed away from that invisible force. The stars sprang back to their rightful places. The sky returned to its blue-black hue; and Henrì and Olivia were back where they were, still cuddled up and looking at the grave marker.

There was a darker side to that invisible force, he knew; and he knew its name the moment he felt its powerful draw, and it was called *temptation*. With the celestial power he possessed to reform and destroy matter, *though not to create it*, he could be a god amongst men…if he chose to. Having touched that dark force for himself, he had a better understanding why a third of the celestials had challenged God for godhood and had rebelled when it was refused.

Olivia looked at him over her shoulder. Her eyes were still glossy. "Before you go to confront that creature, go see your mother and Thaddeus," she said, her voice drowsy. "Ask them to stay with us until you return. Being here with us will give her some comfort, I'm sure. Henrì would like it, too—especially so." She sighed gently and turned around.

"I'm sure they would like that," Jared said. He was impressed that she had broken free of his control over her consciousness, at least for a short time. But then again, he thought, she was no ordinary woman; and she was far more than just an art professor, but one who—thanks to his tutelage and she being an adept student—could sense the thoughts of others when she had a mind for it, as was the case now.

"Tell her I would love to have her here," Olivia said.

"I'll let you know when I'm going, all right?" Jared said to both of them. Henrì slowly bobbed his head in reply. Olivia lolled hers to the side.

Jared turned and walked out of the garden, and then released his hold on their minds. He moved the lifeforce out from his chest and pushed it into every part of his being. He glowed anew as he altered the density of his body from that of steel to helium, becoming lighter than air and rising from the ground. With his arms at his sides, he soared high into the sky and looked down at them. He spoke to Henrì by thought of mind.

If I die, Yikan will come for Metatron's tome. It's the only thing that can stop him and we both know he'll kill anyone to get it. I don't plan on failing, but if I do, it'll be up to you to keep it safe and to find someone new who can translate the Chant of Changing and stop him. So pray, Henrì—pray hard. Let's hope God is listening.

CHAPTER 3

Jared soared for hundreds of miles upon a jet stream shooting north. It was near daybreak when he arrived in Chicago, and then flew east, out past the suburbs to a small town, Homer, Illinois, where he grew up; where his mother and stepfather, Thaddeus, still lived.

He lowered down in the backyard and hovered inches above the neatly trimmed grass. The light was on in the kitchen. He glided over to the window and peered between the half-shut wood blinds. He spotted his mother sitting at the table in the breakfast nook; she had a newspaper in one hand and a cup of coffee in the other; her reading glasses were perched on the end of her nose.

He swept around to the front door. By thought, he reached for the deadbolt on the other side of the door and turned it, and then with that same force, pushed the door open. He moved inside and was nearly down the hall, when he remembered the front door never shut all the way unless there was a good push behind it; and he hadn't given it one, which, as a child, he had always forgotten to do. Even as a warrior of God, not much had changed, yet, on the other hand, a great deal had, he thought. *Angel or not, she'll whip my behind if I leave that door cracked open.*

'I'm not trying to heat the outside, boy!' she would scold, he reminisced. At the time, he had found nothing amusing about her fussing; back then, it was just one more complaint about what he was not doing right. Though now, he thought, he could see the character building in her criticism; and it only took travelling around the world with a thousands year old Egyptian, almost being killed by a demon, and becoming an angel to realize it. *'Boy—if you don't act like you got good commonsense and close that door right, I'm gonna get up from here and make sure you do —you hear me?'*

"Mom," he called from the hallway.

"Jared?"

He walked into the kitchen. "Hey mom."

"Thought you were going to surprise me, hmm?" she said, looking up and smiling at him. Her hair was in pink rollers and in rows from front to back. Time had yet to make an appearance on her cocoa brown skin, despite being in her early fifties.

"I thought I'd give it a try."

She watched him as she blew at her steaming coffee and sipped at it. "I knew you were coming."

Jared played along. "How's that?"

"I prayed," she said, with an air of authority. "I asked the Lord to let me see you again, and again, and as many times as I can before you go away. You were here last month, and then two weeks ago—weren't you? You didn't stop in, but I swear I felt you near. That was you, wasn't it?"

"Uh…yeah," he muttered, a bit in awe, for she was right. He had come to check on them…to watch her and Thaddeus from afar. He had hidden his thoughts, or at least thought he had. Still, she had known; she had felt his presence, just like Olivia always seemed to, no matter how surreptitious his arrival. "I'm supposed to be the one who freaks people out by saying stuff like that, not you, mom."

"It's called mother-sense, child," she said. "I get my feelings about things here and there, too. You *ain't* God's only warrior." She grinned with pride. "I keep telling you that God is a good God."

He walked over and stood behind her, and then leaned over and wrapped his arms around her. "I can't stay as long as I would like to," he said. "I just wanted to see how both of you were both doing."

"Well, Thaddeus is still sleeping," she joked.

"I know. I could hear him sawing logs from outside."

"And I'm just fine," she said, as though her well-being was nothing for him to worry about. "But you know that anyway, I would guess. All you gotta do is take a look in here." She tapped a roller on the side of her head. "So, as I said, my mother-sense has never failed me yet." She swiveled around and faced him. "You going to tell me what's wrong?"

He nibbled on his bottom lip. "It's just something I need to do."

"Does it have to do with that Yikan creature?"

He nodded.

"It's dangerous, isn't it?"

"I'm an angel, mom," he said. "Yikan's nothing but a hybrid man-demon. You don't have to worry about me."

She pursed her lips and raised her brow. "I'm your mammy," she said, reverting to her southern drawl.

"I'm a warrior of God, remember?"

"And barely a man," she countered.

Jared groaned. "Sounds like you been talking to Olivia."

"No, sir."

"Henrì?"

"Go ahead and check." She closed eyes and waited.

"Mom! I wouldn't do that."

She huffed and turned around, and then began taking her rollers out. "Do or don't, it's all the same. I haven't heard from them in weeks." She freed a lock of hair from the roller; it sprung loose and dropped, bouncing on her shoulder. She unsnapped the next one and stopped; her hands were still on the clip. "Should they have?"

"No," said Jared. "You just…just sound like them."

"And this is about Yikan again, huh?"

He nodded.

"I know you have God-given power to lay Yikan low. But what worries me is that thang is older than dirt, and smart, and you're still just a baby-boy, at least you are to me."

Jared moaned at her *baby-boy* remark, though too, her unabashed motherly love made his lifeforce grow warm. As much as he hated hearing it and protested it's use—it making him feel as though he was still, and always would be a child—he hoped she would always use it, for he knew on the day he would have to leave, he would miss hearing it.

"Yeah," he grumbled, agreeing with her. "I get that he's older than me by a few thousand years, but—"

"But what, baby?"

"He's the one running from me," Jared said. "I'm not the one jumping from state to state, or crossing into and out of country after country—*he is*. Before I became an angel, he had the power. But things are a lot different now. I have the power. He's the one who should be afraid."

"And he's got some thousands of years of experience that you don't," she said. "People in power aren't always strong, but they're always smart. And they're always the ones that come out on top—aren't they?" He looked off, but nodded in agreement. "I guess that's what we're all trying to tell you, child. That thang, Yikan, is a dirty, filthy snake, just as much as Lucifer is himself. They don't have the power, but they're slick and sly. Shoot," he chuckled, "they're so slick, they'll make you think black and white is the same as pink and blue if you're not careful. Yikan may be half a demon, but he's got the whole heart of one."

Jared pulled the letter from his back pocket and handed it to her. "He left this for me. You might as well know now."

She hesitated before taking it, and handled it by its edges when she did, as though the paper itself bore a curse. She read it, and then looked up at him; tears crested at the edge of her eyelids. She read it again, and then handed it back. "That poor child," she said softly. Jared slid his hands into his pockets and looked at his feet. "Lord Jesus!—he better not harm Christopher. You're not going to let Christopher get hurt, are you? Jared?"

"I want you and Thaddeus to go and stay with Henrì and Olivia," he responded, dodging her question.

"Why?" She wiped the tears from her eyes.

"It's just...I'll feel better knowing you and Thaddeus are there."

Her face became grim with worry. "I don't like the sound of that."

"It's just a precaution, mom," he insisted. "I'll be back in a week or so, or whenever Yikan calls out for me, and then I'll just handle it." He nodded and smiled. "I'll get the tome and Chris." He looked her in the eye, trying to assure her, though only believed half of what he had told her, which did not include Chris being brought back safely.

She shook her head. "When do you want us to go?"

"As soon as possible," he replied. "Today would be good."

She sat back; her eyes were wide and wild. "Today?"

"Henrì will charter a jet to fly you down."

"Thaddeus and I will have to let the church know first thing that we'll be gone for a while." Her brown eyes darted side to side. "I guess...I suppose the other associate pastors can cover for Thaddeus, but they're going be twisted up trying to find a replacement for me to keep that church office running. It was a mess and a half when I started there."

"Then you'll go?"

"I don't think I have a choice, baby," she said, and then smiled, and then stood. She reached up and cupped his face in her hands. "I'm still not calling you Mizel—you know that, right? You're still my baby to me."

He grinned. "I know, mom."

The alarm clock sounded off in the bedroom down the hall. "Oh Lord, look'a' here!" she exclaimed, turning around and looking at the clock on the wall. "Six o'clock done snuck up on me like a snake." She turned back around.

Jared was gone.

She looked around the room and glanced down the hall. He was nowhere to be seen. She huffed and half-grinned. "I know that boy didn't just scoot outta here like that!" She went to the bedroom. Thaddeus was still asleep despite the obnoxious, pulsing beat of the alarm still going off. She rounded the bed to his side and shut it off. She looked at him. He was still sleeping soundly. "I guess I got two children to see to."

She took hold of his shoulder and was about to shake him awake, though stopped. Instead, she pulled the blanket up further on him and sat down next to him; he grumbled, snorted a few times, and then resumed his throat-rattling snoring.

She patted his chest. "Go on and sleep, big bear. You're gonna need it once I tell you what that boy is up to now. And we're going to need some powerful prayers for him and for that poor baby, Christopher...mmm-hmm…yes, Lord. But I know one thing. No matter what happens. My God is a good God."

* * *

Jared arrived in Nuxta, Mississippi, just past nine that same morning that he left his mother's home. Every mile he traveled he expected to hear a chant upon the wind—Yikan's call. The wait was already sending his lifeforce around in a tizzy, for every moment was now precious. He knew if he was going to retrieve the tome, and possibly—he dared not even hope—Chris too, then he was going to need more than just the power of an angel to win the fight. He needed something that could counter any trick Yikan could possibly throw his way. He needed something unstoppable.

Jared came down in the parking lot of his father's church; an ol' country church is what folks called it; it was set back from a one-lane dirt road that left a fine film of dirt on every parishioner's car by the time they left. Though, this early on a Sunday morning, there was only one car in the parking lot in front of the white, wood slat church.

The front double doors were open. Phineas was inside; Jared could hear him humming a spiritual; its tone was deep and trembling. He walked in. His father was carrying a wicker basket of bulletins and paper fans, and was placing them at the end-seat of each pew.

He didn't want to ask Phineas for help, but he needed it. Phineas could weigh the confrontation with Yikan in his favor. He was also a shit father, he thought…or at least he was before he found God. Though to Jared, Phineas's turnaround—wanting to be a real father to him—felt shallow. He was thankful to Phineas for risking his life to save his family from Shazadeh years ago. However, the burn from Phineas not claiming him as his son for most of his life had yet to cool, or even just become warm for that matter. As a child, he couldn't find the words to describe that feeling of abandonment. Though now, as angel, it still wasn't any easier. That feeling of worthlessness as a child still burned. It still hurt. He had always thought his fatherless birthdays, holidays, his first catch of the ball…his firsts of this and that…would have been tolerable if they had just been bittersweet, not just bitter.

Phineas had abandoned him and his mother, and then moved on and married, and tried to start a new family. Though his wife, who had been dead for almost a year now, had been sterile and had never given him a legitimate offspring to proudly claim as his own. And now Phineas was alone; a situation Jared was none too sad to see him in, for now it was he who got to decide when or if he wanted to have anything to do with Phineas; not a helpless child who only understood the world one foot in front of him and who blamed his mother for their abandonment. The misdirected pain he had inflicted on his mother as a result of it, was just one more reason he had in turning down Phineas's invitations over the last few years to visit more often, to come and talk, or even to pray together. Still, love him or resent him, Jared needed him now.

Phineas was a protected mortal of God; he was one of the three of good who balanced out the three of evil. He was part of God and Lucifer's holy covenant, which is that, good and evil being in equal measure upon the earth, man may freely choose his path—righteousness or sin; Heaven or Hell. And somewhere in the world there were two others of good just like Phineas, just as there were three of evil, whose sole purpose was to inflict pain and suffering, and to tempt mankind. He recalled the words of The Lamb—the Christ—as he lay dying upon the cross, and had spoken of the covenant between God and Lucifer. *'Three mortals of light and three of darkness there shall always be. Woe to those who seek to harm but a hair upon their heads, for the Covenant shall not be torn asunder. So sayeth my Father.'*

"How are ya, Phineas?" Jared called to him.

Phineas turned and squinted. "Jared? Son? That you?"

"Yes, sir."

"It's…good to see you, son." He scratched his head. Gray had nearly supplanted the black on his head and beard.

"I need you, Phineas."

Phineas smiled; though sour it was. "That's fine, son. I told you I'm here for you. Whenever you need me, remember?"

"I do."

"I hope you believe me, 'cause it's true."

"You can always say 'no'."

"How about you just tell this old man what you need from him?" Phineas set the wicker basket down on a pew and walked over to him.

The closer Phineas came, the more Jared realized just how much he resembled him. They had the same thick jaw and dark brown eyes set beneath a heavy brow; their broad noses and full lips were mirror images. "It's Yikan. It's Chris, too," he added. "And I have a chance to get Lucifer's tome."

"And Chris?" Phineas slipped his hands into the pockets of his gray dress slacks.

"Yikan is using him as bait to get to me and to get his hands on Metatron's tome," Jared replied. "So you can basically figure out Chris's chances from there."

"I'm sorry about that, son," Phineas said. "I can't imagine what that feels like to have your friend put in that kind of danger."

Jared looked into his eyes. He believed Phineas. "Thanks for that."

"Anytime…anytime," he said, and then smiled demurely. "What do you need me to do?"

Jared recalled the first time he had seen the church. Its windows were shattered, the parking lot was littered with timber and glass, and the ceiling had been blow apart by a bolt of lightning—an unnatural one. He looked up at the ceiling, and no sooner did spot the patch marks from the rebuild, even though he could tell it was heavily painted over; and to the mortal eye, only a foot-close inspection might reveal the flaws of the carpenter's skill. The circular patchwork above the seating area glared at his celestial eyes. Shazadeh and Yikan had confronted Phineas, though to their utter regret. She was nearly killed by the three-faced celestial that was bound by the covenant to protect Phineas, and imbued with the unstoppable force of The Ghost to see it done. Had they not fled, it would have killed them both.

That's exactly what I need, Jared thought, *something that can tear apart the biggest demon there is. If I have that, then….* He was afraid to even think about rescuing Chris or the fear he was likely feeling at the moment. But, yet again, he caught himself in the moment ruminating and gnashing upon Chris's fate, when he knew his focus had to be on killing Yikan and retrieving the tome. Though thinking about not thinking about it sapped a great deal of mental acuity, too; it pushed and kneaded him like a needy child.

"Yikan is going to call for me. And when he does, I need you and the Order by my side."

"Yikan best have an army if he's gonna fight my guardian angel."

"Its actually an Order," Jared corrected. "Even without it having the force of the Holy Ghost to keep the covenant intact, its not a being you want to mess with."

Phineas bobbed his head in agreement. "Even better still."

"But Yikan has to know that, too," Jared said, insisting upon it. "That's what bothers me about this whole thing. He knows I can't, and won't, negotiate with him. So what's his game, Phineas? What's he been planning that I still don't see?"

For the first time, he had admitted out loud that Yikan might have already outfoxed him; and he had just admitted it to Phineas, of all people. But why him? he wondered, though knew in his lifeforce that it had something—and everything—to do with a long abandoned childhood wish of having a father who was there to help guide him when he felt lost; to have that strong, sturdy someone to hold onto in the midst of a storm.

"I've faced him before. Twice, if truth be told." Phineas said proudly. "And that demon-woman was with him both times. She couldn't do nuthin' against my angel either."

"Are you sure the Order is still with you?"

Phineas chuckled. "Oh, I'm pretty darn sure. If I was still a sinful, bettin' man, like I used to be, son...*like I used to be*," he said, and held Jared's gaze, "I would bet the car, house, and all the mice inside that the Order is still right next to me. You see here, I was coming back from uptown and got up to a stop sign. I stopped and then took my turn, but some young-tail white boy didn't and dang near t-boned me. His car never hit mine, but Lord, it hit somethin' hard." Phineas nodded slowly and spoke. "I mean real hard. I heard a bang, and then I heard a crunch, and next thang I know, the front of his car is all smashed up, like somebody done stepped on a pop can, and mine ain't got one single scratch on it."

"It's still with you," Jared whispered, clenching his fists. It was the best news he had heard since receiving Yikan's letter. It gave him hope that perhaps Chris's fate was not quite sealed all the way.

"What you need me to do?"

"Nothing right now, but that'll change very soon," Jared replied. He turned and walked toward the doors. "I'll be close by. When Yikan calls, I'll come for you. And from there," Jared shook his head, "we'll see what Yikan has up his sleeve." He stopped and looked back at his father. "I want this to be the last time I ever see Yikan alive. After what he's done to all of us, I want to make him a memory to everyone who's ever heard his name."

Jared left the church and walked out to the road. For a while, he just walked, like Tamen had told him he used to do to pass the years of immortality. After he passed through Nuxta, and the town after, and the one after that, he took to the air and flew, and circled round and around Nuxta…waiting and waiting, watching as the townsfolk went about their mortal lives, clueless that their immortal souls were in grave danger.

Hot July became scalding August, and still Jared had heard nothing from Yikan. He visited with Phineas again, though this time stayed longer, and this time there was little talk about Yikan or covenants, or angels, or demons. Phineas had broached their past and Jared had listened to it, though said nothing in reply to Phineas's tearful confession of being a whiskey swilling, womanizing preacher, before finally finding the one true path to salvation. His sincere sounding apologies, which came throughout his story and profusely at the end of it, did not open Jared's door of forgiveness any further; though he did begin to see his father as more of a mortal—a fallible human, as all mortals were—instead of a monster who had used his mother, and whose absence from his life had made him doubt his self-worth for most of his life. Two days after that visit, he heard Yikan's chant upon the wind.

However, he then heard another chant, though it was deeper than the first, which made him question if the first had been Yikan's at all. The notes of the chant were intertwined; they fell and rose together. The thought that Yikan had used Lucifer's tome to create another half-breed to aid him seemed a likely answer to the twin chants. And if he could create one, Jared thought, then Yikan could, with enough time and patience, create more. He was certain he could handle Yikan. However, fighting two of them at the same time, and with them in possession of the tome and having Chris as their hostage, he felt his chances starting to diminish even more than they already had.

He flew to Phineas's house, interrupting him in the midst of breakfast. Phineas had just taken a bite of grits and still had the spoon in his mouth when Jared came into the kitchen. Jared picked him up, cradling him, walked outside and took to the air, and began following the chant back to its source before it could fade away.

Phineas gulped his food and looked down. Nuxta and the surrounding towns had become but a quilt of square and rectangular plots dotted with houses and farms. He squeezed his eyelids shut. "Lord Jesus, don't let me fall, son."

"I won't," Jared said. "But you might want to try and get used to it, because we might be flying for a while."

"You don't know where we're going?"

"No. But we'll find out when we get there. And when we do, I need you to be ready."

"You point and I do, son."

Jared nodded at him.

"Let's me and you take this sonofabitch down for good."

CHAPTER 4

Jared was right when he told Phineas they may be in for a long journey, though it was a far longer than even he expected. The chants he followed had led them east, and to Phineas's dismay, out past the American coastline, and then for thousands of miles across the cold, restless waters of the Atlantic. After three days of travel, only stopping on passing cruise ships and oil tankers to get Phineas food, they came upon their first landmass, the island, Dakar, of Senegal, a former slave port, where the captured had passed through the island's infamous Door of No Return on a one-way journey to a hellish existence in America's roaring, slavery machine. However, the chant didn't stop there; it continued east.

Two days after crossing the west coast of Africa, they arrived in Aksum, a northern city of Ethiopia, where legend said Makeda, the queen of Sheba, had brought the Ark of the Covenant; and where some say it still resides. It was there that Jared felt the last, faint warbles of the chants.

Jared hovered hundreds of feet high above the spot where the chants had ended. Phineas pulled away the thick, quilt blanket Jared had wrapped him in to keep the burn of the frigid wind at bay. He took a hesitant peek over Jared's arm and looked down.

"I can't even see the ground—my Lord! How far up are we, son?"

"Far enough that I'm not going to tell you," Jared replied, looking down and seeing what Phineas's mortal eyes could not see from nearly a thousand feet away. He spied steles—stone, pylon-shaped monuments with false windows carved on its four sides; their tops were shaped like crescent moons, with the points facing up.

There were many steles, though there was one that was far taller than the rest and stood nearly a hundred feet high. Some of the steles were toppled and lay in pieces across the ground, as were many of the stone buildings that had once stood near them. Amongst the standing steles, and ruins of others, he saw three figures gathered together; and behind them, off to the right, were two others.

"We have a bit of company down there."

"They can have all the company they want," Phineas said, his voice low and daring. "It ain't gonna matter, 'cause you still got me."

Jared appreciated his optimism, though could feel Phineas's body betraying his spoken words of confidence. He felt Phineas's heart racing; and he saw sweat—a thin film of it—forming just above his brow despite the frigid air around them. Phineas was trying to stay brave for his sake, just like a father was supposed to, just as he had always wanted a father to do, that is, if he had had one who wanted him. Jared pushed that past back into the past. Right now, he yearned for his father's strength of mind and will; and his father had offered it like a father; and for the moment, he leaned upon it like a son, allowing a bit of forgiveness to seep past his barricade meant to keep Phineas out.

"Hold on," Jared warned. "I'm going to lower us down. And try to calm yourself, Phineas. They can't touch you—you're safe. You here to make sure I win."

"I'm here to make sure don't nobody hurt *you*."

Jared choked up. "Thanks...Phineas," he muttered.

Phineas shook his head. "You don't have to call me nothin' I haven't earned. And I haven't earned *that* title just yet. OK?"

Jared nodded soundly and looked down. "Hold on tight."

* * *

"Yikan and Chris are on the platform with someone," Jared said to Phineas, as they lowered to within a hundred feet of the ground. "And there's someone else hiding behind that monument on our right, and another one in those bushes behind Yikan."

Phineas scanned the area Jared had pointed out. "I don't see'em."

"Don't worry, you will," Jared assured him. "Remember what I told you. If you get a chance, go for the tome."

"What about Chris? If I try and get the tome, and they go to hurt—"

"It doesn't matter," Jared said. "Getting the tome is the mission." Phineas closed his eyes and began mumbling. "What are you doing?"

"I'm praying."

"Now?" Jared was a feet from the ground.

"It ain't ever too late to pray."

It is for me, Jared thought, as he landed and set Phineas on his feet. They were in the gravel parking lot of the ancient graveyard, though now, the final resting site of the dead was a tourist attraction for the living. In front of him were stone stairs that led up to the graveyard, and at the edge of those steps, many of which were broken or fractured, and about to break, was Yikan. He wore a white robe, though it was not near as ghastly white as the bald, ancient Egyptian himself. His pallid skin, along with his liquid blue eyes—they going round and around, like water down a drain—made Yikan seem more inhuman than he already was.

Jared moved in front of Phineas and raised his arms out to his sides. He channeled the lifeforce from his chest out and into his arms, and then into his hands, where he condensed it, and then released it. Streams of fire burst from his hands like it had come from a flamethrower. The fires hit the ground on either side him and set the dirt aflame, creating bonfires the size of tumbleweeds. Some of the dark of the ancient burial ground was driven away by the yellow-red glow of the fires, creating shadows that danced queerly around them.

"Mizel—angel of God, I welcome you to Axum," Yikan pronounced heartily. "We have anxiously awaited your arrival. And I have brought what I have promised." He looked down at gold tome of Lucifer lying at his feet, and then turned to the side and looked at Chris.

Jared looked at the white man standing next to Chris; he had a glow about his skin much like Yikan's. His eyes sparkled. He was no longer human, but a hybrid of mortal and demon, he surmised. He looked to right and pierced the dark with his celestial sight, where the light of his bonfire could not reach. He spotted a woman standing next to a story-high stele. The woman had yet to make a single movement, not even the bend of a leg or twitch of a finger, or some random, unconscious motion that all mortals engaged in, though immortals did not. He knew what she really was, and human wasn't it. The mystery of the two chants made sense to him now.

"Building up a pantheon of gods?" Jared asked.

"No," Yikan said, and then grinned. "There is only one god...Aton."

"For once you done told the truth," Phineas quipped. "There *is* only one God, but it ain't you. It won't ever be you."

"Good preacher!" Yikan called out in mock admiration. "The last time we met, did I not tell you we would meet again some day? And here you are with the look of a killer in your blessed eyes, just like your son, Mizel—the Angel of Balance. After thousands of years of life, you both seek to end my time, for you believe me evil—a vile creature to be expunged from humanity." He moved back and stood behind Chris, and put a hand on his shoulder. Chris cringed at his touch. "And I have brought your dear friend, as promised. He is unharmed, though a bit changed from when last you knew him."

Chris was as short as Jared remembered, barely the height of his shoulder. However, his girth was gone, as well as his thick glasses. Instead of his clothes straining to contain him, as they always had as a teen, the shirt and khakis he wore now draped him.

"You said you want to give up the tome *and* Chris."

"For Egypt," Yikan added.

"Then take it," Jared said, calling his bluff, "and give me what you promised—both of them. It's as simple as that."

"Come-come now, Mizel," Yikan chided. "We both know you cannot stand for that. You are an angel of God, a protector of man! You cannot allow me to remain amongst the mortals. You're here to kill me." His swirl of his eyes slowed. "Why else would you have brought the preacher with you?"

"I guess the same reason you brought him," he said, nodding at the immortal next to Chris, "and her." His eyes darted to the right, where the female hid in the dark. "And there's another one behind you—I didn't miss him either."

"So you are observant," Yikan panned. "But so am I. In the thousands of years that I have lived, I have observed a great deal, indeed. Zoe'el and Mala died, but I lived. And then Shazadeh and Tamen came and went. Yet, it is I who remains. But now there is you. So what must be done now?"

The woman moved out of from the shadows and stood next to the bonfire. She was Mexican, young and built thick like a weightlifting man, and wore a white tank top. Her black hair was trimmed tight in a crew cut. Little about her hinted at femininity, though much screamed maleness.

"Make as many immortals as you like," Jared said. "It won't up your chances."

"No?" Yikan asked, though slowly began to smile. "For years I had wondered how Tamen taught you to chant without Shazadeh or me hearing it. Then it came to me...*ah-ha!*" He raised a finger. "It was in an illusion that he had taught you to decipher the chants. How clever of him. Tamen always was sharp, even as a child, which is why Mala and Zoe'el chose him for godhood. So I took a lesson from my former acolyte, and taught Eric and Miranda the sacred chants in illusions.

"Miranda was a member of Shazadeh's Church of the Imperial goddess," Yikan continued, "as was Eric. They both showed promise before, but under my tutelage, they became great and deciphered the chants of the tome."

"You couldn't translate the tome," Jared said. "You needed Tamen to do it for you, and then you turned against him. Now you've taught two mortals the chant by yourself?" Jared huffed, and then gave him a smarmy smile. "I don't buy it."

"I am certain Tamen has distorted much of our past," Yikan said. "I can only imagine the lies he has nursed you on. But alas, 'tis one thing that is true…in the art of chant magic, he was my better." He gave a deferential bow of the head, as though Tamen was there to receive the compliment. "And 'tis true that I tried to kill him, though I fell prey to my own revenge and helped create the demoness, Shazadeh—inadvertently, mind you. But fear not, Mizel!" His voice was of ridiculing hope. "I did not survive Shazadeh without learning a very valuable lesson. She, too, had assistance in becoming, not just an immortal, but a celestial through and through, and immensely powerful, just like you. *His grace* has promised me that such will be so for me."

"Astaroth," Jared said in a hush.

"The duke of Hell," Yikan said, with a corrective tone, "who is now regent of the realm while Lucifer sleeps. His Grace has grown very powerful, Mizel." He placed his other hand on Chris's shoulder. "I once shunned such demonic sorcery, for I wanted nothing to do with demons, or angels for that matter. But as I have said, I learned my lesson. And so I sought out the dark arts with fervor. I read the ancient grimoires and tomes, searching for those spells to summon the duke. And with my own knowledge of magic combined with it, I succeeded in summoning a visage of His Grace. He taught me and guided me, and showed me the true power of the tome." He raised his arm at Eric. "Behold what I have wrought! I, too, have created wonders."

"We're not gods, Yikan," Jared said. "And your making deals with a demon to become something you can never be. God is God—not you, not me."

"But we *are* gods in every sense of the word," he said, refuting the claim. "Though we will never possess the Gift of Life, it matters not to me, or to the duke. God forsook his creations long ago. Even he, in all of his infinite wisdom, must have known that mortals were doomed the moment he breathed life into them. They're cruel and spiteful, and rife with jealously toward one another. And after thousands of years of inflicting torment upon themselves, they are on a new quest to turn this world into ash with nuclear armaments."

"And you're the god to get them in line?" Jared shook his head. "How can you pass out peace and harmony, when you've left nothing but a trail of dead bodies behind you?"

"Peace and harmony?" he asked, with wry lift of the brow. "I prefer to call what they need, order."

"You want slaves," Phineas blurted.

"You are ill informed, preacher," Yikan chastised. "We have different interpretations of what is and what is not, though one is wrong and the other, right. From the moment I chanted my first spell as a priest of Amon-Ra and felt that power course through me, I knew then—without doubt—that I was born to be a god. I surpassed the skill of my master in just a few years time. Mala and Zoe'el recognized my unique talents and called to me, and offered me immortality and an even greater power. They offered godhood! They knew I was more worthy of it than they ever were. None of this that has happened...Tamen, Shazadeh, the tomes, Mala and Zoe'el...has come about by chance. And neither have you, Mizel." He moved away from Chris and walked to the edge of the stairs. He folded his hands in front of him. "I bring an offer from The Duke."

Now comes the temptation, Jared thought. "And that's what?—other than giving me Chris and the tome."

"He offers you lordship over the earth," Yikan said, "with me as its godhead."

Jared figured as much. *You only want the earth, huh? That's it? Why not ask for the entire galaxy while you're at it.* "You're wasting your breath, old man. You might make deals with demons, but I'm not crazy enough to go there with you. Astaroth is taking you for a ride, and you're going to get all of us killed. Astaroth will never keep his promise. *He's a demon.* Why would you expect him to?"

Yikan rubbed his narrow chin and looked up, mockingly giving due diligence to Jared's warning. "The Duke will keep his promise," he asserted. "And I will remake this world into what it should have been four thousand years ago before I was stumbled by Tamen. Your acceptance of his grace's offer was hoped for, though not expected. In the likely case of your refusal, The Duke wisely suggested that I have contingencies in place."

Jared looked at Eric, and then glanced at Miranda; her hands were balled into fists, her expression a scowl. Jared was unmoved.

"You're gonna get yourself killed, lady," he said to her. He looked at Eric and raised his brows. "You too...if you don't back down."

"You are quite powerful, Mizel," Yikan said. "You're an angel of the Most High, and have been given authority over the elements, whereas we lowly immortals must chant at them and force them to do our bidding. We, of course, cannot fight you head on and expect not to fall. But as I have said...*boy*...I have not survived the ages by power alone." He called out over his shoulder and said, "You may come out, Blain."

Blain moved out from the bushes and walked over, and stood next to Yikan at the edge of the stairs. The red-amber of the bonfires glowed upon his tanned, white skin. His short, curly brown hair was invaded with gray throughout. He was average in build, though had a paunch for a belly that hung over the waist of his black slacks. Jared guessed him early to mid-fifties. However, that was all Jared could ascertain from the man, for he tried to probe the man's thoughts and could not; all he could see was an undulating shroud of white mist.

Jared was certain that Blain was mortal, though was no ordinary mortal. In fact, Jared thought, Blain was unique...like Phineas, whose mind he could not read either.

Blain eyed Jared up and down. "So this is a real angel, huh?" Blain said to Yikan. "He looks like a kid."

"He is the Angel of Balance," Yikan said. "Be not fooled by his handsome, boyish face." He held out his arm to Blain. "Let me introduce Blain Edward Hopps. And as you have likely come to the conclusion, he is not what he seems to be. You see, Mizel, Blain has quite the craving for flesh. So observe, preacher...you are not unique. Where there is light, there must also be darkness in equal measure. Where there is good, so too there be evil—that is the covenant."

Blain shrugged innocently. "I've got some bad habits—always have."

"So modest, this one," Yikan admonished in jest. "The truth being, Blain is a killer like no other. I have seen men and women of vile dispositions come and go throughout the ages, and Blain has rightfully earned his place amongst the most heinous of them. His handicraft is perverse. He is efficient...meticulous...and without remorse. And—but most importantly—he is unstoppable, like your father."

Blain grinned. "I am what I am," he said modestly. He reached behind his back and brought out a straight edge razor; he flicked it open. He walked back and stood behind Chris, and then placed the blade at his neck. He looked over at Yikan and said, "Just say the word."

Chris pulled his head back and yelped. "Jared!" His big, brown eyes pleaded for Jared to save him.

"Leave him alone!" Jared cried, forgetting in that moment that the tome was his primary objective. Seeing Chris just a flick of the wrist away from death quickly reorganized his priorities. Yikan was trying to throw him off by playing on his feelings for Chris, just like Henrì and Olivia said he would. He understood that; and it was working like a charm. At that moment, he wanted nothing more than to save Chris.

Miranda took a step forward; she was one shy from crossing into parking lot. Jared spun toward her and held up his hand. "If you can't see that Yikan is just using you and doesn't care if you get yourself killed or not, then you're a fool, lady. Last time…don't do it."

Miranda cocked her head and dared another step. She gave him a crooked grin. "You gonna take all of us on, heh?" Her voice was laden with bass. "Why you think we called you here? pretty boy. You thought Yikan was just gonna hand over your boyfriend and tuck the tome under your arm? Or maybe you thought you were gonna come here and kick some ass, and take your shit home? *No-no-no,* angel-cake."

"I'm afraid Miranda has a point," Yikan quipped, batting his eyes, as though compelled to give witness to the truth.

"I was no angel before I joined up with the Church of the Imperial Goddess," Miranda volunteered. "Then I found out that bitch, Shazadeh, was all bullshit…got herself toasted by a flock of angels, and took that Egyptian down, too. But I've done some nasty shit myself, heh? right?" She nodded at him. "Hell is real…ya hear me, *Jack?* Me and everlasting fire ain't gonna do too well together. So I get a deal where I can stay here on earth and rule it like a queen, and all for the low-low price of one dead angel." She smiled. "Yeah…I like that deal." She looked at Eric.

Eric dipped his head and began walking down the stairs and moved to the left of Jared, positioning himself opposite of Miranda. Phineas turned and faced him, protecting Jared's left flank.

Phineas spoke to Jared in a hush. "What they doin', son?"

"Trying to split us up," Jared said, turning his body halfway between Yikan and Miranda.

Eric wouldn't attack Phineas out of fear of the Order arising, Jared figured. Still, Yikan and Miranda could double-team him; and if they were quick enough, overwhelm him before he had a chance to go on the defense, let alone offense. *And then Blain slips in, gets a touch, and here comes a demon I'm powerless against.*

Miranda started chanting. Her hands began to glow red, and then burst into flames.

Jared knew only moments remained before she finished the spell and struck. Though, the difference between her and him was that, he had no need of the chant any longer, once he had become an angel. His command of the elements came from the lifeforce within him, that invisible energy of the cosmos, that inexhaustible Godforce. He channeled his lifeforce into his arms and down to his hands.

He slid Phineas to the side with an elbow at his shoulder and faced Eric. And from there, with Eric in his line of sight, he released the energy from his hands in the form of a fireball, it nearly the size of his body. It hurtled toward Eric—sizzling and crackling, and rolling with flames— like a blazing meteor flying sideways.

Eric crossed his arms in front of his face as the fireball closed in. It struck him at chest level and exploded with a boom. He cried out as the impact knocked him off his feet and sent him tumbling away into dark.

"*Storra-nicksum!*" Miranda yelled from behind him. Fire erupted from her outstretched hands by command of the chant she called forth.

Jared spun Phineas around again, placing himself in the line of fire. The scarlet-red fire engulfed him. His skin and short afro began to sizzle. He began to grow hot on the inside, as he roasted on the outside.

Jared struck back. He drew in that invisible energy of the cosmos, and brought that power into his core—his chest—, bolstering his lifeforce with it, which already, he was funneling into his hands. He released the force against her.

Twin-tornadoes of blue fire burst from his hands and met Miranda's streams of red fire head on, and pushed it away from Jared. He willed his lifeforce to flow faster and drove Miranda's flames back until they were midway between them. Their fiery forces raged upon each other. It was a ferociously beautiful display of red and blue plasma exploding upon one another and spraying globs of super heated gases on the ground, melting it.

"I thought they said you were tough," Miranda said, and then chanted once more. With each word of the sacred chant she spoke, her fire grew darker and hotter. "Alum-pak...disorath...Alum-pak...nuet!"

"I thought I told you, *you should have listened to me*," Jared replied.

He pushed more of his lifeforce into his hands and formed lightning around his twin fires, turning them blue. The lightning crackled and spit out charges, and raced around his blue fire, spiraling toward Miranda's dark amber flames. The electricity struck her flames and peeled them back like a banana being stripped of its peels all at once.

Jared pushed her flames nearly back to her hands. He could hear her over the roars of the fires trying to chant quicker. "Your fire is hot, but mine's a lot hotter, lady. It's called angel-fire!"

He yelled out and released all of his force upon her. Her fires extinguished in a flash as Jared's blue, electric fire pushed in, and then spread out and surrounded her.

Her skin was akin to Jared's—tough and dense like steel. Though, whereas his had withstood her chant-conjured flames, hers did not hold up under the force of his angelic ones—blue fires born of the stars and lightning hot enough to melt metal. Her skin began to bubble and burst. She dropped screaming to her knees. She reached out her arm at Jared and tried to speak; she tried to chant, but only managed bits of the sacred words.

Her bubbling, popping skin turned black all over. Her outstretched arm gave way first; it became liquid and plopped to the ground. The rest of her body followed suit. She became liquid all over and collapsed upon herself, and spread out on the ground and bubbled like pancake batter on a hot grill. Jared shut off his flames and lightning and turned to Yikan.

"Her death is on you," Jared accused. His roasted skin was already repairing itself; it was changing from flame-darkened brown back to his normal, warm chestnut hue. The cost of lifeforce to kill Miranda had weakened him, though already he felt the ambient energy flowing back into his core, replenishing what had been lost.

"Utterly amazing," Yikan professed, looking at the bubbling, black goo that had once been Miranda. "Though she was a hybrid of mortal and demon, I did, however, expect much more of a fight out of her. God has made you powerful indeed, Mizel."

"God did—not you," Jared said. He pointed at the bubbling goo, but looked at Yikan as he spoke. "Gods don't die, Yikan."

"No," Yikan said, agreeing. "They persevere through the ages, as I have."

"Then do it," Jared challenged. "Go live your eternal life…live as long as you want. Build yourself the biggest palace on the highest mountaintop. You can chant up bricks of gold and diamonds, and bathe in it." He stepped up even with Phineas. "You just have to stay away from mortals."

"We can't do that," Blain said, keeping the knife steady at Chris's throat. He walked Chris forward to tome. "Yikan said you were powerful, and I believe him now. But…," He looked at the black goo and shook his head in disappointment, "you can't do that to me. I've seen what I turn into when I'm in danger—Yikan set it all up and recorded it for me."

"I'm surprised," Jared panned.

"Trust me…when that demon comes for you, it ain't a pretty sight when he's done," Blain said, shifting his weight to one hip, looking as though he were just in casual conversation with a friend. "Even as a kid, I've never believed in God. I always thought he was just a fairy tale to keep kids in line. If you're a bad boy, you're going to Hell, so obey your parents…*do as they say*…don't sin. I was a good boy for my parents and I did as they said. But my problem is that, *I like to sin.*"

"Indeed!" Yikan verified.

"I'm going to Hell for those sins," Blain said. "I know what I've done, and I know what I saw on that video of me changing into that *thing*. So if demons exist, I thought, then God does, too. But if God exists, that also means down there is real." He nodded at the ground in reference to the infamous realm of fire. "I know you think I'm a sick-o…a pervert…a monster, and a lot more than that, right?" He waited with wide welcoming eyes, as though ready to be unfazed by a concurrence of his self-assessment. He smiled and then said, "But even monsters feel pain."

"You sow what your reap," Phineas said.

"Not always," Blain objected. "Yikan is going to do for me what he did for Eric and Melinda, and make me immortal. Once Yikan becomes a celestial and you're out of the picture, the balance will be thrown off, and there won't be any End Days. Lucifer won't be able to get his hands on me and God can't break his own covenant. Yikan wins means I win." He looked down at Chris with a sorrowful expression and bobbed his head. "You seem like a good guy—you really do. But it's either me or you, kid. That's how life is, you know? It's a dice roll. Not everyone wins. Sometimes its snake eyes."

Phineas raised his hand. "Wait now! Just wait." He stepped forward. "Now look, you…you're only gonna make what's coming to you ten times worse. If you believe in God now, then you should know what God is. God is forgiveness. And he'll give it to you, if you ask for it and mean it—no matter what you done did. You ain't gotta go down that road to Hell."

Blain shook his head. "Sorry reverend, I'm already at Hell's door," he said, though not proudly. "And the thing is, I'm not sorry for what I've done—not at all. I'm on my thirty-first kill. This will be number thirty-two. And if you want the truth, seeing as there's no reason to lie to any of you, I'm pretty eager to get back at it. So reverend, I'd say my soul is already well spoken for."

"It belongs to The Duke, now," Yikan added, with all due reverence. "Do as he asks, Blain Hopps, and you will live forever. You will never step foot in Hell."

Blain turned to Jared. His eyes were wide with innocence. "It's the best offer I got."

"He *will* kill the boy," Yikan said to Jared. "Do not doubt him; though instead, make your choice as I have. The Duke shall do what was thought not possible. He will recast this hybrid form of mine into that of a celestial. Though it shall be of demonkind, it is of no matter; I will become your opposite, your balance in every way. Then, like you, I shall be able to draw upon the dark energies of the cosmos, as you do, though you have not figured that out yet. That is but the first of many lessons which The Duke and I can instruct you in. There is much more you have yet to discover." He extended his arm to Chris and the tome. "Come and grasp that which you desire the most. Die here or rise with me from this hollowed ground of Axumite kings and ascend to godhood."

Yikan beckoned him.

Blain shrugged helplessly.

Jared took a step forward.

"Be careful son," Phineas said, his voice warbling.

Jared looked over his shoulder at Phineas. His lips formed into a faint smile. "You need to remember your Bible a little better." He turned and approached the steps.

"What is your decision, Miel?" Yikan posed. "Deification or death?"

"I choose neither," Jared replied, ascending the stairs.

Blain pressed the blade harder against Chris's neck; blood began trickling down. Blain looked at Yikan, as though wondering whether to wait or not wait...cut or not cut.

"Yikan told you I was loaded with power...and he was right," Jared said to Blain, as he climbed another stair. Less than ten feet now separated them. "I can change matter or raise a storm here in a moment." He raised his arms to the sky, and then lowered them.

Jared looked at Chris; he was shivering. *Get just a bit closer. One more step, and just maybe....* Jared took another step, and then stopped. "Celestials do God's bidding," Jared said, speaking loud enough for Phineas to hear him clearly. "And God's usually wants it done pretty quick, like with Abraham, when he was going to sacrifice his son, Isaac!"

Jared turned and glanced at Phineas. A fleeting look was all the time he had to signal Phineas to remember Abraham's test—that he should sacrifice his son to God, only to have his hand stopped at that very last moment by the swift hands of an angel.

Jared pushed all of his lifeforce into his legs and released and flew at Blain and Chris. Rocketing with Godspeed, he reached for the blade with his thumb and index finger. In one moment, it seemed as though he stood midway on the stairs, and in the next, he was in front of Blain and Chris, and the blade in the firm grip of his finger and thumb.

He pulled the knife out of Blain's hand, careful not to touch any part of him, not even his clothing, and tossed the knife away. With his other hand, he shoved Chris down the stairs, and with a kick of his foot back-wards at the tome, he sent it tumbling right after him. Jared pushed off with his feet, turned around and raced back down the stairs, and had nearly made it to the bottom, until he was tripped.

Though Yikan was slower than Jared, he still managed to slide his body in front of Jared's, like a runner sliding across home base. Jared tumbled down the stairs and fought to stop his roll. But even then, Yikan, who was still on his side, was on the move.

Yikan reached for Blain. Blain reached for Yikan's outstretched hand and took it. He yanked Blain over and his prone body and flung him at Jared and Chris.

Jared looked up. Blain was moments from reaching him. But right next to him was Chris and the tome. And even though Phineas was run-ning for them, he was too far away to help. Jared knew he had to act now or not at all; the time for debating the consequences of pushing Chris and tome toward the safety of Phineas or stopping Blain from reaching all of them was gone. He acted. He pushed Chris and the tome away, and reached for Blain and caught him by the arm.

That fleeting bit of contact was all it took for Blain's metamorphosis to spur into action. Jared released his hold on Blain's arm, but Blain's other hand—it no longer white, but becoming darker by the moment—reached out and grabbed hold of *his* arm. Jared tried pulling free, but the harder he yanked, the tighter the hold became.

Blain's eyes rolled into the back of his head and were replaced with ones that were black from corner to corner. The rest of his skin, like his hand and eyes, also took on that same oily-black hue, which glimmered in the glow of the bonfires.

Its jaws snapped and popped, separating the top one from its bottom one. It opened its mouth; dagger-sharp teeth pushed away Blain's mortal ones and formed double rows, top and bottom, like a shark's. It grew tall, bringing Jared up along with. It's spindly arms were nearly the length of Jared's body. Its hands formed into claws; its feet became hooves, like a goat's.

Yikan scrambled up the steps on his hands and knees. Eric was just returning from having been knocked back and away by Jared's fireball. Though upon seeing Blain transform, he stayed in the shadows, away from the demon. Phineas reached Chris and the tome, and covered them both with his body. He looked up into the black eyes of the demon holding his son.

"Who are you that has dared to harm my mortal?" the demon demanded of Jared, as it continued to morph. Its head flattened on the top, and its mouth—already inhumanly wide—ripped at the corners and spread up to its pointy ears. It was unholy; it was foul; the sound of its deep, trembling voice shook the air and stirred up dust from the ground. *"The covenant must be fulfilled! So sayeth The Father."*

Phineas pushed off of the tome and stood. He looked down at Chris. "Stay here. And don't move from this tome, boy."

Phineas ran up the stairs and stumbled, and fell, whacking his forehead on stone stairs. The demon looked at him. "I know what thou are, mortal."

Phineas looked up at it. His forehead was gashed and blood was trickling down from it into his left eye. He began crawling up the stairs toward the demon. "I know what you are, too! You're a devil! A demon! —straight from the bowels of Hell. And I curse you in the name of God!" He pushed off with his leg and reached for the creature. "By the glory of God, I cast thee—"

Phineas never finished, for at that moment—not even an inch from touching the demon—he was no longer Phineas Boremon, a reformed father, a one time alley cat and now servant of God. In that shallow breath of a moment, he became God's warrior upon earth—a celestial imbued with the power of The Ghost to carry out God's divine command, which was to keep his covenant sound, unblemished, and *holy*.

Phineas glowed a luminous white-blue all over. His body grew in length and width, nearly tripling in size and then some. His head swelled like a balloon being inflated. His nose, lips, and eyes sank into his expanding face, which was quickly replaced with three other faces. One face was positioned in the middle of the head; the other two were on either side of it.

"*Muchenlay*," said the center face of the Order that now stood in place of Phineas. The Order was nude and had no genitalia to speak of; its brilliance outshone the bonfires, making them seem as nothing more than sparks in its blue-tinted, white aura. "What game is at play that you and I have been summoned to this place of the dead?"

"Subterfuge, Oriziel," Muchenlay said, replying to the androgynous face in the center of the Order. Muchenlay looked at the male face on the right; its brow was thick and hung low over its glowing, white eyes; its nose was broad; its lips were plump and dark blue. "It is by hoax and ruse that we are here. Is this not so, Nigiel?" Muchenlay didn't wait for a reply, though instead, looked to the female face on the left and said, "What say you, Palis? What say thee all?"

"'Tis' the Egyptian who has wrought this," Palis said, her voice fair and light, though firm and without equivocation.

The two celestials, one of light and the other of darkness—of Heaven and of Hell—turned their collective gaze on Yikan. And as those ancient eyes bore down upon him, casting fault, all became silent in the graveyard of the Auxumite kings of Africa.

"He schemes with the keepers of the damned," Nigiel said, his voice deep and throbbing.

"He swears allegiance to Duke Astaroth, not to the Morning Star, our holy lord," Muchenlay crowed, with a shake of her hand, which Jared was in, flopping him about like a ragdoll. She held Jared out toward the tri-faced celestial, using him to point with. "Astaroth was once favored by the Morning Star; though now, the Duke of the West has become his adversary."

"You cling to blasphemy," Oriziel professed. "There is but three of the trinity; they who are one, and one who are three."

"There shall be a fourth," Muchenlay prophesized humbly. "The Morning Star shall have his deification, and will be given his rightful place amongst them. Is he not firstborn, the most perfect of all creations of the Father?"

"Such madness is what damned legions of thee and thy kind to Hell," Palis said.

Muchenlay switched Jared to her other hand, clamping him at the chest, and piercing him with her claws. Jared yelled out as her talons sliced through his dense, celestial flesh. He concentrated his lifeforce into his fists and pounded at the creature's arm, though to no effect; its grip did not lessen in the slightest, but instead grew tighter. He was trapped, and the demon knew it, for she gave full attention to bantering with her fellow celestial, and not a scant bit toward him—her securely trapped prey.

"The angel is still mine," Muchenlay claimed, holding Jared up to the Order, like he was a trophy. "He sought to harm my mortal."

Oriziel, Palis, and Nigiel's eyes darted side to side, as though they were in counsel within their shared head. "Do you know who it is you hold captive?" Palis asked.

"I know full well who he is."

"Still, that is of no consequence," Nigiel opined, as though continuing out loud the inner debate with Palis and Oriziel. "The Child of Balance is no more; his mortal duty is complete. Now, he is Mizel, archangel of the third celestial sphere—the Angel of Balance."

"With whom I may do with as I dictate," Muchenlay said haughtily, as though it still were not fully plain enough. "That is the covenant! It is holy law. It cannot be corrupted, even by an Order as great as thou are. What is mine is mine, and no other's!"

Palis looked forlorn. "He is yours," she conceded. "The covenant must not be torn asunder."

"It cannot be!" Muchenlay protested. Black saliva spooled from her lips and to the ground, freezing it. She stomped her foot, shaking the ground; the ancient steles wobbled on their bases. "I shall not kill him, for he is a most uncommon prize. Though, I shall bend his back and place him at my feet. He will serve as the footstool of my throne." Her knuckles popped as she tightened her grip on Jared. "Do you challenge my right?"

The heavenly celestials again went into counsel in their shared head. A few moments passed, and then Oriziel spoke. "Though Heaven may shed bitter tears for the loss of Mizel, thou are correct, Muchenlay—the covenant cannot be trespassed against."

"Know, however, that thy time is short," Nigiel said, his voice grave. "Mizel shall be avenged a thousand times come the last Great War, when your kind is banished back to the ether—to nonexistence."

Muchenlay waved her hand dismissively. "You cling to a prophecy that shall never be, yet you call me a fool? My lords, you have danced too close to the stars of Heaven, and it has addled your brain. If any are to be cast into the ether, it shall be the Holy Hosts of Heaven, not I—not us!"

"So sayeth you," the Order said, speaking as one, blending their three voices into one pure tone. "In that hour, known only to the Father, we shall find thee and deliver your final judgment, and gladly so."

"And I shall be waiting with sword in hand."

"As shall we," they said.

Jared stopped struggling to break free, though within, he was scrambling to prepare to fight. He realized strength alone would not break the demon's grip, no matter how strong his celestial body was. However, blasting his way free just might work, he thought. He began drenching his core with the dark energy around him until he felt himself overflow with it. The excess energy began oozing from his mouth, eyes, nose, and ears.

Muchenlay turned him around to face her. She smiled, showing her double-rowed teeth. She brought him closer, positioning his nose against hers, which was no more than just two black holes in skin.

"*You are mine!*" Muchenlay professed. The force of her voice sent shockwaves through the air and tremors along the ground. The towering stele behind them fractured from its base to its center. Chunks of stone broke from it and smashed to pieces on the ground.

Muchenlay began returning to where she had come from, taking Jared along with her. Her body began to shrink. Her arms and legs retracted, as though they were stretched rubber bands returning to their original state. She brought Jared to her chest and wrapped her other arm around him, and began enveloping him.

Jared saw everything around him suddenly stop as Muchenlay's skin began swallowing him; Chris's mouth was stretched wide in the midst of a yell; Yikan was running for the tome and had one foot in mid-air and was pushing off with the other. Space and time—*space-time*—was warping around him, pulling him away from one existence and into another.

Jared was drenched with dark energy. His lifeforce spun madly as he drew in even more of that invisible force, knowing that he had to strike now and strike hard. Yet, he needed more power.

And then, suddenly, he remembered God, and what had happened the last time he had looked to the cosmos in search for him. In the darkness of space, he had found a hint of God's power. Now, as he had before, he sent his thoughts off to the cosmos in search of God. And in that formless, nothingness of space between trillions of far flung stars, nebulae, black holes, and galaxies, he again caught a glimpse of God's power. With his mental hand outstretched—he reached for it and touched a hint of it.

A force of energy suddenly rushed into his hands and spread out through his entire body. Muchenlay's morphing body enveloped him into her, surrounding him in darkness. Though, with his infusion of power, he shone like a sun of pure white light and pushed the darkness away him.

Jared looked around. There was only he and the darkness, nothing else. There was no up or down, no left or right. He felt as though he were standing between life and death, they equal and in perfect balance.

I gotta do it now! he thought, as the power he'd absorbed began to burn from within.

He released his lifeforce, the dark energy, and that spark of Godforce he had dared to touch, and exploded in a brilliant white flash. The darkness fled, though now, in its place, he saw a light blue color, and then felt himself falling—hurtling. Fire raged and crackled all around him. He stopped abruptly, though not on his own accord, and everything went dark.

* * *

"Jared!" Chris cried out.

Jared was gone—vanished along with the creature. Though now, some one familiar to him was back. Blain Hopps was sprawled face first on the stairs. His head was pointed downward; he was naked and unconscious; the shreds of his clothing were strewn around him.

Chris looked up at the Order and yelled. "Where's Jared? Where did he go?" He bordered on hysteria. "Why didn't you help him?"

The Order turned its head, giving Chris a full view of Nigiel's face. "He has gone to the lair of the Dark One."

"He is in the land of Phenóx!" Oriziel proclaimed. "There, pretended gods sit upon thrones and profess themselves holy."

"In his palace, Lucifer lies in sleep upon a slab of platinum, never to wake until the End of Days—so sayeth the Lord God," Palis told him. "There, Mizel is no more than a pet for Muchenlay, who is lady of that infernal realm of bitter ice, and home to the most vile of souls."

"How...how do I get him back?"

"There is no coming back," Yikan answered gaily. He and Eric descended the steps, giving the celestial ample quarter. They walked over to the tome, which was on the ground in front of Chris.

Chris quickly backed away from them, inadvertently moving closer to the Order. Though at that moment, Chris was less worried about the glowing celestial behind him, than of the two who had held him prisoner and tortured him.

"Do not fret, child," Yikan said. "I have no more need of you now that your friend is far, far away from here, and likely dead already; patience is not a virtue Lady Muchenlay possesses." Yikan glanced at Eric and pointed at the tome. Eric bent down to retrieve it.

"Stop!" Oriziel commanded. Eric looked up at the celestial; his hands were mere inches from the gold tome.

Yikan glared at Eric; his liquid eyes whirled, making they almost seemed solid. Yet, Eric did not move, though stood there, as if waiting for the tri-faced entity to strike him down.

Yikan gazed up at the being. "Have no fear of the Order. It has but one duty, and that is to protect the preacher from harm. It, however, cannot harm you. It is bound by the law of—"

"The covenant," Palis said, with all due reverence. "We give warning to thee, Egyptian."

"Aye," Nigiel said. "Turn from this dark path, before thy actions tear asunder Heaven, Hell, and earth."

"Astaroth allies with no one," Oriziel said.

"He has usurped lordship from his own grandfather, Beelzebub, and taken his cursed lands for himself," Palis said.

"Along with the power embedded within them," Oriziel added.

"Only one lord of Hell still stands against Astaroth," Nigiel said. "Though soon, he shall fall, as the others have. And then to Phenóx Astaroth shall go—"

"And there," Yikan interrupted, "he will slay Lucifer and take his power, as I shall now take his tome. Your knowledge shall serve you not, celestial; what is done is done. *Eric!*" he called. Eric snatched the book and quickly backed away from the Order. "See there, Eric, there are rules that must be adhered to. The Order cannot harm you—it has a duty; that is one rule." He spoke slowly, stretching out his words, as though explaining physics to a toddler. "The other rule is that good and evil must be in perfect balance before his lamb—the Christ—may return to earth to save the mortals. And right now, dear lad, the world is in balance, and the Lamb may come at any moment. Who knows that day and hour of judgment other than the Father himself?" He pouted playfully. "Though now, Mizel is gone. That wretched whore, Shazadeh, is thankfully no more. And the world is in balance, though…I say not for long."

"How weary the arms of Astaroth's puppet," Oriziel opined.

"Soon those strings shall be cut," Palis warned.

"Your greed will doom all of creation, even thyself," said Nigiel. "Mark my words."

"And mine," Oriziel said.

"Agreed," Palis called out.

"Mark our words, Egyptian," they spoke as one, "thou shall surely reap what thou hath sown."

"Aye!" Yikan concurred. "For thousands of years I have sown the seeds of godhood. Though, all mine eyes see now is a meticulously cultivated field of ripe grain bathed in the warm, orange glow of a harvest moon." He spoke glowingly and poetically, though his tone quickly became brash. *You have lost, star-dancer.* Go sail amongst the moons and stars, and forget you ever knew a place called earth, for true salvation has come this day."

"There is only one God," Nigiel said.

"There was, my lord." He grinned, and then chanted and began rising from the ground.

Eric scooped up Blain and held him like a rolled up rug; the tome was tucked under his other arm. Blain groaned and raised his head; his eyelids were half closed. Eric called out a chant and rose into the air, bearing both the tome and Blain with him, and disappeared into the night sky.

Chris looked the ancient graveyard. The bonfires Jared had created had waned and were now just pale yellow flickers of light. It was his first opportunity to take in where he was. The paralyzing fear of Blain about to carve his neck had made it impossible for him to think of anything else; all he had wanted was to live, and all Blain had wanted to do was cut. Yikan had forced him to watch Blain trap and torture and mutilate his victims, and then start upon them again and again, until his vile lust was sated for a brief time. And then he would kill his prey and go off on the hunt again for fresh ones to toy with. He knew if Blain had pulled the knife across his throat, it was going to be bone deep.

"You are troubled, and so you should be," Oriziel said to him. Chris looked up at the Order.

"The world is now balanced," Nigiel said, "though, it will not stay as such for long if the Egyptian has his way."

"Astaroth will remake Yikan," Palis said.

"As a demon," Oriziel added.

"Or…," Palis said, and paused for a moment "so Astaroth has told him."

"Astaroth is a liar…they all are," Nigiel professed. "It is their core nature to deceive."

"There's gotta be a way to get Jared back," Chris said. "If he got there, there's gotta be a gettin' back from there."

"From that lair of evil?" Nigiel said, with a grim look on his face. "Within that palace sleeps a power that only the Father, the Ghost, and the Lamb hath dominion over."

"He was first born," Palis said.

"And perfect in every way," Oriziel chimed in.

"He was the morning star of Heaven," Nigiel professed reverently.

"Til' he fell," said Palis.

"Thy friend is lost to thee," Oriziel said.

"Give up hope for his return," Nigiel advised.

"Do not despair, brother," Oriziel countered. "There is always hope."

"But so thin that hope is," Palis remarked. "If Muchenlay does not kill him, then it shall be at the hands of Lucifer that he is sent to the ether, for the Fallen One feeds on all that is in Phenóx."

Nigiel turned his face to Chris. He spoke solemnly. "Live what life thou hath left to live, mortal child, for the fate of this world and all those upon it, lies in the hands of the Egyptian."

"I'm not gonna give up," said Chris, with tears at his eyes. "You could help us if you—"

"We cannot," Palis said abruptly.

"We are forbidden to interfere in the affairs of mortals," Nigiel said.

"Although," Oriziel said, "there is one who may offer assistance in this great time of need…*Mekka-Nuat.*"

"The Throne," Palis said.

"Aye, the Great Wheel," Nigiel added reverently.

"Its sight can pierce all realms, even that of Hell," Oriziel said.

"Then ask him to help us," Chris implored.

"*He?*" Oriziel said, and then smiled. "Mekka-Nuat is no he. Nor is the Great Wheel a she. Mekka-Nuat is of Thrones of the first sphere—they are the greatest bodies of the cosmos. There is no need to beseech Mekka-Nuat, for the Great Wheel has already heard thy plea, for even now," the Order looked to the star-dotted sky, "it watches and listens from across time and space. Come Mekka-Nuat now or come never, there is no knowing the Great Wheel's intentions."

The Order turned Palis's face to Chris. "Farewell mortal. We must return from whence we have come—our duty here is done."

Just as Muchenlay had inverted its body inside out and transformed back into Blain, so did the Order, transforming back into Phineas. Its face swirled in, and Phineas's rose up from the sides. Its white, luminous skin lost its glow, and the Order began to shrink. They spoke into Chris's mind as one. "Pray to the Father, the Lamb, and the Ghost; it is thy only hope."

The Order was gone. The bonfires were dead; and the ancient burial ground of African kings was returned to utter darkness. On the steps in front of Chris, Phineas lay unconscious.

Chris gathered the scraps of Phineas's clothes and covered his nude body with them. He shook and called to Phineas, who mumbled incoherently, yet did not wake. Chris relented and sat down next to him, and looked at him; he was sleeping peacefully.

He pulled his legs in and wrapped his arms around them, hugging himself tight; he tried not to cry, but the tears came anyway. And instead of trying to stop them, he let them flow; he let his ache come out in sobs, for now it was Jared who was in danger, or likely dead.

He realized he was free of one prison only to be put in another, though this one was bigger, and he shared it with billions of others; and they would all share the same fate under Yikan's rule. Without Jared, there was no stopping Yikan.

He did as the Order suggested. He went to his knees and closed his eyes, and folded his hands in prayer. *God, I know Jared is probably dead and I'm just an idiot for even thinking he isn't. Yikan screwed around with my head and says he fixed me...that I'm not dumb anymore; but I still am; I gotta be for even thinking Jared's alive somewhere. He's my best friend, God, ya know? He's my bro. So...please, if you could give me—and everybody on the planet—just one miracle—and that's all we'll ask of ya—give us Jared back. He can make this right. I know he would. I know he can.*

He opened his eyes and looked about the cemetery. *I don't even know where here is.* He looked down at Phineas, who had begun snoring lightly.

"Shit," he muttered.

CHAPTER 5

Jared had followed the road into the forest. The trees had appeared monstrous from a distance, though up close, they seemed like skyscrapers to him, though ones, he figured, that were made by dark sorcery. As the sound of riders on horseback grew louder—closer—he strayed from the road, and sought refuge within the forest. His lifeforce had yet to renew, his muscles still felt like rubber, and he knew running from them was not going to be an option; though, neither was fighting. He was too weak. The run to the forest had sapped what strength he had recovered since falling.

The forest was silent—absolutely. Other than the rustle of dark green leaves by his own making, he heard not a sound…not a bird, or squirrel, or any animals rustling about, which made what was odd, queerer yet, for it was a lush, green wonderland if ever there was one, he thought. Dark green ivy carpeted the forest floor; and they were as high as his shin, and were dense, making it felt as though he was tromping through foot-high snow instead of leaves. And scattered throughout the forest were all manner of plants of every color and size and shape and height, and some soaring fifty feet high, with leaves the size of two men stacked end on end. Everything seemed perfect; too perfect, just like the soul, Ellen, kept saying. Though, for all of the wondrous beauty around him, it all seemed dead to him. That is, until a voice—a female's—spoke into his mind.

*"Not since the Lamb descended into our realm and freed the damned, has
someone from Heaven come unto us,* she said. *I saw you fall, angel of God.
You were like a star. You escape the hands of Lady Muchenlay, whose grasp,
it is said, cannot be broken—but you did! And you have won your freedom
—for now."*

Jared ran for the largest tree in front of him. A ring of shrubs and
bushes surrounded it, and nearly extended to the next behemoth of a
tree. He pushed past branches and leaves, and fought his way in to the
thick of it.

He reached out with his thoughts to try and locate her. Though, as he
projected his mental force outward, all he could see in his mind's eye
were vines and leaves squirming amongst one another like a den full of
snakes. With a mental swipe of the hand, he brushed them away. And as
soon as he did, they came back, though thicker. Jared was incredulous.
She's blocking me!

"Of course I am. This forest is my home, my land, *my womb*," she
said, though this time, the sound of her voice came from the floor of
vines, and from the shrubs, and came down from the trees, and out
through the leaves of the plants, and even from the leaves of the bushes
he was hiding in. The clapping of horse hooves were louder, though had
slowed to an intermittent clip and clop. The horses whinnied. Their
masters spoke to one another, though Jared could not understand the
language they were speaking. "There is no escape from Varencia—my
realm of eternal life. My duke's soldiers have come to claim you, and
they will have you. Resist them, and you will suffer the ether. Submit,
angel—if you are wise."

Jared peeked through the leaves toward the road. He saw three creatures on horseback; all of them wore black chest armor. One was by far
the largest of the three…a dark-brown male with bulging, sinewy muscles. On the side of his head were ivy-white horns curved like a ram's.
The horse he rode who stood a good two feet above the others, and was
nearly twice their width.

Another demon moved its horse up next to the horned brute, though
this demon was a shadow of the size of his companion. His skin was dark

green and glistened like it was wet. He wore a black circlet with a red jewel atop a head of kinky, black hair.

Jared looked for the last creature, though did not see it. He chanced moving a few leaves and looked to his right. No sign of it. He then looked to his left. Nothing.

He looked back to the two creatures. They had dismounted. The green one seemed like a child in stature next to his muscled comrade. They looked at one another and spoke, and then together, looked up to the trees, and with a whoosh of air, leapt straight up; they flew like rockets and disappeared into the canopy of leaf-laden branches created by the trees.

Jared crouched and went still. He looked up, and from through the leaves of the bushes he was hiding in, searched for sight of them. Though he did not see them, he could see the branches sway and hear them creak, and that sound moving toward him, though in different directions. One was moving toward his right and the other to his left.

"Na nasinna li-ado sundi na ortos mi lida-porra," the lady of the forest called out through the leaves and vines and plants of the forest.

The foliage of the forest in front of Jared began to move at the lady's words. He looked out and saw the massive trees in front of him—three of them, side-by-side, and shrubs crowded at their base—begin to part. Two of the trees bent to the left, while the third one leaned right, groaning and moaning as they did. The shrubs, vines, and plants followed suit and parted, and created a path of green that led directly to the shrubs he was hiding in.

A figure—a female—stepped onto the path and began approaching him. She wore a floor-length white skirt and a breastplate, like the males. Her skin was as dark as the black chest-armor she wore, which bore a gold, oak leaf insignia in the shape of a mobius continuum. Her hair was a mass of yarn-thin black braids that hung straight, all the way down to the top of her bosom. He looked at her face again—her almond-shaped eyes; those full lips—and there, his gaze lingered.

As she passed through the 'v' shaped threshold of parted trees, shrubs, and plants, they straightened back, resuming their original position. She stopped, and then looked up to her right. "Li, Thamuz, luk-aht lida sorra." And to her left she said, "Caym…aht na porra zu dralla-abo." She looked at the shrubs Jared was in. "Come out, creature."

Jared went still, though his thoughts were frenzied. He realized he was flanked on either side and blocked by the female in front of him. Though not only that, the other female who spoke through the plants was still somewhere out there. He forced what scant lifeforce he had into his legs and prepared to flee if need be, to try to outrun them if he could, which he had already figured would be fruitless.

The dark energy within the realm of earth fed his lifeforce; though here—in Hell—he felt nothing to draw from. Without dark energy, he was powerless, save the strength of his body, which too, was still recovering from the fall. Regardless, he knew he had to try.

"There's no place to go," the female in front of him said. Her voice was heavy, though calm—steady and composed. "I don't think you'd care to come upon the lady Pnemoxsis, whose forest you are in. Her hospitality would suit you ill, I'm sure."

Jared glimpsed movement in the bushes to his right; though as soon as he saw it, he caught a shadow moving on his left. In front of him, the female continued her approach. The vines at her feet parted where she stepped and rejoined as she passed. His muscles began quivering with fear, and the need for self-preservation itched at him to run for it. He pivoted to the left on the balls of his feet and dashed out of the bushes, running for a line of shrubs between two massive trees.

He was about to leap through the bushes, when a figure—the green one—stepped out from them. His black eyes were the first to shed its camouflage. The creature's skin suddenly turned a darker shade of green than the bushes he had blended into; the breastplate he wore shimmered and changed from green back to black. Jared skidded on the vines and slipped, and then scrambled back to his feet.

"Did you not hear Lady Zimarantha, angel?" the creature said, as its skin and clothing completely shed their mirage. It gazed around the forest lovingly and smiled. "You're in my home. There's no escape for you here."

Jared spun to his right. The green one's companion had already come down from the trees and was already waiting form him—staring at him with piercing yellow eyes like a cougar. In front of him, the female was staring at him with a look of bewilderment.

Jared spoke to her. "What do you want from me?"

"What do we want from *you?*" she asked. "It is you who have come to our realm uninvited."

"I'm not even supposed to be here," Jared offered.

"Obviously," said the green creature.

"Then let me be," Jared demanded. "Just—just let me figure my own way out of here, and I'll be gone. I'll get out of your realm. And that way, this doesn't have to go the wrong way."

"The wrong way?" the green one asked, though more of himself than Jared. He looked at the towering brute across from him. "Thamuz...is that earthly lingo he uses? *'The wrong way?'*"

Thamuz crossed his arms; they looked like overlapped logs. "He is warning you, Caym. He thinks he will best you."

Caym chuckled. His teeth shined brilliantly white against his glistening green skin. He shook his head and said, "What a foolish creature you are."

"Hold on," Jared blurted. "Look...I don't want to be here as much as you don't want me here." Jared looked at the female. "I'm not trying to start a war."

"Too late for that," Caym quipped.

"War is already upon us," Thamuz added, deeply and somberly.

"Submit, angel," the female commanded, "for your sake."

"Lady Zim," Caym called, "his kind never submits. May we just take him and be done with it?"

"Give him a chance, my lord," Thamuz implored gently. "Perhaps he will see the wisdom in coming along without bother."

"Father says angels never surrender," Caym said. "You have said the same yourself, Thamuz."

"Aye," Thamuz uttered, low like a growl. "Though, that is in battle. This, however, is a most unique situation, to say the least. Tis' not every passing of Wormwood that an angel of The Father falls into Hell."

"Do you submit or do you not?" Lady Zim asked again, with a tone far cooler than even before; it spoke of no more chances to come.

Jared looked from one demon to the other. He moved his head slowly side to side, knowing he did not have the strength to fight them. "I can't do that."

Lady Zim sighed. She extended her right arm out to the side. A beam of white light passed out from her black glove and extended down to the vines at her boots. The light pulsed—brightening and darkening—, and then it dimmed and became solid—formed into a black-handled sword with a gleaming silver blade.

"Surrender freely or not, the duke will still have you," she said, raising the sword out to her side.

The duke, Jared thought. At Lady Zim's mention of him, that night in Axum all came tumbling down on him like an avalanche. Panic drove his thready lifeforce into a mad spin. First, Astaroth tried to kill him, though now, he fretted, Astaroth wanted him as a prisoner—a slave, or worse. He had denied Astaroth his first choice, and now, he planned on doing the same with his second.

Caym was behind him. Thamuz was on his right. Jared decided on the smaller of the two evils.

He bolted to the right, feigning as though he were going to charge Thamuz, though stopped and spun around, and then sprinted for the gap between Caym and Lady Zim. Between the two of them, there was a hill covered with vines and monstrously tall plants. If he could dive through it, he figured he might have a slim possibility of losing them in it…possibly even escaping, if he was lucky.

Jared closed in on Caym and cocked his arm, ready to strike the demon if he tried to block his way. Lady Zim, however, was the one that spurred into action. In one brief moment, she was standing on Jared's right, and in the next, she dashed to his left; her speed was so swift, she left ghostly trails in her wake. She stopped in front of him with her sword raised.

Jared jammed his heels into the vines and slid to halt. He stopped mere inches from the tip of Lady Zim's blade. He turned and raced for Caym. He cocked his fist. Caym didn't flinch.

Jared poured his lifeforce into his fist and swung for Caym's face. His aim was true, however, his strike was halted.

Caym caught Jared's fist in the palm of his hand, stopping its momentum cold. Jared tried to pull his fist away, though was denied; Caym's grip crushed upon his knuckles, holding him firm. Jared cried out as his knuckles cracked, threatening to pop open like a kernel of popcorn; his knees were moments from buckling.

Caym yanked Jared's hand and spun him around. Caym saddled up to Jared's backside and wrapped his left arm around his neck. In turn, Jared took hold of Caym's arm; and giving every bit of strength he had left, he began pulling at it. Caym's grip slowly began to loosen.

Though, just as freedom seemed within his grasp, the foliage around him began to die. What was green and appeared full of life, suddenly became brown, and then turned black and began to shrivel for feet around him in a circle. As the forest withered, Jared felt Caym's grip upon his neck tighten. What ground he had gained was suddenly lost; and the hold about his throat became twice as tight as before.

Caym held out his other hand and conjured a sword from his palm, as Lady Zim had. It burst into flames from tip to hilt. He swung it up, replacing his hand around Jared's neck with the flaming blade inches from his skin.

Caym moved in until he was cheek to cheek with Jared. "It would be unwise of you to move, angel. I have never been known to slip, but there's a first time for everything. Having fallen into our realm, you should know that better than anyone."

"Cease, my son," the lady of the forest called out. Caym lowered his sword. Jared quickly moved away from him, though not far, for Lady Zim and Thamuz were but a few steps in front of him. "Your father has asked for the angel alive, has he not?"

"Yes, Mahti," Caym said and respectfully bowed his head. He transformed his sword back into light, which then returned from where it had come—back into the palm of his hand.

Caym glared at Jared, though then abruptly looked off to the side of him. His glower quickly faded. He bowed at the waist. Lady Zim and Thamuz turned and looked in that same direction; they bowed also. Jared turned around to see what they were seeing.

Coming toward them was a female in a white robe sitting upon a throne composed of leaves, which was borne forth upon a story-high wave of them, which moved like water. The rolling wave of leaves brought the throne and its occupant in front of Jared and set it down. The female had dark green skin like Caym's and eyes just as black. Atop her head of dark green braids, she wore a crown with a red jewel at its center, though larger than the one her son was wearing.

"In these troubled times, my son, we must follow our lord's commands exactly as they are given," she said. "For what purpose the duke wants this angel alive," she looked down at Jared, "I do not know. But it is he that the duke wants, and we shall give him to our lord as he is…unharmed."

"I'm not going to be used by Astaroth," Jared vowed.

Lady Zim turned to him. "Astaroth? The duke of the West? He is no lord here. This is the realm of Duke Chax and Lady Pnemoxsis. You will find no allies of Astaroth in Orsha-Na, lest they be traitors."

"And these are the duke's soldiers," Lady Pnemoxsis said. "Though he," she looked at Caym and smiled proudly, "is the duke's son as well."

No sooner had she spoken, than children—green skinned ones—came scrambling out from behind her throne. There were eight of them, and none of them appeared more than ten years old in age. They wore vines for clothing, which were in constant motion, swirling around them and concealing their private bits. Some came and sat at the foot of her leafy throne; others lay on their backs on the vine-covered ground next to it; two of them stood on the left of the throne.

A male child, who appeared no more than a mortal of four years old, crawled up Lady Pnemoxsis's white robe and sat on her lap. He laid his head upon her breast.

"You forgot about us, mommy," the child said and pouted, and then stuck his thumb in his mouth.

Lady Pnemoxsis kissed his forehead. "Mother never forgets her lovelies, Iban," she assured him, and then looked at Jared. "Astaroth has stolen much from us."

"And we plan to see him to the ether for it," Thamuz added.

"My blade shall fall upon his neck," Caym boastfully predicted.

"It will take more than blades to fall Astaroth now," the lady said. "He was great before, though now, he has grown immensely powerful. Though I begin to wonder if you are not just another part of his plans. Is this why my mate covets you?" The children turned and stared at Jared, waiting for his reply. Even the child on her lap had stopped sucking his thumb, and just held it in his mouth, waiting for Jared to speak.

"I was tricked into coming here," Jared explained. "Astaroth was behind it."

"That is no surprise," Lady Pnemoxsis said. "His plots run deep. Your presence on earth altered the balance of dark and light, though now, it is in balance with you gone from it. So to what advantage does your absence have for him? one wonders." She stroked the back of Iban's neck.

Iban looked up with wide, innocent black eyes. "Perhaps Pahdi knows."

"He knows everything," opined a young female on the left of the throne.

"Yes-yes," the lady assured them both gently. "Your father is Sky God. And he is very wise." The children smiled with pride. "We must take this angel to him at once. Your father commands it."

"May we go with brother to see Pahdi?" asked a male-child, who sat at the foot of her throne. His legs, and waist, and tummy were covered in a restless wrapping of winding ivy. Tiny green leaves wormed through his wooly hair.

No, my sodi," she replied, with a look of despondency. "We should not worry your father, for much is on his mind in these dark days of Astaroth's uprising. Until we are summoned, we shall stay here in Varencia. Though never forget," she turned to all of them; a mother's comforting smile upon her dark, full lips, "that he loves you all. Your brother, Caym, shall bear our love to the duke for us." The children groaned and moaned. The one upon her lap kneaded her breast with his head and whined. He grabbed hold of one of her green braids and diddled with it, as though it was his sole consolation in all of creation.

"Where are you taking me?" Jared asked.

"To Palace Adoja, in Hedun," Lady Zim said.

"It is the home of a god," Lady Pnemoxsis clarified proudly.

Jared cast a look of disdain upon the lush green land around him. The plants were of all shades of green, from a pale sea foam to near black jade; and they were thick of stem and leaf; some of the plants were as tall as two story buildings; the trees were as wide as trucks, and with their soaring height, appeared to brush the sky with their tops. The scent of fertile soil and perfume-rich flowers infused the moist air. It wasn't beauty that was all around him, he thought, just vanity run amok. *You demons aren't gods—not even close. You're everything God isn't…everything that's wrong.*

He looked back at Lady Pnemoxsis. She was scowling at him. Her dark eyes had turned murky green. In that poisonous look of hers, Jared realized that she had listened to every word he had just thought, and was none to pleased at what she'd heard.

She turned from one side to the other, looking upon all of her children. "The angel of The Father believes I overflow with self-aggrandizement." The demon children of the forest turned their dull, green-eyed gaze upon Jared. "What say we ask father if we may have the angel once he has concluded his dealings with *it*?" she proposed.

"I think that is a wonderful idea, mother," said a young female, who appeared to be but nine or ten.

"Yes, mahti…do ask him," another said.

"Please, mahti," came another, and then another, and yet another.

The whole tribe of pre-adolescent demons filled the jade forest with high pitch pleas. She brought them to silence with a refined wave of her hand. Her children stood and crowded around the throne.

"How can I refuse?" she offered, in mock innocence. Her lips parted; they looked equal parts desirous and deadly. "I am sure that father would not refuse his lovelies, now would he?" They grimaced and adamantly shook their heads side to side. "Am I not the goddess of life?" They nodded up and down. "The scryer divine?" They bobbed their heads eagerly. "Then if I say, I have peered into the scrying pool and seen father granting all you your wishes, then shall it not come to pass?"

Iban uncorked his thumb from his mouth and looked up at her. "I want his pain, mommy."

A boy on the left of the throne said, "I want his heartache."

"I want his envy," another said.

"His sorrow," said one at her knee.

"I want his avarice."

"His shame."

"His deceit."

"Denial."

"Regret!"

"Mother!" a voice called out from the hill of ivy, yards off to her right.

Jared looked to the ivy hill. He didn't see the demon amongst the dark ivy leaves until the creature stood and provided some contrast between his green skin and the leaves behind him. The demon stood upon the ivy floor, which then came alive, moving as though it was solid, though undulated like waves of water, bearing him down and in front of his mother's throne. He stepped off of the ivy, which then snaked away and back to the hill from whence it had come.

The demon bowed before his mother—one arm in front of his bare stomach, and one arm behind. Despite his green skin, pointed ears and black eyes, and the squirming ivy wrapped around him from ankle to waist, he appeared as no more than an adolescent male; even his dark green skin had an unnatural glow about the cheeks.

"I want his despair, mother, if you please," the male-child said humbly, though nobly, as one who had been properly schooled in the etiquette of aristocratic manners. He looked over his shoulder at Jared and took his measure from top to bottom, and sneered.

Just then, Jared felt a touch to his shoulder and startled. He spun around and saw a young, green female coming up from behind him. She gave him a tight-lipped smile and an unambiguously seductive narrowing of her eyes. Her cheeks were plump, as were her lips; ivy-covered her curvy hips and perky breasts. She walked over and stood next to the adolescent male, placing her torso next to his, and her cheek to his cheek. The ivy they wore flowed from one to the other.

"I want his lust," said the female.

A little demon, with the appearance of a three-year toddler, climbed onto Lady Pnemoxsis's lap and sat opposite of her sibling perched on the other knee. "Mahti," she said, "everyone has taken all of the best and left nothing at all for me. I don't want to be left with some silly old *gluttony*. Look at him, mahti! He's all bones…and it's not fair. They'll be absolutely nothing to have." She looked at Jared and squished-up her tiny, broad nose.

Lady Pnemoxsis hushed her and caressed her cheek. "Now-now, Ortan, my love. We cannot always have what we want, can we?" She said, with a slow wag of her finger. "Sometimes we must accept what we are given and make the best of it. Do you understand? That's how little forest nymphs like you mature to become spirits of the forest, like Belayphion and Surratta." She nodded at the teen siblings who were nestled side by side.

"Ortan," Surratta called, "I have a surprise for you." She smiled devilishly at her sister.

Ortan closed her eyes and turned up her nose. "If it's not the angel, then I don't want it."

Belayphion winked at Surratta. "You might change your mind once you see them, Ortan."

Ortan quickly perked up. "Them?" she asked, and then gave them a wary glance from the side.

Surratta beckoned her over with a wave. Ortan hopped down and surfed over to them on a flowing wave of ivy leaves. Surratta took her sister's hand and knelt, and tugged at her to do the same. Surratta and Ortan were on one side; their brother, Belayphion, knelt and faced them on the other. Surratta began slowly waving her hands across the ivy on the ground between them.

"Modo lodo, lota dadun," Surratta said to the ivy. A tendril of green smoke came from her lips and spiraled down and into the vines. "Give me my Damned."

The vines began to squirm and twist, and loop through each other. The leaves and vines then raised a foot from the ground, only to begin receding from the center of the mound it had just created. As the vines moved away, they revealed a body hidden beneath their greenery. It was a male demon covered in peacock feathers; his plumes of bold greens, yellows, and blues, dazzled; his eyes were as blue as a clear day on earth. Ivy snaked bore in and out of his body from head to foot.

"Look at his plumes, Ortan," Belayphion urged. He waved his hand up and down the vine-bound demon. "They are all nearly perfect. He has fed on many sins of The Damned to have come so close to perfection."

Caym moved over and looked at the captive demon. "Was he wearing colors?" he asked Belayphion and Surratta.

"Red and white armor, brother," Belayphion answered, respectfully lowering his eyes.

Caym turned to his mother. "It's one of Astaroth's dogs."

"We caught them sneaking through the northern edge of the forest," Belayphion said. He turned and pointed to a tree a few yards to his right. "Give me my Damned," he called out to the massive oak. A swirling plume of green smoke passed from his lips; the curling tendril of enchantment hit the tree, and then broke apart and dissipated. The moss covered bark began shifting; some pieces moved up, and the others down. From behind the bark, the body of a white, female demon with blond tresses pushed through, though only half of her—the back half of her body was still trapped within the bark. "Here is the other. Once I ran her down, she tried casting an enchantment upon me, though obviously, to no avail. She must have forgotten whose realm she was in." Belayphion looked at his mother and smiled. Lady Pnemoxsis bowed her head approvingly.

"Well," Caym said, dividing a sneering gaze between both bound demons, "now you may both enjoy the company of my brothers and sisters. I wish thee both a long, slow journey to the ether."

"Do I get to choose first, Surratta?" Ortan asked, her voice hopeful.

Surratta performed the sign of the cross, but then finished by touching the center of her chest. "The Morning Star be my witness, I haven't touched one of their sins...promise."

"See now, Ortan," Lady Pnemoxsis said, though was staring at Jared, "look at what wonderful surprises come to those who are patient."

Ortan grinned smugly and nodded. She passed her hand over the feathered demon. A vine from her waist snaked up and circled around her torso, and then moved on to her arm and down to her hand. It shot out and plunged into the demon's feathered chest. The demon cried out and writhed in his grave of ivy.

Ortan looked up at Surratta and smiled with glee. "I have his regret!" She paused for a moment and squinted. "He regrets joining with Astaroth, because now, *of course*," she rolled her dark green eyes and shook her head at him, "*...now* he feels the draw of the ether." Belayphion and Surratta stood and looked at each other with self-satisfying grins, leaving their sister to feast on her treat delight.

"And now," Surratta said, speaking to Belayphion, "we have another trespasser in our lands, and one who has insulted our dear mother at that."

Belayphion gave his sister a curious gaze. "Then we should pray to father that he be returned to us soon."

"Rightly so," Surratta said.

"Bear him hence to your father," Lady Pnemoxsis called out to Caym. She raised her arm and flung her hand toward Jared. Green mist flowed from her hand and then dove to the ground. It flowed over the ivy, and upon reaching Jared's feet, it sunk between the leaves and vines, causing them to come alive and squirm.

Dark green vines as thick as broom handles shot up from the ground and wrapped around Jared's wrists, binding them. Jared instinctively tried pulling and twisting out of them. The vines, however, resisted him and yanked his hands down, and then coiled even more of themselves around his wrists, binding him even tighter. He struggled against his ropes of ivy shackles, though to no avail.

As the enchanted vines bound him, Jared saw the great oak off to Lady Pnemoxsis's right begin to shudder, and then sway as though a quake was rocking it at its base. The moss-covered bark turned black, and then became gray; it became ash! It collapsed under its own weight and spread its greasy ash remains across the forest floor. Moments after, the ash began to melt like ice under the glare of a summer sun and seeped away between the ivy. The stench of burnt wood was the only memory that the tree had ever existed at all.

Lady Pnemoxsis turned and looked at the spot where her great tree had been. She frowned, and then turned back around and said to her

children, "Worry not for the loss of Akunun, our great tree, for your father shall see it raised back anew and greater than ever before." Her
throne of leaves began moving backward, receding into the depths of the
forest from whence she had come. "Soon, the angel shall be returned to
us, Father Chax willing. And we shall know his sins well, until his
screams are raw with agony and he has gnashed his teeth to dust. Then,
my loves, we shall conclude our prelude, and then upon him, truly commence our first act. We will show this angel of God what Hell truly has
to offer."

Jared stopped struggling against his enchanted bonds. With every
move of his arms and hands, the vines readjusted themselves around his
wrists—coiling around them even more and tightening harder. He relented; he was their prisoner and powerless to escape. Though, even if he
did, where would he go? he thought, glancing about the forest, and
knowing that outside of it—if the stories of the Bible were true—there
were legions upon legions of his sworn enemies who would like nothing
more than to see him dead, or to the ether as they called it.

He was bound. He was trapped. He was at the mercy of those fabled
for having none.

Chapter 6

Jared followed behind the soldier's horses, led by a leash of squirming ivy held by Caym. He looked up at the sky. He had no way of telling how much time had passed; the sky had not darkened since he arrived. Had it been two hours so far? Three? he wondered.

The sun-demon—the curled-up, fire-encased creature moving across Hell's sky—was of no help in time management. When he was led in ivy chains from the forest and once again under Hell's white light, he had spied the sun-demon in front of them; though now, it was almost directly above them.

Time was distorted in Hell. Physics was perverted. Actually, he thought, everything about the place was just plain warped.

As they traveled toward Hedun—the capital—he could feel his life-force slowly starting to regenerate. Though, even if his force was at full strength, he doubted he could break the mystical tethers; they were constantly twisting and coiling about each other, countering every shift of his hand or flex of his wrist; and yet, they weighed like lead.

They followed the road out of the forest and past the crater he had made crashing into Hell. For what seemed like miles, the road inclined and declined like a roller coaster. The apex of each hill offered a stunning view of the rolling landscape on either side. Fields of flowers and pockets of trees dotted landscapes that seemed to just go on for miles.

They climed yet another hill. They crested it. Down below was a town. The travel to it was long enough for Wormwood to pass from over them.

The structures of the town rose two and three stories tall with flat roofs, and were tan in color. Their thresholds and fascias were painted in rich hues—bold blues and rich greens, sun yellows and fire reds; they gleamed in the white glow of Hell's sun-demon. They were reminiscent of medieval African dwellings, when great kings and queens ruled empires that were centers of world trade, intellectualism, and culture. Though, such was not the case with one of the structures, Jared spied. This one was conical—not flat and square like the rest. It rose stories above the others.

Even stranger to him was that, he had yet to spot a single inhabitant in the vibrantly painted, seemingly just constructed, stone and brick town. Throughout the town, and especially the further in they went, he saw shops with tables and racks out in front them with wares on display, as though a mob of shoppers was expected at any moment. Some shops sold necklaces and bracelets, and others had bowls, cups, and various other pottery and wares. Some displayed scarves and robes next to their lintels and posts; and not just a few did he see with signs of advertisement hanging above their doorways, written with swooping, calligraphic symbols that reminded him of those inscribed within the gold tomes of Metatron and Lucifer.

"Where is everyone?" Jared asked, curious why such a place of such structural and aesthetic vibrancy was as lively as a ghost town.

Lady Zim and Caym glanced back at him, though it was Thamuz who replied. He spoke over his shoulder. "Behold the work of Astaroth," he said.

"Aye, but it is," Caym uttered.

"You have fallen into the midst of a war, angel," Thamuz said. "Your timing is ill, which is most unfortunate for you. Though for us, your presence here is an omen. Be it for our victory or defeat, only the duke has the power to discern which it is. The green forest of Lady Pnemoxsis, and this town, Hafah, are territories of the northlands—Duke Chax's sovereign realm. Astaroth has dared to lay claim to them, and has absconded with the souls we once hunted around them."

Jared gave a queer, puzzled look. "Hunting souls? For what?"

"For power," Lady Zim said.

"He does not know these things," Caym said. "He is ignorant of Hell."

"Spoken true, my lord," Thamuz said, edging on his horse a bit more with a nudged to its flanks.

"The fire pits are in Sheol, the realm of King Purson," Caym said. "That is where you will find your land of fire and brimstone. Hell is of beauty and the pursuit to improve upon it, until it stands just a hair below perfection, which is only The Morning Star himself—made by The Father to be perfect in every way."

"Perfection gained from torturing souls," Jared remarked, with a sour look.

"If your soul is bound here," Lady Zim said, "it is because—and only because—it has been judged and found deserving of punishment for its mortal sins. There is, and must be, consequence. And this is the consequence for those who are damned."

"Their suffering gives us life," Thamuz added,

"And power," Lady Zim added.

"Whoever has dominion over the souls has the power of Hell," Thamuz explained.

They entered a circular courtyard. Streets, which led into it from all around its perimeter, broke up its continuity. It was there that Jared again saw the cone-shaped building, though this time unimpeded by the other structures. Now, it was clear to him what the building was, for a story-high frieze of Lady Pnemoxsis was set above its entrance; it was painted dark green as she was, with ivy wrapped around her legs, waist, bare breasts, and outstretched arms. Frescos of her children's smiling green faces gazed up at her from within the tangle of ivy at her feet. The Lady Zim, Caym, and Thamuz lowered their heads reverently as they passed by her temple. He heard Caym speak low, calling out to her. "Watch over our steps, mother—blessed lady of green—goddess of life."

He looked back at Jared. "I suppose you find my mother's temple as awash in vanity, as you do her forest. But, do not worry yourself with answering, for I'm sure mother already knows your answer."

"You cannot hide what the Scryer Supreme of Hell wishes to know," Thamuz cautioned.

"But why a temple in Hell?" Jared asked. "There are no mortals to worship her here."

"But there are souls aplenty," Caym said. "Well…there were. When the realm teemed with the damned, they did come to worship her, and to freely sacrifice their most precious gift to her—*that sin that brought them in.* If their prayers were enough to sway mother toward kindness, she would grant that wretched soul a passing of Wormwood free from torture. However, The Damned do not give up their sins readily. They cling to their lies and profess their innocence. They fight and struggle to hide all of the evil they have committed, which in turn, makes their essence that much sweeter to partake of. It is done meticulously, one sin at a time, until we reach that great one—the one that has damned them to Hell. Though, by confessing that sin—*freely so*—the power of their essence is multiplied. And then, once we are done, their bodies are extinguished…*destroyed.*"

"And are brought back at the next passing of Wormwood," Lady Zim said. "They are born anew in the Lake of Fire."

"Mortals are the vilest creatures ever created by The Father," Thamuz opined.

"Monsters, to be sure—practically every one of them," Caym declared loudly. His voice echoed through the town. "Enjoy thy respite…it shant last long. By my father's will, the hunt will soon commence again."

"How sad for you," Jared grumped.

"They have sinned, not I," Caym uttered. "Twas' not I who drowned a child to spite a spouse, or murdered a parent whilst they slept, or swindled and thieved, sending innocents over the edge of despair and to their utter demise—twas' not I! Mortals know full well the cost of their actions—praise The Father or disobey and pay your due to me the other."

"The Father has clouded your eyes," Lady Zim said. "In him, you see benevolence, though that is a lie. He is vindictive."

"Cruel," Thamuz added.

"Dishonest," Caym attested.

"And if he gave you the Gift of Life, you might think otherwise, right?" Jared asked, with a wry raise of his lip. "Isn't that what you're really after? He won't give it to you, so you refuse to accept your place as one of his creations."

Caym sneered. "My place—you fool—is upon a throne. I am the child of Duke Chax and the green goddess, a direct descendant of The Morning Star, who, is more than worthy of the Gift of Life."

"There's only one God."

"There are many gods, but only one Father...one Creator," Caym retorted.

"Do not tire yourself bantering with *it*," Thamuz advised. "His mind has been awash in the great power for far too long."

"The great power?"

Thamuz sighed and grudgingly obliged, though he had just sworn Caym to desist. "It is the force that keeps all as all. It's what binds the fabric of existence. It is what mortals say is dark energy; though having no idea that it is The Ghost—the living will of The Father that their instruments cannot detect, though logic has told them is certain and is real."

"But Hell is closed off from that great power. That is our unjust consequence," Lady Zim said. "As a result of that, we must draw sustenance from the sins of The Damned. Thankfully, the ill nature of mortals has kept us awash in souls; that is, before Astaroth rose up against the other lords and took their lands, and the souls within."

"His next move is to lay siege on Phenóx," Thamuz said. "It is the realm of The Morning Star, where he lies in sleep until the last days of earth."

"Once The Morning Star is dead," Lady Zim said, "Astaroth will have his power, and all of the souls frozen upon the Lake of Phenóx. He will move onto earth next."

"He can't," Jared argued. "You—you said the portals were closed between earth and Hell."

"The power of The Morning Star is surpassed only by that of The Father, The Lamb, and the Ghost," Lady Zim explained. "Let there be no doubt in your mind; if Astaroth attains that power, he will pierce time and space, and pass into earth's realm unimpeded."

Thoughts of his mother suffering in a world ruled by Astaroth came to his mind first, and was soon joined by all of the others that he loved...Thaddeus and Chris, Henrì and Olivia, and even Phineas, too. And there were billions of others around the world, who, along with his family and friends, would share their same, dark fate. He glanced down at the squirming vines and felt helpless to protect them, especially when he couldn't even protect himself at the moment.

"I have already pledged to give every ounce of my lifeforce to see Astaroth fail," Caym said to Lady Zim. "I will see him to the ether."

"As will I, my lord," she said.

"Aye," Thamuz pledged heartily.

"Astaroth ruled Phoenicia as the goddess, Astarte," Lady Zim said. "In Babylon, he was Ishtar, where he found the sorceress, Shazadeh, and remade her as one of us." Lady Zim yanked on her reigns, bringing her steed to a sudden halt. She raised her arm, signaling the others to do the same. Jared expanded his hearing, focusing it on the road in front of him, which led out of the courtyard and back into the town proper.

'Leave me be!' He heard a woman cry out. *'Please don't...I beg you! Spare me this passing.'* Her wrenching pleas induced a reply, though it came in the language of demons...two of them; a male and female.

Lady Zim nudged her steed to move forward and signaled the others to follow. They proceeded slowly down the street and stopped where the street ended and another began. Lady Zim moved up to the crossroad and looked left and right down it.

"Caym," she said in a low voice, pointing left.

Caym handed the leash of vines to Thamuz and dismounted. He walked over to the tan, stone building on his left and put his green hand on it. His fingers, and then hands, took on the stone's hue, and gritty texture as well. It spread up his arms and over his face; even his black, wooly hair and dark green eyes became sandy brown. His chest armor and clothing underneath took on the appearance of stone as well. Try as he might, and even with his celestial sight, Jared couldn't spot Caym standing against the wall.

"I shant be a moment," Caym said, though his voice had come from in front of Jared, out by the street.

Caym was gone for a few minutes, and then returned, shedding his tan hue as he stepped away from the wall and walked over to Lady Zim. "Tis' Junna and Yurias of the first legion," he said. "And," he paused a moment, "they have Mary Susan with them."

"*Traitors,*" Thamuz seethed.

"Astaroth must not have Mary Susan," Lady Zim said; her tone was of urgency.

"Father would be upset with us, indeed," Caym said woefully. "She is his prized soul."

"What's going on?" Jared asked, looking at Lady Zim.

"We are about to have an impromptu execution," she explained. She lowered her right hand to her side and conjured her silver sword. Caym and Thamuz produced theirs as well. "They're trying to take Mary Susan to Astaroth as an offering. I am sure of it."

"Perhaps being a soldier of my father no longer serves them well," Caym quipped. "Maybe once they fall upon my sword, they will find the nothingness of the ether better suited for them."

"I should be allowed to dispose of them myself," Thamuz said to her. "His Grace's soldiers are under my command, and I under yours. It is my failing that they desert the duke's legions. It should be my duty to give punishment for the crime."

"Tis' my father they betray," Caym countered, with a wicked grin thrown Thamuz's way. "Besides, the big lurch will simply sliced them in half, whereas I," his green eyes sparkled, "will make them suffer."

Thamuz grinned. "Tis' a matter of preference, my lord."

"One to each of you," said Lady Zim.

"Fair enough," Caym said and shrugged, and then mounted his horse. "And their lifeforce?" Caym raised his brow and smiled.

Lady Zim was silent; her dark brown eyes roved about the street in front of her. "Take it," she said. "The duke shall praise us for having sent them to the ether."

Thamuz moved up and handed Jared's tether to Lady Zim, and then kicked at his horse's flanks, spurring it into a gallop. Caym did likewise. He sped around the corner and off after Thamuz.

"Come," Lady Zim called to Jared, giving a firm tug on the leash.

She led him down the road. Though already, he could hear the clanging of metal echoing off the stone and mud-brick walls. As they came to the end of the road, Jared saw a white-winged demon crossing to the left in front of him, scurrying backwards on clawed-feet, and struggling to ward off Caym's swift swings of his sword.

He looked right. Kneeling in the middle of the road was an old, white woman with gray tangled hair curtaining her face. To the right of her, was Thamuz. He was walking toward them with his prey seized at the neck, and lifted from its feet. He flung the demon down on its belly. It flipped over on its back and rose up on its elbows. Its face was white, and his singular horn—marbled black and white—curved up from his forehead and rose to a needle's point.

"Spare me, Thamuz!" he cried, shaking his head. "I beg thee."

Thamuz placed the tip of his sword at the center of the demon's chest armor. "Tell Lady Zimarantha what you just told me, Yurias. Or I will make you suffer long before I send you to the ether. *Be quick!*"

"I—I said," he closed his eyes and gathered himself. "I said I would cut the lady's throat if you help me steal Mary Susan." His lips quivered as he looked up at Lady Zim. Thamuz pushed the tip of his blade against the chest armor, piercing it. Yurias quickly clasped his hands together. "And—and I said the Duke of the West would reward him princely."

Lady Zim smiled coyly at him. "My head on a platter is worth only a prince's wealth, not a king's?" She cocked her head. "I'm insulted, Yurias. What did you expect to gain for your treason? a kingdom in Hell or upon earth? Astaroth must have offered you much for Mary Susan."

"I suppose this one wanted some equally grand title," Caym called out from the other side of them. He led the winged female toward them with his sword poised at her back. "Kneel, beast."

The female demon knelt beside Yurias. Her right wing bore slash marks where Caym had struck; her left was cleaved nearly in half and hung limp on the ground. Her face was mostly skull; flaps of brown skin that once covered it hung at her jaws. Her left eye was gone—just a black hole was there now. The other bulged at the rim of its socket. "Mercy, Lady Zimarantha."

"There is no mercy for one such as you, Junna," Lady Zim said. "You know as well as I that mercy has long since left Hell. You've made your choice, though, unfortunately for you, it was the wrong one."

Junna lowered her head and shook it, and then gazed up. "My lady, Astaroth cannot be stopped. Duke Chax is mighty, though even he cannot stop Astaroth now—no force can. He has taken the east and the south, and—"

"Moves now upon the north?" Lady Zim said. "Mayhap he would not, were it not for traitors such as you."

Caym placed his sword under her neck. "My father has vowed to lead us in the Great War, and this is how you repay him?"

Yurias held up his hands to Lady Zim. "What then?...when Astaroth takes Duke Chax's lands and the last of the souls held beneath Palace Adoja? What then, prince? Shall we be left here with nothing? No souls? No sins to nourish us?"

"We all hunger, Yurias," Lady Zim said.

"But some less than others," Junna said, fixing her eyes upon Lady Zim, as if daring her to deny it.

"We are His Grace's royal guards," Thamuz insisted, as though she had forgotten.

"Who are fed well indeed," Junna said, turning her defiant gaze toward him. "We mere soldiers must sit and thirst, while His Grace makes hollow promises of defeating Astaroth and returning the souls back to the land. Astaroth has the Train of Souls, my lady." She shook her head. "Duke Chax's rule is over, as is Beelzebub's and Agares's. The great forest, and all of Varencia will soon be ash. Hedun will burn as well. Palace Adoja will be next, and then, Duke Chax will fall. Do you hear me? There is no road that leads to victory for Chax. Release us and go with us! Lead us as only you can. Let us present the foul, child-killer to Astaroth," she pointed at Mary Susan. "He would welcome a two-tongued enchantress like you with open arms. He would seat you on his right."

Lady Zim looked up and away, as though weary of gazing upon her. "Better now than later to discover the weak links in our defenses."

"You are a fool, my lady," Junna admonished.

"I?" Lady Zim asked, still looking about. "'Tis' you who are kneeling."

"It shant be long before you, too, will kneel," Junna said.

"Be done with them," Lady Zim said to Caym and Thamuz.

Caym took a step back; his sword turned to green mist and dispersed like smoke. From the palm of his hand, where the sword had materialized from, an ivy vine shot out from it and dove into the back of Junna's neck. More vines sprang from the one embedded in her spine and began piercing her back, shoulders, and head. Junna cried out and began choking on her own screams as the ivy turned her into a pincushion. She flung her arms up and began jerking, as though a seizure had set upon her. Her stark white skull began turning black, and then to grey; it became ash, as did the rest of her. Her wings fell to the ground first, and then her body came tumbling next.

Caym's eyes grew dark. His skin shimmered. He smiled as though he were in the grips of ecstasy.

Yurias's face was of horror and fear after having watched his fellow deserter turned to ash and sent off to the ether. He looked at Thamuz. "Please spare me, my lord. I will rejoin the ranks and pledge my undying—"

Thamuz seized him by the neck, strangling the words in his throat. He pushed his fingers into Yuria's neck knuckle deep, and began moving them around in the muscle, as though massaging it from the inside. As Thamuz began taking the creature's lifeforce, its coal, black eyes turned grey, as did its white skin all over. It crumpled into a pile of ash at his feet.

"Well, that was barely satisfying," Thamuz remarked offhandedly. "Had he given up his sins freely, it would have been almost worth the effort."

"Was it typical?" Caym asked.

"Yes-yes," Thamuz uttered, slapping his hands up and down, dusting his gloves free of the ash. Under the glare of Wormwood, his gleaming black skin looked more like moving oil. "It was the same old sin...*tempt the mortal into what they wanted to do in the first place*—nothing remarkable." He and Caym mounted their horses. He looked down at the ash and grimaced. The ash was disappearing; soon, it was nothing at all. He sneered. "And they wondered why they had risen no higher than foot soldiers."

Jared was repulsed by the entire spectacle. Listening to Caym and Thamuz chatting about it casually only made it that much sicker to him. Still, they were fallen celestials, he remembered. What semblance of civility was to be found in them anyway? What ounce of good? What hope then, for redemption? All that was left for them was the ether.

"What is it?" Jared asked, he again being led by Caym, continuing their way through the town. "What's the ether?"

"It's nothingness," Lady Zim said, "which is where we have all come from, by the word of The Father. He pulled us from nothing, and gave us form and life. And that is where we return when our lives are at an end."

"We are not souls," Caym said, "who, no matter how many times you destroy their bodies, they are reborn anew to continue their punishment."

"Perhaps," said Thamuz, "we should have apprised the angel of this back in the forest. Maybe he wouldn't have been so quick with his tongue if he knew that upon his death, there would be no afterlife for him—just ash." He chuckled heartily. "Which is why, when I swing my sword, I do not miss, young angel. I take no threat as hollow, and see every aggression, no matter how small, as a death duel."

"Aye," Caym called.

Jared began thinking of everything he knew about God, The Christ, and The Ghost, and what he understood the afterlife to be. For mortals, their options were either Heaven or Hell. Though for celestials—both the Heavenly Host and the Fallen—he knew nothing of their shared fate upon death.

He looked up and caught Lady Zim watching him from over her shoulder. He stared at her dark brown eyes; they were nearly black, like her skin; and for a moment, neither of them spoke; they just looked at one another, drawing that moment out far longer than moments actually were and should be. Lady Zim abruptly looked away, though Jared, however, did not.

"You doubt our words," said Lady Zim. "You think we're incapable of telling the truth, when in fact, it is the truth that we are actually known for. Perhaps you will see."

"Very soon, in fact," Caym added.

They passed out of the town. The road before them declined; it was buttressed by lush fields and vibrant flowers, all of it borne of magic, and all of it beautiful to behold, yet demonic in nature; it was all false, like the demons who had him, he thought, even as he continued watching Lady Zim from behind, looking away whenever she looked to the side. Or was she looking at him? he wondered, and began worrying why he should care if she was, and then grew increasingly bothered that, perhaps, she was not.

He spotted structures off in the distance. The building situated in the midst of the others seemed large enough to fit all of the others inside of it. With each step he took, the structure grew larger in his sight; it was a mile wide, if not more, he guessed—it was its own city within a city.

They came unto a forest that lay on either side of the road. Though it was sweeping and covered much of the land around them, it was barely a mention to the previous one. Still, he saw that the power of Lady Pnemoxsis extended to this wonderland also, for between the trees and shrubs and plants and flowers, he spotted green bodies darting through them—two of them—Belayphion and Surratta. At times he spotted them on his right; and then, as he walked on, he spied them on his left...sometimes next to a shrub, or in front of a tree, or laying on their bellies by the end of the road with their heads on top of their folded hands, like innocent green cherubs.

Though they appeared as smooth-skinned, cheery-faced adolescents, whom just happened to be green, he knew they were anything but that. They were demons on the hunt and he their prey. He was certain of it, for he could see them. And if they truly wished not to be glimpsed, they could do so, though had chosen not to. They wanted to be seen. They wanted him to see them watching him. No matter where he spied them, left or right, up in a tree or down on the ground nestled in ivy and leaves, their dark, muddy green eyes were always locked on him.

They were passing out of the forest. On his right, he saw Surratta crouching by a plant with leaves as tall as men. She lolled her head to the side and grinned, and waved goodbye as though assured of his imminent return.

Once out of the forest, the great building was once more in his sight. It was monolithic, an ostentatious emblem of pride.

Though, it was even more than just that, he thought. It was the home of a fallen celestial—the palace of a self-proclaimed god. He feared it, and who was inside it.

CHAPTER 7

"Boy am I glad you're rich as ol' king Midas, my man," Thaddeus said, opening the door and greeting Henrì at his own doorstep.

"Me too," Henrì said, glancing over his shoulder at Chris and Phineas who were standing behind him. "They would still be Africa if I wasn't. Thankfully, I still have some connections over there, but they weren't cheap. These two got lucky. That's the only reason they're here right now."

He and Thaddeus shook hands; he felt a tremble—an unease in Thaddeus's grip. He knew Thaddeus loved Jared like a son; and the pain that came with knowing that someone that close to him was in Hell, was something he never wanted to even imagine. Everything borne of evil was born in Hell, and Jared was surrounded by it, that is, he thought, if he was still alive, which didn't seem likely at all given the story Phineas and Chris had told him as they travelled back to America. "How's Dorthea?"

"Worried sick to death," Thaddeus said and grimaced. "To tell you the truth, I don't even know what to say to her."

"Mr. Robinette?" Chris called out, moving around Henrì and walking up to him. "Remember me?"

Thaddeus looked down and squinted. "Lord, if ain't you," he said, giving Chris the once over and back again. Thaddeus hugged him, and then held him out at arm's length. "We never gave up on you. Jared never did—now that's the truth. He wasn't going to stop until he found you. The thing is, you're safe now, you hear me?—you're safe."

Chris disagreed with a slow sway of his head. "Yikan's free to do whatever he wants. There's no place on earth that's safe from him."

"After seeing what we done seen, I can vouch for that," Phineas remarked. He came around and shook Thaddeus's hand. "I've seen demon's from the pit of Hell walk this Lord's good earth with my own eyes. We gonna need the power of God to survive what's coming."

"That was supposed to be Jared," Henrì panned. "And we don't have him...they do."

"It was a trap and he fell into it," Chris said, turning and looking at all of them. "He tried to get the tome, but...Yikan was never going to let Jared get it." He looked around the circular foyer, and then walked over and looked at a painting on the wall. It was of pre-colonial Africans at market; the women wore wide brim, straw hats, and the men styled themselves in turbans and floor-length robes. He looked up at the foyer's glass, domed ceiling. "Nice house, Henrì." He began walking down the hall to his right, and over his shoulder he said, "I think I wanna see Ms. Dorthea now."

Chris paused a moment at the first door on his right, and then moved on. He turned to the door on his left, and then looked away from it, and walked over to a door on the other side.

Phineas put his hand on Henrì's shoulder. "He ain't never been here, right? Has he?"

Henrì shook his head 'no' and waved his hand for Phineas to be quiet. He was not quite sure what Chris was doing, though whatever it was, he was deliberate in it; he paused at each door on either side of the hallway, raising his hand in front of each one. He stopped at another door on his right and paused a moment. This time, he took hold of the doorknob and entered. Henrì and the others began walking down the hallway after him.

Thaddeus huffed. "I'll be if that isn't exactly where Dotty and Olivia are. That's not the same boy I knew," he said to Henrì.

Henrì was thinking the same thing. He had known Chris as long as Jared had, having watched the two become friends and witnessed that bond turn into brotherhood over the years. Chris had always been a happy critter, even with all of the bullying he endured; though that was when he had Jared around, who was that someone who had always liked him for him, and now loved him as a brother. Though now, Jared was gone, and Chris's joy with him. Still, he suspected there was more than just that troubling Chris.

"He's been held hostage for years," Henrì said, "and by one of the most evil people there ever was. You bet that kid's different—and he's not even a kid anymore. He's a man. Yikan stole more than just his childhood. I guarantee you that." Henrì huffed. "That son-of-a-bitch made Jared choose between the tome and his best friend. There was no choice—Jared knew that. And so did Yikan. And now, Jared's lost the tome and Chris, and himself as well."

"I don't believe that," Phineas said. "I'm not giving up on my boy."

"Me either," Thaddeus said.

Henrì withheld his support of solidarity. He felt if there were at least a suggestion of hope tucked into the slimmest of chances, he would've been the loudest, if not the first, to profess his unwavering resolve in getting Jared back. Though, with Jared gone and Yikan free to prey upon the world, he couldn't bring himself to indulge in delusional optimism with them. Tamen's greatest fear was Yikan ruling the world and stealing salvation from man in the process. And now, Henrì thought uneasily, it had come true. The mad Egyptian was free to do as he willed, and the only one who could stop him was in Hell.

I haven't given up on you either, Jared, he thought. *But it's not looking good for us on this end, and probably even worse for you on yours.*

* * *

Henrì felt his heart drop when he walked in and saw Chris and Dorthea hugging and crying into the other's shoulder. Olivia was perched on the edge of a chair, watching them through tears of her own. He looked at Olivia. He shook his head and sighed.

Chris and Dorthea broke their embrace. Her eyes were red; his were, too. "We're going to get him back," she said to Chris, and then turned and faced the others. "And he's going to make everything back to the way it was. And he's going to do it, too. That's why God chose him to save this world in the first place. And God always keeps his promises."

"You might be onto something there," Henrì said, walking over to Olivia and standing behind her chair. "God's covenant with Lucifer was for man to choose a life of good or evil in a balanced world. And right now, it's balanced." He crossed his arms and leaned them on the chair. "What if, what Phineas and Chris have said is true? that Astaroth is going to remake Yikan as a demon. If Yikan wants to survive, he has to unbalance good and evil somehow, which means, technically, Yikan is still vulnerable. Until he's a demon, his power over earth won't be absolute. I think we all know Yikan well enough to know that he won't leave that end untied. He's going to take out even the smallest threat." He looked at everyone, pausing at each face, and then said, "I still have Metatron's tome. He'll come for it eventually."

"What happened out there?" Thaddeus asked, looking to Phineas and Chris. "Tell us what happened from the start, and—and don't leave nothing out. That just might be that one thing we need to save Jared, so he can save us."

And they told them; Phineas and Chris told them everything they could remember, from Blain Hopps, to the demoness, Muchenlay, who rose out of him. Chris spoke more on Eric and Melinda, having been forced to spend years with them. And then, Phineas rejoined the tale, repeating the grim tidings of the three-faced celestial. The tale, however, did not end there. Chris recounted his time as a prisoner of Yikan; how he had been a plaything for Yikan to practice his skills on to create his other immortals. He told it all; he told the bad...the worst...*the horrifying.*

"Even if we knew where Yikan was, what can we do to stop someone like *him*?" Olivia asked.

"Nothing," Henrì replied bluntly. "Yikan's weak as far as immortals go. Still, we couldn't take on his weakest one. We might as well be fighting a mythological god come to life."

"They're nothing like God," Phineas argued.

"They don't have to be," Henrì said. "With Jared gone, they can do whatever they want. That's god-like enough to rule earth."

"We need Jared. That's the only way to stop Yikan," Thaddeus said. Dorthea concurred with a bob of her head.

"Of course we do," Henrì replied, with a coarse edge to his tone. "Our problem is how? We *know* where Jared is, but we can't get to him. We *don't* know where Yikan and his crew of monsters are, and can't do a thing to him even if we did."

"Well for one, we need to get that tome from him," Phineas said.

"Preferably before he uses it again," Henrì quipped. He took his cell phone from his shirt pocket and held it up. "Damn."

"Darling?" Olivia said, gazing up at him.

"No signal," Henrì grumbled. "Let's say you were going to take over the world. What would be the first thing you would do?" He held up his phone. "You cut-off all communication. And in this day and age, when a cell tower goes down, and our precious smartphones don't work, we lose our collective mind."

Thaddeus his phone out. He held it at arm's length, and then began moving it around, waving it through the air. "Man…I think you right about that."

"He is," Chris said. He walked over to the fireplace, and then ran his hands across the mantle. He sat down facing it. "I've heard Yikan talking to Eric about that more than a few times."

"And?" Henrì came from around the chair and stood behind him. "Go on, Chris," he urged gently.

"Cut off communication first. That will send them into disarray," he said. "That's exactly how Yikan said it. I remember it…word-for-word." He moved his head back and looked up at Henrì. "And then we move on to the houses of worship."

"Say what?" Phineas asked, coming toward him.

"He wants mankind to feel hopeless and lost," Chris explained. "So when he comes to them as the god, Aton, the world will greet him as a savior, or something like that…I guess. That's what I heard."

"Destroy their faith in God," Henrì stated, nodding his head, concurring that it was a masterful plan for Yikan, though not for everyone else. "If he gets his hands on—"

"The power grids?" Chris asked, looking down and back at the fireless fireplace. "Yikan's already thought that one through. He knows where every country's electrical grid is and the companies that control them. He can bypass their security systems with a thought."

"If he shuts them down," Henrì said, "then—"

"We're back in the Stone Ages, folks," Chris finished.

Henrì looked down at Chris with a start. His mouth hung open. He knew Chris had changed over the years, but *this change* he didn't see coming. Chris had read his mind, which was an ability that even he, with Tamen and Aria's tutorage, had failed to master. He had only ever known Chris as a special education student, who, despite repeated instruction, failed to comprehend the simplest of concepts in math and reading, and science, let alone understanding what the term 'concepts' was.

He sat down next to Chris. He wanted to give him a hug, to give him what comfort he could, though at the moment, Chris didn't even seem at home in his own body. He was just staring off into the ashy, lifeless fireplace.

"I'm not daydreaming, I'm just not looking at you, Henrì," Chris said. "I feel sad and angry, but mostly angry at myself. It's my fault all of this is happening."

"No, it's not, honey," said Dorthea. "You were tricked, just like Jared was. How were you supposed to know all of this was going on?"

"But I did, you see?" Chris said. "Jared told me everything…about what was happening with Tamen and Henrì, and the tomes, and all of it. He made me promise not to open my big mouth, and I did anyway. Yikan and Shazadeh wouldn't have known you were in Mississippi if it wasn't for me. A lot of people died because of what I did."

"You were manipulated by creatures that shouldn't even exist," Olivia told him. "You are not the first person they have tricked. There's no way you could have known what was going to happen."

"I do now," Chris said softly. "But I went and did something really dumb. I guess no one thought that was a surprise coming from me."

Henrì squeezed his shoulder. "C'mon, Chris. Don't do that to yourself." The others quickly joined in to assuage his guilt. "See? No one blames you for this...not even Jared."

"I know," Chris said. "But I still blame myself. I'm not gonna make another stupid mistake this time—I can't. Yikan saw to that. I guess if I wanted to do something dumb, I could, because that's free will. But that's illogical. Why would I knowingly make a mistake, unless I know the consequence from that mistake is really my goal? Otherwise, without those variants, it remains illogical when looked at in its base form— right?" He looked at Henrì, as though waiting for the teacher's approval.

Henrì turned and gave the others a puzzled glance. He leaned into Chris. "What are you trying to say to us, Chris?"

Chris spun around on his rear, and looked up at the others. "The guy with Yikan is Eric Lightner. He was with Yikan when Shazadeh was still alive. He was a member of the Church of the Imperial Goddess, like Miranda, the one that Jared killed. He wanted to make them into immortals to fight Jared, but neither one of them could decipher the tome. That's when he began studying dark magic, and buddied up with Astaroth. Astaroth showed him how to fiddle with the brain and change it. He tried it out on me first, because it didn't matter if I died.

"Each day, for years, he would put me into an illusion, and then get inside of my head. On a good day, it felt like I had teeny-tiny worms crawling through my brain. The other times, it was like I could feel him cutting the brain matter in my head, and changing it...moving it around. I would come out of the illusion and find out I'd peed my pants, or chewed up my tongue. And I would ache all over, like I had worked every muscle in my body at the same time. Some times, afterwards, I couldn't move for a day or two. I could think and feel and see, but I couldn't even wiggle my toes.

"And then," his voice rose a little, "I started feeling different. I started to think different, too. When we hopped from country to country, trying to stay one step ahead of Jared—and he got close a few times, too —I started learning the languages just by listening to them. Yikan began showing me theorems on things like, theoretical physics and calculus, and I got it—I understood it. I hated basic math when I was a kid, because I just never got it, and it frustrated me, and I just didn't want to do it anymore, so I goofed off and acted up sometimes because of it...*but I understood this!* But Yikan was more interested in the part of my brain that processed language, because that was the key to deciphering the tome. So he experimented on me first, and then Miranda went next. He saved Eric for last. Eric is loyal to him. And because Eric gives it without a thought, Yikan keeps him close."

"But you read my mind, Chris," Henrì said, prodding him. "How far did Yikan take you with this?"

"He wanted to turn me against Jared," Chris said, looking at Henrì. "He had already read my mind. He knew I hated being stupid, and hated myself because of it. And he used my self-hatred against me. In the illusions he would put me in, I began to decipher the chants of the tome. When Yikan realized I could, he knew his fiddling with my brain was working. He began teaching me chant magic that he had learned in Ancient Egypt. But it was to make me like him, and to turn me against Jared. He said I could be like him if I wanted to, and that those same people who used to make fun of me, would one day worship *me* as a god —as a deity. As he fiddled up in here to make me smart, he also put in the idea—over and over again—that Jared had abandoned me; that he was just like the others who always laughed at me, who always told me I was worthless...a fat ass...a nobody...a nothing."

Chris moved to his knees, and then began placing logs from the copper wood rack onto the fire grate. He sat back on his haunches and placed his hands on his thighs. "As he taught me the Ancient Egyptian chants, he tried to teach me to hate Jared, only I couldn't, because, well...it was Yikan's fault, actually. He made me smart—too smart; and smart enough for me to see what he was actually doing. Hamlet said, *the lady doth protest too much, methinks.*" Chris grinned. "Yeah, I read Shakespeare—all of his works. Imagine that, Henrì...me reading Shakespeare. But it taught me what Yikan was up to. Why was he trying so hard to turn me against Jared if he was so sure of himself?"

"Well, I didn't turn against Jared, and he stopped instructing me when he realized I never would. They would leave me chained up while they spent hours and days in illusions learning the chant. And I read and read, because that was the only thing to do when you spend time with people, who to them, time doesn't matter."

"But you did learn something, right?" Henrì asked; his voice eager. Olivia moved to the edge of her seat; Thaddeus and Dorthea straightened up, too. Phineas edged in closer.

Chris held his palms up at the stack of wood in the fireplace, and then closed his eyes. A few moments later, while they watched in silence, a puff of white smoke rose from between the logs. A small flame appeared at the edge of the top log, which then grew and spread across and down toward the others, setting it ablaze.

Chris opened his eyes. "I learned a few things."

"The tome," Olivia said in a hush, as though afraid to even mention it.

Henrì bobbed his head at her. "I know."

Though suddenly, Henrì felt Chris intrude into his thoughts. He was shuffling through memories of his past and his present. Henrì watched the images flash by his mind's eye and was unable to control them. His thoughts were no longer his.

"You want me to…" Chris stopped and cocked his head, "You want to know if I can decipher the tome." He looked at Olivia. "And you're thinking that I can." Olivia nodded.

"Can you do it, boy?" Phineas asked.

"I don't know," Chris said, turning around and sitting on his rump; his back was to the fire, and it cast a swaying, dancing shadow of him along the rug and up on the wall—the living shadows of the mansion oozed over to his silhouette, as though to inspect the new arrival. "I've seen the chants from Lucifer's tome, but not from the one you have, Henrì. And I…I didn't learn all that much before Yikan stopped teaching me. He offered me everything I could ever want. But I guess he didn't read my mind well enough, because being a god was not what I wanted the most. Having Jared back was. Seeing Ms. Dorthea was. Running into Mr. Thaddeus at the rec center was, because it was nice having someone say something good to you, and about you…especially when you didn't like yourself. What I want the most is still what I want the most—getting Jared back and alive. And if I can kill Yikan while doing it, then even better."

"Get in line," Henrì quipped.

"It's a long line, boy," Phineas warned.

Henrì stood. "Thaddeus...Phineas...I have some shovels out in the shed behind the gardens. I'm going to need some help."

"With?" Thaddeus asked.

"The tome is buried out back, underneath Tamen's headstone," Chris answered, before Henrì could divulge what only he, Olivia, and Jared knew. "He wants you to help him dig it up, but...there's a problem with your plans, Henrì."

"Which is?"

"Even if I find the Chant of Changing, and even if I can make myself into an immortal, I don't know if I can beat him. Yikan's had thousands of years of practice with it, and I'll only have a few moments, because when he hears the chant, he'll come running. And he'll kill us all." Chris looked at each of them. "You don't have to worry about me, Ms. Dorthea; I'll die trying to kill Yikan. But it's still not going to bring Jared back."

"You're right, boy," Phineas said. "But it's a start."

"Dead right on that," Thaddeus agreed. "Yikan's got that Eric fella, and that murderer on his side. He got us squeezed in tight."

"Well, we have Phineas on our side," said Chris, nodding at him. He turned and looked at Olivia, and stared at her. She nodded her head.

Henrì looked from Chris to Olivia. He shook his head. His face grew tight. "I can't read your mind; and I don't know what you just told her, but I know what you're thinking, and the answer is *no*. Olivia is not going to get shoved into the middle of Yikan and his little band of killers."

"Wait...what ya'll talkin' 'bout?" Thaddeus asked.

"Chris thinks he can teach me to chant and help decipher the tome," Olivia said. Chris grinned at her. "It wouldn't just be Chris against Yikan and Eric...it would be Chris and *me*. It would even the odds a little— not much—but it would definitely help. And we need every bit of help we can get." She looked at Henrì.

What Henrì knew was that Olivia would be put in danger, and it re- minded him of losing Tamen, and of that gaping hole in his soul that it left. He enjoyed the money that Tamen had given him, but he did not love it. He loved what money could not buy, and what he had always wanted, and that which Tamen and Olivia had given him, which was a feeling of being wanted, which he had never had until Tamen rescued him. And now, having lost Tamen and found that feeling of safety in Olivia, he had no plans of relinquishing it.

"I mean 'no', Olivia."

"I'm saying 'yes', mon chére," she replied. "We can't stop this by holding back—Yikan certainly won't. If we see an opportunity—a chance—we have to take it."

"No we don't," he insisted. "Not this chance."

"Darling, don't you see?" she said, rising from her seat. "I was supposed to come here and be with you—*all of you*. God works through people."

"Amen," Dorthea called out, and was seconded by Thaddeus and Phineas.

"You live in a house filled with the shadows of the dead, and I can sense them," Olivia said. "The chances of two people like that meeting doesn't sound like fate, but faith—having faith in the will of God."

"Maybe or maybe not," Chris cautioned. "But you're here now, and I know you have some innate abilities. Your presence is in everything around here. I knew you were here before I knew you were here. I knew you were different from the others." He looked at Thaddeus and Dorthea. "Tamen taught chants to his African people. The power Tamen gave them is nearly gone from your ancestors, but a few still have it." He looked at Olivia. "We know you love her a lot, Henrì—we can all see that, and why. But the others can't feel what I'm sensing from you. You hide in the bayou, away from everyone, because you fear what might be coming for mankind. And Olivia is the only person you ever opened up to about that…that demons will alter the balance and damn mankind. Your love for her is strong."

Olivia grasped Henrì's chin. He pulled away like an obstinate child. "This isn't just about us, Henrì," she said, her voice was low and poignant. "Billions of lives and souls depend on what we do now, and they have no idea what's even going on."

"Not for long," Chris said. "Yikan won't take long to get started."

"I know you don't want to see me get hurt," she said, "but if we don't stop Yikan, I will be. He's not going to spare any of us. He's going to make us pay for having stood in his way, that's what he's going to do. He's in league with a demon, now. When he comes for us—and he will eventually—he won't be merciful to any of us, Henrì."

Henrì took her hand, but couldn't look up at her. He wanted to, but was afraid it would become another memory to have of her were she to be lost to him.

"Olivia is already lost to you, Henrì," Chris said. "You're already lost to her." He pointed at Thaddeus and Dorthea. "You're lost to her, and she's lost to you, and even you, Phineas...you're already gone, even though you're still sitting there." Chris stood. He was barely as tall as Henrì's shoulder, but spoke as though he towered over him. "The life you and Olivia have is already over—you just haven't accepted it yet."

The lights went out suddenly. The orange glow of the fire cast the room in gloom. Nervous shadows moaned from dark corners. One passed across the ceiling. "The Egyptian! Wickedness!" it bemoaned. It moved across the ceiling and down across the mantle, and under and up the chimney it went.

"Get the power grid first and then—" Chris began.

"The churches and temples," Phineas finished.

Chris nodded. "The world as we know it is already over," he said, glancing around at everyone.

Henrì walked over to the patio doors. "I'm going to the shed," he announced, prompting Phineas and Thaddeus to begin walking over. Henrì waved them off, and then said, "Alone, fellas. I'll let you know when I get to the tome."

"You don't have to do it alone, Henrì," Phineas said. "This ol' back still knows how to move a shovel."

"I appreciate it," he said, "but I rather just be alone right now." He rapped his knuckles against his head. "I'm trying to square having to sacrifice my wife, to protect my wife...and it ain't working."

"If we can't stop Yikan, then like the boy said, you've already lost her," Phineas said.

"Yeah," he snapped, "I got it the first time Chris mentioned it." He glared at Phineas, but then looked down with shame and hurt aching at his heart. "I'll be back." He slammed the door on his way out.

He knew he was acting childish, though did not care. He just wanted to be out of that room and away from everyone, especially from Olivia, who—though he hated to admit it—, was right. They would need more than just Phineas and Chris fighting for them, if they were going to have a chance at stopping Yikan. What they really needed was Jared.

Though, like it or not—and he didn't at all—Olivia and Chris were their best bets. Though, whether they were successful or not, or whether they could chant from the tome and somehow destroy Yikan or not, it would not change the final outcome for Olivia and him; that if she became an immortal, she could die fighting Yikan—and they would be parted. Though, too, if they somehow defeated Yikan, they would still be parted by the unceasing march of time, whereas he would age and she would not. Chris was right, he thought grimly. *It's already over.*

He went into the shed and flicked on the light. He grabbed a shovel from the wall and went back to the garden where Tamen's grave was. He set the tip on the ground and lazily spun it round and round. "We thought it was going to be over once Jared transformed, huh papà?" he said, looking at the obelisk. "We're in a big mess…even bigger than the one you and I had. We're just mortals and we're up against creatures that think they're gods. At least back then we had you. You could always think one step ahead of Yikan. But us…" he paused and sighed. "We're just…just wandering lost."

He gripped the shovel and pushed down into the moist, bayou soil. "If you can hear me, wherever you are…if there's anything at all you can do, I know you will." He pulled up a clod and threw it, and dug back in.

"Astaroth," Henrì said, sneering, and then chuckling at the insanity of it all. "Yikan might have started all of this, but it's that demon, papà; it's Astaroth who's behind this. And Jared is down there with him." He dug into the moist soil again and threw…and dug and threw…and dug and threw.

CHAPTER 8

"I am Astaroth. Many of you know me by the ancient names…Ashtoreth to the Canaanites…Astarte to the Phoenicians…Inanna to the Sumerians. To the Akkadians, the Assyrians, and my beloved Babylonians, I was Ishtar. Though soon, all of earth shall know me by my true name." Astaroth paused a moment and gazed down at those seated below his white, marble throne. "God," he said.

He was white, pale like chalk. He wore a blood red, shendyt. Draped over his shoulders and wrapped around his right arm was a silken shawl, dark red like his skirt.

"We shall reassume our mantles of godhood," he announced. "All of you have pledged allegiance to me as your god-king and shall reap rewards exponentially. And who but the princess of Hell, Lilith, should be first?" He looked at her. She was seated to his right on a chair of white stone. And to her right were two more chairs, and across from her, three more; all were occupied.

Lilith lifted her chin, raising her silver-crowned head higher than it already was. Her skin was white, though showed a hint of color—rose at the cheeks and dark red at the lips. Her hair was black as coal.

"Your majesty is gracious," Lilith said, with much ado.

King Purson, the ruler of Sheol—home of the Lake of Fire and smothering brimstone—, was seated next to Lilith. His head was that of a lion's and his body of male. To the right of the lion-headed king was

Count Morax, whose face was covered with black hair, and who had the nose of a bull, complete with a brass ring through it. Across from Lilith was King Moloch, a thick-bodied, white male dressed in a tight, white tunic; he had a black mustache that curled up at the ends and a braided goatee that extended down to his chest. To his left was Count Aka Manah, whose head was that of a ram's, and who had three eyes; the third one was at the center of his forehead. Curled horns—black and white striped—adorned either side of his head. Upon the last great stone seats was the dark-skinned, Marquis Leraje—the great archer. His nose and lips were handsomely broad; his muscular body was loosely draped in a pale green cloak.

"God is good!" Astaroth exclaimed, with a voice that sung out through his hall, it painted in bright blues, reds, and greens, "or so he doth professes to the mortals." He grinned, amused by his own words. "The Father claims he is omnipotent, though I say he is not, for there is one thing he has not yet seen." He paused to wind his shawl around his other arm. "For all of his supposed wisdom, The Father—who has always existed—knows not what it means to have been *created*."

"Aye," King Purson called out, bearing his fangs.

Aka Mana bobbed his horned head and slapped at the stone armrest with his black, fur-covered claws. "Here-here!"

"The Father knows no creator," Astaroth said, his voice falling low. "My lords, know that I do take The Father at his word, that he is Alpha and Omega, that which is the beginning and end. And you must accept this, too, for are we not his children? Did he not bring us from nothingness and give us shape, and consciousness, and command of all that he hath created?" He looked to those on his right and left, they separated by a rectangular reflecting pool. "Of course he did! He has created all that is. Though in Hell, we take his damned souls and craft their essence into objects of beauty—including ourselves." He looked out at the hall. The stone walls were painted blue and adorned with white, marble reliefs of himself in his various guises throughout the ages. On his right was Ishtar, as he was to the Babylonians— a bare-breasted female with wings, who had talons for feet, who was the High Mother Goddess of fertility, love, *and war*. Next to it was Ashtoreth, a wide-hipped woman with straight hair down to her waist; in her right hand she held a star, and in the left, a spear. On the other side of the hall were his likenesses of the Phoenician goddess, Astarte, and of the Sumerian goddess, Inanna; both were sculpted as voluptuous women with thick lips and noses, and whose gazes could easily be seen as wisdom or seduction, or both.

Astaroth leaned forward. "By our very nature, we, as celestials, can never be compared to mortals." His mouth was still ajar, as though struck and stuck in disbelief at the audacity of the two having ever been compared at all. "Show me a mortal who can form one creature into another, as we have done with what mortals now call prehistoric animals. The mortals named them dinosaurs, for that is the best that they know. We, however, knew the creatures when they were cellular, having no shape or form about them."

Astaroth grimaced as he fell into thought. *If we should bow to you, Father, then why not the mortals to us?* he reasoned. *We are gods to them, as you are Father to us. They are sinful in every way…lust, envy, spite, greed. They fill the Lake of Fire from end to end—they overflow its banks. Yet…in your infinite wisdom, you set us—we who dance amongst the stars—in balance with them?*

No, Father. No.

"My lords," Astaroth said, "mortals are ignorant to what we are, except as gods of the old worlds. Their ancient history is but a passing moment to us, for we *are* ancient. We are not them, my lords; we will never be." Lilith nodded and gave him a smarmy smile. King Moloch concurred with a pout of the lip and a regal bow of the head. Marquis Leraje smiled and called out several *ayes*, right along with the others, who all eagerly agreed with their would be god-king.

"The Father did not care for the creatures we turned into beasts of beauty," Astaroth said, his voice low. "The Morning Star—our sleeping prince—pleaded our case at the steps of The Father's throne…*but nay!*" He looked off to the right, as though it was he who had been impugned and was reliving that very moment.

"Nay, sayeth The Father," Astaroth said once more, though this time slowly, and with a look of illness on his face. "From his own mouth, The Father has declared himself a jealous god, and I take him for his word.

He is jealous of what he has created, and fell us for it, depriving us of the power of The Ghost, whose essence flows through all that is, leaving us only The Damned to sustain ourselves on, so that we may once again see ourselves as we once were and should be—; that is, beautiful to behold." His voice carried to the end of the cavernous hall and flowed back in whispering echoes. "Yet, in Hell, we have once again performed miracle after miracle, over and again, and have recaptured beauty for the sake of beauty, for there is nothing more godlike than beauty and the perfection of it. And though we were unjustly fallen, did we not proceed to rule mortals for centuries, whilst The Father was absent?" King Purson roared like the lion he was—at least from the neck up. The bull-faced, Count Morax, slapped his fur-covered hands vigorously.

"We, who are the gifted of all created, gave mortals a way forth—a true way," Astaroth said. "As their gods, we gave them a choice…Heaven or Hell. It was as simple as that, was it not?" He paused and looked at each one. "But The Lamb, at the behest of The Father, ended our age on earth. He descended into our realm and released those he judged worthy of redemption, and sealed the doors between our realms; though not completely, it would seem."

He grinned. He was lovely to behold…crimson hair, green eyes, all sheathed in porcelain white skin, which made the smooth muscles of his chest and stomach appear as though they were carved from stone.

"Why…an angel has come into our midst," he said in mock surprise.

Count Aka Mana furrowed his gray, furry brow, and moved to the edge of his chair. Count Morax was slack-mouthed. Marquis Leraje glanced around at the others and tapped an ill beat on the armrest with his fingers.

"Aye, tis' true," Astaroth said to them. "An angel has fallen into Hell. Though I tell you all, he did not come from Heaven, but from earth. Into the Northlands of Chax he came hurtling down. I assume Chax has already imprisoned the angel and plans to drain it of its lifeforce in a futile attempt to stop me. How desperate they must be…he, Agares, and Beelzebub. But I tell you this, my pantheon, no power shall stop me from placing all of you above Hell and Earth both—Heaven be damned!"

Astaroth stood and raised his head. His pantheon of demons stood and bowed. "I will tear down the black dome of Phenóx and march legions to the top of the platinum palace; and there, I shall stand over our sleeping prince and pierce his chest." He looked down at them. "As I have claimed the lands of Agares and Beelzebub—and soon that of Chax; for he too shall fall—I will take Phenóx and every one of its vile souls for my own.

"There is no power greater than what lies in sleep in Phenóx, for he was The Father's first creation, and is perfect in every way. Aye, my lords, I will have his power and light for mine own.

"With the power of The Morning Star in my hands, I shall open a portal and step onto earth's plane, and unbalanced what is now balanced.

"I will halt the coming of the end days forever.

"And upon my head I shall place a crown." The demons knelt before him. "As king and god, shall I rule!"

* * *

Astaroth dismissed them all, except for Lilith and Leraje, who drew near and stood at the foot of the stairs leading up to his throne. He commanded King Purson to return to his fire realm of Sheol, and ordered him to double the number of souls being brought to the Westlands. "Let the Train of Souls scream as it never has before," Astaroth directed of the lion king. "Strip the lake of every soul, for it is their essence that shall tear the dome of Phenóx apart."

He ordered Count Morax, his general, to prepare the legions for war. And to the pale, King Moloch, he assigned the duty of scouring the Eastlands and Southlands—realms he stole from Agares and Beelzebub—for the last remaining souls hiding in them. To Count Aka Mana, he gave guardianship over the Enchanters—tentacle-legged demons, who were used to corral souls with their mind-warping mist to make them docile; to make them see what they desired the most.

Astaroth sat down and leaned back on the throne. "Great archer," he said to Leraje, "what news do you bring of the Northlands?"

Marquis Leraje put a foot behind the other and bowed. "Your Grace…two of my scouts, I fear, have been captured in Varencia. I can only assume it was by the hands of Lady Pnemoxsis and her brood of salamanders. The two traitors, who were to steal Mary Susan away, have yet to show face, or hide, or wing of themselves. I presume their fate is no better."

Astaroth looked at his likeness of Inanna, admiring his beauty in her guise. She sat cross-legged; her hips were ample and her breasts full; her face a cheerful smile of seductive fertility. He sighed. "Great-uncle Chax," Astaroth plead, as though burdened with empathy for him, "when will you see that all hope has already abandoned you?"

"Chax refuses to fall, your Grace," Leraje said.

"Oh...he *will* fall," Astaroth insisted, and then grinned. "Even The Morning Star—the greatest of us all—can fall, and so will Chax. Taking the angel's lifeforce will not save him. I possess command of the Train of Souls, not he." He looked to Lilith. "Is that not true, my lady?"

Lilith bowed her head. "Most certainly, your Grace. Lord Flagon conducts the train, and he loves me, as do I love thee, though only more. He is mine, and I am yours."

"My lady is ready for her godly crown, I see," Astaroth said, most impressed with her enchanted cunning. Lilith was only a few thousands years old...created by The Father as a mate for Adam, the first mortal. Though, there came a time in the garden when Lilith refused to submit to Adam...to lay under him. On top, she had demanded, and for that, was cursed, and then fallen by The Father—turned into a demoness and cast into Hell. For one so young in demonhood, he saw her power of seduction and hunger for greatness as admirable traits, indeed. Though it was the Train of Souls that he had wanted most of all, and she had delivered it to him. And for that, he found her worthy enough to seat on his right, and had even began considering her for one of his mates.

"Send Lord Khonvoum and his legions to the Northlands," Astaroth said to Leraje. "Let us see how much force it takes Chax to stop them. And then attack again and again. Do not cease until Chax has used every ounce of force from his lands and all of Orsha-Na lies in ash."

Leraje bowed and departed. Astaroth rose and walked down the stairs. He extended an arm to Lilith, and they began walking down the hall toward the doors. "Hell is nearly in your grasp, your Grace." She stroked his arm. "What of the mongrel, the Egyptian, Yikan? He has failed you."

"Aye," Astaroth grumbled, "he was to kill the angel, and now Chax has him…that is true. But Yikan is—as you have said—a mongrel, my lady. He was born of flesh and blood, not flesh and bone as we are. You can only expect so much from one such as him. However, he did rid the earth of the angel."

They approached the double doors that led out of the hall; they were two stories high and made of stone, and painted dark blue and overlaid from top to bottom with swirls of wrought gold. With a sweep of his hand toward them, the stone doors opened and revealed his western province, it of painted, terraced-buildings and dwellings adorned in hanging plants and tropical trees; it was Babylon remade in all of its vibrant blues, reds, golds, and yellows.

In front of them, far off in the distance away from the sprawling stone city, stood the Tower of Babel—the original one he had conceived and commanded his Babylonian people to construct on earth. It was the same one that God had fell. The spiraling, white stone structure reached hundreds of stories into the sky of Hell; and with the glaring rays of Wormwood upon it, it gleamed like a cone of glass.

"Still, Yikan has served me well," Astaroth told her, walking her out and stopping at the edge of the steps. "One must not overlook his lofty ambitions, which has risen him from man, to one who thinks he will rule as a god." Lilith chuckled softly, tucking her chin and looking up at him with a bashful gaze. "I know, my dear. Humorous, isn't it?" He smiled. "Who, but us, could appreciate such foolishness? I did, however, nearly tempt myself into giving him some obscure region of the earth… perhaps as a sea spirit, or something of that sort; some place where he would be out of the way. But you must be careful of his sort, for whether he be mortal or celestial, or a combination of them both, Yikan will suffer no lord above himself."

"Tis' most true, your Grace," Lilith said.

"He has survived far longer than he should have. That, itself, is reward enough for him. In the end, when I kill him, he will come to understand this, and perhaps, be glad for it. Whether he knows his place within The

Father's cosmos or not, it does not matter. There are mortals, and then, there are gods—there is no intersection between the two.

"I am Ashtoreth, my lady. I am Inanna and Ishtar." Lilith dropped to her knee and bowed her head. "I am Astaroth.

"I am god!"

CHAPTER 9

They came to a halt at the gates of Adoja, palace of the demon called Chax. Jared looked up at the palace walls in awe at its stories-tall height, though also in dread of the one who possessed the power to have created it. Demons patrolled the gatehouse and walkways above; and down below they stood guard in front of the massive doors. Like Zim, Thamuz, and Caym, the soldiers wore breast, arm, and leg armor that shielded the front and was open in back. On their breastplate was the oak leaf twisted into an infinity emblem—forever green and unending.

The demon guards were male and female, though also, some were part animal, and others part plant it seemed, and yet others were amalgamations of each, they having taken on aspects of beauty from nature and claimed it for their own in the pursuit of perfection and godliness. They were beautiful, Jared admitted, though grudgingly, for he knew the cost of their sleek ivory horns, and their colored, feathered and furred bodies, and their vibrant blue, red, green, and yellow eyes; and their luxurious straight, locked, curly, braided hair; and their silky black, white, brown, peach skins…emulations of men and women, and of animal and of and nature, all at the cost of a tortured soul—dark sorcery in its base form.

A guard approached Lady Zim. He was white as snow and had large, reflective black eyes that took up the majority of his face. "Lady Zi-marantha," he said. "We saw riders approaching, but we did not know it was you. You were gone for some time. We sent for more guards out of precaution." He glanced over his shoulder at two demons that were just then riding up from the side.

"We cannot be too cautious in these passings of Wormwood, captain," she said. "How goes the wall?"

"None have come in who shouldn't be in," he said. "But there are reports of more soldiers deserting."

"We caught two of them…Junna and Yurias," Caym said, raising his brow. "They were trying to abduct Mary Susan, though paid the cost. Still, his grace will not be pleased to hear of your shortcomings at the wall, captain."

The captain's eyes seemed to grow larger than they already were. He leaned over and looked at Mary Susan, and then turned his attention to Jared, and lingered there with a curious look on his face. "My lord, forgive us," he said, looking back at Caym. "It will not happen again. I will have the patrol around the walls doubled."

"It's not me you should ask forgiveness from," Caym said. "My brother and sister apprehended two others in the forest and dealt with them accordingly. Perhaps they should command the defense of the city, if you are not up to the task. Do not let it happen again."

"My lord," he replied humbly and bowed. He stood straight and looked at Lady Zim. "His Grace is awaiting your arrival. He has gathered the nobles at the palace doors to welcome you back. He said that he is, *most eager*, to see what you have brought him."

Lady Zim turned and looked at Jared from the side. "As His Grace commands," she said to the captain.

The captain looked up to the gatehouse and called out. "Open the gates!"

The word was quickly passed along. The massive, wood doors began swinging in. Lady Zim led them inside. Thamuz and Caym followed behind her; Jared and Mary Susan picked up the rear.

Jared was in awe of the stone and brick capital of Hedun—the city surrounding Palace Adoja. The flat-roof structures were stories higher than those in the town they had passed earlier, and in similar fashion, were painted in dark and startling bright hues. Though unlike the other town, which was deserted—except for the deserters, and the haggard old soul, Mary Susan—, this city bustled with life of those who had been fallen.

The demons on the street paused in their conversations to stare and leer, and look at him with unchecked, wide-eye amazement. From above, he saw them leaning out of windows; sometimes two or three were in the same one, using their elbows to jockey for a better position to see him. From one to the next, each demon seemed more beautiful, more exotic, and more bizarre than the next. Though, the way they were looking at him, with expressions ranging from curiosity to repulsion, it made him feel as though he were the oddity, not they, some of whom appeared to him as part animal or flower, or were covered in scales or fur like a minx, or who had three eyes or a horn, or one eye and many horns—a magnum opus of perfection in nature gone awry.

On his left, a female demon stopped in mid-stride and gawked at him. She had glistening black scales for skin. Her pupils were vertical like a serpent's. She wore a floor length, white tunic that hugged her curvaceous body. Next to her, seated on a round stone bench, was a blue-eyed female covered in white feathers like a goose; she was engaged in conversation with a handsome black male with a prominent nose and almond-shaped eyes; he wore nothing but a shendyt-skirt, displaying his smooth, muscular chest, arms, and beefy thighs for all to see. They both turned and watched him with open mouth silence. The further they traveled into the city, the more demons Jared saw coming out; their number was growing exponentially. Hundreds quickly became thousands, and then many thousands, and thousands more upon that... legions of them!

A shadow passed overhead, and then a series more of them followed. Jared looked up and saw a group of winged-demons circling above; they proceeded to follow him like vultures having spotted something almost dead. On the other side of him, to his right, a male demon with Asian eyes, an African nose, and white skin was arranging large, crystal orbs on a stand in front of a shop; and having spotted Jared, he startled and dropped the one he was holding. The orb smashed to pieces, releasing a swirling black smoke into the air.

He was the demon's object of fascination for many steps and many streets. Palace Adoja towered in front of them. With each step he took toward the stone behemoth, he felt as though the last slivers of hope were receding by two. The onlookers on either side of the road began to thin and their numbers replaced by soldiers lined up in formation.

They came to an archway and passed under it, and into the palace courtyard, which was filled with hundreds of demons attired in lavish robes and adornments. They stood silently on either side of the court-yard, creating a path leading directly to the palace doors.

Lady Zim led them to doors and stopped. A dark-skinned female with translucent black wings, like a dragonfly, was standing in front of them. "Welcome, my prince," she said to Caym, bowing her head and curt-seying.

"It's a good passing if we are still alive, Lady Esra," he opined, with a kind, lingering smile.

"Your father has been anxious for your return," she said, looking at them all, "and to see what you have brought with you."

Lady Zim, Thamuz, and Caym dismounted, and handed their leads over to waiting soldiers; Caym kept hold of Jared's ivy leash; Mary Susan straggled alongside him. Lady Esra took a step back and looked out to the crowd.

"Prepare Orsha-Na," she called out. The throngs of nobility bowed their heads. "His Grace, Duke Chax—god of the dead, Lord of the Northlands—*approaches.*"

The massive doors of the palace creaked and began opening inward. A rush of power followed, and flowed over Jared like a wave of heat es-caping an oven. A golden paw broke past the threshold and stepped into the courtyard; the rest of it followed. It was a lion, though no ordinary king of the jungle. As all else was in Hell, it was a perversion of its earthly counterpart. It was as tall as a horse and had paws the size of an elephant. It's amber eyes swept to and fro, as though on the hunt.

Riding atop the lion on a black saddle was its master, the duke, wearing a black hood and cloak that concealed all of him in layer upon layer of silky fabric. His face was masked also, though the fabric was pulled tight enough to show his strong, broad nose and plump lips. He wore a crown—a band of gold affixed with a fist-sized ruby at its center. The duke stopped the lion in front of Lady Zim and the others.

"Lay thee down, Farfal," Chax said. Farfal did as commanded.

With feline grace, he eased down his front paws first, and then the back ones. Chax dismounted and greeted Lady Zim, Thamuz, and his son with a respectful tilt of the head. Thamuz and Caym bowed; Lady Zim curtseyed low. *'Your Grace,'* said each in deference. Chax flipped the long cuffs of his layered cloak out to the side of him, and began walking around Lady Zim, moving toward Jared and Mary Susan.

Jared looked up at Chax. He was barely eye level with the creature's shoulder. The urge to step back made him shiver and shake. Though even if he had wanted to retreat, he could not; Caym was holding the ivy leash taught. Chax neared him, though abruptly stopped and looked over at the soul beside him.

"*Mary Susan!*" Chax called out, as though happening upon a dear old friend not seen for some time. "I thought you were lost to me, my dear. They told me you were abducted. I asked…'How can this be?' And they said…'Oh, your grace, but it is so. She is…*gone!*'" His voice was heavy with despair.

He bent at the waist, placing his shrouded face inches from her sagging, wrinkled one. She cowered and began weeping. "How could I ever live without you, my Mary Susan?" The moments of silence that passed were broken only by Mary's whimpering. Chax stood and turned to the nobles on his right; his voice soared high and across the courtyard. "Twas' I who gave you your heart's desire; and twas' you, Mary Susan, who paid that costly price to attain it. You conjured me, not I, you." He glanced back at her. "Remind me again, dear midwife, how many newborns did you throttle before they could even take their first breath? It slips my godly mind, it does. Was it twenty? Perhaps thirty? *Am I close, dear?*" He paused, and then looked to those on his left. "How many infants died at your hands before you were discovered—*found out*—and then covered in tar and burned in a pit as a witch? Hmm?" He tilted his head. "Do tell."

She fell to her knees and rocked, and grabbed at her matted hair and yanked at it. "I didn't kill'em," she muttered, and began gnawing at the gunk under her nails. "I swear! I never did those—"

"Oh Mary...*dear Mary.* Will we play that old game again?" Chax said, groaning to the nobles, as though pleading with them to empathize with his burden. "Or shall we just have at it, and let it be done? Either way, my dear, I shall not be disappointed." She wobbled her head side to side. "The Morning Star wanted you as one of his frozen treasures in his palace, but it was I who went to the dome of Phenóx and begged him to give you to me. 'I nurtured the witch for some time, my lord,' I said to him. She gave me the blood of infants and I gave her a Spell of Death for each one, I said to him, explaining as passionately as I could, in hope The Morning Star would understand my dilemma and be merciful to his most loyal and humble servant." He looked at the nobles on the other side. "Mary Susan kill those she envied...oh yes, indeed! And The Morning Star, being benevolent in that moment, he gave her to me. He heard my pleas." He turned, facing her. His voice was cold, like mist rolling off of a grave. *"And here you are."*

Chax straightened the front of his cloak and sleeves, and walked over and stood in front of Jared, casting a shadow over him. For a moment, Chax said nothing, though then beckoned him closer with a finger. Jared didn't move, but then suddenly felt his body being pushed forward. The invisible force moved him up just inches from Chax, who then leaned over and put his face in front of Jared's.

"Tell me, Miel—angel of The Father—Angel of Balance," he said, "do you know where you are?"

Jared stayed silent. The force emanating from Chax was making his head woozy and his body weak. He began swaying back and forth.

"I've never known one of the Heavenly Host to be so," Chax paused, "silent. Though, too, I have never known of an angel to be trapped in Hell. There have been many firsts in The Father's vast, unending cosmos; an angel in Hell will certainly not be the last of them." He looked down at the vines winding around Jared's wrists. "You've met the Lady Pnemoxsis. I trust that she has extended her welcome accordingly."

Caym turned around. "Father...a moment?" he asked.

Chax nodded and beckoned for him. He leaned down, allowing Caym to whisper in his ear. When Caym had finished, he bowed to his father and returned to his place.

"It seems the lady's welcome for you is not yet over," he said to Jared. "I'm told that my family wishes you to return to Varencia, so that they may know you intimately. But my lady is mistaken." Chax spoke for all to hear. "This angel is not our enemy, but our guest." He passed his gloved hand over Jared's ivy bonds. The vines halted in mid-twist and turned black, and then gray, and became ash. They fell from his wrists.

Jared rubbed at his sore wrists. "Lady Pnemoxsis could have killed me if she wanted to, but didn't. They could have, too." He nodded at Lady Zim and the others. "Obviously, you can. So why haven't you? What do you want from me?"

"Me from you, or you from me?" Chax replied coyly. "Perhaps you think a trick is being weaved around you—one misstep, and you are caught!" He shook his head. "I assure you, there is no subterfuge here. I say that no citizen of Orsha-Na shall bring harm to you. That is my word. That is my bond. I may be many things to you, but do not let foolish be one of them. True enough, you and I are enemies. Though in these dark passings of Wormwood, we must be allies, for now, there is more than just the ruin of Hell at stake."

"Says the one who put it that way," Jared said. "I wouldn't even be here if—"

"If Lucifer had not sought deification," he rattled off, dismissively waving his hand. "'Tis' the oldest story in creation, and one that has been greatly distorted. Yet, what does that matter now, angel? Does your belief in one version of that story now lift you out of our realm and return you back to earth, where you should not even reside at all? You, yourself, are not so innocent in all of this, Miel. Though we cannot freely pass into earth's realm, there are those of us who can see past the barrier into yours —my lady, Pnemoxsis, being one of them. Had you left earth, as you should have, and gone to your heavenly realm, perhaps you and I would not be having this chat at all. Your accusation of guilt, is at best, disturbingly tenuous."

"If you know that, then you should know that I couldn't leave without both tomes," Jared said.

"Sacrifices must be made," Chax opined.

"Not that one."

"You say 'no', but now that is no longer your choice to make," Chax said. "The Egyptian is still in possession of the tome, not you, Miel-angel. How rotten the fruit borne of your self-righteousness." He turned and began walking, and beckoned over his shoulder for Jared to follow. "In these passings, we are not enemies. We cannot afford to be. The fate of earth and Hell are now one and the same. If one falls, so does the other. There is no undoing what has already been done. It is far, far too late for that now."

Chax walked over to Farfal and rubbed his head. Jared stopped next to Lady Zim.

"There is a path to earth from Hell," Chax said to him. "Though, it has never been travelled by anyone. And it cannot be—not without the assistance of those you hold in such disdain."

"A deal with the devil?" Jared chuckled, despite his fear. The idea of making a Faustian pact to save mankind seemed ridiculous on its face, knowing that such pacts were always never really a pact at all, but a wager, and there was only ever one winner—*the same one*—, each and every time.

"A deal?" Chax said. "No, my lord. We wish to forge a covenant…one as strong and as binding as that between The Father and The Morning Star."

"We?" Jared asked. His lifeforce slowed and became heavy in his chest.

"The Lady of the East and Lord of the South have gathered at Adoja," Chax replied. The noble demons passed the news along to the rear in waves of whispers and murmurs. "We are all most eager to speak with you." Chax mounted his lion. "Rise thee up, Farfal." The beast obeyed, and then shook its mane. Chax looked down at Lady Zim. "Escort the angel inside. Perhaps we shall forge a covenant betwixt us that may save both our worlds."

* * *

Jared followed them into the palace, and was led into a cavernous hall with stories tall, white statues on pedestals placed about. Mary Susan—Chax's prized soul—was led away by guards in a different direction; her whimpering pleas of innocence and for mercy were ceaseless echoes.

Jared walked in line with the others behind Chax atop Farfal; he was free, though not free. Zim was to the right of him. Caym was next, and then came the hulking brute, Thamuz.

"Hold, Farfal," Chax called out, stopping the procession. He pointed up to the statue on his right. It was of a young woman with thick braids holding her arms up waist high. In one of her cupped hands she held a dove; and in the other, a dagger. "That is my child, Nuna. She is becoming a great goddess of peace and war." Chax turned and looked at Jared. "She takes after me, I am proud to say."

They walked on a few feet and Chax stopped them again, this time to point at a young male whose body was covered in ivy. Jared recognized the boyish, though devilish Belayphion immediately. Across from him was his sister, Surratta.

They passed more statues of his brood. Chax stopped to wax on about each one. They came to a set of double doors. Reliefs of Caym and Lady Pnemoxsis were on either side; she was on the left and he on the right. Their hands met in the middle over the doorway, she with hers cupped, and his just lightly resting in it, as though presenting her beloved son to the world.

"And here we have the duchess and prince, my mate and first-born—wife and heir," Chax said, as they passed through the doorway. "Seeing all of my children reminds me just how much I miss them." He called for Caym. "See the lady and my children here to Adoja before the next pass."

"Yes, father," Caym said obediently.

They walked into what looked like a coliseum to Jared. There was seating, which soared stories high all around the circular hall. There was no roof, just blue skies above, and now Wormwood, he directly above it, curled up and wagging his arms as he beamed down light upon them.

"Behold me as I was, angel," Chax said, pointing to the right and up, even as he turned Farfal left.

Jared looked. On the top of the coliseum was a colossal, white statue of Odin—the one-eyed king of the Norse gods. The tips of his winged helmet seemed to touch the sky. And upon both shoulders were ravens; the one on his left looked out, and the other turned toward his ear, as though whispering the secrets of the cosmos to him.

"As I was Odin, so was I Zeus," Chax said.

Jared looked straight ahead. Perched on the top of the coliseum was another statue. This one was of Zeus sitting upon his throne. In his right hand he held a staff topped with an eagle. In his left hand, which rested on his thigh, he cupped a globe of the earth.

"We were everything to mankind," Chax said, leading them down the middle of the coliseum. "We have led every nation on earth. I, Odin, sent the Norsemen down through Europe and across the ocean to America. I, Zeus, shepherded Rome and Greece to greatness, which has led man's footsteps ever since."

Chax looked to his left. Opposite of Zeus, was a black statue of Atum-Ra, the Egyptian king of the gods. His arms were crossed in front of him, with a crook in one hand and a flail in the other. "Twas' I who made Egypt the envy of the world," Chax said, his tone casual, as though remarking upon a triviality.

They approached a set of stairs that led up to a dais with two, white stone thrones upon it. Above it, another set of stairs led to a second dais, though this one was wider, and had three thrones arranged side by side on it. The middle throne was empty, though the two on either side of it were not. Like Chax, the figure seated on the left wore a black cloak and netting over its face. The creature was hunched over and squirmed in its seat, never stopping for more than a moment. The one seated on the right was cloaked in white. Its face was concealed like the others, and the hood of its cloak was down past its eyes. It sat still, completely unmoving like a statue.

Chax came to the foot of the stairs, and then gave Farfal a nudge on either side of his flanks. The lion roared and leapt, and began pouncing up the stairs, crossing four and five of them at a time. It reached the top, turned around and roared again. It lay down, allowing its master to dismount.

Chax walked over and stood in front of his throne, and then looked straight up. On top of the coliseum directly above him, was a statue of a black-skinned male sitting on a throne with a snake coiled around his shin.

"Above all of the gods that I was, I was both Adroa and Adro the serpent...good and evil. There is no Atum-Ra, or Odin, or Zeus without Adroa; they came from him and he from me. Though Adroa is father god to all and sits upon a throne worthy of The Father, he is still, nonetheless, but an incarnation of my very own creation." He sat down on his throne. "Know thee now who I am. I am Chax!"

"Angel," the figure in white called out; it was a female's voice. "Whereas man dare not look upon the face of The Father, we have sat at his footstool and looked upon him with our celestial eyes. I am the duchess, Agares—Lady of the Eastlands. Though, too, I was also Mawu —goddess of creation."

"Tis' true, angel," the other in black said. His words sounded as though he were gargling them. He jerked forward and backward, and swayed to the side, never resting. His head bobbed beneath his hood, looking as though it were about to pop off at any moment.

Chax extended his arm to the squirming and jerking creature. "His Grace, Duke Beelzebub," he said, with a regal flair. "Were it not for the Lord of the Flies, there would have been no Ba'al—god of Ekron. And thus, there would have been no *us*."

"Beelzebub taught man how to worship us," Agares said.

"Aye," Beelzebub croaked, with weave and bobble of his body. "I was Ba'al and Hades, too. I gave men gluttony."

"And then men gave us all that we asked for," Chax added. "Show me a mortal sated in his life, and I will give you my crown and rule of Orsha-Na."

"I suggest you do not take His Grace up on his offer, Miel-angel," Beelzebub warbled. "There is a counter-cost that must be wagered. And it would be a fool's bet...*on your part*."

"And you want me to make a covenant with you?" Jared asked, with a wry grin.

"That is all together different," Agares replied.

"Being double crossed—no matter what I choose—doesn't sound all that different to me."

"To believe we do nothing but lie is a lie itself," Chax said. "Being possessed of a counter opinion is not a lie. We know that we are gods, but the Heavenly Host does not agree. Show me the subterfuge therein."

"And where does rebellion fit in there?" Jared quipped. "Who are the real traitors, Chax?"

"Your disrespect may be rewarded with my sword across your neck," Caym advised.

"You must not punish the foolish for being foolish, dear nephew," Agares said to Caym. "He speaks upon the war in Heaven as though he were there...as though he knows what he speaks of, yet he speaks from ignorance."

"I sent many of the Heavenly Host to the ether in that war," Chax said, "and many of my brothers and sisters fell into that nothingness along with them. Thousands of legions of celestials fell in the Great War. But what you call rebellion, we call justice."

"You want to stop the next war," Jared said, "because you know you can't win. But Astaroth is holding the End Days hostage, not you three. Now it's a bad thing because you're bowing to him?"

"Foolish angel," Beelzebub gurgled.

"We are more than prepared for the final war, Miel," Agares said, her voice flowing out almost in a whisper. "We see victory, where you see inevitable defeat. Though again, that is fundamentally a matter of opinion, not a lie."

"If anything, we welcome war," Chax said. "Though now, there may not be one at all. And at your feet I must lay this blame, Miel-angel. That worm of a creature—the Egyptian—has possession of The Morning Star's tome, and has become yet another pawn of Astaroth that surround us from all sides. If they succeed, Hell and earth will be under Astaroth's dominion, and not even The Father will be able to stop it, for He gave His word, and His word is power itself."

"Neither one of our worlds can stand alone," Agares warned. "You cannot save the earth without saving Hell."

"We have no wish to be sent to the ether," Chax said. "Self-preservation is perhaps the only thing we have in commonality with mortals. Now that all of our lives are in peril, then *what-oh-what* shall we do? I must say this has weighed heavily upon my thoughts."

"And on mine," Agares said.

"Aye," Beelzebub garbled. "It has made the light of Wormwood seem dim and cold."

"My great nephew—Beelzebub's own grandchild—, has taken much from us," Chax said. "He has claimed lordship over his grandfather's lands, and that of his aunt's, the lady, Agares. He now possesses the souls of those lands and all of the force embedded in every blade of grass, every stone, every twig on every tree—it is all his."

"Not only that," Agares jutted in. "He has taken command of the holy Train of Souls, the transport of The Damned that funnels souls to the realms of Hell. Duke Chax's Northlands is all that remains out of Astaroth's grasp...but he reaches for it. Astaroth is as relentless, as he is unique."

"He is a demon-deuce—a dual spell caster," Beelzebub said. "He swings with a sword, as he speaks spells from his mouth. We elevated him and placed a crown upon his head, and called him duke, Lord of the West. We had created a god!"

"True-true, Your Grace," Chax agreed heartily.

Agares turned to Beelzebub. "You raised him up as Ishtar and Astarte."

"To be sure," Beelzebub concurred proudly. "And while I did, he attacked from behind. He made pacts with King Purson and the lady, Lilith, and all of those traitorous others, and expelled me from my own lands. And then he came for you, duchess."

"He seized power from my hands," Agares said, turning her masked gaze back to Jared. "Now it is the Northlands that he desires, and from there to Phenóx. Earth will fall soon after."

"See now, if you did not see before, Miel-angel," said Chax. "Hell is at war. Earth teeters on the brink."

"All will fall," Beelzebub said.

"If 'no' is your answer," Agares added.

"It depends on what the question is," Jared said.

"Does it?" Chax asked. "Or does it depend on what is at stake? With the souls of the east, west, and south under his command, Astaroth is unstoppable…or so we thought, until we saw you fall. And if there is one thing I know to the depths of my bones, is what a falling angel looks like."

"Just as we thought all was lost, here came you," Agares said.

"An angel," Beelzebub remarked.

"And not just any heavenly celestial, but the mortal who became Miel —the Angel of Balance," Chax said. "Your fall into Hell may just have saved both worlds."

"How?" Jared asked.

"By giving of yourself to us," Agares said in hush.

"Freely," Beelzebub chortled.

"Give us your lifeforce," Chax said, "and save your world and all upon it that you love."

"Deny us…." Beelzebub said.

"And all of mankind will suffer," Agares warned.

Jared walked to the foot of the stairs. "You're out of your minds."

"Quite the contrary," Chax said. "We have explored every avenue there is in stopping Astaroth. There is no other way."

"You hold the fate of both worlds in your hands," Agares said.

"If you know another way, then speak it now," Beelzebub warbled.

Jared didn't, though felt that somewhere within their scheme lay his downfall. *There's a catch to it. I know there is. There has to be.* Jared looked from one cloaked creature to the other. *I'm just not seeing it.*

"You feed off of me and you get power," Jared said. "How does this help me get home?"

Chax turned to Agares, and then to Beelzebub. "There is only one way home for you," he said. "And that path is through Phenóx and ends in the palace of The Morning Star, where The Father has laid him down in sleep until the End of Days."

"He is surrounded by the guardians of the three evils on earth," Agares said.

"You came to Hell by way of one of them," Chax said.

"To return to earth, you must leave by way of one of them," Beelzebub chortled.

"The only way to enter Phenóx is to burst the black sphere around it," Chax said. "Only a great and awesome power can do that."

"Astaroth has nearly amassed such power," Agares added.

"If he breaches the dome of Phenóx, he will have expended a great deal of force to do it," Chax said. "It will be his only moment of weakness and our only opportunity to strike him down."

"But we cannot, unless you give us your lifeforce, Miel," Agares said. "It must be given freely, for that is when it is the most powerful. You escaped the inescapable grip of Lady Muchenlay. You have great power, Miel. And great power is what we need—"

"If Astaroth is to be stopped," Beelzebub said, finishing with a bobble of the head.

"The only way is through Phenóx?" Jared asked, looking from one to the other. "Now I know you're up to a trick. The place I barely got out of, is the one I have to go to, to get home?"

"Were it only that simple," Chax said. "There is great risk in attempting to return to earth. All that is in Phenóx belongs to The Morning Star. He drains every frozen soul within it of its essence. Once you step into that realm, he shall begin to drain you, too. And as you wait for a guardian to be summoned to earth, to ride upon its flesh back to your world, the Morning Star will feed upon you. If you are fortunate, one will be summoned soon."

"And if not?"

The Lords of Hell were silent.

"If you feed off of me, I'll be drained of force when I reached Phenóx," Jared said. "I'll be helpless."

"You are a celestial," Chax said. "You will replenish your natural force, albeit slowly."

"I'll still be going in weakened."

"Most true," Agares remarked.

"Therein lies the risk," Chax said. "But we risk much ourselves. This is no longer about winning a war, but of surviving one."

"Lest all fall to ash," Beelzebub added.

And what if all did?—fall to ash, Jared thought. There was more than just his family and friends to worry about. The welfare of billions of mortals now weighed upon his shoulders, and it was a heavy weight, indeed.

"As proof of our earnestness," Chax said, "I will see you to the hall of The Morning Star. Lady Zimarantha, Captain Thamuz, and my own son, Prince Caym, shall accompany you and safeguard your journey as far as their swords and spells can take you. If we are successful in defeating Astaroth," he raised a hand toward Beelzebub and Agares each, "we will have the power to reclaim my son, and my general, and my captain from Phenóx. You, however, will remain. And in the name of The Father, The Lamb, the Ghost, and the Morning Star," the lords made the sign of the cross, though added one more move, touching the center of their chest as Chax said, "we pray you will return to earth and kill the Egyptian. Return the world to balance and let the final war come about. He who knows victory is to come, does not fear the war to claim it. I am Chax."

"I am Beelzebub."

"I, Agares."

"That is the terms of *our* covenant," Chax pronounced. "Give us your lifeforce freely; release the power of the Angel of Balance, and let us feed. Do so, and we will kill the usurper and give you passage into Phenóx. It is the only way back to earth.

"Sign the pact."

CHAPTER 10

Jared looked out over the city of Hedun from his room on the upper level of the palace. Far off in the distance, the enchanted forest of Lady Pnemoxsis brushed the pale blue skies with its leafy tops. Down below, throngs of demons were making their way to the palace, heading toward the great throne room. They were arrayed in flowing robes and shendyts; their jewelry sparkled under the white glare of Wormwood, making them appears as bodies moving through a sea of diamonds. And they were all coming to see him, he thought, gripping the edge of the window and cracking its stone ledge.

He looked at his hands and clenched them. He could feel his force nearly returned, though for what little good it was, he thought. Though he was no longer technically a prisoner, he still felt like one. There were thousands of them pouring in below, and each one of them, his sworn enemy, and he theirs. *And all I have to do is help save them, if I want to save earth.* He closed his eyes and sighed.

He walked over to the floor mirror in the corner at looked at himself. He was wearing the white robes given to him by an old, black soul who came rapping at his door earlier; he was thin as sticks and hunched over, and looked ready to break apart at any moment; each step seemed his last. The robe was light, as though it were made of spider silk; it felt barely there at all, he thought, running his hand across it. The black boots he had been given were loose when he had put them on, though when he stood, they shifted and shrank to fit him; they conformed and reformed with every step he took.

He looked at his face. The face of a boy having just become a man looked back at him…smooth brown skin, dark eyes, a heavy brow, and strong jaw…all the markings of when the foolishness of male youth begins its transition to pensive wisdom; some faster than others; some slower; and some never.

"You're still a kid to me, Jared," Henrì was fond of reminding him. 'The more I find out about these celestials—creatures like you—the more I'm in awe of them,' Henrì had said. 'They've been around for eons. Some of the oldest of them are nearly as old as the universe itself; those are the most powerful ones. They're not only ancient, but also immensely wise. Just imagine…they've watched man go from amino acids floating in sludge in the ocean, to a walking, breathing, cognizant creature imbued with a soul. That's what makes them so dangerous. They know us inside and out, but we think we can fool them—we always think we can. But we're like rats trying to outwit the scientist. You may be a celestial like them, but when it comes to knowledge—the only real weapon there really is—they've got you beat hands down They'll use what you want the most to seduce you. And you'll never see it coming. They're masters at seduction.'

A rap came at the door. "Come in," Jared called.

"Good passing," Zim said, walking in and closing the door behind her.

"Is it?" Jared replied.

He already knew what he wanted the most; and that was to get home and kill Yikan, and to set everything back to right. The seduction part already seemed in play, he thought, looking at her from the reflection in the mirror. His eyes roved up and down her body. She was wearing a robe that was of layers of sheer white cloth. It was loose at the shoulders and neck, exposing the tops of her bosom, and snug at her hips.

"Do you like it, angel," she asked, following his eyes as they roved over her.

His cheeks were warm with lifeforce. "Yeah…nice. I mean, you look nice," he stumbled.

"It was made by Lady Leox," she said, glancing down at her robes. "She made yours as well, by command of His Grace."

"You here to convince me to make the pact?"

"No. I'm here to accompany you to the gala...in your honor."

Jared chuckled and turned toward her. "First I'm a prisoner, now I'm the guest of honor?"

"You are free to come and go as you please," she replied. "By the duke's decree, none in Orsha-Na may bring you harm. In truth—if anything—we would protect you. You are our last hope."

She spoke earnestly and passionately for her cause. It was the first time he had heard anything from her that was not rigidly pragmatic. She had willingly exposed a weakness. *Though, was it to seduce?* he wondered. If it was, then she had dressed the part as well, he thought, trying to keep eye contact and not allow his eyes to wander about her body any more than they already had.

"Do you know how wrong this is for me?" he asked.

"As wrong as it is for me, I suppose," she replied, with a slow raise of her brow. "I believe the Morning Star should have a seat amongst The Father, The Lamb, and The Ghost. I believe him to be divine and holy, whereas you do not, and you are willingly to lay down your life to see him—and all of us who worship him—to our death." She stepped closer. "Yes, Miel-angel...I do understand how wrong this feels to you." She stared into his eyes for a moment, and then walked over to the window. She sat on the ledge and looked out at Hedun. "Who will you trust, Miel?"

"Me."

"And since you cannot escape our realm without our assistance, who will you put your faith in?" she asked, but continued on. "We have never deceived mortals. When they came beseeching us for wealth and love and revenge, they all knew the cost of their actions. They agreed—*and signed in blood*—because, no matter the cost—in this life or the next—they wanted their heart's desire. And now, century after century, the mortals have only become worse, not better...just as The Morning Star prophesized. The mortals worship greed and violence. Their leaders are corrupt, and they exalt them for being so. The heart of man is rife with evil, and gluttony which fuels it, making it burn hot and remaining ever at the forefront of his mind." She turned away from the city and looked at him. "There are some mortals who eschew such immorality. And believe it or not, I would love to bestow gifts and wonders upon them, had I the chance again." She bobbed her head. "I am not evil, Miel. I was benevolent to the mortals that deserved it. Though now, my role is to punish the wicked and sinful." She looked back to Hedun and smiled. "Do you know why the lords conceal themselves? Their power is all that keeps what is left of Hedun still standing. The drain on their lifeforce to keep it as such has stolen their beauty, so they hide beneath shrouds, concealing their great sacrifice from us."

Jared sighed. "We're back to beauty again."

"And what is wrong with beauty?" she asked, pursing her plump lips. "Perfection is next to godliness. *You were so perfect in every way, from the day thou wast created.*' That is what we say in prayer when we look to Phenóx, over there, beyond the great forest." She pointed above the green realm. Jared came over and looked.

Zim got up and walked over to a large, round wood table in the center of the room. The top was inlaid with a mosaic of the god, Neptune, half-seated on an open seashell with trident in hand. His head was turned, looking off over his watery realm with a stern look on his face.

"Norum-dei stum alt infenio-tu," she said, waving her hand over the table. The pieces of glass from the mosaic rose up and transformed into bits of grains. "Storuk abo ahbek." The particles swirled, and then began arranging themselves into miniature structures.

Jared came over and stood opposite of her, watching as the sand-like bits formed into a physical map, complete with a glass dome over the entire structure. There was even a likeness of Wormwood at the apex, and below it, in the center of the map, was another dome, though this one was black and opaque.

Zim waved her hand over the dome. "This is the sky of Hell," she said. It fell away like sand. She pointed to the black dome. "And this is Phenóx; it is at the center of the four realms, and each realm is connected to it by a bridge."

Jared recognized Chax's medieval, African palace and the replica of his mate's great forest at the top of the map. To the west was Astaroth's stone and sand realm of mud brick Babylonian structures, complete with its great tower of Babel. Southward was Beelzebub's realm of flat-roof buildings, though was dominated by a colossal, Aztecan stepped-pyramid. In the east, in Agares's domain, the style was Greek—pillared, white temples surrounding a great mount that was home to a grand, lavish palace with a gold dome.

"Come here, Miel," she said, pointing to a spot in red in the Westlands near Phenóx. "This is Sheol, where the Lake of Fire is. And these rail tracks that lead out to the four realms is for the Train of Souls—the ferry of The Damned. Astaroth is concentrating all of his might upon his Westland bridge to Phenóx. And that is where we must go to confront Astaroth. That is your only way in and the lords only chance to stop him. But...." She held up a finger and pointed back to Sheol. "This is King Purson's realm. He has sided with Astaroth and feeds him souls from Sheol, depriving the lords of theirs. To get to the Westlands, we must pass through his realm and ride the Train of Souls to get there."

"Right into the middle of Astaroth's army?"

"Precisely," she replied. "Though army suggests thousands. Astaroth has amassed legions of The Fallen, and has a never ending supply of vulags to attack the dome with." Jared cocked his head. She looked at him and smiled. "Vulags are souls that have been meshed together and flung by catapult. When they hit their target, their essence is released as energy."

"And then after that, Phenóx," he panned.

"One of the three gods—the guardians of the three evils on earth—must be summoned."

"While Lucifer is feeding on my lifeforce."

"Yes...until you become just another of his many frozen treasures."

"I can't wait there forever."

Zim looked him in the eye. "No, you cannot. But it is your only way home."

"It sounds like a sure way to die."

"As is inaction."

"How long do I have to decide?"

"Midpass. That is the duke's command," she said. "Miel...*Jared*...you have more than one route." She held his gaze. "It is a path that does not involve suicide, for that is what it will be if you linger in the hall of The Morning Star. You cannot return to earth...it is nigh impossible. But in Hell, you would be a king and a god. If you aid the lords in defeating Astaroth, there is nothing they will not give you."

"And here it comes," he quipped, shaking his head.

"What is that?"

"The trick!" he said, waving his arm at her. "The deceit and double cross, and all that. You know the drill, don'cha? Huh *goddess?*"

Zim didn't flinch. Instead, coolly, she rested her hands on the table and leaned over. "Instead of anger toward your ignorance, I'm compelled to pity you instead, Jared." Her eyes were wide and earnest. "I know compassion is the last thing you would expect from a Fallen One, but it's actually quite a common trait amongst us. And I have a great deal of this for you right now." She lolled her head to the side. "You actually believe you have a chance of returning home."

"I have to."

"You must do nothing you do not wish to do," she countered.

"But this isn't just about me."

"The mortals," she said bluntly.

"Yes," he said. "Billions of them. I have to believe there's a chance of getting back, no matter how small it is."

"Infinitesimal, I would say."

"Then I'll take it."

"Or choose a kingdom," she suggested. "We would welcome you with open arms." She looked away, but then glanced up coyly. "All of us would."

He caught her eye, but looked away. Was it the trap that had just been sprung? he wondered. Or was it some thing more basic in the way she was looking at him and making his lifeforce race around in his chest? Was it something primal he was feeling?

She walked over to the door. "Until midpass arrives, we shall mark this passing with a celebration of life and resilience, and of hope." She opened the door and stood to the side. "Shall we, Jared? There are more gods of Orsha-Na waiting to meet you."

* * *

The gala had already begun when he and Zim walked in, they entering below the statue of Zeus to the coliseum filled to capacity with demons. Slow, eerie notes from violins and cellos that had been wafting through the air suddenly stopped upon their arrival. The noble demons, who had been chatting and laughing, and mingling between groups, stopped and turned toward them. As a collective, they lowered their heads.

Zim curtseyed and bowed hers. "My lords," she replied in humble deference.

The demons parted, allowing them a path to the center of the room, and then up, toward the daises. "Lady Diadooah," some said in greeting to Zim and bowed again as she and Jared passed. Others called out the name Zimarantha, and yet others spoke to her in the language of demons.

Jared heard others calling out as well, though to him. Some spoke with their mouths...others with their minds, directing their thoughts into his. *'Fight for us! Miel. And I will give you treasures beyond measure,'* one said to his mind.

"Seal the pact," a pale, winged demon called out, who was standing just in front of them. His eyes were as blue as the sea; his hair was golden, and his wings as white as snow. "Do it. And I will smite all of your enemies." His eyes flashed white for a moment. "I vow it!"

"I will show you the past of any day of any time," said a svelte, copper-haired female from the other side. "Knowledge is the ultimate power, my lord." She bowed as they passed and called out, "Sign it!"

A brown-skinned female with feathers for hair called out to him. "I will see your lust fulfilled."

A white male with the horns of a buck deer stepped out in front of them, halting them. He put one hand on his hip, and twirled the other in the air with a flourish as he bowed. "I will feed your gluttony for a thousand years, if you would but…" he looked up at Jared and winked, "sign it, my lord." He smiled and stepped back into the crowd.

"I will give you love," one called out.

"I will give you *lovers*," said another.

I'll drive your enemies mad, a female promised him in thought. *Sign it!* He looked around to find her. Was it the one with Asian eyes and dark skin and pouty lips? he wondered, spotting her, and then turning to look at another. Or was it the dark skinned female holding up an orb? or the dark blue one with white eyes that glowed? He looked back and forth as they barraged his mind with promises, if he would just….

"I'll make you irresistible."

"I'll torture your enemies."

"I'll give you a legion of my men for a hundred years."

"I'll make it a thousand!"

"I'll give two!"

"Sign it!"

"Sign it!"

Sign it!

"Welcome, angel of The Father," Chax called out, with a boom to his voice that shook the hall. The noble demons became silent and faced their lord, and bowed their heads.

Zim leaned in and whispered. "Come on, Jared."

He nodded and began walking. Lady Pnemoxsis was seated on a throne on the first dais, and across from her was Caym; both wore crowns affixed with a ruby in the center upon their heads. And below them, seated on the steps, were the dark green children of the forest, the spawn of the duke and duchess. Chax, Beelzebub, and Agares were seated on the top dais, concealed in their shrouds and face nettings.

Jared and Zim stopped at the foot of the stairs. Chax stood.

"Each pass of Wormwood is a blessing from The Morning Star," Chax pronounced. "We must cherish each pass and live each to the fullest. For no god knows when it may be our last. I speak not as a pessimist, but as a realist, which I am, by my nature. But this I do know…I will give every ounce of force that I have to see Astaroth pay for his treason." He looked up to the sky and spoke with a solemn voice. "Morning Star, be merciful and see us upon a field of victory. Give us the strength to destroy your adversary. Sharpen our spells and make swift our swords. Let us send Astaroth to the ether. This we ask in the name of The Father, The Lamb, The Ghost, and The Morning Star." He performed the five pointed sign of the cross. The nobles quickly followed.

Chax looked down at Jared. "What we fight for, Miel-angel, is worth fighting for. It is worth risking the ether," he said, and then look to the nobles on his left. "Countess Asani! Come hither."

Jared and Zim turned around. On his right, the nobles began to part. From within their mist came a brown-skinned demon with rope thick braids down to her waist. She approached the stairs, and then slid her right foot behind her and curtseyed.

"Patron goddess of the arts," Chax said to her. "Dance the Rise and Fall for our esteemed guest." The nobles whispered and gasped in awe; the news spread like waves throughout the hall.

Countess Asani passed by Jared and looked at him from the side. "My lord," she offered in respect, with a bow of the head.

The sky rumbled. Jared looked up and saw the blue skies beginning to cloud over. He turned around and glanced up at Chax, who was looking up to the darkening skies. He raised his gloved hand at them. They turned pitch black and blocked out the light of Wormwood. Chax swept his arm out and away at the hall. The metal braziers throughout the hall suddenly burst alight with roaring flames, casting the room in a deep orange glow.

"You're in for a delight," Zim said, smiling at Jared.

The countess turned around. She removed her pale blue robes one layer at time, twirling them out and away from her body as she unwound them. With the last piece gone, she stood before them with her breasts and nether region covered in sheer white cloths. She was tiny at the waist and curvy at the chest and hips. The whole of her eyes were black, the same color as her plump lips.

The countess sprang into an allegro, bounding high and fast toward the nobles who gasped as scuttled back and away. She twirled and jumped, moving around clockwise until she had come full circle, and had created one. She moved to the center of it.

A white, goateed male in a shendyt stepped out from the onlookers and into the circle, just at the edge; he held a violin and bow in his hands. Jared noticed his odd looking hands right off; the fingers were unusually long, like they had an extra knuckle. The countess bowed to him and knelt, and then lowered her chest to her thighs and looked off to the side.

The violinist began! The first note struck was low, slow, and strong; it was the darkest of nights captured in a single note.

Countess Asani wrapped her arms around her chest. "She is the Morning Star," Zim whispered to him. "He is in the ether and is nothing, for in there, there is nothing."

The countess unfolded her arms and reached into the air as she rose to her feet; though she did not stop there, for upon a pair of sleek, muscular calves, she elevated the full weight of her curvaceous form upon the tips of her toes—en pointe. From her toes to the tip of her middle finger, she was an absolute straight line.

"He rises from the ether by the word of The Father," Lady Zim said.

The countess moved her right leg out, gently touching the floor as she stretched out her arms like they were virgin wings being unfurled. She looked to either side of her; she appeared lost. And then she looked up. Her black eyes were wide with wonder.

"He realizes he is alive...*he is sentient*—aware of himself. And he is beautiful and perfect in every sense of the word."

The countess began moving around the circle. She spun and then sauntered forward, gliding almost, as though she walked on air. She extended her arms out in front of her as though she were wading in a sea of delicate flowers, parting them gently, as if their welfare was her only concern. Her body flowed effortlessly from movement to movement...from kick of the leg, to bowing, and parting of those gentle flowers to the side; her display of *adagio* was mercurial. She twirled and paused, and then rose upon en pointe and twirled around slowly like a jewelry box ballerina. She bounded off and leapt into the air with both feet together, and then landing on both, performing a flawless *assemble*.

She rose and began twirling on one foot, performing dizzying pirou-
ettes around the perimeter of open-mouthed, wide-eyed gathered nobles.
Her angles were sharp. Her twirls were without the slightest bobble.

She stopped in the middle of the circle and looked at Jared. The violin
struck low and lingered there.

Zim leaned close and whispered. "He has come to the throne of The
Father, but refuses to bow. Instead, he claims divine seating as the fourth
to their trinity. Witness now, Jared, what has started eons of conflict between our kind."

The countess rose on en pointe, and with the other leg, curled it behind past her back. And as she moved her leg up—foot pointed—, she
brought her hands out and up, and touched the tip of her foot. She was
a straight line from tip to toe, and a perfect circle around her torso with
her curled leg and arms.

"He is the flame of life!" Zim said. "He is the spark of creation. He is
unique. Perfect. Flawless."

The violin hit a discordant note. The countess came down from her
perch of perfection. Her expression was at first forlorn, but quickly
turned fierce and vengeful.

"The Father has fallen him," Zim said. "But now, he stands in his own
godhood and makes a wager with The Father...god to God. The Great
Covenant is struck. In a world balanced with good and evil, mortals will
choose evil, so the Morning Star wagers; The Father does not agree. Each
vows not to interfere with mankind, and The Morning Star is commanded to sleep, only to be awoken upon the last days of earth, when all
shall be judged."

The countess rose back up on en pointe for a moment, and then came
down to her knees. She lay back and stretched her legs straight. She
folded her hands at her waist and closed her eyes.

The dark skies dispersed. The light of Wormwood shone bright in the
hall once more. The applause began and quickly spiraled into a roar of
cheers that shook the hall like thunder.

Chax sprung from his throne and clapped vigorously. "Bravo! my lady.
Bravo!"

The countess lay still as the applause grew. The lords, Lady Pnemoxsis, and Caym remained seated, though clapped heartily they did. Belayphion and Surratta stood and commended her. Their green siblings were anything but composed; they were naughty. They squealed and began jumping and tumbling across the dais, funning about just for the sake of it.

Two bone-white, muscular males came forward and lifted the countess to her feet. She strolled toward Jared, flipping her locs away from her face. She stood nose-to-nose with him.

"I will give you that dance, angel," she said, in a husky voice. "No mortal who sees it will ever say 'no' to anything you ask of them. I will enchant your limbs to make you move like the wind and flow like water. I will give this to you, my lord…if you will sign the pact."

Jared was about to reply 'thank you', but 'no thank you', when Zim suddenly turned and looked behind. He did likewise and saw Lady Esra —the gossamer winged demon that had been at the palace doors—fly across the dais toward Chax. She landed and curtseyed. He beckoned her forth and leaned over to listen. She drew near and began whispering to him.

The crowd was still applauding when suddenly an explosion went off that shook the hall. All applause and chatter ceased. And just then, another explosion went off right outside the hall that was strong enough to wobble the monolithic statue of Odin. The nobles yelled out in a startle. Others seemed shocked and locked in silence.

Chax stood. "Orsha-Narians!" he called out. Every eye turned to the duke. "We are under siege once again. Our enemy has sent legions to raid and destroy our lands. Those who were once your brothers and sisters of Orsha-Na, now stand outside of our gates ready to fight for the enemy and are prepared to send all of you to the ether. We know what game Astaroth plays at and it has worked to his advantage each and every time." Another nearby blast rocked the palace; the stone columns by the entrance under the Odin statue cracked. The nobles looked at one another and around the trembling hall with trepidation marked on their faces. Chax, however, spoke with a voice that was clearly unmoved from his resolve. "We do as we always have to protect our lands. *We fight!*" He looked down toward Jared and the others. "Lady Zimarantha!"

Zim took Jared by the arm, bringing him along as she hurried up the stairs. She curtseyed before the duke. "Your Grace."

Chax glanced at Lady Ursa, who was standing off to the side of him. "There is a legion of Astaroth's soldiers at the city wall."

"A legion?" Caym said, coming up behind Zim and Jared. Thamuz had already made his way to the footstep of the dais and was looking up at them. "We have barely ten legions left, father." His voice was low, hushed, and of alarm; the words he spoke went no further than to those upon the dais. "How many more of our soldiers shall desert after this assault?"

"Astaroth shows his strength, yet he still fears mine," Chax said, with an agreeing, hesitant nod. "Worship him or be slowly worn away to nothing, like water dripping on a stone. But I am still stone. *I am still Chax.*" Another blast hit nearby, rocking the floor. "Lady Zimarantha."

"Your Grace."

"Take lead of the forces," Chax commanded. "Kill every one of Astaroth's soldiers. Send them all to ether."

Zim bowed her head and hurried down the stairs. With a flick of her hand at Thamuz, he tore off his robe, baring himself down to his loin-cloth and following behind her. Thousands of the nobles did likewise; they shed their shimmering robes and dresses and shendyts to the floor, as though they were no more than rags, and began following Zim and Thamuz out of the hall and to battle. Lady Pnemoxsis stood and called her children to follow her up the stairs. She walked over and stood off to the right, behind Chax's throne. Their green-skinned children crowded around the three thrones; Beelzebub reached down and picked up Ortan and sat him on his lap. Ortan sucked on his thumb and turned, and glowered at Jared, as though all that was happening was his fault.

"Bring my horse," Caym called to the soldiers who had come to stand guard by the dais. Two of them sped off; the other two remained at their post.

Chax slowly wagged his finger at Caym. "No, my son. Not now. My command is that you keep watch over the angel. Keep him safe from harm."

Caym protested. "I'm a soldier, too."

"You are what I say you are, and that is a warrior and a prince...*and my son.*" Chax looked over at Jared, though continued speaking to Caym. "Perhaps, very soon, I will have a far greater need for you than routing Astaroth's vermin from our lands. Perhaps, soon, you will go off to battle and come back to us as the prince who saved Hell, and earth. *Perhaps.*"

Caym walked over and stood next to Jared; he raised his head, tipping his jaw out. "Angel of the Heavenly Host...I will give the last of my life-force to protect you from harm. As prince of Orsha-Na, the Northlands, I so swear it," he said with a regal air. He turned and looked at Jared. "Your enemies are now mine, so sayeth Sky Father, Chax."

If he was lying, Jared couldn't see it no matter how hard he searched for a telltale sign of subterfuge. Not a flicker of the eyelid, a sly grin, or a twitch of the chin did he see. He nodded at Caym, accepting his words as truth—at least for now.

Another explosion hit the stadium beneath the statue of Odin. Jared ducked and turned away from the blast as it turned rock and stone into projectiles, crushing demons—turning them to ash—, and knocking others across the room. Huginn, the raven perched on Odin's left shoulder fractured and began wobbling. The nobles below yelled and screamed, and began scrambling as the stone raven teetered and came tumbling down. Some escaped; those with wings flew off; and those who hurriedly cast spells of flight in time escaped the hurtling chunks of stone; though hundreds of others, who were caught in the mob trying to flee on foot, were not so lucky. They shrieked and cried out as their flaw-less, beautiful bodies were smashed—pulverized—and turned to ash.

The flaming projectile that had wrought such damage and death was in pieces and scattered about the hall. Arms and legs...heads and feet...torsos, too, were littered about the floor and rolling with flames. A chunk of it that was mostly still together, had rolled and come to rest near the foot of the stairs. It was a menagerie of flaming body parts that had been meshed together; heads were affixed to legs, and legs to arms, and hands to backs. As it was with the demons that were turning to ash, the tangled heads, limbs, and torsos, began to also, once again beginning their journey back to the Lake of Fire to be reborn in its purifying flames.

Chax stood with a start as another vulag burst upon his statue of Odin. The statue exploded at the chest, and sent the shoulders and head of it tumbling down the stairs and crushing those below.

Chax spoke as though he could barely catch his breath. "*My Odin!*" He stared at the broken pieces for some time, and even as another barrage of explosions rung out deep within the city, he did not move. He began walking down the stairs. "Bring the angel forthwith," he said to Caym. "Let him see what happens when a god is angered."

"My horse," Caym called to the soldiers.

Chax stepped onto the lower dais. "Farfal...come to me," he said, as though the great lion was right next to him. Though in moments, it responded with a roar as if his call had been right at his ear. The echo of Farfal's answer to his master came out of the hall beneath the statue of Atum-Ra. The nobles near that hall went on the scramble again, this time not fleeing from flung, flaming body parts and chunks of stone, but clearing the way for the great lion. Farfal bounded into the hall and dashed for the stairs; and it leapt them in two, swift powerful thrusts of its brawny legs. It circled around Chax and then lay down next to him, awaiting his next command.

Caym mounted his horse in one swift swing of the leg. He extended his hand to Jared.

Jared hesitated. As much as he wished he could, he couldn't shake the feeling that he was falling deeper and deeper into their trap. Trust was a commodity he was not willing to give just yet, or at all.

Caym urged him on. "Come angel. Do not be leery of me. You should have a care for what is out there," he said, nodding toward the city. He gave a smarmy grin. "Fear not. I will protect you. I've given my word, remember?" Jared relented and took his hand, and swung up behind him. "You might want to hold on tight. We'll be pressed to keep up with Farfal."

Chax looked back at Caym. He spoke simply, though commandingly. "Follow me," he said, and then bent down toward the lion's head. He ran his hand across its tawny mane. "Become wind, Farfal. Take me into battle."

Farfal hunched down on his front legs and raised the rears ones; he lowered his head; his muscles bulged beneath his fur. He leapt, cracking the stone with the force of his thrust. He roared as he soared over the stairs. He landed, cracking the stone floor. Caym called his horse to follow with a swift kick in the side. It lunged. Jared quickly wrapped his arms around Caym's waist, suddenly no longer concerned that he was holding on to a demon.

The horse galloped flawlessly down the steps, and then broke out into a full sprint when it reached the floor, following the path through the nobles made by Chax and Farfal. They turned right as they exited the hall, and then sped down a long road, heading toward the front of the palace where the main road was. There was no sign of Chax and Farfal.

Jared looked up. A flaming ball of souls was streaking across the sky, leaving a trail of black smoke in its wake. It exploded blocks away to his right, though the buildings all around him trembled from the blast. The screams and wails of the injured and dying soon followed.

Caym took a sharp left and leaned into it. Jared locked his hands and matched his tilt, squeezing Caym tight as momentum pulled him to the right as the horse pulled him left. The horse had its way and brought both riders with it, never breaking stride. It charged out of the courtyard and into the city streets, where now, the clanging of swords and cries of battle could be heard. Now on the straightaway—hundreds of yards ahead of them—Jared could see Chax's black shroud flopping about.

Caym snapped the rains. "Heeyah!" he called to it, demanding more speed and receiving it. They chased after Chax and Farfal.

Jared spotted the city wall ahead, it seeming to grow larger and larger as they drew near it. They were gaining on Chax and Farfal, he thought for a moment, leaning to the side and spotting them; but then looking closer, he saw that Chax had simply slowed his pace, and had set Farfal on an easy stroll. There were soldiers from both sides all around Chax; his own troops were barely clothed, they having shed their garments to come and fight; Astaroth's demons wore red and white breastplates, and leg and arm armor. But none of them were fighting. They had all ceased trying to kill one another, and had lowered their lifeforce-fueled swords to their sides as Chax moved amongst them. They parted to either side of the road. Chax's soldiers looked upon him with expressions of relief... Astaroth's with trepidation.

Caym caught them up to his father. Jared looked down at the mixed forces on either side of him. They were staring at him as much as they stared at Chax, whose presence—judging by their expressions—was obviously not expected.

They moved into the courtyard. It was filled with soldiers from both sides, who, upon Chax's arrival, proceeded to create a clear path toward the mangled doors of the city. One of the doors was off its hinges; its metal frame was warped and its wood on fire. The other door was on the ground, clinging precariously to its bottom hinge. The soaring walls on either side of the gate had been heavily assaulted, and were now just mounds of rubble, which Astaroth's soldiers had been scaling over; though now, they were simply standing there dumbfounded, watching Chax and the angel behind him approach.

Chax raised his hand to the sky. It quickly began to cloud over and grew dark, blocking out the light of Wormwood at its master's command. In mere moments, billowing clouds as black as night raged overhead. A bolt of lightning careened out of the clouds and headed straight for them. The hairs on Jared's neck rose. He and Caym shielded their eyes with their arms as the white energy bore down toward them.

The lightning did not hit them, nor did it hit the ground; it was aimed at Chax, who caught the rod of electric fire in his gloved hands. A boom followed and shook the ground, and tumbled even more of the city walls down. Astaroth's demons began slowly backing away as Chax continued his approach; though now, he wielded in his hand a bolt of pure, crackling energy shaped like a staff.

Just then, three of Astaroth's soldiers stepped in Chax's path. They raised their swords at him. Chax brought Farfal to a stop.

"You grow weaker with each pass, Chax," one called out in taunt.

"You cannot persevere," said the one next to him. "You can burn a thousand of us and we will be replaced with twice as many."

"Know when you are defeated, my lord," the third one said.

"Know when thou are already ash," Chax retorted, as he goaded Farfal forward and extended his lightning staff at them. Three jagged bolts darted from the staff and struck the soldiers. Their bones glowed blue-white beneath their flesh, making them look as though they were moving x-rays. They jittered and jumped and seized as the electric fire cooked them from the inside out, turning them to ash. Their armor fell and clanged on the ash-covered ground, as though they had simply vanished.

Chax's soldiers formed up behind him. Zim and Thamuz moved up next to Jared and Caym; they kept their swords forward and at the ready. Their faces, arms, and armor were dusted in the ashy remains of the fallen.

Zim glanced up at Jared. The whole of her eyes were black. Her face was drawn tight with fury. And even still, despite her warrior's façade, and despite the current situation, and despite himself, and even despite who she was, he found her just as lovely to look at now as before.

"Halt!" someone bellowed from beyond the ravaged gates of Hedun. Astaroth's soldiers stopped their retreat, though many of them looked at one another questioningly, as though not quite sure it was a good idea to have stopped at all. "I didn't give the goddamn order to stop. So why in Hell aren't you fighting, you fools?"

The one deriding the troops marched over the ravaged doors and into the courtyard. He had the body of a male, but the head and spiral horns of a gazelle. His eyes were blood red. Fangs extended to his chin. His other teeth were equally as sharp.

"If that dual-casting bitch, Zimarantha, has got you on the run," he yelled to those on his right, and then turned and scowled at those to his left, "then you deserve to go to the ether." He looked forward and saw Chax, and startled to a stop. His eyes widened. His mouth gaped.

"Lord Khonvoum!—Huntsman of the Bush. You've destroyed my Odin," Chax said lightly, as though merely informing him about it. His voice then turned cold. "That shall have to be answered for."

Khonvoum looked around at his troops, who were now staring at him, waiting for his reply. He pulled his shoulders back and formed his snout of a mouth into a half grin. "Is that all you care about, Chax?... your old glory? Well, its over. You are Sky Father no more. That age has passed and a new one has risen up right beneath your godly nose. How come your green lady didn't see that coming? Has something gone awry with her scrying pools, great necromancer? Or is it just...just that Duke Astaroth is the only Lord of Hell truly fit to rule? How can you say he is not, when he has made fools of Beelzebub and Agares, and now of you? It is a certainty that Astaroth will rule both worlds, and yet, here you are foolishly holding onto yours with every ounce of lifeforce you have left. You and the other lords hide your true selves beneath shrouds to conceal your true, fallen forms. You drain your land of its essence to defend the indefensible, when you could combine that strength with Astaroth and walk behind him when he conquerors Phenóx."

"Astaroth will march into Phenóx only when I am ash," Chax said.

"That can be arranged, my lord," Khonvoum quipped. "Though, truly, none of this is even necessary. There is only one war, and that is against the Heavenly Host of The Father. We are but a step away from winning that war without a single one of us going to the ether for it."

Chax spurred Farfal into a slow walk toward Khonvoum.

"If you were to bend your knee," Khonvoum said, "you, Beelzebub, and Agares could rule both worlds with him."

"I think you meant to say, *under him.*"

"I did." Khonvoum smiled. "But what would it matter anyway? You would be assured of going on, or you could choose to go to war with the Hosts of Heaven and wager against falling into the ether." He nodded at Jared. "Look at you, Chax. You've fallen in league with the enemy to fight your own people."

Chax drew within fifty paces of Khonvoum and pulled Farfal to a stop. "I am much like the Heavenly Host," he said. "I cling to my god. I am not swayed with schemes and plots to undermine him, and to reap power as a reward for my betrayal. No. Not I. Never Chax."

"All of Hedun will be ash before you strike down a thousand of our legions. And what then? What does the preeminent Chax do when he has exhausted every ounce of essence from his lands, and there are ten thousand legions falling on his right, and ten more on his left? Does he drain his captured angel of his lifeforce? Still, it will not save you...*my lord*."

"And what will save *you* now?" Chax asked.

"His Grace shall," Khonvoum said, with an air of starry-eyed reverence. "Once he has claimed the power of The Morning Star, he shall bring us all back from the ether."

"There is no coming back from the ether, fool."

"Mayhap not for you."

"For anyone," Chax said, insisting. "You have been sold false promises."

"We all know The Father loves the mortals to no end, though, too, he cannot break his own covenant. Astaroth will forge a new covenant with The Father and will have us restored; that will be The Father's only recourse once Astaroth has claimed earth. And then, we will rule as the gods we were meant to be. It will be done."

"Orsha-Na still stands, Lord Khonvoum. And while it does, so shall I."

"Not for much longer." Khonvoum held his hand up. White mist came from the palm of it and formed into a bow, though one that was alive. Two snakes, with their tails tied in a knot, formed the upper and lower end of bow. Their intertwined heads and the rest of their bodies served as its string.

Khonvoum raised the serpentine bow and aimed it at Chax. He squeezed the heads of the snakes between his fingers, and like strings, drew them back. The serpents opened their mouths; they glowed red inside, like twin furnaces. Khonvoum released the heads; the snakes spewed out balls of fire. And he fired again and again; his hand moved so quickly it blurred.

Farfal didn't move a paw as the blanket of sizzling fire bore down on them. Chax swung his lightning staff at the fire. The red hue of the fire turned black, and then turned to ash and fell apart, littering the air with snow-ash. As the ash wafted through the air around him—vanishing as it did—from behind him, across the courtyard, the buildings of Orsha-Na began to shake and rumble.

Jared turned and looked.

Three of the buildings shuddered as though an earthquake was rocking them. And then, they stopped abruptly and transformed from one matter into another—from tan brick and rock, to gray ash. They crumpled under their own weight, spilling ash into the streets of Hedun; and that ash—it barely settling to the ground—began to disintegrate into nothing.

"You'll see you're entire realm in ruin before all of this is over, Chax," Khonvoum warned, even as he pulled back on the snake-heads of his bow. "Bend thy knee and live; and take your seat beneath Astaroth."

Chax said nothing. He sat motionless upon Farfal. However, his storm clouds above were not so coy. The storm grew darker. The clouds moved faster. Lightning began streaking within it and crisscrossing the roiling storm in all directions. Though, as Chax churned his storm into a fury, he paid the cost for it. Building after building behind him transmuted from stone to ash and came tumbling down in heaping piles. As the storm grew, so did swaths of Hedun's structures fall.

Khonvoum dropped his bow to his side and waved his hand in surrender as thunder began shaking the ground. His bravado had suddenly waned. "Chax wait!" he cried. "Astaroth is your only salvation…and mine—us all!" He looked to his soldiers; they had their swords half-raised, though fear was set squarely in their eyes as they looked up at the raging storm. "Will you not seek reason?"

"I have," he replied simply. "And in such, I see victory."

Khonvoum stared at him for a moment, and then looked down, and then, suddenly, he lunged. He yelled as he swung his bow up and aimed it at Chax. His fingers reached for the snake heads.

As Khonvoum was reaching for those serpentine strings, Chax hurled his lightning rod at him, moving his arm so fast, it blurred. If not for the ghost-trails his arm left behind, it would have seemed as if he had not moved at all.

The lightning rod pierced Khonvoum's chest and exploded with a flash of light. The thunder's shockwave warped the air as it rippled out, knocking his soldiers from their feet and sending them tumbling across the ground. Not a speck of Khonvoum's ash was left. He had been vaporized…extinguished from life…sent to the ether from whence he had been risen eons ago.

Chax looked to the sky; it was furious!; it was black; it churned with lightning.

He raised his arms. The clouds obeyed and stopped rolling; the lightning stopped flashing. It was as if the storm had become a painting in the sky—*Once Upon a Stormy, Hellish Night*. He spoke to all those around him, amplifying his voice in their ears with his dark sorcery. He spoke quickly. He spoke defiantly. He said, "I am Chax—there is no other. I will not be ruled, but will rule. In this pass of Wormwood, know that I am still Chax, and that I bring death to mine enemies."

The storm roared back into motion and began discharging lightning strikes upon Astaroth's soldiers, who were now attempting to flee over the rubble of the crumbled wall. The lightning roasted them to ash in their armor. When their celestial bodies could take no more of the electric-fire borne of dark magic, they exploded like balloons full of dust. Beyond the shattered wall, where the rest of Astaroth's soldiers were, lightning spiraled down upon them like tornadoes. The lightning strikes began sweeping across the staging area where the catapults and the rest of Astaroth's forces were, incinerating everything in their twisting path.

Chax lowered his arm and the storm ceased. Even more of Hedun came rumbling down in piles of ash behind him.

Chax looked over at Zim. "Lady Zimarantha," he called, "the herd of traitors should be well thinned by now. Finish them and take their life-force, and take the souls they brought with them, if there are any left to be had."

Zim and Thamuz bowed and were already barking orders at the soldiers before they had even turned around to face them. Thamuz lined them up. Zim had a horse brought to her and was quickly surrounded by her officers.

"Soon my entire realm will be as this—powder and ash, and then nothing," Chax said to Jared. "I no longer have the power to repair what has been destroyed this pass—not this time. When Astaroth marches on Phenóx—*and soon he will*—we, the Lords of Hell, must face him at that moment when he is at his weakest; when he has expended his stolen souls and his lifeforce to crack the black dome. Though as you see, Miel-angel, with every action I take, I diminish myself." He looked past Jared and at what was left of the buildings behind him. Where buildings once stood, piles of ash lay. "For your own sake, make the pact. Save yourself, Miel-angel. Give us your lifeforce—freely so; it must be given freely to release that power within in you that you have yet to realize you even possess. You were the Child of Balance, and now are the Angel of Balance. You were never meant to be, yet here you are—a creation of The Father to give balance back to earth. You are unique. You are powerful. You are what we need, if any of us—Heavenly Host, Fallen, or mortal—are to survive. With your aid, we will destroy Astaroth. I am Chax—I have never broken a bond. Save us all, Miel-angel." He was silent for a moment. "*Sign the pact.*"

The time to deal with the devil had come, Jared knew. Fight for The Fallen and have a chance at saving himself and earth, and every mortal upon it. Refuse the Lords of Hell, and they would likely take his lifeforce anyway; though, if Chax were to be believed, they would still fall before Astaroth.

"Give your answer," Caym said.

Jared looked up at Chax and nodded, knowing full well that he was wagering his life and the salvation of billions of others on the word of a demon by the tip of his head. He made his intent even clearer. "I'll give it to you freely, Chax. You just be sure to keep your word and get me into Phenóx, and into Lucifer's palace. Like you said…I broke free of Muchenlay, and I wasn't supposed to be able to do that—no one is. But *I* did it. I found the power to do it." Jared lowered his brow and his voice. His renewed lifeforce swirled slowly within him. "If you cross me, I'll find that power again…and I'll come for you."

"They'll be no need for that, Miel-angel," said Chax, his voice again genial. "I will keep my word. After all, I am Chax."

CHAPTER 11

"You don't have to leave, Ms. Dotty," Chris said to her. He opened his eyes. He was lying on a rug in a bedroom upstairs. The fireplace off to the right of him was aglow in orange flames. The heat felt good to him in the cool night air that had crept into the mansion. "I really should be back practicing."

Dorthea closed the door. She walked over and sat down on the bench at the end of the bed and crossed her legs. She clasped her hands and rested her chin on them. "How's it coming?"

"Hard."

"I didn't figure it was going to be easy," she said, more to herself than to him. "Can I see it?"

"The tome?" She nodded.

He came to his feet. The glow from the fireplace cast his shadow over her; it was truly a shadow of what it used to be. He thought back to his old self—the chubby one, the awkward one, the special education kid who was the outcast. Where this new, thinner and smarter Chris belonged amongst those groups, he wasn't sure; he didn't know how to fit the new Chris in, for it seemed like he belonged nowhere. What he was certain of was that, he didn't feel like himself anymore. He didn't who to feel like.

"*Chris, honey*," Dorthea said, with a rise of her voice. She had been calling his name for a while, though to no avail.

He focused back on her. He gave her a coy smile, as though he had just now seen her. "Hi, Ms. Dotty."

She frowned and looked at him from the side. "Chris, you're not OK, honey."

"Yeah, I am," he said. "I really am. I'm just a little…off." He blinked a few times, as though he was trying to clear his vision. "After everything that's happened, you should be worried if I wasn't acting a bit funny, huh?" He raised a brow. "I look in the mirror and I still can't see that fat kid I hated so much—I really hated being me. And then I got my wish wrapped in a nightmare, and I wasn't me anymore." He took her hand in his and squeezed. He liked her warmth; it was comforting. It helped soothe the ache of blame, which was his constant companion. "You've never seen the tome have you?" She shook her head no. "It was written by the angel, Metatron."

He helped her to her feet and walked her over to a round, wood table, where the tome lay open. He pulled out the chair in front of it. He had been in that chair for the past week, and Olivia beside him, they trying to crack the language of the tome. Their hope being that, one of them—if not both—could find and decipher the Chant of Changing, and transform into an immortal strong enough to defeat Yikan. When the electricity went off three days ago, they resorted to using candles and flashlights.

"It's beautiful," Dorthea said, as she sat. Her eyes grew wide as they passed over the silver, celestial symbols set against a backdrop of gold-leaf pages.

Chris sat next to her and took her hand, placing his over top of hers. He passed their hands just above the pages. "As God created all of the planets and stars, and everything in the entire universe—people, too—the angels watched and sang, and Metatron wrote those songs in this tome—that's the power of the chant." He turned the page. "Somewhere in here is the song the angels sung when God created celestials—when he pulled them out of nothing and made them something. That's what we're looking for and can't find." He moved the tips of her fingers across a symbol that swooped over at the top like an 's', and at the bottom, it had three diagonal lines through its curved bulge. The symbol next to it had the same curled top, though no bulge at the bottom, but a series of lines and dots there instead, as though it were some type of alien mathematics.

"The way to get Jared back is in here somewhere," she said.

"Somewhere," he repeated. "I can memorize the symbols and then go under." She looked at him oddly. "I mean, create an illusion in my head. I bring Olivia in so that we can practice out loud. She can make fire now, ya know?"

Dorthea grinned. "I didn't."

"She's pretty good at it," he said, turning the gold-leaf page back to where it was. He looked at it, and then turned to Dorthea. "Breaking down the chant comes more natural to her than it does to me. Yikan may have made me smart, but that's all he did." He paused and glanced up. "What I'm saying is, is that intelligence by itself can't crack the code. It was written by celestials, who, according to the laws of nature, are breaking every one of them. Celestials don't make sense; I guess they were never suppose to...at least not to us, huh?" He grinned for a moment, and then looked away. "When you chant, you have to feel it." He held his hand up and rubbed his thumb and finger together. "The chant lets you feel the actual matter that makes up everything around us. And when you feel it, you can change it. You can make it do what you want it to, if you have the right chant. When I chant to make fire, I can make those billions and billions of bits that make up that piece of wood heat up. I can force it to do that, if I chant it correctly." His eyes were wide, and bright, and full of wonder, but it quickly turned sour. He looked at the tome. "But you can't plug a feeling into an algorithm. "

Dorthea eyed the tome suspiciously. "It's a big book."

"There's a lot to go through—yeah."

"We don't have much time," she said. "The longer Jared is down there, the harder it's going to be getting him back." Her voice broke; her eyes became glassy. "I keep saying that word, 'Hell', over and over in my head. It's like—

"It's not real," Chris jutted in, bobbing his head. "It's one thing to have faith that Heaven and Hell are real, but knowing that they *are* real, keeps me up. It makes me sick. And I can't stop thinking about Jared being there."

Dorthea wiped her eyes. "I can't make sense of it."

"Can we make sense of any of it? We're not supposed to know about any of this. Celestials and demons are supposed to be in the background...out of our reality. We're supposed to be like fish, huh? They don't know there's a whole 'nother world above them. All they know is water. But we...we got yanked out."

"And can't breathe," Dorthea added.

"But that doesn't mean we're not gonna try."

She gave a firm nod of the head. "You and Olivia *can* do this."

"And then after that...?" he asked. The question lingered unanswered. "That demon took him, so we know there's a way into Hell, and possibly, logically speaking, a way back. But we need to remember we're not dealing with logical things. Getting Jared back is the unknown; it's the X in a big equation."

He began computing the possible scenarios, putting a *'what if'* here and a *'then that'* over there. There was God to consider; there was also Lucifer to factor in, as well as the tomes and Astaroth, and Yikan and Eric, and the psychopath, Blain; and there was Jared, too.

For days he had done this: arranging all of the factors in various combinations, oftentimes to the point of making himself dizzy. And then his forehead would begin thumping, he feeling as though his brain was swelling with each throb and pulse. The memories of his past with Yikan began accompanying the headaches, making what was already physically painful, mentally excruciating, too. One of the darkest memories was with Blain Hopps and being forced to watch him indulge in his hobby of torturing, and then dismembering the trusting, the foolish, the innocents who wandered into the path of a fairly handsome, middle-age white man with a fondness for perversity. Yikan's experiments with his mind was equally dark, though painful, even in remembrance of the burning and shocking, deconstructing and rebuilding of brain tissue, to rewire billions and billions of neural networks; he would come out of the illusions and find himself soiled and his tongue chewed raw—his mouth full of blood.

"We gotta pray, and hard," Dorthea said. "It's the only way."

"I never did before," he admitted. "You know I do now, right?"

"It's never too late to start. The Lord will answer you," she said. "He'll give you the answer you need, but it might not be the one you want. But one thing is for sure—he'll always answer you."

She still had hope, and Chris was glad for it. He figured one of them should at least have some. He was never going to give up. He was for trying anything that might save Jared; but hopeful about it? It was hard to have any hope at all. He had seen the razor-toothed demon that took Jared, and had looked into Yikan's swirling blue eyes, and been in the same room with Blain Hopps, knowing he was just as likely to shake your hand, as he was to cut your throat; and they made all difference between what was rationale hope and what were dreams of fancy.

He blamed himself for all of it. The others had been kind in reassuring him that it wasn't his fault, but that he had been a victim of deceit and cunning by creatures eons old; Dorthea was the most vehement. They hugged him; they gave him their love. Dorthea had taken hold of his cheeks and pulled him close—forehead to forehead—and swore she didn't blame him a bit. It was cold comfort in allaying his guilt.

Now, the very ones he had brought misery to needed his help, and he was stuck. He had only learned a few chants before Yikan stopped training him, realizing that the dark magic of Astaroth could, indeed, reshape the mind and increase human intelligence, giving one the knowledge to decipher the songs of celestials.

He looked down, suddenly ashamed to cross eyes with Dorthea. It hurt him to see such sorrow on her face, and to hear fear in her voice, especially since he was the one who had caused it. "Why don't you stay and help us?—me and Olivia."

She gave him a queer look. "Me?"

"I can teach you the few symbols that I know, but after that," he shrugged, "you'll know as much as I do as this point."

"If you'll think it'll help, I'll try it then," she said, her voice suddenly eager. "All I'm doing is pacing the floor and watching Thaddeus go in and out of that kitchen. He's about to eat himself right into a sugar coma. I'm more nervous watching him be nervous."

"I used to be like that. I'd get upset about something and reach for anything sweet, greasy, and crunchy."

She chuckled. "You sure could eat."

"Now...I don't eat. I'm just not hungry anymore. I just think and think about things...over and over, until I figure it out. And this," he sighed, looking at the tome, "I can't figure out."

A knock came at the door and opened. Thaddeus stuck his head halfway in and shined the flashlight around the room. "Ya'll in here?"

"We're over here," Dorthea called, waving at him.

He stepped in, and ran his hand up and down the wall. "Where the mess is that light switch?"

"The powers back on?" Dorthea asked.

"Yes ma'am, it is."

Chris closed his eyes. He found the half-inch plastic switch and grabbed hold of it with his mind, as though he were actually using his fingers. He pushed it up, turning the chandelier on.

"Thank *you,* Jesus," he muttered, slipping in and quickly closing the door behind him. "You know...it's bad enough walking around in the dark, but those shadows make it ten times worse. If I move here...they move there." He pointed left and right. "I look there...and here they come lurkin' right after me."

"They don't come in here," Chris said. "I think they're afraid of the tome—or me."

"Good," Thaddeus said. "Sounds like I need to spend more time in here with you then. That—that real-real tall one is the worst of all of'em; I forget his name. That uh—"

"Jackson Lovell," said Dorthea.

Thaddeus pointed at her. "*That's him!* That's that thing I can keep seeing walking around. Those other ones are like shadows; at least they look harmless and stick to the walls and floors. But that Jackson fella, he—"

"Looks alive," Dorthea jutted in. "Olivia warned me about him...said he had only been around for a few years, I guess."

"One minute that joker looks like some old, black man, and then—*poof*—gone like a genie out the bottle."

"I told you their harmless," Dorthea said, "—even Jackson. They're not going to harm you. Spook you, maybe; but that's all. They're just spirits not wanting to go on just yet…can't be alive and don't wanna be dead. Lord help'em."

Thaddeus huffed and chuckled, and then grinned. "I ain't buyin' that, Dotty. You go right ahead and believe that mess if you want. Me?—uh-uh." He pursed his lips. "I'll avoid them, and I hope they start doing the same to me." Thaddeus's eyes darted around the room, as though expecting a reply. "Anyway, we need ya'll to come downstairs."

"Something about Jared?" Dorthea asked, with wide, hopeful eyes.

Thaddeus bit his lip and shook his head. "Naw, honey. We got a channel to come in. It looks like someone from the White House is going to speak…maybe the president. Right now it just says 'breaking news', but they always say that…this is breakin' and that's breakin'. But I think this time it's true. Maybe we can find out what's going on out there. Out here in these back wood swamps, we wouldn't know if the world was on fire or not."

"God's truth," Dotty said.

"Ya'll come'on now," he told them.

* * *

"My fellow Americans," the president said, from behind his desk in the oval office. "For the past week, all across America, we have experienced partial or complete blackouts. This has been a result of a coordinated attack on our electrical grid—our power supply. Let me be clear in saying right now that this is not just an attack on America's electrical supply, but an attack on our way of life.

"There have been rumors that this is the act of the Russians or Chinese, or religious fundamentalists. That is not true." He paused, and then repeated himself. "Our intelligence agencies have verified that nearly every nation across the globe has experienced a complete and total loss of power, as we have. But if you are listening to me now, that means that our soldiers, engineers, and scientists have been making headway in restoring full power to the nation. This will happen. It will be slow, but…but…."

"What's going on?" Phineas asked, looking at the screen that was now just a sea of static. Henrì walked up to the TV where he was standing and banged on it. It didn't work. "Is this cable or antennae, or what—?"

"Shhhh!" Henrì waved his hand. "It's coming back on."

The picture was fuzzy at first, and then flickered and cleared up. "Are we on?" the president asked, looking to someone off camera. "Are we back up?"

A female responded. "Yes, Mr. President."

The president quickly looked back into the camera. He was just moments too late in changing his worried expression to one of presidential calm and fortitude.

"Our intelligence agencies," he cleared his throat, "were able to track the source of the attack back to the Middle East, where, unbeknownst to any of our counterterrorism agencies, including those of our allies, a man who calls himself 'Aton' has created a base of operation for these cowardly acts of aggression. My fellow Americans, this is terrorism, plain and simple. And at this moment, we are at war with this individual.

"This terrorist—this man who calls himself Aton—believes he is a god. He has demanded the surrender and—*these are his words*—the unconditional obedience of every human on earth. He has called for the dissolution of all governments as well—this all coming from the mind of a madman, who was smart enough to shut down our grid. That, in and of itself, makes this man dangerous, and America's number one enemy; and as we stand together with our allies, he has become the world's number one enemy.

"We are the United States of America," he said, his voice deepening with conviction. "We do not negotiate with terrorists; neither do we surrender to them. We take the fight to them, and we win.

"As I speak, our armed forces in the gulf region have been put on the highest alert. Make no mistake about it, we will stop this terrorist and bring him to—" The signal went out again. The electricity died with a snap and fizzle right after.

Chris was sitting on the sofa next to Dorthea. He scooted to the edge of his seat and stared at the blank television. "He's doing exactly what Yikan wants him to do."

"What's that, boy?" asked Thaddeus, standing behind him.

"The president is starting a war he can't win." Chris looked around at the others.

Chris knew what Yikan was capable of, because Yikan had showed him…showed him in illusions what a beautiful life with Aton as god would be like. The world would revert into a modern day semblance of Ancient Egypt, reclaiming the old, while embracing the new. He showed Chris the temples he would erect to himself, and the obelisks and pylons he would build to signify his glory. Yikan had even showed him how he would build the pyramids anew, though twice as large as the behemoths residing on the Giza Plateau. Yikan was like a child drawing pictures of all of the goodies he ever wanted in the whole-big-wide-world. His glory would know no bounds, Yikan promised.

"There's nothing we can do about it, is there?" Olivia asked. She was standing across from Henrì; the cold dance they danced over her learning the chants had yet to thaw.

Henrì crossed his arms and grimaced. "They don't even know what they're dealing with."

"They think he's crazy," said Phineas, "because believing demons exist doesn't make sense to them—that would be crazy, right? Sounds to me like the perfect way for the devil to slip right on in."

"Yikan *is* insane, but he's smart," Chris said. "He knows the military needs satellites to control their missiles. If he's attacked the grid, then he's already tampered with the satellites, too…they just have no idea. What they don't know about him is that, he's obsessed with godhood; it's all he ever talked about. It was always about Aton—just Aton. He's studied us. He knows that we depend on electricity for everything, and that every encryption program has a weakness." Chris looked around at everyone. "He already knows our first step and our last resort."

"Nukes, you mean," Thaddeus said.

Chris nodded. "He's going to send a very large message to the world. Worship me or die."

"Jesus! We'll all be living in the stone ages," Henrì said.

"That's Yikan's first step," Chris said. "What's the point of becoming a god if the real one comes back and takes you out? Yikan has to stop the

End of Days if he wants to stay a god, and that means he has to remake himself into a demon to throw off the balance of good and evil. Astaroth promised him he would, if he delivered Jared…and…he did."

"You've gotta crack Metatron's tome. Soon!" Henrì urged, with brows low and voice heavy. "Jared figured it out. Tamen did, too. Hell…even Yikan managed to half-ass his way through it and taught two more to do the same. If we're going to have any chance of stopping him, we're going to have to sacrifice everything," he looked at Olivia for a moment, and then closed his eyes and turned away, "*and everyone.*"

"We need to get my baby back," Dorthea said. "He can stop this." She looked at Chris. "The angel that came…the one that watches over Phineas…" Chris nodded, "it told you there was another who could help us, right?"

"They called it Mekka-Nuat," Chris said. "It's a Throne."

"And…?" asked Dorthea.

"I—I don't know," Chris said, looking about, his eyes settling on nothing as he tried to remember if he'd forgotten something The Order had told him. "They told me it would choose to help or not help. That's how they left it."

"What if we summoned Phineas's angel?" Dorthea posed. "Maybe it can convince the other one to help us…maybe." She looked at everyone. "Isn't it worth a try?"

"Everything is worth a try," Olivia said, and then smiled encouragingly at her.

Dorthea looked to Phineas. "You'll have to kill yourself."

Phineas's eyes bulged. "Say what?"

"Not for real, Phineas," she replied, with a wobble of her head. "The angel won't let anything hurt you, right? So if you were to just *act* like you were going to kill yourself, wouldn't it come to stop you?" She stood. "And if it did come—"

"It might get that other one to help us," Thaddeus said, with a sharp clap of his hands. "I think you did it." He walked around the sofa and kissed her on the forehead.

"Ok—Ok," Henrì mumbled, his eyes darting left and right, seeped in thought. "I'm with Thaddeus on this. I think you might be right about that, Dorthea."

"And if it doesn't work?" Phineas asked. "I'm just dead as a doornail then?"

"It means that plan didn't work," Chris said, his tone matter of fact. Phineas raised his brow at him; his mouth hung open. Chris shrugged. "We have to sacrifice everything, remember? You could die if you try it, Phineas. Or, you could summon The Order. Actually, I'm not sure if it's one celestial or three of them in one."

"Add it to our growing list of what we don't know," Henrì panned. "But you're right, Chris. We're going to have to try everything, because we don't have much time. Anytime a president announces we're going to carry out strikes, that means he's telling us what he already did, or is just moments away from doing it—you know how they are. And that means Yikan is about to strike back. We need that Chant of Changing cracked before Yikan can become a demon, because once he does, we're all done for. If it's immortal against an immortal, then we might have a prayer. But, Yikan as a demon against an immortal?; even two of them?" he looked at Chris and Olivia, "and we ain't got a prayer, folks. We can pray all day and night for Jesus to save us, but if Yikan gets his wish, it'll never happen. I vote we go with Dorthea's plan. It's shaky, but…."

Henrì stopped and shut his mouth, and simply raised his hand. He looked at Chris, who quickly swung his up. Olivia, Dorthea, and Thaddeus raised theirs right after.

Phineas was the only one with both arms still at his sides. "Dotty-girl," he said, calling her by the nickname he gave her years ago before Jared was born, while he was still stalking the alleys like a cat; before demons, angels, and celestial-human hybrids had become part of his physical world. "For years I didn't do right by you and Jared. But, Lord knows I've been trying to make it right. I don't need to raise my hand to make that decision, ya' see, Dotty-girl? He's our boy." He nodded at Thaddeus. "He's yours, too. You raised him when I didn't have the sense to. I told Jared I would do anything for him, and I meant it."

Henrì put his hands on his hips and cocked his head. "So…how do you wanna do it? I have a .45 upstairs that I've never used. I bought it for protection, but the shadows keep any nosy visitors far away, so…I've never used it. Or, I have a butcher's knife. If you sat in the tub, or if we put down some plastic, you could cut your—"

"Que Dieu nous aide," Olivia blurted out in French for God to help them. She closed her eyes and shook her head.

Phineas gave him a half-grin. "I'll take the gun."

CHAPTER 12

Yikan reached for the ballistic missile headed for him with the power of a chant. At the moment it was zooming just above the atmosphere, making it difficult for him to focus on and grasp hold of. Though, eventually he did, as he had done to the others that had been launched from Europe. The other nuclear missiles sent from France and their allies, Belgium and Italy, he had turned around and sunk into the Atlantic. Though the one headed for him now, he had other plans for; this one he wanted to use. He only needed one to make his point. He had promised fire and destruction if the nations of earth attacked…and they had. He was eager to keep his end of the deal.

"Kurra-samah a'tah…abebo durro nah-tut, Kurra-samah a'tah," he chanted, sitting upon a throne of white marble he had fashioned from sand. His eyes swirled around like whirlpools, as the energy from the chant soared high into the thermosphere—that place just below space—where the missile was starting to curve down, beginning it's descent to release hell on earth.

Yikan grabbed hold of the missile and sent a jolt of electricity through it, short-circuiting its computer boards. The thrusters shut down; the missile began coasting along the edge of space. He began curving the missile to the right; bring it around full circle. Chanting harder and faster, he began it on its new journey, sending it back to the country it had come from. England, that is; and into London, precisely.

He chanted faster. His pitch soared. The power of those celestial words he sung in repetition pushed the missile back to near its original speed.

He began pulling down harder. With his mind's eye, he saw the lush green island come into focus as the missile broke through the clouds. London's buildings, streets, and homes seemed to expand exponentially, as the missile rushed down upon them.

He reached for the warhead and slowed his chant; he spoke the words softly, it was barely a whisper at all. He searched for the uranium; thanks to the mortals he already knew what to do with it; it was science after all, and had been readily available to him at the touch of a key. He began flooding the uranium with neutrons, beginning the process of fission.

He released the power of the atom. The nuke exploded above the city. Even with his mind's eye, for moments, he saw nothing but the white light of the blast. When the glare faded, he could see the rolling clouds of fire sweeping out in all directions.

The skyscrapers directly below the blast were blown apart by the shockwave; their stone, rock, and rubble were rattled away to dust. The other nearby buildings shattered, as though they were made of toy blocks. For miles around, the sweeping wall of fire flash-incinerated all that was not stone, steel, and mortar; and miles further away, set fire to what was wood and flesh, and the scraps and tatters left of London.

Yikan slumped in his throne. His muscles quivered with exhaustion. His throat felt raw, as though the chants had scorched it.

He had never tried anything like that before. It had succeeded, but it was taxing. It had weakened him. His limbs felt heavy. His head was even woozy. The drain reminded him of his limitations of being half-mortal and half-celestial. He was powerful; he was great, indeed, but he was not all-powerful—not even close; which meant that he was still vulnerable. And that, he thought, simply would not do. He still needed Astaroth to help him become a celestial—fully and wholly, through and through.

Though, I fear it is a promise you have no plans on keeping. You must think me an absolute fool, Your Grace. He pushed up in throne, and gripped the armrests to stop from sliding back down. He laid his head back and closed his eyes. *No, Your Grace…I did not survive all these years to be undone by a mad demon. You have no plans of staying down there, do you? You want the earth for yourself…your kind always have.*

But you'll never have it. You'll never step a cloven hoof on earth. It's mine!

"My lord, Aton," Eric called softly—respectfully.

Yikan looked down at him; he was standing at the bottom of the steps. The swirl of his blue eyes was slow with fatigue; it took a moment for Eric to come into focus. Eric was wearing a white robe that reached to the top of his bare feet. His hair was golden. His eyes were as blue as sapphires, and sparkled like they were. His plump red lips and thick jaw gave him a dashing look. His physical transformation was perfect—from homely to handsome; it all bestowed by the power of the chants.

"What of old Britannia?" Yikan asked.

"The city burns, my lord…and everything in it," Eric replied. "That—that's all I could sense before their screams overwhelmed me. Forgive me."

"Eric, my son," he said, "there is nothing to forgive. It takes much practice to enter another's thoughts when they are calm, let alone when they are burning."

"I practice daily, as you have directed."

"Yes…but you must master it," he said. "This will not be their last attempt to destroy us. I will give them their power back for a short while and see if London turned to ashes has changed their minds of attacking again. If they are foolish enough to do so, then I will dismantle their grids permanently, and we will start this world again from scratch." His eyes danced around in thought. "And perhaps, that is the best thing, Eric. Look where the mortals have brought themselves to: murder and war…thievery and deceit. Perhaps a fresh start is not such a defeatist idea after all."

Eric bowed. "Very wise, my lord."

"Indeed."

Yikan looked out across his hall. It was incomplete, though nearly finished, and it would have been, if not for the missiles sent from the West, diverting his attention from reforming sand into stone, rock, and marble for his palace in front of the Sphinx on the Giza Plateau. Now free to unleash the power of the chant, he used its power to lay the foundation and to build up the walls of the football length palace. He created hundreds of lotus, lily, and papyrus topped and bottomed pillars to support the ceiling. On the walls, he inscribed images of his godly-self—a sun surrounded by light rays; and around them, written in hieroglyphs, his story—the story of Aton as would be told in his new age to come. He was about to begin chanting, carving the image of Aton on the other side of the hall, when the missiles from Europe had come calling.

He stood up and walked down the stairs. Eric stood solemnly as he walked past, and then followed behind him. He looked around at what he had created and was pleased by it, though was not yet decided on declaring it fit for a god—not yet, that is. A wall painting of the old gods, Atum-Ra, Horus, and Isis bowing before Aton, covered the entire left wall of the palace. Gold braziers hung from the ceiling in a row down the center path, and others were scattered throughout the hall; their fire-light sparkled off the metal of the other, creating a network of reflected light, casting the hall in an amber glow, like a sunset after a hot summer's day. It was tedious work, and physically and mentally draining on him. Still, the majesty he had created was just a reminder of who he was not.

The power of the chant was too limiting to him. He had created wonders, but he had yet to create marvels as celestials could, for unlike him, they did not need the chant to reform and mold and control matter. Their power was not within the word of the chant, but within themselves—their lifeforce. And with that great power, some of them had chosen to rule as gods, though were fallen for it. However, to Yikan, the age of demons influencing the course of mankind was over. He had outwitted the demons and killed his enemies. He could think of nothing left to prove that he alone deserved earth's crown and glory. All that was needed now, was to finish it, he thought...to once and for all secure his godhood for the never-ending age of Aton that was to come.

"Our footing is not yet firm," Yikan said to Eric. "The preacher and Christopher still have Metatron's tome. I'm sure they are with Miel's family and precious friends, and are now trying to devise a plan to stop me...trying to do what Tamen could not, what Shazadeh could not, what Astaroth plans on trying to do, though, he too, shall not. They will chant from the tome—I am sure of it to my bones. The ages have taught me to be wary, and if not anything else, to be patient; and I have been patient for a very long time. To be cautious, Eric, is a precious virtue to possess. The preacher and his friends will try and stop us. Astaroth seeks to trick us. And now, the mortals have tried to burn us. If we are to live, we must suffer no enemies to survive."

"We still have Blain, my lord," Eric offered meekly. "Not even Astaroth is foolish enough to confront him."

Yikan curled his lip in disgust at the sound of Blain's name. "Where is that perversion?"

"He's in the city—Cairo, my lord."

"No doubt indulging his nature," he said, and then scowled. "That man is repulsive to me. I despise everything about him, even his innocent, pragmatic charm. The demons may adore his murderous proclivities, but I do not. We must look at him as nothing but a tool...a piece to be strategically moved about, and with the utmost care, mind you, lest we arouse his demon familiar. Though when his purpose is served, we shall part, never to meet again. Though, until we have the tome—until that time—we will hold Blain Hopps close and call him brother, and cosset him."

"And the preacher and Christopher?"

"Aye. Have no fear. One way or another, they will make themselves known to us. Christopher despises us, though me more so than you," he said with pride. "He will help them, I'm sure. And he will fail—I am certain."

"He could have been great."

"He already is," Yikan said. "From the pitiable sow that he was, to what he is now; that is greatness to be remarked upon for a mortal. I do, however, see your point. You of all people know what it feels like to rise from the cesspool of humanity." Eric bowed his head graciously. "Your face was once hideous to behold, and now you shine like a demi-god, because your faith in me has never wavered, even when it seemed as though I would forever be Shazadeh's slave. Your faith has made you great, Eric; Christopher could never find his in me, but you did, and you held fast to it. And for your unwavering faithfulness, I will anoint you and place a crown upon your head, and the mortals will call you king."

They walked out of the palace and into the light of the midday Egyptian sun. Yikan turned around and looked at the Great Sphinx and the pyramids behind his palace; they all a reminder of the glory that Egypt once was. His memory of the pyramids as a child was nothing close to what they were now—just weatherworn stacks of rocks. The great tombs that he remembered seeing were encased in polished limestone. The largest one, Pharaoh Khufu's pyramid, had flaunted a gold capstone that was a beacon to travelers for miles away; the Sphinx's headdress was painted bright blue and green in alternating stripes; and the surface of it was smooth, like glass. Then—those many thousands of years ago—they were truly wonders to behold, he thought, remembering back upon them fondly, back when he was still a child of Egypt with dark brown skin and dark eyes, and still a worshipper of the sun gods and of his pharaoh—the living incarnation of the god, Horus, and upon his death, becoming Osiris, god of the dead.

And then he found magic, and Zoe'el and Mala, the immortals masquerading as the gods of Egypt, found him. They taught him the ancient language of celestials, and then led him to the gold tomes and bid him to discover the Chant of Changing...to join them, and become a god as they were. And he did. Though soon, he came upon the opinion that it was he who should rule their pantheon as king of the gods. They disagreed. He took the crown anyway and subdued them for a short while, until Tamen aided them and imprisoned him in The Sphinx that he was now looking upon.

"That was my prison for many years," Yikan said. "Zoe'el, Mala, and Tamen bound me between life and death within the Sphinx...sentencing to remain so for all eternity. Though, who stands and looks upon The Sphinx now?" In his mind's eye, he saw the world beyond the pyramids of Egypt remade with his godly hands, and he knew *it would be good*.

"One must know who they are," Yikan offered. "I have seen this moment since I was a child. I was different, and I knew it early on. I took to magic as an Ibis to flight—I excelled at it. I surpassed my masters. I have stepped over every enemy put in my path, save one...Astaroth." He waved over his shoulder for Eric to come closer. He turned and looked at him. "Zoe'el and Mala never saw the hand of Astaroth at play in all that they did. Mala never questioned the water spirit who showed her to the tomes. Zoe'el did not care who had written them—what their true source was—only that it gave him power and immortality. But…nor did I at the time. And we all paid the price for our complacency. Another mistake will be our last."

"Can we trust anything the demon says?"

"How can we?" Yikan decried. "Astaroth did not conquer the other demon lords to content himself with Hell."

"He would have plenty of souls if he did."

"Aye…if it was just Hell that he wanted. But it is not. On earth, his power is not limited as it is in Hell, where he must feed on the souls of The Damned. Here, he could draw upon the limitless dark energy of the cosmos."

"As you will, once you are transformed."

"Aye," Yikan said. "Do you see now? Astaroth has no plans of allowing me to grasp that power. I know this to be true, for were it I, I would act in the same manner—I would suffer no rival."

He looked at the pyramids and envisioned replicas of them in every city, and upon each side of them, an image of Aton; they would signify his glory and fulfilled destiny in becoming god of gods. And he thought, what greater genesis tale could there be, than of a man born to greatness of mind, who became an immortal, who then became a god? And as the age of Aton carried on never ending, the memory of other gods and God would eventually fade away.

"I *will* not suffer a rival," he professed. "When Christopher and the others chant and we find them, we will kill them. For what I care, Blain may have them all to do with as he pleases. Let him carve the flesh from their bones. No preacher of God will stop me. No demon will usurp me.

"And every mortal will bow their knee, for they will know in that day that I come unto them by you, Eric—my only begotten son—that I am Aton. I alone am god.

"And I will have no other gods before me."

CHAPTER 13

Jared leaned on the stone window with his arms crossed at his chest. He looked out over the town of Hafah—the first town they had passed—, which lay past the walls of Hedun. Though Hafah was deserted, all seemed well with the town. Though, below in the city of Hedun, where Chax himself had waged battle, he could see the ruin that had been made of the city built from the torment of souls. Now drained of the dark magic that had created them, swaths of city blocks were no more. He understood that as the buildings of Hedun disappeared, and their power along with them, Chax's ability to protect him from Astaroth diminished, too.

"I had to make a choice, Henrì," he said softly, speaking his dilemma to no one, though wishing Henrì was with him to help him. He turned his gaze to the forest of Lady Pnemoxsis, whose land they would have to pass through to reach Phenóx. "This is the only way I know how to fix things."

"As do I, angel," Zim said from the doorway; she was leaning on it and watching him.

Jared turned around. Seeing her there made his lifeforce quicken, like it did in the forest the first time he saw her. Back then, he had attributed his swirling lifeforce to fright and fear—which was true—, though now, he struggled to find something other than her lovely, dark face and shapely body to blame it on.

"I've known war in some manner, shape, or form for most of my life," Zim said, walking in and closing the door. She went over to the table and picked up a glass goblet; she eyed it like a lost lover who had come back to her. "The first war with the Heavenly Host is what started the wars in Hell we now fight. After the first war, the lands were divided into four, and one given to each of the most powerful of us…Chax, Beelzebub, Agares, and of course, Astaroth. Though, we only knew peace for a short while. Now, once more, there is war."

Jared came over and sat at the table. She sat opposite of him. "Chax was Odin and Zeus, among others," Jared said. "And Beelzebub and Agares were various gods, too, right? So who were you then?"

"Guess." She half-smiled and tilted her head. "Let me gauge how wise you are."

Jared returned the smile. "I—I don't know. Really."

"Oya," she said, rounding her full, dark lips. "Have you not heard of me, angel?"

"There are lots of gods."

"There are many who are fallen," she said, concurringly. "I was Oya— goddess of the storm and spirit of the river Niger. And in other ages, I assumed the mantle of Bast, the goddess of war, and of Aphrodite, goddess of love and—

"And?" Jared blushed, knowing what came after that 'and'. He was too embarrassed to speak it.

"And 'beauty', my lord."

The lifeforce rushed to his face, causing him to glow for a moment. She smiled and looked away.

"Before…" he cleared his throat, "before the portals were shut, you mean?"

"Yes." She set the goblet down and pushed it away from her. "We were many gods before The Lamb sealed us in Hell. Upon his death, The Lamb descended into Hell, atoning for those who were here and had been unable to before he became the mortal's sacrificial lamb. He took the repentant with him to Heaven and sealed the portal, banishing us here. You may think our exile is of benefit to mortals, but you would be in error. Mortals do not require our influence to commit evil—they never have. They are fully capable of such acts on their own accord, whether we are upon the earth or not. Sin is simply in their nature."

"And a demon's nature?"

"Demons?" She raised a brow. "We were once part of the Heavenly Host, also."

"And then we're back to the Heavenly Host against The Fallen, and who's right and who's wrong, which brings it back to us…I mean *to this!*" he said, quickly replacing the ill-timed word. He got up and went back to the window, and sat on the ledge. "You know why this is hard for me."

She nodded. "I do, Miel."

"It's Jared," he told her. "I'm Miel, too. I guess I haven't gotten comfortable with that name yet." He glanced out at the town. "I don't like being controlled, and that's how I feel…like everyone is moving me around. I chased after Yikan for years, and then I found him and screwed it up. Now, I have all of you pushing me to trust you by giving up my lifeforce."

"Duke Chax has made no mystery of his desire to rule Hell once Astaroth is disposed of. That is the truth, Jared." She came to the window and looked out over Hedun as well. "We of Hell—The Fallen—do wish to reclaim our godhoods. Though we are fallen, and you believe our innate nature is to mislead and to deceive, remember that we are like you in every way; we are celestials, also. If we were on earth, we could bathe in the power of The Ghost, which flows through all, just as the Seraphim, Archangels, Principalities, and all of the other of the Host do." She looked at him. "Whether it pleases or displeases you…we are you, and you are us, Jared."

Jared looked at her, allowing himself to finally appreciate her beauty without hating himself for it. In those long moments that he did gaze at her, he felt more mortal than when he was actually a mortal. He suddenly understood the meaning of the word *desire* and how dangerous it really was, and how foolish it could make one become pondering the 'what ifs, maybes, and possible possibilities of what could never be.

Reality, however, was a shrill alarm clock.

She was a demon. He was a warrior of God. What more was there to consider? he wondered, though was bothered by the fact that it remained a question in his mind at all.

"What happens after they take my lifeforce?"

"Then we will move against Astaroth," she said. "The lords have forged a plan, though even they readily admit it is tenuous at best."

"Tenuous?"

"Perhaps after you hear it, you may think I have framed it too optimistically."

"I'm really sure I don't want to hear this."

"I'm positive you do not," she said, "but it is our best course. We will have to travel by horse and then on foot; we cannot risk flight. Astaroth commands the skies with legions of The Fallen who were once Virtues; there are none who are as swift as they; and we must conserve every ounce of our lifeforce for what we face.

"Once we are past the lady's forest, we will travel to Sheol, the realm of King Purson. It is because of King Purson that Astaroth holds Hell in his hand. King Purson is a guardian of the realm; he was to have loyalty only to Lucifer and to Hell…no other and none other. But Purson broke his vow and bowed at Astaroth's feet. His land, Sheol, is where the souls first arrive from earth, and where they are reborn when drained of their force and torn asunder in Hell. The Train of Souls then shuttles them equally to all four realms…the Northlands, Southlands, Eastlands, and Westlands. In these dark passings of Wormwood, the Train of Souls now runs only one way, and that is to the Westlands, Astaroth's realm, where he will launch his attack on Phenóx."

"We get through Sheol—"

"The Lake of Fire."

Jared gawked. *"We'll be in the lake?"*

"You are a celestial, not a damned soul," she chastised. "But make no mistake about it, the fires will be hot on your celestial skin. The fire of the lake is meant to baptize the damned—to purify them with anguish, as only fire-meets-flesh can do. To use The Damned as fuel, a greater heat is required. We will find that on the Train of Souls, which we must board in order to reach the Westlands."

"You're right," he said, with cocky grin. "You were being way too optimistic. How—how are we supposed to travel with souls and we look nothing like them. They'll—"

"Lady Pnemoxsis will conceal us," she said. "She will lay an enchant over us. Whoever looks upon you will see just one of the millions of The Damned who will be there. The lady will sacrifice much of her land to cast the enchantment, though, it will only last for one pass of Wormwood."

"Is that enough time?"

"No. But it's all we have."

"And we do what when the enchantment fades?"

She smiled. "I suppose we are both in agreement that 'tenuous' was not the best choice of words to describe this."

"Uh, yeah," he muttered, and gave a wry look.

"I know the path is dangerous," she said, her voice turning calm and soothing. "Once we are in the Westlands, we still must travel through Astaroth's legions and across the bridge to Phenóx. There, once he breaches it, he will be weakened and vulnerable, and you will have a way home; and the lords will have their opportunity to kill Astaroth. If, and when, our enchantments fade—no matter what—we must do what we must to be at the end of that bridge when wall of Phenóx is torn asunder. If we must fight, then we must! But if we are fortunate and steal across the bridge unnoticed, then we can use it to bottleneck Astaroth's troops until the lords of Hell have come. And when they come, we will let the lords of Hell have at battle, while we steal into Phenóx. But time is our enemy, Jared." She leaned in to him. Her eyes grew wide. "It is only by the grace of The Morning Star that Astaroth has not attacked Phenóx. Astaroth does not have Duke Chax's realm, and he would like nothing more than to have its power behind him when he attacks. But who knows the mind of a mad celestial? He may choose to attack without having Chax's lands, and that is what we fear he may do. That is why the lords must have your lifeforce now—without delay. What awaits you in Phenóx, is what you should be wary about, not your pact with the Lords of Hell."

"Oh, don't worry about that," he said, and winked. "I've been giving that one a lot of thought, too. It's kind'a hard to forget. And I hate to say it, but...I hope one of the Three of Evil on earth is being very, very bad when I get to Lucifer's palace."

"Pray that is the case," she said. "If you linger too long, The Morning Star will add you to his realm of frozen souls and will drain you for all eternity. All that is in Phenóx belongs to The Morning Star. Other," she paused, "options still remain."

For a moment, they looked at one another and said nothing, and moved not at all. A knock came at door, jarring them both back into motion.

"Lady Zimarantha?"

"Enter," she called, and then looked at Jared. "It is time."

The door opened to Thamuz and Caym standing in the hall. Both were bare-chested, and wore only shendyts and calf-high boots. Jared followed Zim out of the room and down the hallway. Thamuz and Caym walked behind them like soldiers marching a prisoner to the gallows. They traveled deep into the center of the palace. At the end of a hall lit by torchlights on either side, they came to a set of double doors bearing Chax's oak leaf and crossed swords insignia split between the two.

"This is the duke's holy sanctum," Zim said, turning to him. "Some of the greatest magic has been perform in there...magic that has changed the course of life on earth. I now commit you into the hands of His Grace."

She sounded almost hesitant, he thought, which either meant she felt similarly for him, or was just empathetic about what he was about to endure. Still, both ways were troubling.

"I guess this is the ultimate test of trust," he said.

"Remember," she replied, her voice low, "it is not us that you should worry about, but what is inside the dome of Phenóx."

"You'll just have to blame me, because," he looked at the oak leaf insignia and nodded. "I'm worried about this—a lot."

"I don't," she said. "All I can do is say that, I will see you once all is done. You may trust in that, Jared."

Caym and Thamuz came around them with torches in hand. They each pulled on a door, opening up a room that was lit by gray, stone braziers lining the walls. They turned and looked at Jared, waiting for him to enter.

Jared walked in. The doors closed behind him.

Zim's trust—a demon's trust—was all that he had to hold onto now. It was that or nothing. And right now, he really didn't have a choice. He chose trust.

* * *

The air was sweet with incense. The room was aglow in the pale red light of the braziers placed along its perimeter, and from the ones in the center of the room—seven of them; black—arranged in a circle. Chax and the other lords were nowhere to be seen. It seemed to be just him, the red gloom, and the crackle of the fire.

He walked over to the circle of braziers. Inside of it, there was a mosaic of a pentagram with Chax's insignia in its center. Above the points of the star, Jared recognized the arcane symbols from the golden tome naming each of the four elements…fire, water, wind, and soil; the last one he saw said tree, though there was a stroke at the bottom of the symbol that he did not recognize.

"It says 'oak', Miel-angel," a voice said from the right of him, answering his unspoken question.

Jared turned to look. There was nothing there, though he was certain the low, lyrical voice belonged to Chax.

"We bid you welcome," a female voice said to his left.

It was Agares this time. Though like Chax, she too, was nowhere to be seen.

"An angel of The Father has come to us as a savior—a lamb, just like *The Lamb*," another said from behind.

It was Beelzebub, Jared knew. There was no mistaking the buzzing and croaking of the Lord of the Flies.

Something stirred to his right, catching his eye. It was tall and moving toward him hidden in darkness, like a shadow moving within a shadow. As it neared, the shadow transformed into a black robed figure bearing a crown affixed with a ruby. It was Chax, Lord of the Northlands, Duke of Hell. Chax glided across the air, stopping just a foot shy of where he was and looked down on him. Jared looked up at his shrouded face.

"You have chosen wisely, Miel-angel," Chax said. "If there is a way to Earth, then you have stepped upon the path leading to it."

"As you begin your journey, so do we," Agares said from the left. He turned and saw her billowing milk-white robes break from the darkness. She approached and stood opposite of Chax.

"We will break Astaroth's grasp on our lands," Beelzebub croaked from behind him. Jared started to turn around, but ice-cold hands suddenly gripped him at the shoulders. He heard flies buzzing behind him, and then suddenly, the droning cacophony was right at his ear. Beelzebub was bending over him, and had placed his shrouded face right next to Jared's. "Miel-angel…step into the circle."

Jared looked at the pentagram for a moment. He sighed, resigning himself to committing the act that he was quite sure he wasn't sure about at all. Though now, with all options gone, it was the only way to save the earth. He walked to the center of the circle, and then turned around and faced them. The fires from the braziers around the pentagram flared and turned from red to dark blue. The lords promptly began whispering amongst themselves, and then suddenly became silent. As one, they turned their shrouded faces toward him and stared.

"What's a matter?" Jared asked, looking from one cloaked face to the other, more suspicious now of their intent than even before.

"Tis' a good omen—the flames," Chax replied, and began walking to the left. Agares went the other way around the pentagram. Beelzebub wobbled where he stood. "The sacred circle of magic knows an angel of The Father when it senses one."

"And a powerful one you are, indeed," Agares said, walking over and standing to the left of Jared; Chax stood opposite of her. "You are no ordinary angel, Miel."

"Indeed," Beelzebub said. "Celestials were created for the pleasure of The Father."

"Except Lucifer," Chax said.

"And now—" Beelzebub began.

"There is you," Agares said. *Sign the pact*, she whispered to his mind.

Save thyself, Beelzebub told him.

Give us your lifeforce, Chax urged.

And we will show you home, Agares said, her voice as smooth as milk and honey.

"Make your mark at your feet," Chax said, holding up his finger.

Jared squatted. With his index finger, he began signing his name. Where he traced the letters, the stone began to glow yellow, like gold. He finished and stood.

"Now invite us in, Miel-angel," Agares said. "Only by your word may we enter the sacred circle."

Jared sighed. "Beelzebub!" he called out. The Lord of the Flies came wobbling into the circle. Jared looked to his left. "Agares!" In she came, flowing on air. Jared turned to Chax and paused. He took measure of the Lord of the Northlands from crown to boot, and then said, "Chax!"

Chax stepped into the circle and moved toward Beelzebub, who then began lurching to the right. Agares moved to the right also...she following Chax, and they all now circling Jared counterclockwise.

Beelzebub passed by. "Give it to us—*your lifeforce!*"

"Freely so!" Chax said, coming around.

"It must be given freely," Agares urged, as she passed by him. "Unbound and unfettered."

"We desire all that you are," Beelzebub croaked.

"All thy losses," Agares said.

"Thy grief," Chax added.

"Thy sorrow," Beelzebub said.

"Thy despair!"

"Hopelessness."

"*Give it to us.*"

"Freely!" Beelzebub said.

Speak it, Chax's said.

"Freely!" Jared called out.

For a moment, nothing moved. The blue flames of the braziers were frozen in time, as were the Lords of Hell, they each hovering over him—Chax and Agares on either side and Beelzebub in front of him. Or were they? he wondered, just as the room began spinning clockwise. Or was he the one who was going around? Suddenly, he couldn't tell what was right or left, or who was to his right or to his left, or who was in front of him. The lords began moving again, opposite the spin of the room. The blue fires resumed dancing in their braziers.

"Fix your mind on The Father," Chax said, swirling past him. "Recall that spark of life when he made you into what you are—"

"From mortal child—," Agares said, sweeping past him.

"Into a celestial, that was created for one purpose," Beelzebub said.

"To bring the world into balance," Chax said. "And to see it be done, The Father has made you powerful."

"Strong!" Beelzebub bellowed.

"Unique," Agares whispered.

"Mighty enough to escape the inescapable grip of Lady Muchenlay… *indeed!*" Chax professed. "It is that power that we need."

"Burn bright, angel," Agares said, passing by.

"Release thy lifeforce, Miel," Beelzebub told him, hobbling around, taking her place.

Jared closed his eyes. His lifeforce felt strong. He did as Chax instructed and began thinking about God. As he did, he saw a spark of light with his mind's eye. It reminded him of that night in the desert, when Heaven—that Godly realm—had opened up, revealing itself through a rip in the fabric of space and time; and within that realm, he had seen hundreds of thousands of his celestial brethren, and felt millions more that he could not see. They had come to witness his birth— that spark of life that would transform him from mortal to celestial. It was that power the Lords of Hell sought to drain from him.

His lifeforce began spinning faster. The white light grew brighter, though was not harsh—it did not hurt—, but instead emanated warmth and a sense of peace. He moved the mental projection of his body toward the light, but as he drew closer, he felt it washing away, leaving nothing but his consciousness, just as it had when he exploded with light and escaped Muchenlay's hold. The light grew brighter, expanding and surrounding him. His lifeforce surged in reply.

Everywhere he looked it was white; there was nothing. And then darkness came over him suddenly, like someone had flicked off the light. The darkness was as complete in blackness, as the white had been void of color.

In the darkness there was nothing—*it was without form, and void*. It was nonexistence. Jared now understood where he was; it was the ether —the great void. But even clearer to him was that, even though the ether was of utter nothingness, everything there was in creation had come from it...from nothing came everything, and therein lay the greatest power, which he had released upon Muchenlay and broke her grip.

The clarity of thought brought on by darkness was suddenly marred by a milk-white light in the shape of a figure. It pulled him away from his oneness with the dark and back into his physical body inside Chax's sanctum.

The white figure in his mind was still moving toward him, only now, it was clear to him that it was Agares, Lady of the Eastlands. She swept around him once and then stopped in front of him. She pulled away her hood, face-shroud and all. Jared recoiled at the sight of her. Her skin was like curdled milk—serosal yellow and lumpy, and hung from her face like rivers of wax down a well-used candle.

"I will have your lust, angel," she said, reaching up and caressing his cheek with the back of her wet, sticky hand.

A spiral of red, glowing smoke spooled from Jared's mouth. *There!* he heard Agares whisper, as an image of Zim appeared in his thoughts. She was nude. Her black skin glistened, as though she had been rubbed with oil from head to foot. She smelled like lavender, and it made him woozy, and excited—mentally and physically. It made him want to say—

"*Yes*...Miel-angel," Agares urged, as the red smoke began circling her. She pulled the shroud from her shoulders and let it fall to the floor, exposing the rest of her bubbled, oozing body. "You find her beautiful... *desirable*." Her voice teased. "You doubt your resolve when you see her, and question The Father's plans for you when she is near, for you believe you cannot have what you want—*but that is not so*."

Jared tried to rid his mind of Zim's image, though the more he tried, the more vivid she grew; her lips became wetter and fuller, her skin softer. No matter how hard he tried to replace her, he could not, and then remembered that he had given himself over to the lords freely, and they were the ones now in control of him, not he.

Touch her, the duchess whispered, commanding him.

He did. He could not resist—he didn't want to, though did want to.

Taste her. He leaned in and kissed her deeply, parting her lips with his, which were equally as plump. Her lips were even softer than they looked, he thought, caressing them with his tongue; and they were sweet, too.

Love her!

And he did. He gave in to that sin.

He surrendered his angelic flesh to unchained lust with each thrust of his pelvis. And she—beneath him—met his plunge with a rise of her hips, giving him all—and more than he ever imagined there being. Ecstasy took hold of him...*she took tight hold of him*...rising and peaking, only to rise higher yet. And the further up he spiraled—one climax following the next—the weaker he felt, and the less he cared about anything or anyone else but her, for he had found sexual Nirvana, and there was no coming back from it.

But he did come back—*abruptly.*

He was in the sanctum again. Zim's illusion was gone and Agares was walking away from him. Her nude body was completely transformed from the monstrosity it had been. Now, she bore the image of a cocoa brown, green-eyed beauty with shoulder long, brown hair. From his mouth to hers, his red lifeforce spooled out in the form smoke. She inhaled greedily, until she had the tail of the tendril past her lips. She faded away as Beelzebub lurched forward and took her place in front of him.

Beelzebub jerked at his shroud, ripping it away and releasing thousands of flies upon him. He swatted at them, as they swarmed and buzzed around him. The flies suddenly retreated back to where they had come from and molded themselves back into the form of Beelzebub. The Lord of the Flies bent over and stared into Jared's eyes.

"I will have thy resentment," Beelzebub croaked, from mouth and lips made of crawling flies and squirming maggots, as was his entire body. "It has been denied for a very long time—until now." The flies and their larvae began melting and flowing into one another, and reformed into the image of a brown-skinned, middle-aged man with wooly, salt and pepper hair.

"Phineas?" Jared mumbled, as looked at the spitting image of his father.

He knew Phineas was not real, but knowing he wasn't suddenly didn't seem to matter. The Phineas before him was existent to his mind—it was reality at its clearest. But then, Phineas began to shrink. He grew younger. His hair filled out and turned black. His wrinkles faded and his skin took on the glow of youth. He looked to be seven or eight years old, and oddly, Jared thought, Phineas looked remarkably like he did when he was that age—gapped teeth, hair in neat, tight cornrows, large brown eyes, and all.

"Slap me!" Beelzebub commanded, speaking through the child.

Jared did, and hard; the smack across the Phineas-child's cheek was sharp. The boy yelped and covered his injured cheek. Tears came to his eyes.

Dark purple lifeforce began oozing from Jared's mouth, twisting and twirling its way over to the boy. The boy reached out and caught it in the palm of his hand, where it began spinning around, forming a sphere.

"That was for me abandoning you, wasn't it?" Beelzebub asked. "It hurt, didn't it? I left you to the wolves. I gave you over to a world already lined-up against you. I made you stumble from the moment you could walk, and you have ever since—even now. It made you feel as though you didn't exist to me, and you were right—you didn't. And it stung like a slap to the face. Only, the sting of abandonment lasts so much longer. It hollows a man, and creates a pain that is a hole that cannot be filled. *Now slap me!*" The boy stepped forward. "Make me know how it feels."

Jared swung harder this time and knocked the child to the ground. Everything Beelzebub had said was true. Phineas was trying to make amends, but the hurt he had caused ran deep. And that hurt, he knew, had become a part of him in many ways. It made him question who he was as a black man, and of what value he had, if any, especially since his father had saw none in him.

The boy stood. "I made you feel like shit; I knew I was doing it, too. Every day I was gone from your life, I knew you were struggling to live life without me. So I got real good at forgetting about it. I drank it away and I screwed it away, just so that I didn't have to think about you. And I got up every Sunday and stood in that pulpit, and preached the word, like nothing was even wrong...Sunday after Sunday, while you're up north crying about a daddy who doesn't want you. I just didn't care, and you knew it in your bones." The boy smiled and spoke softly. "Hit me."

Jared punched him in the nose—straight on—shattering his bridge and sending him on his rear again. The boy struggled to his feet. Blood pooled from his nostrils into his mouth.

"Not bad," the boy said, wiping his nose, stopping the blood for only a moment before it resumed streaming out. He bobbed his head. "I felt that one real good. So—so that's what it feels like when you fault your mother for the sins of your Father...*youch!*" He chuckled. "How many tears did she shed?—you making her feel like a whore and blaming her for all the wrongs in your life, when it was really me?" He raised his arms out to his sides. "I'm here for ya. You've always wanted to beat the living shit out of me, so here's your chance...*son.*"

Jared lunged and swung. This time, he knocked the boy to the ground and straddled his chest. He struck him in the face with alternating fists. "I hate you!" he screamed, as he swung and cracked the boy's jaw, it sounding like a branch snapping in two. He hit again, and then again; and his lifeforce grew weaker with each strike. Soon, after raining down blow upon crushing blow—curses along with them—he felt like he was hitting a bag of mush and bits of bone, instead of the child's face. But then, suddenly, he realized he wasn't hitting the boy at all, but had been pummeling the stone floor, and had crushed it into jagged bits.

The illusion of the boy was gone. The pulverized stone began repairing itself—reassembling and becoming as though nothing had ever happened. Beelzebub was back standing in front of him...nude, muscular, a strong face with a thick jaw, and skin as dark as night. He began walking backwards.

"You have replenished me and more," Beelzebub said, disappearing, fading away with the echo of his voice.

Tears streamed down Jared's face. He had finally released the rage he felt toward Phineas. In his dark thoughts, he had always wanted Phineas to suffer like he had as a child. He wanted Phineas to finally understand that 'I'm sorry' doesn't mend the wound that he caused. And Beelzebub had given him that wish on a silver platter, and he ate it greedily—*freely so*. But it was at great cost to his lifeforce. Much of it had been taken. He could feel the drain of energy in his muscles...in his bones. He stood and wobbled. His knees threatened to buckle.

"That's it, Miel-angel," Chax urged, speaking from behind. Jared shuffled around and struggled to raise his head. Chax reached out and took hold of his shoulders, steadying him. He lifted Jared's head by the chin, and cocked his head, as though wrought with worry for him. "You have given much lifeforce with your pain and desire. But there is far more of you to partake of, for there is one sin that we celestials all share."

Jared looked at Chax. His shroud and veil were gone. In place of skin, Chax's body was covered in bark, like a tree. The brown bark was mottled all over with white and green fungus, and reeked of decay. The great Lord of the Oak—mate to the Lady of Green—was simply just of rot.

"Know what it is to be like us—those who are fallen," Chax said.

The ether enveloped him once more. And again, in the nothingness, he spotted a glint of light. It looked so far away that it appeared like a sole star in an empty heaven. But in the breath of a moment, the light rushed at him and exploded, shooting out rays of every color, from the faintest pastel to the darkest hue.

Jared reached out to a blue beam of light that was in front of him. It was solid, not ethereal, as he had thought it would be. He grabbed hold of it. As he did, the other rays of light around him began fading away. The darkness returned, but now there were stars twinkling all around him. He looked down and startled; there was nothing beneath his feet, just space and more stars.

A note, pure and full of vibrato, broke the silence, *and physics,* by calling out in the vacuum of space. A multitude of ghostly shapes in white robes began forming next to him, and behind, creating a circle of bodies that stretched for thousands of miles in circumference. As they coalesced out of nothing, they sung, adding their voices to the mezzo-soprano's. Their faces and heads were an assortment of the wild and fantastical. Some had heads of animals—sheep, oxen, lions, and bulls, and more. Others had humanoid faces of varying hues…pale white to ink black, and every shade and hue between them.

Jared looked up. There was another ring of celestials miles above; and above them, there was another ring, and another, and another—nine in total. The last ring consisted of sparkling, heavenly bodies—hundreds of spiraled galaxies slowly turning around, looking like giant eyes in the heavens.

A piece of dust came floating in front of his face. It was quickly joined by other pieces of dust that stuck to it—accreted with it and formed into a solid ball, which began pulling in larger pieces. The ball flew to the center of the ring of celestials.

Time—*for the little planet that could*—suddenly began to speed up.

Thousands of fire-engulfed asteroids suddenly came hurtling in from all directions and crashed into the fledgling planet. The celestial's voices rose as the planet spun and absorbed the impacts. The surface of the planet began turning from red hot to cool blue, as oceans began appearing. And in the midst of the blue waters, a supercontinent rose and then broke apart, and began spreading out across the globe. Upon the landmasses, bits of green began to appear, and with it, Jared knew, the seeds of human life were soon to grow.

Creation had begun.

He was witnessing it from its birth. But also, he knew, as a celestial he could shape it and mold it; he could alter what had been made, even though he had not created it. He could become god of all there was below. All he had to do was to descend down to the planet—to the earth—and claim it.

"It is yours, Miel-angel," Chax said, his voice coming from all directions. "The earth was once ours. And we loved it and cared for it, and lorded over it as gods. And now, Miel," his voice turned cold, "it is yours —take it from The Father's hand!"

Jared did, unable to resist the draw of godhood, having freely given his will away. He lowered down to where earth's atmosphere and space met. The earth slowed its spin at his approach, as if waiting for its new master to take possession.

Jared moved his left hand out and away from him—a system of clouds appeared and began journeying around the earth. He grasped the African, European, and Asian continents with his mind, and commanded them to shift to the right, and they did; he could see their lands rumbling as the quakes he commanded into being pushed them to the side. He raised his arms above his head, mentally pulling at the earth's molten core. Lava spewed from the Atlantic Ocean, and then cooled in the frigid waters, forming a landmass, and then turned green.

Whatever he desired the planet to do or to become, it obeyed. He was its master. It was his servant.

"You are earth's god—immortal and beautiful," Chax said. "You have dominion over all that moves across its lands and swims in its waters. The earth is your loom; the mortal your yarn; the cosmos your home. All that remains is for you turn your back on The Father and bow to The Morning Star. Denounce him!"

Jared looked upon his earth. He could feel the creatures great and small beginning to move upon it and swim in its waters; the mortals would arise next. A great sense of self-righteousness came upon him, and he thought it good, for in his hands, he knew he could guide the lives of mortals far better than God, who had made a mess out of his own creation, putting them all in the dire positions they were now in.

What kind of God is that? He creates mortals and then punishes them. He puts out temptation, but says don't touch it. He's just setting us up to fail. And then, a wonderful idea came to him—or so he thought, though did not care, for it seemed like a very good one—a pragmatic one. *I'm not going to let that happen. I'm gonna save the earth from God. I'll be its god.*

"Yes!" Chax whispered into his mind.

Jared began thinking how wonderful it would be to bless the poor and punish the wicked. He could save lives, as well as snuff out the ones that didn't deserve to live. He could build, destroy, reform, and reshape all that he wanted and all that he saw—all that he was lord and god of.

Denounce him!

Jared felt weaker than he did after crashing into Hell; but his will to rule and govern and save the mortals was strong. God was to blame for all that was wrong, and he was the one who needed to be stopped, no matter the cost, Jared reasoned.

"I denoun—" Jared began, and then paused. He tried again. "I denoun—denounce…"

Say it. Speak it. Release the Godly force within you! Betray The Father.

"I denounce God!" Jared yelled.

He suddenly felt as though he was falling, hurtling through space. In the spark of a moment, he fell no more; he was on the stone floor of Chax's sanctum lying on his side with his knees pulled up to his chest. White smoke oozed from his skin and crept across the ground to Chax, where it swirled up around his wood-rotted legs and to his thighs, and then circling his chest, arms, and head. His decayed bark began flattening and smoothing out, turning from a moldy green to a glossy dark brown. Dark tan striations ran vertically from his head to feet, giving him the appearance of well-polished wood.

Chax held his arms out and turned them over, and then back again, appraising them. He looked down at Jared and smiled; his black eyes glimmered. "I am renewed!" he professed, "It has been at great cost to you, and at great pain. Though, do not fear the vision I have shown you, for to dream of being God is a dream all celestials have dreamt." He bent at the waist, drawing closer to Jared. "You, Miel-angel, are no different."

Jared tried lifting his head, but couldn't. His muscles felt like pudding. He could barely feel his lifeforce at all. It was as though his chest, and every part of him, was empty—just a shell of flesh. But he still had the power of thought. And he remembered the earth, and what he had seen, and what he was able to do to it, and what he had said to God, and he knew it to be wrong. Even though he had given himself over freely, he could feel a part of himself that was still under his own influence, and it gave him a sudden, fleeting jolt of strength, which he used to eek out a mumble.

"I…*still love God.*"

The braziers shot blue flames feet into the air.

Chax gasped. "I was right!" He knelt beside Jared and lifted his head, bringing him close, as though he were about to kiss him. "Once again, you have done what could not be done." His eyes were wide with wonder. "First you escape Lady Muchenlay, and now this—breaking a spell sealed with a freely given mark. How great did The Father make thee?"

Chax opened his mouth. Jared's lips parted also.

Glowing blue lifeforce began flowing from Jared's mouth…surprising him, as he thought he was all but depleted. But he was wrong, he saw and felt, as more and more of the blue lifeforce came pouring from his mouth.

His vision began to blur and go dark, though this time, it was no illusion; the emptiness of the ether was real, and he was beginning to spiral into it. He was dying—he was sure of it. His suddenly renewed and unexplained resurgence of lifeforce was quickly being drained away. *Give me more!* he heard Chax cry out to his mind, as the darkness closed in around him.

"There is only God," Jared mumbled.

"More angel," Chax demanded.

"He's God of gods."

"More!"

"He's Alpha."

"More!"

"And Omega."

Chax stood up and backed away from him. Another quickly took his place, kneeling down beside him and smelling of jasmine. He opened his eyes. Zim was there looking down at him with a grave expression on her face. She cradled his head and picked him up as though he weighed nothing. His body drooped in her arms.

"Care for him," Chax said to Zimarantha. "We have taken him to the point of death, and he will be weak for some time. Watch over him, dear lady—my Zimarantha. Nurse him and prepare him for what is to come."

Chax leaned over Jared. Chax's breath was warm and smelled like the forest on a spring morning, just at daybreak. His handsome face was a fusion of wood and skin. Chax smiled at him; Jared could see his reflection in his black eyes.

"We are remade because of you; and I even more so, for we did not sense, but always believed, that you were no ordinary angel of The Father."

Chax's voice began fading away as Jared slipped out of consciousness.

"The Father has imbued you with great might to see his covenant stay whole and holy. Though with such power comes great peril, indeed!"

Jared drifted away.

"Temptation be thy enemy now."

Jared's mind shut down. For the first time as an angel, he slept like a mortal.

* * *

"The angel looks remarkably well," Lady Pnemoxsis remarked, appraising Jared who was standing before her. Zim was to his left, followed by Caym and Thamuz. Lady Pnemoxsis was standing next to Chax, who was sitting on his throne.

"He's barely the worse for wear," Chax added, and then leaned across his throne to look at Beelzebub, who was seated on his right, and then to Agares on his left.

Beelzebub concurred with a nod and a grumble. Like Chax, he wore only a white shendyt, proudly displaying his renewed, black body and handsome face; a thick gold necklace hung about his neck. Upon his head, he wore a band of gold.

"Three passes of sleep has done him wonders," Agares opined, eyeing Jared from the side. She wore a white skirt and twirled cloth over her breasts. A gold circlet was upon her head, though now, her curly brown locks were in cornrows.

"I wished I felt as good as I look," Jared said, referring to his dearth of strength, as well as his clothing. He and the others had been given the attire of The Damned to dress in—tattered brown pants for the males, and a coarse, one piece dress for Zim.

Beelzebub leaned to right and pointed at him. "Time will restore you again, Miel-angel."

"And perhaps sooner than you think," Chax said. "The power you have been imbued you with astounds us. We are Seraphim," he extended his arms out to Beelzebub and Agares, "the highest choir of celestial there is. Rarely does The Father give a low ranked celestial great power. The archangel, Michael, was given power to subdue The Morning Star in the first Great War in Heaven—*because of purpose.*"

"Now there is you, Miel-angel," Agares said.

"The Angel of Balance," Beelzebub added.

"Created and imbued with great lifeforce to keep The Father's covenant intact," Chax said. He stood and extended a hand to Lady Pnemoxsis. They walked over and stood in front of Jared and the others. Chax's skin was like polished wood come to life; the lady's was dark green, *and of life*. "The Father, having created you so strong, may have just saved us all—Hell, Heaven, and earth. Your unique lifeforce has given us much to fight Astaroth with."

"You took a lot of it," Jared accused. "You almost killed me."

"But I did not," Chax snipped. "And I would not. We have pact, Miel-angel…remember?"

"Can't forget it," Jared replied, arching his brow.

"Will what you have given us be enough to stop Astaroth?" Chax shook his head. "I do not know…nor does anyone. You have given us great power, but the sins of mortals has filled Hell with multitudes of The Damned; and it is an awesome force; one that Astaroth now commands."

"I have looked into that future, and it has turned gray," Lady Pnemoxsis said, looking at Jared, and then to Zim and the others. "Your futures are uncertain."

"'Tis' better it is unclear, than to scry certain defeat, my lady," Beelzebub opined.

"Aye, my lord," she said.

Chax looked at Jared and the others with a solemn gaze. "A dark path lies ahead. You must steal into Sheol and board the Train of Souls. But know that if King Purson apprehends you, he will flay you and serve your remains to his master. Survive that and you still must get yourselves to the bridge when Astaroth attacks. He has not attacked Orsha-Na since you have slept, Miel-angel, which tells me he prepares to march on

Phenóx soon. We must be there when he does and strike him when he is weakest."

"Though first," Lady Pnemoxsis said, "to make it through Purson's realm, you must have the cover of illusion."

Chax returned to his throne. Lady Pnemoxsis took a step back and began speaking in the language of demons; and as she did, a circle of green fire rose up around Jared and the others.

Her eyes turned black. "Turum-pak, anissi de putumbuk," she said, walking around them.

Jared's left cheek began to twitch; his right began soon after. And then, as though his skin had become putty, it began to reshape itself. He could feel his nose and lips shrinking. He looked at his hands. They began to wrinkle before his eyes. He felt his cheeks sag and his head start to itch. He rubbed his head. All of his hair was gone.

He turned to Zim and the others; they were changing as well. Zim's nose grew long and hooked over, and her skin and hair became white. Caym's green skin and eyes turned brown; his toned body shriveled away to barely skin and bones; Thamuz shrank and morphed into the image of a potbellied, middle-aged white man with snaggled teeth.

"*Turro baye, sudarra,*" Lady Pnemoxsis said, finishing her spell of concealment upon them. The green flames died away. "For one pass of Wormwood, my enchantment will conceal your true form from all eyes, even Astaroth's—were he to look upon you. Though, once Wormwood has crossed the sky, the enchantment will begin to fade and you will be vulnerable." She walked over and stood in front of Caym. "To you, my beloved son, I give you dominion over all of Varencia, and the Great Forest as well." She puckered her lips and blew. A stream of green smoke passed from her mouth into his. His eyes glowed green for a moment. "May the power in these lands grant you victory over the usurper, and see you back to me alive and whole." She offered her hand.

Caym took it and kissed it. "Yes, Mahti."

"Then this is farewell," she said, glancing back at Chax. He nodded approvingly. She turned back and addressed them all. "Soldiers of Orsha-Na, and angel of The Father…the fate of Hell, Heaven, and earth now rests upon your mighty shoulders. If you fall, then we all shall. So, I will ask only one thing from all of you…" she paused, "*do not fall.*"

* * *

The enchantment that concealed them as The Damned had cost the lady much of her forest, Jared saw. He, Zim, Caym and Thamuz were passing through Lady Pnemoxsis's green wonderland on horseback. Though now, the forest was not as dense as it had been before. Swaths of her sky-tall trees, shrubs, and bushes were gone—*vanished*—as though they had never existed at all. The grasses, plants, and vines that had blan-keted the forest, were now just parcels of dirt, dust, and rocks. Though seeing the lady's loss was actually a comfort to him. He had sacrificed his all. He expected them to do the same. Still, he remembered fondly, there was at least one of them who had gone out of her way to assure him of their earnestness.

Jared looked over at Zim; she was riding next to him. Caym and Thamuz were on her other side.

"Thanks for the last few…." He struggled for the word.

"Passings?" she said.

"Yeah," he replied. "I've never slept before…as a celestial, I mean. It was pretty strange."

"And a bit frightening, too, I can imagine," she said. "To be utterly defenseless in a land of your sworn enemies *should* induce such a feeling, among many others, I would say."

"I won't lie…it still does," he said. His body had rejuvenated some of his lifeforce already, though much of it—nearly all—had been taken. When he had woke and saw Zim sitting next to his bed, he barely had the energy to reach his hand out to her in search of comfort. Though amazingly and disturbingly to him, his will and need for her reassuring touch overcame his fatigue.

"His Grace has commanded me to keep you safe to best of my skills," she said.

"I'd like to be able to defend myself somehow," he said. "You all have your swords and your lifeforce."

She cocked her head. "They are one and the same."

"Though not for you, my lady," Caym said, with an admiring glance.

"True enough," Zim said. "Your lifeforce is your weapon, whether it is to manipulate the elements or to forge into an actual object to direct an expression of your force. There are some demons who can express both simultaneously, such as me."

"And Astaroth, unfortunately," Caym added.

Thamuz leaned over and looked at Jared. "What exactly were you planning on doing come the last Great War?"

"If there be one at all," Caym droned.

Zim gave Caym a curt glance. She sighed and turned to Jared. "Your lifeforce, forged as a weapon, can pierce celestial flesh and counter magic —if it is strong enough, that is." She held out her right hand. From her palm, white mist arose and took on the shape of a sword's handle; and from it, a silver blade extended out, rising to a point. She held it above her head. The rays of Wormwood peeking through the treetops danced on her blade.

Jared concentrated the lifeforce he had recovered into his hand. A stream of fire erupted from his palm and struck the trees above him, setting them on fire. "Whoa!" Jared yelped.

Caym leaned over and glared at Jared, who replied with an innocent shrug. Caym extended his hand to the burning trees and spoke his demon tongue to them. The fires immediately extinguished.

"Will you try not to burn my mother's forest to ground? Where we're going, we will need every ounce of power from every leaf…that is, if you don't turn it all to ash before then."

"You must focus on your weapon," Zim said, bringing Jared's attention back to her. "Picture in your mind what you wish to conjure. Focus your lifeforce into making it so."

What lifeforce? he thought, holding up his hand, where a flame still danced on his palm. *I barely got this to work.*

"Try again, Jared," Zim urged.

He did as she instructed. The flame at his palm vanished, though soon, white smoke started trickling out where the flame had been. He pictured a sword in his mind; one with a long handle and a pointed cross-guard on either end. His lifeforce began swirling in his palm, and then began taking on the shape of a handle. Though, just as the blade began to emerge, it dispersed, disappearing like smoke.

Jared groaned. He tried it again, though came upon the same result. He hung his head, as though the weight of saving earth already on his shoulders had just been doubled. "I don't have the strength."

"Not yet. But eventually you will," she encouraged. "And once you do, you must learn how to wield your lifeforce through it."

"Will you instruct him then, my lady?" Caym asked, his voice full of cynicism. "When the last Great War turns us to enemies again, what you've taught the angel may very well send many of our kind to the ether."

"His inexperience—*now*—may result in our deaths," Zim countered. "Perhaps, my lord, it is wise that we have every possible means of defense and offense at our disposal."

"Aye," Thamuz concurred heartily. He pointed ahead. The canopy of trees was coming to an end. "We're coming up on Galak—the last town of the Northlands."

"Once we are out of the forest, we will no longer have the protection of the lady and the duke," Zim said. "Astaroth has claimed Galak as his. We must be watchful of his soldiers."

They passed out of the enchanted forest. In the distance, Jared spotted the tops of Galak's buildings. As they traveled along, he listened eagerly as Zim instructed him in the art of weapon conjuring and how to focus his lifeforce through them once he had created them. Once—nearly twice—he had managed to form a sword, though still did not have the strength to keep it solid.

When they reached the gates of Galak, they were open and un-guarded. Jared and Zim immediately ceased their lesson and rode through the deserted city without speaking. Thamuz and Caym took the lead and steered them away from the main road, and on through a maze of smaller streets and back alleys.

Jared, like the others, was ever watchful. He scanned the streets and the flat roofs of the buildings, moving his head in a sweeping pattern from side-to-side. He looked backwards also, giving that direction al-most as much attention as what was in front of him. The absence of life and the dearth of sound—save for the clip-clop of their horses—put him further on edge.

Jared felt his cheek, and then his chest with the palm of his hand. Both were warm. "It's heating up."

"It's going to get hotter," Thamuz promised. "We're nearing Sheol—the legendary hell of mortal nightmares."

"The mortals fear it more than anything," Caym said. "Though it's not the fire they should fear…it is us; the servants of their punishment."

They stopped at the end of a road leading to gates out of the city. Zim sent Caym to scout ahead. He returned a short time later declaring it all clear.

They rode up to the gates; they too were open like the ones they entered the city through. From here, Jared saw his final destination in the distance; and seeing the immense, black dome of Phenóx—which looked like a world unto itself—his dreams of returning home suddenly felt like pure fantasy. Ripples, like water disturbed by a tossed pebble, emanated down from the top of the dome. And it gleamed, like oil in water.

"Phenóx," Thamuz uttered, gazing up at it and performing the five pointed sign of the cross. Caym and Zim promptly followed his lead.

Jared moved his horse up next to Caym and Thamuz. The lifeforce he had regenerated stuttered in his chest at the sight of the dome. He looked back at Zim and shook his head.

"How does one describe the realm of a god as old as the cosmos itself?" she posed, moving her horse up beside his. "In the midst of that realm is where The Morning Star's palace is…where you must go."

"This already seems impossible."

"The same thing was said about Astaroth usurping Hell's power," she said. "And he did. He wrested control of the Southlands from his own grandfather."

"Beelzebub?"

"Aye," she said. "Once the Southlands fell and he took its power, the Eastlands tumbled soon thereafter. What was thought could not happen, has indeed. You must fix your mind in the same manner if you are to be victorious. You must believe the impossible is possible. That is the only way to survive what is to come." Zim prodded her horse, moving past them and continuing down the road.

The lush, rolling hills on either side of them began looking less and less vibrant. Dense grass was soon replaced with dirt and rocks and gravel. The trees and shrubs and plants became sparse, and soon were nowhere to be seen across the rock-strewn landscape.

The further they went, the hotter it became. Jared sniffed at the air and grimaced; it was thick and bore a stench that assaulted his nose and stung his eyes. "What's that smell?"

"Brimstone and roasted souls," Thamuz answered, and then inhaled deeply and held it. He looked at Jared and smiled.

"A baptism of fire for the wicked," Caym ascribed, and half-grinned.

The road led them to a curved, stone archway with a black bell hanging from its center like a chandelier. Atop of the archway was a statue of Chax gazing up, his regal chin jutting out. His left arm was raised to the sky and his right held a spear the length of his body. His legs straddled the archway they passed under, which led out to a train yard with no trains, but single tracks that crisscrossed and led into—and up out of—hundreds of tunnels that looked like massive sinkholes.

"They come up out of the holes?" Jared asked.

"*It*," Zim corrected, though she was glancing up at the sky. Wormwood was nearly above them, drawing closer to its apex over Phenóx. "There is only one Train of Souls. It departs at the ringing of the bell, on *umandi-de*—midpass—, which gives us time to get into Sheol. But right now," she glanced at Wormwood again, "we should get going."

"Which hole does it come out of?" Jared asked.

"Hopefully one that we will be far away from," Zim said, and then dismounted. The others followed her lead. "The tunnel walls of Sheol are weakened by the heat from the Lake of Fire. We will have already burst through and be inside Sheol well before the train departs; and hopefully—if all goes as planned—we will be on that train and heading for Phenóx upon *umandi-de*."

Thamuz and Caym led the horses back to the road, and with a slap to their hindquarters, sent them galloping back to Orsha-Na. They regrouped with Jared and Zim and began walking toward the tracks that wound in and out of the tunnels.

"Follow my every move, and do as I say," she said to Jared. "You have not recovered enough of your force to protect yourself."

"Don't worry. I'll stick to you like glue."

She smiled. Her eyes lingered upon his illusionary eyes. "That is very wise."

Jared turned and smiled, and then looked back at her. She was still looking. His smile grew wider. He looked off to his right, toward the first of hundreds of tunnels they were approaching. He peered in as they passed by it. It looked like a cavern to him. He could only see a few feet down before it was too dark to see anything at all.

"We must reach the bottom of the tunnel before the Train of Souls departs," Zim said. "Once it has taken off, there is…." She paused. Her eyes grew large and her lips parted.

"What is it, Zim?" Jared asked. Though before she could answer, the ground began to shake. He looked down at his feet. The ground began cracking; and within the cracks, a red glow shone through and yellow smoke began twirling out from them.

"It's the Train of Souls," she mumbled, looking frantically about the rail yard. She grabbed him by the arm and took off running. Caym and Thamuz sprinted behind them.

"But, you said—" Jared began.

"I know what I said." She pulled him to the left.

He glanced at Wormwood. "But it's not midpass—umandi-de."

"Obviously," Caym replied from behind. "But here the train comes, nevertheless."

"We'll have to get further in, Zim," Thamuz called ahead to her. "We'll be lost in a maze of tunnels if we descend now."

She yanked Jared to the right, moving them toward the center of the rail yard. "I know, Thamuz."

"We need to get closer to the Lake of Fire," Thamuz insisted.

"I know!" she yelled.

The shaking grew worse. Jared felt like he was running on a trampoline that was being jumped on from all sides. Every time he thought he had found firm footing, the ground dropped out beneath him or pushed up against him, or tossed him left or right, or lurched him forward or sent him stumbling backwards.

Zim led them toward a tunnel that was straight ahead of them. Jared pushed what lifeforce he had into his legs, giving them a boost of speed and dexterity. He caught up to Zim, and then began passing her, closing in quickly on the tunnel ahead. He pushed off with his legs and jumped. In midair, Zim reached in front of him and swung her arm back, slamming him in the chest and sending him flying backwards. He slid across the ground, stopping at Thamuz and Caym's feet.

Thamuz—bearing the image of a middle-aged man—though still possessed of his vast, immortal strength, reached down and pulled Jared to his feet. Jared yanked his shoulder from Thamuz's grip and glared at him.

"What was that for?" he yelled over the rumbling, rubbing at his aching chest.

Zim ran toward him. "It's called saving your life!"

A piercing scream suddenly came from the tunnel he had nearly jumped in. Not a moment after it had, the Train of Souls came rushing out in all of its screeching glory and created a windstorm in its wake.

The train was as black as the smolder billowing from its smokestack, which looked like two top hats set brim upon brim—narrow at the top and bottom, and fat in the middle. The coal-black locomotive was as tall as a tree, and nearly just as wide as one. It went speeding off and screaming, and dove into another tunnel, even as its box cars continued streaming out of the one it had come from.

"We must move!" Zim yelled over the scream of the whistle. "The longer we wait, the faster the train becomes. Its winds will fling us about—"

"And throw us right under the train," Thamuz finished.

"We need to get closer to The Lake of Fire, which is that way," Caym said, pointing to the tunnel the train had come out of. The train's whistle blew again, but this time, the scream came echoing out from the tunnel behind them.

Jared looked at them all. "We need to choose a hole...*now!*"

"To the right of the train, and then up," Caym offered. "That'll get us closer to the lake below."

"Then there we go," Zim said, grabbing Jared's arm and taking off running with him.

Thamuz and Caym were right behind them, but by the sound of the scream-whistle, Jared thought, the train was, too. He glanced back and saw that he was right. Not a moment after turning his head, the Train of Souls came shooting out from the tunnel, heading directly for them. Its clouds of smoke covered the sky, dimming Wormwood's light. Though from the train's headlight, it cast a glaring white glow over them.

"Zim!" Jared yelled.

"I know!" She yanked him to the left.

A second later, the train came zooming behind them, narrowly missing them. It screamed! It bellowed! It shook the ground like an earthquake!

They were running back to where they had started, Jared saw. And with a glance to the left, he saw it was still zooming out of the first hole; it seemed unending.

Zim changed their direction again, pulling him to right. He glanced down at the tracks; they intersected every few feet, which meant that the train could come at them from every angle; and it was picking up speed, just as Zim said it would.

They turned left, and then right; and then right again, running further into the rail yard; and at each turn, there came the train from behind them, or from the side of them, or in front of them—blinding them with its headlight and threatening to run them down. They were moving deeper into the rail yard, but the train—it shaking the ground and its wake creating hurricane gusts—was becoming harder to dodge, even with their nimble, celestial feet.

In those scarce moments that the Train of Souls had appeared, it had dove down and up countless tunnels, and changed directions multiple times. Jared couldn't make sense of its pattern, if it had one at all. Though now, with its lines of never-ending cargo freights zooming behind them and to their right, and in front of them, they had an open avenue deeper into the rail yard.

"What about there?" Jared yelled to Zim, over the gusting winds and rumbling of the ground. He pointed to their left. Though, just then, the Train of Souls came rocketing up out of a hole to their right, heading directly for them. Its whistle blared as it zoomed past them. Its wake threatened to snatch them and bring them along for the ride. Jared groaned as he watched it cut-off their exit.

"No-no!" Zim yelled, pulling at him to run to where he had just suggested. Jared ran along with her. "There's still a gap." She nodded toward the two tunnels ahead of them. The closest one was to their left; the one the train was speeding out from. And the other was just above it, to the right, though with no room between them.

"If it flanks us from the other side, we're done!" Caym said, with a fierce sway of the head side-to-side.

"Not if we get there first," Jared yelled back, understanding what Zim was planning. If they could make it around the upper tunnel before the train came, they would have a clear shot to get further in the rail yard. Though if they couldn't, the Train of Souls would have them boxed in and at the mercy of its merciless winds, which were already pushing at them—sliding them backward—taking a step away from every three they took forward. If they were swept up in the winds, they would be tossed against or under the train; and regardless of how they hit it; they would be crushed in moments.

The Train of Souls screamed again, but suddenly, the cry became hollow. It was diving, Jared knew, just by the sound of its fading cry, which returned as echoes from the tunnels around them. But that also meant that the train could resurface anywhere.

They sprinted for the tunnel Jared had suggested. Thamuz and Caym drew up even with them, running side-by-side. They came to the tunnel at the same time, and began sprinting around it. As they neared the first track leading into the tunnel, the Train of Souls screamed and came rushing out of the tunnel to the right, heading straight for them.

"Tis' a bad omen!" Thamuz bemoaned, dashing past them.

"Concur!" Caym said, extending his hand to Thamuz.

Thamuz grabbed his hand and leapt the first track, and then spun, whipping Caym to the other side of the far track. Zim and Jared neared the first track just as the train neared the hole; it was a few hundred feet away and closing in by the moment. Zim grabbed a hold of Jared's hand and reached for Thamuz's. Thamuz took hold of her. And as he had done to Caym, he flung her, sending her twirling in the air, and Jared along with her. This time, Thamuz did not let go.

Zim cried out to Jared even before they landed. "*Pull!*"

Jared landed on his feet, and then yanked with every bit of strength he had. Despite Thamuz's illusion of being a middle-aged mortal, he was still Thamuz—dense as a boulder. But Zim and Jared, together in might, moved the mountain of a demon off of his feet, and yanked him toward them just as the train came to claim him, nicking the tips of his feet.

Jared, Zim, and Thamuz tumbled to the ground, and quickly righted themselves, knowing they had no time to waste celebrating surviving their close call or remaining flat-footed in shock that they had. In front of them were three more tunnels.

"We're going down before it comes up," Zim told them. She led them to the first hole and slid to a stop inches from its lip.

"How far down?" Jared asked, moving up next to her.

"Until we reach bottom," Thamuz quipped.

Caym smiled at Jared. "I don't carry angels."

Jared cocked his head. "I don't piggyback demons, either."

"And I don't nanny," Zim professed sharply, glaring at both.

"Nor do I," Thamuz growled. "Both of you shut your holes and jump."

Zim grabbed Jared's arm. "Wait! I don't have enough—" he began, but Zim leapt, pulling him into the tunnel. The train's echoing scream flowed up, as they careened down the tunnel. He yelled out 'lifeforce' over and again to Zim, trying to finish what he was trying to say, which was that he didn't have enough of it yet to fly. And then, he felt her pulling him close and wrapping her arm around his waist. He stopped yelling as she pressed his head against her chest.

"Rotukamak," she called out. Their plunge slowed at the sound of her word.

Jared held onto her tight and looked up. Caym and Thamuz had also slowed their descent and were drifting down right above them. The scream-whistle of the train echoed up from below. The heat was becoming hotter. The red glow of the rock walls darkened the further down they went.

The tunnel curved and finally leveled off. They landed, and then sprinted for the wall as the train screamed again, sounding closer this time. They lined up with their backs to the wall, though even then, they were only feet away from the tracks.

"Is this close enough to Sheol?" Jared asked Zim.

Zim looked up at the wall. Her illusionary, white face looked dark red under the glow of the cracked, crimson rock wall that oozed out brimstone. "I dare say so," she quipped, with a cock of the head. "Now we just need a weak spot."

"And soon, my lady," Caym said, leaning over and speaking to her. "The train fills all of the tunnels before it departs, and..." he looked at the tracks, "it is not here yet, and its speeding up by the moment. Not good at all, Zim...not good."

Thamuz stepped away from the wall and swung at it, pounding his arm against it. Chunks of rock came tumbling down. He moved forward and hit the wall again, breaking away more pieces of stone, searching for a weak spot. Jared and the others followed him, staying close as they could to the wall.

They moved quickly down the tunnel, stopping only for Thamuz to pound at the wall. With each blow of the train's whistle, Thamuz seemed to double his speed. The train's scream was growing louder. The grounding was quaking harder; and they were in its tunnel, with no way out.

Thamuz moved ahead and slammed his arm into a section of the wall whose rocks were crimson and bellowing clouds of yellow sulfur. Bigger chunks than before broke off and came tumbling down. He backed up and struck the same spot again. This time, foot-wide chunks of red-hot rock broke from the wall and tumbled at his feet. He backed away, crossing the tracks and hunching down like a linesman. The Train of Souls screamed from nearby.

"Make it count!" Caym called to him.

Thamuz's eyes turned black from corner-to-corner. "Dado loto nehu," he said, upon breath that came from his mouth in the form of black smoke. The smoke—his lifeforce—moved away from him and paused, and then came rushing back and seeped into his skin. He looked up at the wall as the wail of the train rung out and the tunnel began rumbling. He ran and hit the wall—shuddering it—managing to embed himself halfway into it.

Jared looked down the tunnel and saw the dark red glow of its walls beginning to lighten. Just then, the train let out a wail.

"Guys?" he called out nervously, as though they hadn't realized what was fast approaching.

Thamuz had already extracted himself from the wall and was already crouched, ready to charge it again. He huffed black mist from his nose like a bull that had been skewered and teased, and was ready to exact its revenge upon those responsible.

Thamuz bellowed as he ran for the wall.

He slammed into it. Red-hot rock sprayed out, followed by clouds of brimstone that came pouring through.

Thamuz, however, kept going through and tumbled out the other side. Zim and Caym ran for him, though Zim was faster, and caught of Thamuz at the ankle. Caym grabbed hold of her arm and anchored his other hand on the tunnel wall.

Jared ran over and stopped just shy of Caym's reach. Caym's face was contorted as he strained to keep Thamuz from tumbling down and away. Jared looked down the tunnel. The glare of the train's headlight was fast approaching. There was only one choice to make, he knew.

He channeled the lifeforce he had into his arms and legs, and grabbed hold of Caym's arm. "On three," Jared cried, and then began counting. "Three!" He yelled and heaved.

They moved Thamuz back up inches. Jared counted again; this time they all pulled and roared. They yanked Thamuz back across the threshold. Jared went tumbling backwards and across the tracks, and into the blinding light of the oncoming train.

"Run Jared!" Zim cried out, as the Train of Souls came screaming and bearing down on him.

Jared hopped to his feet and leapt into a run. He sprinted for the opening in the wall, where Caym and Thamuz were standing side-by-side. They leapt in together.

"Right behind you," Zim yelled, reaching out a hand to Jared.

He grabbed hold of her as the Train of Souls came speeding through the tunnel. She leapt through the hole, pulling him with her.

They fell into Sheol.

Below, coming up on them quickly, Jared saw the Lake of Fire and the millions of bodies writhing within it. The screams of The Damned rose up all around him...that is, until he crashed into it and was submerged beneath its liquid flames.

CHAPTER 14

Henrì slid the last bullet into the chamber, and then snapped the barrel back into place. He handed the gun to Phineas, grip end first. "It's all set," Henrì said, looking him in the eye.

Phineas took the gun and kept it low, below his waist, and aimed away from his body. "Is the safety off? It has a safety, right?"

Henrì nodded. "Yes and yes."

"All I have to do is pull the trigger?"

Henrì grimaced. "Hopefully it doesn't come to that."

They were in the flower garden. Dorthea was next to Thaddeus by the patio doors. Chris and Olivia were just a few steps ahead of them. Henrì walked over and stood by Olivia.

"I hope this works," he whispered to her.

"I can't watch this!" Dorthea blurted, shaking her head. She turned around and went inside.

"I'm coming wit'cha, honey," Thaddeus uttered, following right behind her and closing the door.

Henrì turned to Olivia and Chris. "Anybody else?" Olivia covered her eyes with both hands. Chris shrugged and nodded. "You ready, old man?" Phineas pursed his lips and nodded.

Henrì looked at the gun; it was quivering in Phineas's nervous hand. He didn't blame him a bit for being terrified. He wondered if he could do it; could he cross his fingers and put a gun to his head, and pray for the best. Though still, he thought, if the suicide-trick to rouse the celestial failed, there was going to be more than just a gory mess to clean up. Without Phineas, there was no way of stopping the demon that protects the killer, Blain Hopps. And it would only be a matter of time before Yikan tracked them down and killed them all, and took the tome.

The electricity had come back on, though just long enough for the media to transmit grainy images of the horrors in England. *London was destroyed!* Yikan had turned the Kingdom's nuclear bomb back on them, detonating it above their beloved city, flattening half of it and engulfing the other half in fire, killing millions instantly.

The other nations of the world received Yikan's holocaustic message loud and clear. The president interrupted the breaking news about London to address the American people while he had a chance. His message was clear, though unreservedly troublesome.

America was now under martial law, the president had announced. The military was on the highest alert. He vowed that America and its allies would track down the mad terrorist known as Yikan, and make him pay dearly for his murderous deeds. He even boldly compared him to Hitler, though on steroids. For all of the president's bravado, Henrì knew it was hollow, even before the power went off again and shut down the greatest nation on earth. Yikan was the one in control now; the president, and every other world leader just hadn't realized it yet. The only hope the world had now, Henrì thought, was in a preacher about to shoot himself in the head.

Electricity was the blood of modern civilization, Henrì knew. And without it, society would eventually revert to the Stone Age. There was no weapon that man possessed—satellite guided bombs, drones, warplanes, missiles—or any means of offense or defense that could stop Yikan—; that had been proven in the fires and ash and screams of London. What billions and trillions worth of war machines could not do, Henrì prayed Phineas and a revolver could; which was to find a way to bring Jared back and stop the madness, and the madman.

"Don't pull the trigger too quick," Henrì blurted.

"I don't wanna pull the trigger at all, to tell ya the truth," Phineas said, glancing at it. "I don't think fast or slow is gonna matter much anyway. Either the celestial comes or it don't."

He gave Phineas a stalwart nod, even as he clenched his teeth and fists. Phineas brought the gun to his temple. Henrì turned his head and looked at Olivia, not wanting to be a witness if their plan went wrong. He expected to see her looking away like he was, or at least covering her eyes as she had been. Instead, she was looking at him, and smiling, and that's when he heard the click of the gun, though didn't hear a bang.

He turned and looked at Phineas. Phineas was still standing there with the gun to his head. He shrugged at Henrì. Phineas closed his eyes, grimaced, and pulled the trigger again. Again nothing. There was no bang, just a dull click.

"Is it jammed up?" Phineas asked.

"Can't be," Henrì said.

"The bullets too old?"

Henrì walked over. He took the gun from Phineas and opened the chamber; the bullets were all seated properly. He spun the chamber around and then pushed it back it.

"There's nothing wrong with it." He pointed it in the air and pulled the trigger. It fired with a bang—without a hitch. Henrì ducked and nearly dropped it, not expecting it to fire. From within the house, they heard Thaddeus blurt out a startled *'Lord Jesus!'*

"It's okay, everybody," Phineas yelled to Dorthea and Thaddeus. He turned and spoke to Henrì. "Maybe the celestial won't let me do it."

"They will, but I will not," Olivia said, though it was not her voice coming from her mouth. It was another's voice...a male's; it trembled with authority. Phineas and Henrì looked at one another with mirrored puzzled expressions.

Chris smiled at Olivia and backed away from her. She returned his gesture with a tilt of her head and a toothy grin.

"Hi," Chris said.

"Hello, Christopher Knopfitter," the male replied from Olivia's mouth.

Henrì and Phineas walked over and stood next to Chris. Henrì looked into Olivia's eyes, though knew it wasn't her looking back at him.

"Who are you?" Henrì asked, nearly whispering it.

"I am Gabriel—an angel of The Father."

"Where's Olivia?"

Gabriel lolled Olivia's head to the side and formed a smile upon her face. "She is asleep. She has a beautiful soul, Henrì. You fear her being taken from you—and you should. You should all fear what may come, for what has been wrought upon this earth has stirred The Father, The Lamb, and The Ghost." Gabriel looked over at the patio doors. Dorthea and Thaddeus were looking out at them with puzzled expressions. Gabriel extended his hand toward the door. It unlatched and opened at his command. "Come out Thaddeus, Dorthea…please." Gabriel smiled and beckoned them over.

Dorthea held Thaddeus's hand the entire way, gripping it close to her side. "*Olivia?*"

"Gabriel," he replied plainly.

"Gabriel who?" Thaddeus asked, his face a comedy mask, one side slack with doubt and the other raised in hope.

"I am the angel who whispered unto Mary, and to Daniel, and to Zachariah—he too," Gabriel said. "Though this night, I come bearing grave tidings." He looked at all of them, pausing at each one, and slowly tilting his head to the side and slowly back again. "You all have such faith." His voice became firm. "You will need it." He looked at Dorthea. "Miel attempts to return to earth; to escape that infernal realm that is Hell."

Dorthea went weak in the knees. Thaddeus caught her and held her steady. "He's alive," she muttered, unbelievingly.

"He is," Gabriel said. "Though all of Hell is now poised to fall upon him." He looked up at the star-dotted night. "Mekka-Nuat has heard you, Christopher Knopfitter." He pointed to a hazy, faint light; it was barely even a blur. "There spins The Great Wheel, Mekka-Nuat—a Burning One. *It* has pierced space and time with its thousand eyes and has peered into Hell. It has seen your son—alive; and in the company of demons; so sayeth the Burning One."

Henrì's face went slack. "What do you mean, 'in the company of demons?'"

"They are helping him, as he helps them," Gabriel replied, sounding as though he questioned his own words.

"Helping him?" Thaddeus blurted.

"Mekka-Nuat has seen it," Gabriel assured him. "They journey to Phenóx—Lucifer's realm."

"He's gonna try to get back the same way he went," Chris said. "He came with a demon, so he's going to try and leave with one." Gabriel smiled and nodded affirmatively.

Henrì waved his hands in protest. "Wait-wait-wait! What do the demons get out of it? If they're helping him get back to earth, what did he give them in exchange for it?"

All eyes turned on Gabriel.

"I do not know," Gabriel replied. "But there has been great magic cast in Hell as of late—that we do know. Though, what dark evil has been cast in the Northlands of Hell—where it came from—not even Mekka-Nuat can speak to, for it was hidden from *its* thousand eyes. Only the demon, Chax, —Lord of the Northlands—remains possessed of power great enough to hide from Mekka-Nuat. Pray mortals…pray that Miel has not signed a pact with a Fallen One, for there is only subterfuge and deceit, and doom that awaits he who does."

"But he's trying to get back," Phineas said.

Gabriel looked to the night sky. "The demons were once the pagan gods of old. Though now, they wage war amongst one another. Astaroth has usurped power from two of the Lords of Hell, leaving only one, Chax—the greatest of them all still standing. Astaroth seeks to conqueror Phenóx. And next, he will come for earth and all upon it—that is the fear of the Celestial Host. Even if Miel survives his journey to Phenóx, he still must face its bitter cold and the master of that realm."

Dorthea gasped and covered her mouth. Her eyes welled with tears.

"He's down there with Satan himself," Thaddeus said, shaking his head. "Good Lord help us all."

"The Satan…The Prince of Darkness…The Morning Star," Gabriel said. "Lucifer—The Morning Star—has gone by many names since the birth of time."

"Help us," Dorthea pleaded of him. "There has to be some thing you can do. We—we can't do this alone. Jared never meant for any of this to happen. He loves God with all his heart."

"I know."

"He was trying to stop Yikan," she explained, her voice cracking.

"Yes…the Egyptian."

"And he was going to set things back right."

"And fell into their snare, and became trapped in Hell—I know this, too," he assured her. He stopped and looked at her oddly. "You ask for my assistance, though I have already assisted you, when I should not have. I ask you…does Phineas Boremon still live? 'T'was only by my hand that he does."

"You stopped the gun from going off?" Henrì asked, looking down at the gun in his hands. He looked up at Phineas and suddenly realized how lucky the old man was.

"Nigiel, Palis, and Oriziel—they all; they one—would not have spared his life," Gabriel informed them.

Phineas's mouth went slack. "I—I would have…I almost done—"

"Killed yourself?" Gabriel nodded. "Indeed, mortal."

"Then you *have* come to help us," Dorthea professed.

"Though I have kept the preacher from harm, I cannot assist Miel," he said. "Already, I have done too much…as has the Great Wheel. Man must choose his path, freely so—good or evil; Heaven or Hell; The Father or Lucifer."

Henrì spoke up. "If Yikan gets his way, we're all doomed, Gabriel. We won't have to make a choice between good and evil. It'll be made for us. This will become Yikan's world. Jesus will never be able to return if Yikan unbalances the covenant."

"You are trying to persuade me? That is—*admirable*," Gabriel said, giving him a pitiful smile. His voice went cold and hard, like the color grey—void of any warmth. "I see it, Henrì; I see the world burning in your thoughts. Mortals will fall by the millions—and already have in London—; and then there will be billions more to follow. You will become slaves to a creature who thinks himself a god." He looked at Chris. "A world you never knew existed has been revealed to you in so short a time. And in that span, you have changed greatly, Christopher. Do you remember what you told Jared…that you knew you were meant for something far greater than yourself? *That* something greater is The Father, though you did not know it then, though you do now." He leaned down and whispered in Chris's ear, who then began smiling and nodding.

Gabriel stood straight and lightly bowed his head at Chris. "Farewell mortals. Perhaps we will meet again, when I come with The Lamb and the Hosts of Heaven to wage war upon The Fallen for the last and final time; that is, if Miel can set wrong back to right. Though if he fails—if salvation is taken away from mankind—then this is farewell forever, and ever, and ever…Amen." Gabriel turned to Henrì. "*Now catch me!*"

Like a ghost, Gabriel rose out of Olivia's body and transformed into a true, flesh and bone celestial, clad in just a stark white loincloth. His skin and eyes and lips were darker than the night sky he rose into. From his back, shiny, black feathered wings unfurled and began flapping, sending him higher, fanning a gentle breeze laced with myrrh over Henrì and the others.

Olivia went limp. Henrì caught her and rested her body on his. She struggled to open her eyes, and eventually did, and looked into his.

"He…Gabriel told me to wake up, and then he said goodbye," Olivia said, her voice drowsy.

Henrì squeezed her tight and kissed her forehead. "It's OK, honey… your safe. I got you."

Olivia looked at him strangely. "I'm fine, mon chére. I feel like I just slept the best sleep of my life." She looked at the others. "What did Gabriel say?"

There was a pause amongst all. And then they all looked at Chris.

"He told me that I was right," Chris said, and then looked at Dorthea and said it again. "We need to work on the tome. And I'm going to need Olivia when she's feeling better—"

"I'm ready now," she said, pushing away from Henrì and standing on her own.

"She needs to rest first," Henrì insisted, giving Chris a foul stare.

Olivia grasped Henrì's chin and slowly turned his head toward her. She smiled, though it was of sorrow. "We don't have time, mon chére."

"She's right," Chris said. "And if you're ready to get at it, then I am, too. We're gonna need you, too, Dorthea."

"Me? I—I…." She looked at everyone innocently. "I told you I'll do whatever it takes to get Jared back, but this is beyond me…magic, sorcery…." She shrugged.

"But God is great," Olivia said to her.

Dorthea nodded. "Amen to that. But—"

"That's his name, Dorthea," Olivia said, bobbing her head. "Yes-yes, mon chére. Gabriel means, 'God is great'. You always say that God is a good God, and that you can trust him to lead you right…to lead *you*, so you can lead us. I think that's why Gabriel came." Chris bobbed his head in agreement. "There must be some thing you're suppose to do to help us."

"God is a good God," Dorthea said softly, and then began muttering. "God is good; God is my strength; I am God's strength." Her eyes darted about, and then finally settled on Chris. "It's time we got this tome figured out, so we can get my boy back." Her voice became resolute. "We're going to get this done. And when we do—God be my witness—we're going to send Yikan straight to Hell where he belongs."

CHAPTER 15

The Damned were burning all around Jared.

He and Zim had submerged beneath the liquid flames of the Lake of Fire after jumping in from hundreds of feet above; that was when they lost grip of each other's hand and became separated amongst the burning bodies. Jared surfaced in a sea of flames that moved and behaved like water. And all around him, The Damned writhed and wailed in agony... thousand of them, pushing and shoving at him, all the while clawing at their own flesh, which was being seared to the bone, only to have it grow back anew and begin the burning process all over again. The fire felt hot on his celestial skin, but it did not burn it, not like it did The Damned, where it scorched flesh and charred bone.

Grey, crescent-shaped fishing boats with rectangular black sails moved through the fire, dragging wrought iron nets along either side of their hulls and swooped up The Damned. Demons bearing the colors of Astaroth hauled up their burning bounty like fish; their fire-roasted faces were pressed against the netting; blackened limbs poked through the holes. Others souls had scaled the red-hot rocks on the shorelines to either side of Jared, though even there, Astaroth's demons stood in wait for them with whips, herding them back into the lake with deft snaps on their roasted flesh. Above the lake was a ceiling of rock that was nearly obscured by billowing clouds of rancid, yellow brimstone. The rock-domed lake seemed endless, as did the number of souls who filled it.

Jared searched for Zim amongst The Damned, remembering that she was still disguised in her illusion, which made the task all the more difficult. He called out for her, and then turned toward the shore and called for her again, this time louder, trying to raise his voice above the screams of those burning around him. He turned the other way, and felt a hand suddenly grab his shoulder, pulling at him, dragging him back under the flames.

"*Get off!*" Jared heard a voice cry out.

He turned around and saw Zim swimming toward him, though he also caught sight of the one who had grabbed him. It was a male soul whose face was a black and red sheet of fire-scorched skin; one eye was missing, and in its socket, flames danced.

"*Help me!*" the soul wailed, pawing at him. His teeth were like crushed rock; he had chewed half of his tongue off on one side; it looked like raw meat that had been hacked away with a dull knife.

Zim swam up and swung just to the side of Jared's face, catching the soul in the cheek. The soul released his grip and sunk beneath the flames.

"Knock them away!" she shouted at Jared.

"There's so many of them," he yelled in frustration and disgust, pushing a soul off who came screeching toward him on the right, and then shoving another away who quickly took its place and was trying to crawl over his head to get out of the flames.

"The sins of man are many…and vile," Thamuz called out, as he waded over, pushing The Damned away four and five at a time with swipes of his massive arms.

Caym bobbed up to the surface on Jared's other side. He spat liquid fire from his mouth and gagged. *Euuuugh!* His face…cast in the illusion of an emaciated black man…contorted in disgust.

"I'd rather swim in sewage than with these foul creatures," Caym decried.

"What now?" Jared asked Zim.

She turned around and looked past him, and then nodded. He turned and saw one of the fishing boats heading their way.

"That one," Zim said. She began moving toward it, treading the water and knocking away souls, creating a small, temporary path through the flames. She called over her shoulder to him. "Stay close."

Jared did. And behind him, pressed against his backside, was Caym; and in back of him was Thamuz. They were heading away from the shore and toward the outer reaches of the lake. Between tossing souls off to the side and peeling their frantic, desperate hands away from his body, he caught glimpses of the fiery, Hell of legend.

At the mouth of the inlet on the right was a black volcano spewing yellow brimstone into the air and gushing dark, red lava into the lake from its side vent. From the opening of the inlet and outward, the lake spread out as far as he could see; and upon those endless waters there seemed to him an endless supply of The Damned, and hundreds of ships passing through them, fishing them out.

"*Drop net!*" a demon called out from the boat heading toward them.

"This way, Jared," Zim said, directing him toward the side of the boat.

It was the same idea the hordes of The Damned had in mind. They were all desperately trying to be caught in the nets and pulled from the flames, in hope of respite from their agony, totally unsuspecting of the horrors yet to come for them. Just then, a soul latched his arm around Jared's neck.

"*Help me! Kill me!*" the man shrieked over and again, pleading for Jared to end his misery.

Jared peeled the man's arm away from his neck, though in the process, he snapped the charred, brittle bone off at the elbow. The soul howled like a banshee, and then flung himself back into the flames, where he floated, writhing in agony, only to be submerged by others who were quick to take his place, for it was one step closer to being swept up in the nets and out of the fire.

"*Repent!*" a voice called from the oncoming boat.

Jared looked up. A male demon was standing at the edge looking down at the souls with disgust. The souls howled their confessions to him. They confessed to murder and thievery, and to envy and spitefulness, and to foul perversions, that even speaking them seemed sin enough to damn one to torment for all eternity.

"Now you confess?" the pale demon taunted, and then smiled at them. "It's too late for that. You are damned." He pointed at them haphazardly. "You and you and you...you're all mine, for all time. You took a gamble with your brief, mortal lives and have lost the wager. Go ahead...cry out to The Father and The Lamb all you want; they can't help you now." He called to the soldiers behind him. "Let's get them in."

Zim was by the net. She reached behind and grabbed Jared by the arm, pulling him next to her. She turned around and grabbed the two souls in front of her that were trying to crawl into the net, and pulled them away from it. She climbed into the net and turned again, taking Jared by the hand and pulling him in. Caym jumped in right on top of him. Thamuz flung his body in next, splashing fire over the other souls already in, inducing new wails of agony from them.

The pale-skinned soldier on the boat raised his arm and twirled his finger around in a circle. "Ready on the left!" Another demon called out, signaling that they were. "Ready on the right!" The reply was affirmative. "Raise them up!"

The nets began rising. Jared and the others—along with The Damned —began rolling toward the middle of the net as it sagged. Blackened arms, hands, legs, and even heads protruded through the holes of the net and dripped liquid-fire back into the lake.

"Hey ho!" a soldier cried out, as the nets came to a jarring halt.

"Bring her to port, you *soul-wranglers*," a black-skinned demon ordered. He was standing in the middle of the deck with a grim look on his face. "We have many more souls to net. The more we load on the train and get to the Westlands, the sooner Phenóx falls."

"Aye, captain," the soldiers replied, working the ropes of the nets to balance their bounty evenly on both sides.

"Give it your all," the captain commanded, "and the duke will give you back your godhood—that is your right! It is *our* right. We soul-wranglers will reclaim our dominion over every sea and ocean, and every waterway that runs across the earth. "

The soldiers manning the sails turned them into the heat-borne breeze and began making their way toward shore. They arrived at port and released their goods on the wharf, where Jared and the others tumbled out, rolling over each other. Now that the souls were out of the flames and their skins were renewing, their screams had waned to whimpering and crying.

Jared stood and looked out onto the lake. There were hundreds of fishing boats upon it; hundreds more were heading toward the shore with nets full and nearly dragging in the water; and even more boats—the ones that had just deposited their bounty on the wharf—were already headed back out for more.

Whip-wielding soldiers were waiting for them on the wharf and quickly surrounded them. They began lashing the souls.

"*Get in line!*" one of them barked, and slung his whip at Jared, catching him just below the eye.

"Jesus!" Jared yelped, covering his eye.

The solider that had struck him smiled and walked over; white fangs protruded from his mouth and extended nearly to his chin. He grabbed Jared by the top of the head and stared into his eyes. Jared felt the creature mentally pushing into his mind, delving and searching for *that sin that did him in*, but then, he saw the soldier's brown eyes turn dark green, almost black, and knew it was Lady Pnemoxsis's enchantment taking hold of him. Hopefully, he thought.

The soldier blinked several times, and then began to smile. "You went and poisoned your wife," he said. "Killed the old bitch for the money." The soldier raised his brow. "Told those poor kids that mommy just got real sick, and now she's in Heaven. Well...chances are she is, but you're not. You're a long, long way from there, Theodore Cantor, —*oh yes, you are*. Thought you were going to get away with it, huh? You really thought there was nothing waiting for you on the other side...just darkness, just nothing—nonexistence." He cocked his head to the side. "Surprised you, didn't we?" He nodded slowly and fixed his lips taught like a schoolmaster, who had been born and bred on the principal of never spare the rod, lest the child be spoiled. "You've just begun to feel the burn for what you've done, you vile piece of flesh. We're going to burn you until your ash. And when you come back, we're going to tear you apart from the inside—we're going to make you suffer. You will worship at the altar of the god of *regret*, for forever, and forever. *Now repent!*"

"I...." Jared began.

"'I' what?"

"I poisoned...*her?*" Jared said, almost innocently.

The soldier shook his head and clicked his tongue. "Another reluctant one." He palmed Jared's face and shoved his head. "Good then. Your kind burns the hottest. You'll make the Train of Souls scream loud."

The soldiers lined the souls up—six deep—by the sting of the whip. Jared, Zim, Caym, and Thamuz pushed against The Damned, positioning themselves in the same line. They were then driven toward two bronze doors that were built into the side of a glowing, red-hot cliff. Perched atop of the cliff was a sprawling palace of black stone. From its square-shaped towers, banners flew bearing the image of a lion in profile.

"That is the den of King Purson," Zim whispered to Jared, seeing him staring up at it. "Next to Astaroth, it is Purson who is most deserving of death. Had he not given authority of Sheol to Astaroth, none of us would be here, including you."

"Well, you know what they say about the enemy of my enemy?"

She grinned. "I do, indeed."

They were herded through the gates, which led into a tunnel lit by torchlight on either side. From there, after traveling for a mile under the constant lash of the whip, they came out the other side and were greeted by a familiar, if not haunting sight.

The Train of Souls was in station. The locomotive was steaming; black smoke billowed from its stack, tainting the hot air with the sharp odor of burn. The unholy train had been run hard, though its duty was far from over. Down to the left, Jared saw thousands of The Damned being led up ramps and into the freight cars like cattle. Their group of The Damned was turned and herded in that same direction.

Zim looked around and checked for prying ears and eyes, and then spoke to Jared from the side of her mouth. "This is good," she told him. "The Damned that are housed near the front are the first to die. If we were with them, we would also." Jared darted his eyes toward her. "The fire from the lake is one thing; it is a nuisance to us. But the fire in the belly of the train will incinerate even our flesh."

"Halt!" a voice called out from behind them.

Jared and the others turned and looked, not sure whether to continue trudging along, or to obey the deep call of authority. A soldier in silver armor that was adorned with intertwined, red and white swirls at the shoulder, approached from their rear on horseback. The call to stop was given by those herding them and was accompanied by a burst of smartly snapped whips to see that they did it immediately.

The silver-armored soldier rode up to the one who had interrogated and accosted Jared. He leaned over and spoke to him for a moment—soft and low—; and then raised upright. He nodded deferentially, and turned his horse around and galloped off.

The soldier—the leader of the group—turned around and glared at The Damned. "*Traitors in our midst!*" he seethed. The *soul-wranglers* glanced at one another with puzzled expressions, but then mimicked their leader's scowl and began inspecting The Damned closely for those who did not belong amongst them. "It seems that Chax and his band of deposed lords are finally making their play. Who else would be foolish—and desperate enough—to break into Sheol?"

Jared went stiff with panic. They had been found out, though not yet discovered. He didn't need to calculate their odds now, for they were completely surrounded by the enemy. Lady Pnemoxsis's enchantment had worked thus far, even up close, even when the soldier had sought out his sins. But now, the soldiers knew exactly what, and whom, they were looking for.

The lead soldier began walking around the ragged, fire-scarred group of The Damned. Jared's lifeforce began racing as the soldiers weaved in and out of the lines, peering deep into their eyes, searching for Chax's infiltrators. And then, suddenly, he felt a brushing against his fingers from Zim. His lifeforce slowed at her reassuring touch.

"You've already lost, Chax," the soldier said, staring at them as he walked around them. "Where do you think you're sending your dogs to, Chax? Either way, it doesn't matter. Your traitors will burn in the belly of the train before this *pass* is over. *Move them to the front!*"

"My lord, there is no more room in the front," a soldier told him.

"There is now," he said, with a cocky grin. "We're going to burn this lot, and the next fifty after them. If Chax's traitors are here, the train will burn them just the same."

The soldier he spoke to bowed his head, and then promptly raised his whip. He walked to the front of the line and snapped it, hitting one of The Damned in the face, splitting his cheek in two. "Turn it around...all you." The Damned did as commanded. "The train is going to burn hotter than it ever has before."

They were marched to the ramp of the freight car behind the train's engine. At the top of the ramp, looking down at them, Jared saw a demon that looked as though it had been dragged from a prehistoric swamp. It had the legs, arms, head, and even tail of an alligator, though his had needle-tip spikes on either side near the tip. And instead of two, bulging dark green eyes with vertical irises, the creature had four of them...two on each side...one set atop of the other.

One of the soldiers who had herded them over ran up the ramp, bowed his head and reported to the swamp-demon. "The souls you requested, Lord Flagon."

Flagon clenched his claws and rested them atop of his shimmering, blue shendyt. "Traitors!" he called down to The Damned, "I know you're here somewhere." He inspected The Damned gathered below him at the edge of the ramp, and then looked up and over them, toward the tunnel they had come through. "Or...are you still in the Lake of Fire?" He turned his attention back to the hundreds of souls below him. "You think you will not be revealed? *Hmm?*" He began pacing back and forth, scraping his clawed-feet across the metal floor of the freight car. "Chax and his witch may hide you from my eyes with their sorcery—*for now.* Though, sooner or later, I will discover who you are. And when I do, I shall catch you, and then burn you like a soul. Even celestials can burn if the fire be hot enough!"

Flagon signaled the soldiers with a twirl of his scaled hand. They turned to The Damned and began marching them up the ramp. They stopped each line at the top of the ramp and inspected them before letting them pass into the freight car.

Jared's line neared the top of the ramp. Flagon was standing off to the left, next to a pale blue, female demon with yellow eyes. Unlike the others around her who wore armor, she wore a blood red robe. Jared lowered his head as his lined moved up to be examined.

The soldier at the top held out his arm. "Halt, sinners!" He walked in front of them, pausing and looking each of them before moving on to the next. He called for them to proceed—to follow the other souls into the freight car. As Jared's line was about to step across the threshold, Flagon suddenly tromped forward and stopped them.

"Lady Nura, come here," Flagon said, to the blue demon. She sauntered over. Flagon pointed at Zim. "This one strikes me ill. Know her! *See her!*"

Nura positioned herself in front of Zim. She slowly moved her hand in front of Zim's face and cocked her head. Her tone was unnervingly cordial. "What is your name?"

"Diana," Zim replied.

Nura stared into Zim's eyes, even as she narrowed hers. "Confess."

"I enticed men from their marital bed," Zim said. "I've destroyed many lives to feed my desire."

"Truth, my lady?" Flagon asked.

Nura closed her eyes, and again passed her hand in front of Zim's face. "Yes," she uttered, and then looked at Zim. "She's a dark soul. She is not the one you seek, my lord. I am sure of it."

Flagon pointed at Zim and smiled, displaying rows of knife-sharp teeth "I like you much, my dear. You'll burn hot, indeed."

Flagon moved on to the next soul, and the next one after that one, picking them at random and having the blue-skinned demon read the thoughts of those he found suspect. The inspections and interrogations continued for some time. Flagon seemed determined to find the traitors, though finally, without finding a single one, he relented and allowed them to enter the freight car.

The soldiers herded them into the cargo hold, and then funneled them through a set of doors leading to the locomotive. Jared felt the heat suddenly double inside the black engine room. It was not like the heat of the Lake of Fire, which was hot, though tolerable to his celestial skin.

The heat now upon him had a fury to it that he felt in his bones and that pulled at his skin, drawing it taut. Hanging from the black, steaming ceiling was a large brass bell. Against the far wall there were cages—metal pens—, which the soldiers began funneling them into. Jared, Zim, and the others in his line, were about to be led into a pen, when one of the soldiers leading them through stopped the line and gave them a strange look.

"None of them are enchanted," he remarked, and then looked around the room. He turned to the soldier next to him. "Where are those slimy *enchanters?*"

The other soldier replied with a shrug. "Lord Flagon stopped the loading to search for the traitors. They should have been enchanted then."

"And yet, they are not."

"We'll have to do it ourselves until the enchanters come."

The soldier looked around at the hundreds of The Damned crowding in and grumbled. "That's a great deal of lifeforce to enchant them all."

"If we don't, and the souls see the first pen drop, there will be mayhem," the other warned. "The souls will go insane, and then we'll have a real mess on our hands." He sighed. "Go and see what's taking the enchanters so long. Tell them to get their greasy legs in here before I turn them all into calamari."

The soldier hustled off through the corridor they had come through. The other, who was standing in front of Jared, gave him a weary stare. He snapped his fingers in front of Jared's face. A plume of white smoke snaked out from his finger and thumb, which touched Jared's forehead and vanished.

"There-there now—go on," he said to Jared; all that was missing was an accompanying, patronizing pat on the head. He moved on to Caym and snapped his fingers in front of him, sending out another plume of enchanted smoke.

Jared darted his eyes at Caym, confused about what the soldier had supposedly done to him, as he felt nothing at all, thanks to Lady Pnemoxsis's enchantment. Caym began grasping at the air in front of his face, as though something was there. The soldier that had cast the enchantment had already moved on to the next soul, but then he stopped and turned, and looked back at Jared with a furrowed brow. He came back and stood in front of him.

He nodded at Jared. "Go ahead, sinner," he urged, pointing at the air in front of Jared's face. "There it is. Reach for the cup."

Jared glanced at Zim for guidance. She looked straight ahead, though from the side, he saw her bob her head slightly. He looked at Caym again; he was still grasping at the air. Jared reached for where the soldier had pointed.

"That's it," the soldier urged. "Get your cup...*if you can.*"

"Water!" Caym blurted. "Give me water."

"See?" the soldier said to Jared, and then smiled at Caym approvingly. "Be a good little sinner for once in your life."

"Water?" Jared mumbled, reaching for the air.

The soldier smirked. "There you go."

Jared sighed as the guard moved on, continuing down the row, enchanting one damned soul after another. Jared leaned forward and chanced a look down the row. Once enchanted, he saw The Damned wobble on their feet, and began reaching out in front of them, as though something was actually there.

"What's going on Zim," Jared muttered.

Zim checked the row to make sure no guards were near, and then leaned over to him. "It is The Damned's greatest wish denied," she whispered. "They see a cup of water in front of them...just within their grasp. Though, it is only an illusion to keep them docile for what is to come next."

"And that is...."

"Trust me," she said. "You don't really want to know. And you certainly don't want to find out first hand."

Once their row was enchanted, they were shuttled over to the pens, which had no door or gate to it. Jared followed Zim inside and looked around at The Damned who were filing in, grasping at their cups, begging for just a sip of the imaginary water; and he realized, there was no point of locking them in at all; they were far too preoccupied with their cups of water; and now that the heat was growing hotter, it only encouraged their efforts to obtain it.

The rising heat began stinging his eyes, and already had heated his bones. And he knew what happens to meat when the bone gets hot; it was a trick that Thaddeus always used while barbequing. *You get that bone good and hot, and it'll cook that meat from the inside out. You do it like that, boy...and you got some juicy meat on yo' hands.*

"Finally!" one of the guards called out, turning and looking toward the corridor. "The squids decided to finally show up, eh?"

From through the corridor came a squad of hovering demons, who, from their waist down, had muddy-pink tentacles like a squid. From the waist up, however, both male and female enchanters were dark blue, nearly black, as was the mists they exuded from their nether regions. They spread out across the room, draping The Damned in their enchantments. Once enchanted, The Damned began reaching for their imaginary cups, forgetting all else around them, even ignoring the rising heat.

More of The Damned began crowding into the pen that Jared, Zim, Caym, and Thamuz were in. They pushed The Damned back and made a small spot for themselves in the corner near the front. Now that the souls were no longer roasting in the Lake of Fire, their begging and pleading sounded much different to Jared. Now their cries were tinged with hope.

"*I nearly had it—I did!*" a soul bemoaned from nearby, he having just swiped at the air. "*I could feel it on my hand.*" He did it again, and again, licking his hands after every attempt, as though by some miracle a drop cool, crystal clear water had fallen on it.

"I touched mine!" a woman claimed. She pointed at the air in front of her nose and began weeping. "It was so cold...*so wet.*"

"I got it!" another screamed. She formed her hands, as though she were actually holding the cup. She brought it to her mouth and proceeded to drink from it. She smiled victoriously; her eyes glazed over with madness.

Two men began slinging blows at one another. "Get away from my cup, you sick bastard!" the one said, punching the other dead in the eye.

The assaulted one spun with the punch and came back around, and slapped the other smartly across the face, knocking him a step back. "Rapist!" he seethed.

"Touch mine again and I'll rip your throat out…*with my teeth*," the other promised, refusing to back down, and then swiped at the air and grimaced as he came up empty-handed again.

"Yeah…I'm sure you would, you murderer!"

"Screw you, pervert."

The two men were soon back tussling and slapping and punching one another, as were a few others. However, the vast majority of The Damned was fixated on their own cups and paid no heed to those arguing and fighting. The Damned seemed to try every trick to get that precious cup of water. They reached under it and from the sides it, and then from above. Some paused after each attempt, studying it, trying to outwit it. Others had simply given up and stared at it longingly, or with contempt, or both.

"All aboard!" A soldier near the corridor announced. Two other soldiers promptly closed the doors, sealing the room.

The Train of Souls' whistle screamed. The train lurched, jerking them all forward. A soldier with the head of a brown bear—and girth, too, — stepped into the middle of the room and raised his left paw. He called out the order. "To your posts!"

A cadre of soldiers split into groups of two and double-timed it over to the wall that was opposite of the pens. There, on the floor across from each pen, was a tall black lever, which they each took hold of, one on each side. They looked over at their bear-faced commander, waiting for his next order.

The brass bell above began to sway and rang out a bone-rattling bong. "Box one…*drop!*" the commander called out.

The two soldiers at the far end pulled their lever back, but the sound of metal cranking on metal came from the pen opposite them—as did the screams that followed, as the floor beneath The Damned's feet dropped away and flames shot up where they had once been. The Damned in the pens next to them paid no attention to the cacophony of screams; they were far too preoccupied in gaining hold of their water.

The soldiers pulled the lever forward, raising the floor back and muffling the shrieks of The Damned now below it.

Jared turned to Zim. "Is that the...?"

"The firebox," she confirmed. "You must feed the Train of Souls what it desires; and it desires souls...many of them." She pointed to the corridor they had come through. More of The Damned was being funneled through it, enchanted, and then led over to the empty pen that had just dumped its livestock into the fire-belly of the train. "And if we don't get out of here, the Train of Souls will turn us to ash also."

As the train began picking up speed, the soldiers paused in their duties and began casting spells over themselves, adhering their boots to the floor. The bell rang out and stopped, and then rang again. The call from the commander came right after.

"Box two and three!" The soldiers pulled the floors away with a tug of the lever, and as they did, more of the cup-reaching damned were already being lined up outside of the pen, ready to take their place.

The bell rang again, and then again, and for a short while it continued on ringing. "We're on a run!" the commander bellowed. "Lord Flagon wants the train to run hot enough to melt the tracks, I see. And that means one thing.... *It's time for war!*" The soldiers cried out in preemptive victory. The commander turned around to the soldiers manning the levers. "Ready the entire left side!"

The soldiers mounted their switches. Zim looked at Jared and the others with a steely glare. "It's time to fight."

"If we conjure our swords, our illusions will fall away," Thamuz reminded her.

"The moment we step out of this pen, they're going to know who we are anyway," Jared remarked.

"Then I hope you're ready for a fight, angel," Caym said, with wry glance his way.

"Jared," Zim said, "stay behind me. You are not ready for battle—not yet."

"No problem there," Jared said.

"If you *are* forced to fight, remember what I told you," Thamuz said. "When I swing, I do not miss." He nodded toward the doorway. "Now run!"

Zim ran for the doorway just as the call came for the pens to drop. Jared was right at her backside; Caym and Thamuz were at his, pushing him forward. Zim and Jared crossed the threshold just as the floor to their pen opened, sending The Damned down to their fiery doom. Caym leapt across the threshold as it fell away. Thamuz—belying his massive girth—jumped onto the bars of the pen to his left, and from there, sprang off of them and across the gap, and out of the way of the flames that came roaring up.

The soldiers stopped, turned, and stared at them. The commander, who was facing the wall where the levers where, turned around and looked at them. His grizzly brow furrowed low.

One of the guards pointed at Jared and cried out, "That's the one who couldn't see the cup. He resisted the enchantment. *He's the one!*"

"Spies," the commander growled. "Traitors!"

Jared backed up to the pen. The floor was still dropped and the heat rising from below was beginning to singe his skin. Unconsciously, he lowered his arm. His renewed lifeforce rushed into his hand and out of his palm. Whether fear, or the urge to fight it was the impetus, his lifeforce—black and white mist—exuded from his palm and formed into a silver handle with a black pommel at the base. From the top of it, black and white mist twirled around and solidified into a black blade with a strip of white, glowing metal down its center. Bewildered by it—surprised that he had actually conjured it—Jared raised it up, marveling at its beauty and near-weightlessness. He was so fixated upon the blade, he hadn't realized that his enchantment of concealment was fading away.

"Angel!" a soldier cried out at him, as though it were a curse.

Half with pride, and the other with the hope of intimidation, Jared widened his stance and held his sword in front of him. Zim, Caym, and Thamuz followed Jared's lead, and conjured their swords, shedding Lady Pnemoxsis's enchantment. Thamuz pulled his bulky shoulders back and growled at the soldiers; they stiffened in reply. The tentacle-legged enchanters fled to the sides of the room.

The bear-faced commander looked at his wide-eyed soldiers, and then conjured his sword. "You fear Thamuz, when it is Zimarantha you should have a far greater care for." He pointed his sword at Zim. "So leave the bitch to me."

Zim lowered her sword and turned her head, and eyed the commander from the side. "My lord, Marlek, you could save yourself by just leaping from the train. Or—if you insist—I can see you to the ether." She faced him directly. "A simple choice, no?"

Marlek swung his sword around and up, and then tossed it from paw to paw. "You ought to think about taking your own advice." He called over his shoulder. "Line up!"

The soldiers abandoned the clueless, cup grabbing souls and conjured their swords. They began advancing on Jared and the others, spreading out around them on both sides. Thamuz and Caym, who were on either side of Jared and Zim, turned and faced the soldiers who had gathered to the side of them.

"You wish to fight?" Caym asked the soldiers, who were posturing and pointing their swords at him. He brandished his flaming sword. His eyes and skin turned dark green. "Then come get me."

The soldiers yelled out as they rushed at him. Caym, eager to engage them, ran for them, though as he closed within in feet of them, he leapt up and over them, spinning his body and landing, facing their backsides. By the time the gaggle of soldiers had turned around, he had already jabbed the sword left into one of them, and then in a blur, thrust it to the right, skewering two of them, reducing them to ash, and had already moved on to the next one.

Thamuz charged and roared at the soldiers on his side. His howl startled the soldiers at the front long enough for him to slice two of them into two, straight across their waists. Thamuz jabbed left with both hands on the sword, stabbing a soldier in the throat, and then swung to the right, catching another in the side of her ribs. A soldier broke from the group and ran for him. Thamuz raised his trunk of a leg and snapped it at him, and caught him in the chest with his bear-sized foot, and sent him flying backward—off of his feet—and crashing into those behind him like a slung bowling ball.

Marlek advanced on Zim. She waved her hand behind her back, signaling Jared to move away. He quickly backed up to the pen behind him.

Marlek swung for her neck. Zim deflected the blow and spun around in the direction it had come, and then swung for his leg. Her blade sliced through his leg-guard, just above his knee. He howled and backtracked.

Zim gave him no quarter. She raised her left hand and called out a spell, producing black, twirling mist that shot at Marlek from her fingertips. He parried the enchanted mist, slicing it at the top, middle, and bottom, severing its mystical force, rendering her spell null and void. Though by doing so, he left his right side defenseless. She leapt left and landed on her hunches, and then sprang up at him with her sword leading the way. Her sword cut through his armor and ribs, and came out through the top on the other side. He roared; though Zim quickly muffled his cry with a slash to the throat. Marlek grabbed his neck and fell forward. His brown, fur-covered body turned to ash. His armor—breastplate, arm, and leg shields—fell to the ground before his ashes did.

The train's whistle screamed and started an abrupt, nearly vertical ascent. Jared had only a moment to decide whether to lose the sword and use his lifeforce to secure his feet to the floor or grab hold of the bars of the pen and keep his only means of defense. He chose the latter and gripped his sword while dangling from the pen as though they were monkey bars. Looking below, he saw Zim running across the floor with her sword pointed toward a rabble of soldier who had chosen sword over footing; and because of it, they had no spell to keep them from rolling back and tumbling over one another.

Zim, however, who could wield her lifeforce as a weapon and cast spells simultaneously, did not have to make a choice between sword and footing, and slid into the midst of them with a battle cry, swinging her sword with utter precision, reducing them to ash, two and three at a time. From her left hand, she attacked with spells that spiraled out from her fingers in the form of black mist. The smoky enchantments enveloped the soldiers and rotted them from the inside out. Their skin shriveled away to the bone; and the whole of them, soon after, turned to ash.

The Train of Souls slung itself horizontal, sending Jared slamming hard to his feet. He kept a tight grip on the bars, knowing the next sling-shot up or down could send him hurtling right into the midst of the soldiers. Though now, he saw, there was not much of a brawl left.

Thamuz had a female soldier cornered and was advancing on her with his sword raised and his muscular black frame casting a growing shadow over her. She dropped her sword and held her arms out to the side. She opened her mouth to speak, though Thamuz never gave her the chance. With a quick stab of his sword to her chest, she was already ash before a single sound left her mouth.

Caym had three soldiers left to contend with. They had him from the front and on both sides—outnumbering him and flanking him—though it was they, not he, who looked afraid. He parried their blows with casual ease and a smug grin. When the train dove or careened up—and they all relinquished their swords for firm footing—it was Caym who conjured his sword back first, and then attacked, forcing them into retreat. The soldiers grunted louder with each desperate blow they swung his way, only to have it knocked away, as though it was just a nuisance to him.

"Be done with it," Zim called over to him.

"I would rather make them pay," Caym said, with a quick glance over his shoulder, deflecting blows sight unseen. He turned back around and glared at them. "Traitorous bastards! You risk all of our lives to crown a fool as a god, and destroyed Hell to do it." He swung his flaming sword at the female soldier on his left, catching her thigh guard, and easily slicing through it, cutting her to the bone. The flames of his sword flared as he pulled it up and away from her; its fire was dark red—crimson Hellfire. She fell to her knee. He seethed. "You deserve to suffer."

"Now is not the time," Zim said, her voice deepening.

Caym growled. He swung up at the soldier on his right, knocking the sword out of his hand. The hobbled female one on his left jabbed at him, though Caym was already swinging around and parried her blow off; and with a quick thrust forward, sent his sword through her chest. He retracted it and jabbed it at the soldier in front of him, parrying his oncoming blow, and carrying on straight into his torso. The soldier turned to ash and fell apart around Caym's sword. The last soldier—now defenseless—waved his hands palm out in surrender, begging for mercy. Caym swung and sliced clean through his neck, and then spun around, and began walking toward Jared and the others as the decapitated soldier turned to ash.

Jared noticed a different gleam to Caym's skin and his jet black eyes. He seemed to glow dark green from within. He looked at Zim and Thamuz; they, too, radiated with a similar light, though both of theirs was a dark purple, like midnight.

"Chax gave you parts of Orsha-Na, didn't he," Jared said to both, as it began making sense how they were able to attack and strike with such deadly precision.

"Actually, he gave each of us half of the realm," Zim said.

"The power of Orsha-Na, which once flowed through His Grace, is now ours to command," Thamuz said.

"Leaving him with just the lifeforce he took from me."

"That you gave him," Caym objected smartly, "and freely so."

"This was certainly not the plan, of course," Zim said. "Once Chax and the other lords took your lifeforce, they discovered that it was far more powerful than even they had first thought. You are an unique creation of The Father."

"You have given our mission some hope," Thamuz added. "It's not just Astaroth we face, but Hell itself, for he controls nearly all of it now, and that power is his."

A wet, strangled voice came echoing out of the corridor behind them. *"And he will add The Morning Star's power to his as well."* Jared and the others turned around as one to the corridor. "I should have known Chax's dogs had stolen aboard this shipment." The sound of the voice grew closer. "I'm ringing for more souls and no souls are dropping. And now I come here," he walked into the room; it was Lord Flagon, the reptilian demon.

Flagon walked over and stood in the center of the room, separating Jared and Zim from Caym and Thamuz. He didn't seem at all anxious about having enemies behind his scaly back; he had only eyes—four of them—for Jared at the moment.

"Chax is betting his realm on the pretty boy, I see," Flagon said. "I don't care how much lifeforce you've drained from him, or how powerful you believe him to be...*you will fail.*"

Thamuz and Caym spread out, walking to either side of Flagon. And just then, the Train of Souls dove. Jared fell back against the cage, though the others—Flagon, as well,—remained steady on their feet, using the power of their lifeforce to anchor them to the floor. Jared quickly did the same; he shunted his lifeforce to his feet, making them grow heavy like lead and sticking to the tilting floor.

"Jared!" Zim called out, waving him back and away from Flagon.

"Jared, is it?" Flagon asked, narrowing his four eyes. "So that's the angel's mortal name, eh? It's good to know it, at least before I kill the rest of you, and then deliver him on to His Grace. Zimarantha, my beauty, I thought you far wiser than this." He extended his scaly arm and conjured a gleaming, silver sword in his claw. His spiked tail rose over his head and began to sway side-to-side. "Chax may possess the strength to turn legions of angels and archangels into ash, but I am not them. I was a cherub—a guardsman of the palace of The Father—before being fallen. Yet now, I am the conductor of this holy train of Hell and its power is mine." He crouched on his hind legs. "And its power is great!" His body blurred as he leapt at Zim, with his sword cocked and ready to swing.

Jared leapt to the left as he came hurtling toward them. Zim stood her ground and blocked his blow, and then spun around and went on the offensive on two fronts—sword in one hand and a spiraling black spell spiraling out from the other. Flagon twirled his sword around, slicing her spell and blocking her thrust. From behind, Flagon went on the attack also, swinging his spiked tail, trying to impale Jared and the others.

Jared jumped as the tail came zooming his way. He hopped it. And then, without hesitation, he rushed in to attack. He didn't consider if his lifeforce was strong enough, or if he was ready to put his celestial mind and body to the test and find out if he could mimic the few movements of sword fighting he'd seen thus far. None of that mattered to him; he attacked anyway, and he did it bearing the full weight of billions of mortals weighing upon his mind. But now, there was another that he fought for; and she was beginning to falter under a flurry of blows from

Flagon's sword and his clawed-hand, he alternating between the two—each swing, a swing of death.

Caym came around Flagon's left flank and swung. His blow was deflected by a swing of Flagon's tail, which Jared almost missed hopping again. Flagon's tail came swinging back the opposite way and struck Caym in the chest—its spikes missing him by inches—and batted him away like a ball.

The tail came whoosing back. Jared anticipated it this time, and jumped forward before it could reach him. He rolled on the floor and sprung to his feet, and came up next to Zim. He raised his sword, and just in time; Flagon's sword was coming for him. Jared's sword met his blow—mystical metal upon metal—and shattered Flagon's like it was made of glass.

Zim swung down on Flagon's now weaponless arm and lopped it off at the elbow. Thamuz—on the left—cocked his sword above his head, and gripping it with both hands, drove it into the side of Flagon's scaly flank.

Flagon bellowed and flung his head side-to-side. And then, as though he had nothing else to loose, and feared going to the ether without at least one of them along with him, he slung his head down at Jared, his stretched wide and ripping at the corners; every dagger-sharp tooth was on display and closing in quick.

The fear of doom for all he loved energized Jared's lifeforce like a shot of adrenalin to the heart, needle and all. He swung his sword around like the hand of a clock, and then pointed it up. He gave a battle cry worthy of the celestial that he was and thrust his sword up, just as Flagon's jaws came down. Jared's sword burst through the flesh under Flagon's jaw and came up through his mouth and out the roof of it. Jared yanked his sword back, splaying Flagon's snout.

Flagon fell face first on the floor. He wiggled about for a moment, and then went still, and then began turning black...turning gray... *turning to ash*. He crumpled into a pile of ash and spread out. It began disappearing. And soon there was nothing; there was no trace of the creature that had been fallen by The Father; and now, he had been fallen again, though this time, for the last time.

Caym came walking over, though certainly was not as light of foot as he had been before Flagon rang his bell. He looked at Jared's black and white-sword with a low, dubious brow.

"If I hadn't seen it myself, I would never have believed it, not even from the mouth of my own mother," Caym said. He looked Jared in the eye, and then stated the obvious. "You shattered his blade."

"I can't believe I did that," Jared said. Fear's adrenalin was just now easing off his lifeforce.

"But you did, Jared," Zim said, looking at the sword with wide, curious eyes.

Thamuz eyed it suspiciously. "Indeed," he growled.

"Did you enchant it?" Caym asked. Jared shook his head side-to-side.

"You're a dual spell caster, like Lady Zim," Thamuz offered weakly, his tone a dead giveaway that he already knew that wasn't it.

Again Jared shook his head. "I just swung it."

"And with great lifeforce," Caym opined. "I see you have recovered much of it."

"Most," Jared uttered.

"And now you have answered your own question," Zim told him. He gave her a perplexed look. "You wanted to know how Duke Chax could bequeath the power of Orsha-Na to Thamuz and me, and still have power enough to fight Astaroth." She glanced at Jared's sword. He followed her gaze. "Now you know."

"You were given great power," Thamuz said.

"For all the good it's done me," Jared bemoaned, but then raised the sword and appraised it from tip of the blade to its black pommel. The black blade gleamed; the white center glowed and throbbed like an artery. It felt like it weighed nearly nothing at all, but when it struck, he felt it become solid, dense, and raging with a celestial might he had only ever felt when reaching out for God.

"Hold up your sword, Jared," Thamuz said.

Jared did as asked. Thamuz held his palm up to it and moved it from the tip of the blade down to the guard, and then back again. He looked at Zim and Caym. "It is of perfect balance."

"So is mine," Caym argued. "But mine does not slice through the sword of a Cherub."

"It is beyond the best blade I have ever seen conjured," Thamuz said.

Caym moved his hand in front of Jared's sword as Thamuz had. "Morning Star be praised," he uttered, ogling Jared as though he were some new species set down in front of him.

"You wield the might of the Great Covenant," Zim said, stepping to him.

"Equality and equilibrium...*a balance in all that is visible, and that which is not,*" Thamuz added.

"A blade of perfect balance can render anything asunder, spell or blade —it does not matter," Caym said, his eyes studying Jared and his sword anew.

"And if the blade is of such power, then so too is the angel that wields it," Zim proffered, though almost in a hush, as though such words should not have been uttered out loud, though had did such, only because circumstances dictated that they must be. Her eyes lingered upon Jared for some time.

"I find comfort that you wield the binding words of the Covenant in this moment that has made us allies, but..." Caym said, and then paused to glance at Thamuz and Zim, "if we succeed in our quest—by some great means or miracle—and we are once again enemies with Miel, we shall come to fear him. He will become the bane of our existence, and possibly, the cause of our defeat in the last Great War."

An ill moment of silence followed Caym's phrophecy. Jared looked at Zim. She turned away—grudgingly—and turned her attention to the souls milling about their pens, trying to grasp their illusionary cups of water, they still completely oblivious to everything and everyone around them. The Train of Souls had ceased jetting up and diving down holes, and was gliding along the tracks smoothly, though far from its normal breakneck pace.

"We need to get souls in the firebox before suspicion arises and more soldiers come," Zim said, as though she had not heard Caym's dire prediction.

"I'm not putting people in there," Jared said.

"They are no longer people," Caym reminded him.

"They are souls," Thamuz said.

"Damned ones," Caym added.

"Damned or not," Jared said, "I'm not doing it. It's perverse and cruel."

"Its atonement for their sins," said Caym, with a wicked rise of his brow.

Thamuz walked over to the corridor. "We'll shuttle them down here and into the cages," he said, with a nod at Caym, who then began following him.

"And if the enchanters give us any trouble," Caym said, loud enough for all of the enchanters to hear, "I'll take every limb from their hideous hides." The enchanters hung their heads and stilled their tentacles in a show of obedience.

"Jared...come with me to the engineering cab," Zim said. "I do not expect you to have the mind for burning souls as we do, but we need to run the Train of Souls as hot as we can get it. We must get to Phenóx with all haste."

"If Astaroth attacks and breaches the dome before we get there," Thamuz said, "then all of this is for naught. You will be trapped here... with us."

Thamuz and Caym set off on their task of herding the souls in and having them enchanted, and then placing them in their pens to be dropped into the firebox below. Jared and Zim walked through the corridor, but then took the ladder down to the engineering room.

They exchanged few words.

Zim busied herself with the controls, blowing off the heat—sending the screams of The Damned up and out the smoke stack. Jared was content to let her be. Caym's words reminded him of who she really was to him, which was his enemy. Though still—already—, she was much more than that to him. He saw her as someone who had nothing to do with God or gods, or with the Celestial Host and The Fallen, but simply just as a male to a female.

She turned away from the control panel and looked at him. "I know what Caym said. And there is much truth to his words, but there is truth to mine also. I gave you my word, Jared. I asked you to trust me."

"I remember," he said, with a look of relief. "And I did. I still do."

"Then I'm glad for it," she replied, with a demure smile, which quickly faded and turned grim. "I don't know what the future will bring. But if we are to survive this quest, only to be pitted against each other in the Great War, then I hope we never have to face one another in battle."

"I'm with you on that, Zim," he said, unashamedly looking at her, caring less and less about whose side she was on, and more about who she was a celestial, and as a female.

"Fighting with both sword and spell has given me the edge over every enemy I have ever faced," she said, and then paused, "until this pass. Your actions did not go unnoticed, Jared. It was you who caught Flagon off guard and opened him up to attack, leading to his doom."

"I wasn't going to let him kill you, Zim."

"Which begs the question. Why?" she asked. They looked at one another. Neither seemed willing to disrupt the moment they dared to share away from prying eyes. Finally, Zim spoke. "Show me your sword."

Jared conjured it and raised it, holding it upright between them. Zim moved behind him and positioned her legs, arms, and torso behind his, as though she was just one more layer to him. She wrapped her hand around his, matching him finger for finger around the handle. She placed her chin in the crook of his neck.

"I feel your lifeforce," she said. "You are nearly whole."

He turned his cheek, brushing hers. "I know," he said, as his lifeforce answered her touch by speeding up, and now, was zooming around.

"Let me show you how to wield your sword properly," she said. "Who knows when it may save your life again."

"Or yours."

She moved her face next to his. Had she turned any further, her lips would have been on his cheek. But then she did. Her plump lips pressed softly against his skin, blurring that already faint line that parted them as Heavenly Host and Fallen.

"I trust you, Zim."

She replied with a kiss on his cheek. It was all the response he needed.

CHAPTER 16

Chris watched Dorthea turned around and around in awe at the world he had created in the illusion. He had placed them—Olivia, Dorthea, and himself—in a field of ankle-high grass that stretched out as far as the eye could see. After lulling the women to sleep and taking over their subconscious minds, he fashioned the world around them, complete with a sky as dark as night, and placed the glowing symbols from the tome on it that he had memorized.

"You can do anything here?" Dorthea asked him.

He nodded. "Anything I can think of, I can make real." He held his hand out to the field of grass in front of them. The grasses began to sway and turned from green to blue, and fell upon itself and became water. The grass at their feet turned white, and then fell apart into tiny grains of sand, forming a beach. He waved his hand at the lake and sand he had created. The waves stopped—frozen in time; the sand gathered onto itself, clumping together. The water and sand turned gray and black, and became rocks—a field of them. The ground began rattling. Jagged rock formations burst from the stone-covered ground and went soaring high into the night sky. The world around them had been transformed into a cold, gray desert wasteland. He looked out on what he had made and was impressed by it. He spoke to Dorthea as he continued taking it all in. "It's the power of my mind," he said to her. "Anything I can think of,

I can make—at least in here. And in here, we can chant without Yikan hearing us."

"It feels real," she said. "But I can't help thinking that I'm still laying down on the bed."

"Actually, you are," Olivia told her. She was standing next to Dorthea. "We all are."

"The signals your mind receives is what creates your reality," Chris said. "So now," he looked around his desert world and began reshaping it back into a field of grass, "I'm just feeding it the signals I want it to perceive, and your mind makes it real, because to your mind, it is real."

"I don't know what's real and what's not anymore," she said, looking to the symbols lined up across the sky. "I feel like David fighting Goliath, only I don't have a rock to throw, or a slingshot to put one in."

"But you do, Ms. Dotty." Chris smiled. "You just don't know it yet."

"And you do?"

"Not me…Gabriel."

"God is my strength," Olivia said, reminding her of the meaning of Gabriel's name. "God is great…just like you always say he is. Gabriel was the angel who came, not some other one. And his name just happens to translate into what you're always saying about God; that he is your strength. He's pointing us toward you. You're the key we need."

Dorthea took hold of Olivia's hand. "You're right, girl." She nodded. "I never thought my faith in the Lord could be shaken like this. I've always trusted in him, until—"

"Your baby is gone," Olivia said, quickly hushing her with empathy. "How can you not feel that way? I would. Anyone would. Most people would completely give up on God, but you didn't, chére. He's given you a situation that you think is hopeless, but yet, he says to believe in him —*trust in him*—and to remember that he *is* great; that he is your strength."

"Ms. Dotty," Chris said, pointing to a symbol in the sky. She gave him a resolute nod and looked up at it.

The symbol looked like an 's', though at the top, it became horizontal, and at its bottom curve, there were two slash marks through it. Chris pointed to another symbol, the one right below it, which bore similar, though different features to its upper and lower curve.

"See how its still straight at the top," he said, "but at the bottom, there's wavy marks instead of slashes? The top one you hold the note, but the one below it, where the wavy lines are, you have to add vibrato to release its power. Those bottom slashes tell you how long to hold that note. Eh-zah-eh-zah—*ahhhhh*," he chanted, and then sung it, holding the note.

A breeze came to life around them and swirled Dorthea's hair in her face. Chris held out his hand—palm up—and sung again, though this time, adding vibrato to his voice. A plume of fire popped into life above his palm. He held the note; the fire grew larger. He tapered off of it; the fire shrank, and then disappeared.

"See?" he said. Dorthea nodded, and then looked at the symbols with a suspicious eye. "The slightest change of voice can change the chant."

"And if they're put in the correct order, they can create wonders," Olivia said, looking at them with reverence.

"But if not, the chant doesn't work," Chris said. "Or you create something you didn't want and hope it doesn't kill you in the process. But see, that fire and wind chant could be from any part of the tome. We have to remember that these chants and songs are transcriptions of God in the process of creating a universe of creations. The chants of wind and fire are going to be repeated over and over throughout the tome."

"When God created the Celestial Host," Olivia said, "he gave them dominion over all that was created…some more powerful than others, like Lucifer and Astaroth."

"So," Chris said, "the chant of fire and wind is going to be in the Chant of Changing as well, along with the other elements…water and soil. All four of them have to be there." He shrugged. "That's what we've come up with so far."

Dorthea took a breath and began chanting, and then added vibrato to her voice as she began to sing. "Eh-zah-eh-zah—*ah*…. She yelped as a flame came to life in front of her face. The flame responded to her cry of surprise and quickly grew into a ball of rolling fire, and then flared and contracted like a dying star, extinguishing itself. She turned to Chris and

Olivia slowly. She looked just as shaken as she did excited at what she had done.

Chris feared for her. She had felt the power of the chant, just as he had when Yikan taught him; he could see it in her eyes; that temptation to think of yourself as more than a mortal and something more akin to a god.

He stood on one side of Dorthea; Olivia was on the other. They showed her the symbols they had successfully decoded thus far...or hoped they had. And once they had taught her what they knew, they started again, from the beginning, hoping she could see, or chant, or sing, or feel what they couldn't, and discover the key that would unlock one of the tome's greatest chants—the creation of a celestial. They went on like this for an hour, or maybe it was two or three; Chris couldn't tell anymore. His body wasn't weary; his true form was asleep at the foot of the bed the women were lying in; his mind, however, was taxed, and it began to show.

The illusion began to disappear. The symbols lost their brilliance and faded away like neon lights being shut off. The grasses vanished, leaving nothing but darkness at their feet and all around them. He heard the women call out for him, as the sky, too, went completely dark; as did he; as did they; everything went dark, and then they woke up.

"Just an hour and I promise we'll go back in," Chris said, raising up at the waist and looking over at the women.

"You'll need more than that if you're going to be any help, and you know it," Dorthea said. She and Olivia were upright in bed. "I want to keep at it too, honey, but I don't want us to make a mistake either. How about we all get some rest. And then we hit it again."

Chris complied, because,...well, Ms. Dotty had spoken, and had done such in that tone that she always used on Jared to get him in line and to follow her orders, and not to question them, but to listen to the wisdom of those who had already been to where he was trying to go. They rejoined the others and ate a quick meal prepared by Thaddeus, who since arriving, had never been far from any food in the mansion. And afterwards, Chris returned to the bedroom and slept for three hours, and then laid awake for another ruminating about it all.

Jared had always been there to catch him when he fell and to keep him moving when he didn't want to, and to push back against the bullies at school who made him the target of their angst. Jared always stepped up, even when he knew he would get pushback for it. What haunted him was that he couldn't say he did the same.

It was easier, he thought, to see himself as more of an enemy more than anything. Everything Jared had risked his life to put together—from becoming an angel and avoiding Shazadeh and Yikan in the process, to rescuing him from Yikan's grasp—he had unraveled, and then made worse. Everyone had forgiven him, but that wasn't good enough for him...not even close...because he knew he didn't deserve it, but he wanted to. He wanted to earn their forgiveness; and the only way was to find that spell and transform into an immortal in hope of getting Jared back.

Jared deserved that much from him, even if it meant giving his life, he thought—especially if it meant his life. And he was more than willing to give it.

Jared was his friend.

He was his brother.

And he was going to save him.

Chris felt a shake at his shoulder and realized he had fallen back asleep. He looked up to Dorthea's face hovering over his. She was smiling. Gray had crept into her hair; fine creases were just now beginning to show at the corners of her eyes—if one looked hard enough. Time had only made her lovelier, he thought. She smoothed his hair back, and then wiped at a tear that was just about to crest his eye.

"Chris-honey," she said softly, "time to wake-up."

He had never believed in the power of words. Teachers had tried to get him to believe. Counselors had, too. Even all of the wacky spiritualists and new age gurus his parents were always falling for, had failed to move him forward, only backwards. Dorthea—Ms. Dotty—was different. There was equal amount of authority and motherly warmth to her words...how she said them and looked at him when she did. She was lioness and teacher, giving courage, as well as knowledge. And he felt it; it was palpable. He needed it. And he used it.

He reformed the illusion in their minds strong and sturdy, and had memorized strings of new symbols for them to decode and test. There was a renewed urgency to their work with Dorthea pushing them on, demanding more from them and twice as much from herself. She admonished herself for each and every mistake she made—creating fire when she meant ice; or conjuring a wind when she meant to transform the grass into pebbles. Though when he or Olivia made an error, her words and tone were always encouraging and reassuring.

He allowed himself some joy watching her master what he had shown her, and now she—beginning to surpass him in skill—was pointing out parts of the chant that he and Olivia had overlooked, even though it seems that had been over it a thousand times before. *Magic was in their blood—their African blood,* Chris remembered. *Tamen gave that gift to their people.* And now, because of it, she and Olivia—but more Dorthea —were seeing the symbols and feeling their power in ways he just couldn't.

He felt like they were picking away at a large rock wall and making progress, though obviously not enough. He had to stop often, pulling Dorthea and Olivia out of the illusion to go back to the tome and memorize more chants, which was a good thing. It meant they were making progress, and far more than before, now that Dorthea was with them. Still, with hours now behind them, they were only a quarter of the way through the tome; the morning sun had already come and gone, and had become an evening one, ready to fade away. It was then that the progress they were making came to a halt.

"This row of chants doesn't make any sense," Dorthea said, after trying several times to blend their sounds into each other and it producing no effect, great or errant. "If we've been doing this right," she pointed at the first symbol in that row in the sky, which looked like a nine-pointed star whose tips were curved to the right, "then our voice should fall at the end, not rise...right?" Olivia and Chris nodded. Dorthea's brow furrowed as she mumbled. "Okay...okay, then. But the next symbol says to raise your voice; it jumps from low to high with no bridge between them, which is what we *haven't* been doing, because it doesn't make any sense. But now we're supposed to?" She pointed to the row of symbols just below the others. "It's the same with these, too."

Chris swept his hand out and away from his body. The symbols above those Dorthea were referring to, retreated into the night sky and faded away. With his other hand, he made a pulling motion, as though he were opening a drawer and brought the other symbols closer.

Olivia gave the row of chants a go. She made it past the first symbol, though like Dorthea, could not bridge the low tone with the arching soprano the next symbol seemed to dictate. Chris shook his head; he wasn't even going to give it a try, knowing he could never reach the pitch of an alto or even mezzo-soprano, let alone the soaring, pure pitch of a true soprano.

"I'm going to take us out of the illusion and memorize it again," Chris said, as his eyes roved back and forth across the symbols, trying to spot an errant slash or swirl that he may have inadvertently added, or possibly deleted, or maybe both. He shook his head. He couldn't trust it—not yet, anyway. "What if I didn't put it in the illusion right?"

"And what if you did?" Olivia posed. "But I see your point, Chris."

"You're right," Dorthea said, and then sighed, closing her eyes for a moment. "We can't make a mistake. I want it to be the one so bad. That would put us so close to getting Jared back."

"But every moment that goes by, you see Jared slipping further and further away," Olivia said, with gentle tilt of her head. Dorthea nodded and began tearing up. "Yikan hasn't made his move yet and that means we still have time; not much, but we still have some. And let's use it to be certain about this."

"Absolutely sure, Ms. Dotty," Chris said.

"Then let's get outta here, Chris," Dorthea said, bobbing her head and wiping her eyes. "We're gonna get this right."

They woke. They said nothing as they wiped sleep from their eyes and yawned themselves back to consciousness, all the while moving to the tome to find that passage that did not behave like the others; the one with no rhyme or reason to it, at least as far as their mortal eyes could tell. Chris sat down in front of it. Dorthea and Olivia hovered over him, watching him scan the rows of ancient text to find that mulish passage again. It was Olivia who found it first.

"Right there," she said, pointing at a row of text.

Chris brought the candle closer, holding it inches above where she had pointed. Dorthea and Olivia leaned in to get a better look. Though then, the light from the chandelier above began buzzing and flickering, and then turned on. It had been days since they had power, which should have been welcomed, but instead they paused and looked at one another with fear and apprehension, knowing it was an ill omen.

"Oh no," Dorthea whispered.

A frantic rapping at the door made them all startle. Thaddeus hustled in, not bothering to wait for permission. It was the second time Thaddeus had come looking for them after the power had come on; the first was when the president had spoken after London's incineration. This time, they didn't bother asking why he had come or why he looked as though the shadow he feared, Jackson Lovell, had finally seized upon him.

Thaddeus beckoned with his hand. They followed him out and to the living room—silently—as though they were passing tombstones on their way to graveside. Henrì and Phineas were standing in front of the television, which was broadcasting a hazy signal. Henrì's arms were crossed and his head was lowered; he glowered at the T.V.. Phineas had his hand over his mouth and was slowly shaking his head side-to-side at it.

Chris, Thaddeus, Dorthea, and Olivia circled around the men and looked at the snow-fuzzy picture of a tan, stone wall, with a tunnel leading through it. Latin words were inscribed above the tunnel's arch... *Habemus Papum*...'We have a Pope'.

The Pope's Swiss guards were in front of the tunnel's entrance. They were dressed in their ceremonial yellow, blue, and red striped coats, pantaloons, and stockings, and silver helmets topped with red and blue dyed ostrich feathers. They had forsaken their swords and halberds for military grade semi-automatic weapons. Italian soldiers in camouflage, who were just as heavily armed, had joined them. They all had their backs to the camera and were looking up.

The shot of the scene began moving up; it expanded suddenly, giving a full view of what was above the entrance to Vatican City. Amidst a blue, cloudless sky, a dark, rotating storm cloud hovered above the holy city-state. From within the cloud's center, a white-robed white man descended out of it. In his arms he carried an old, stark naked man, who drooped in his arms like an overcooked noodle. The old man's head was lolled to the side, facing the camera; his pupils were nowhere to be seen, just the whites.

Chris pushed between Henrì and Thaddeus and pointed at the robed man. He turned and looked at the others. "Do you know who that is?" Chris asked them.

"I do," Phineas muttered, speaking through his hand and nodding. "That's the man that was with Yikan...*Eric*...Eric Lightner."

Chris shook his head in disagreement. "Not anymore he's not. That's—"

CHAPTER 17

"I am The Lamb....

"I am the truth, the light, and the way," Eric proclaimed, reciting the words just as Yikan had instructed him to. His voice was amplified by the power of his chant and carried down to the multitude of onlookers, soldiers, and police who had gathered around Vatican City. "No man may come unto Father-Aton but through me, for he is now your god. Bow your heads mortals; a new age has come upon the earth. All of those who cling to the old one shall be purified in eternal fire."

The old man—the pontiff—turned his head and looked up at Eric. His left eye had rolled back down, though was stuck and jittered in the corner of his eyelid; the other was still absent. "You're the...Satan!" the pontiff mumbled, through a deep Italian accent and a throat webbed with phlegm.

Eric looked at him—God's shepherd on earth. The old man's pallid face was a mask of wrinkles. His mouth was twisted to the side and quivering. It was quite clear the old man had suffered a massive stroke or two.

"Satan, and all of the other devils, are in Hell, dear vicar," Eric said. "And by the will of Aton, they will all stay there." His Holiness tried to speak, though all that came out was a gurgle and some drool that oozed over his lips. "Poor Father. You warn your flock that demons will torture their flesh day and night, if they do not pledge their lives to God and worship The Lamb. If you think I am a demon, then you know nothing of them." He lowered his head closer to the Pontiff's. *"But I do!"*

He looked down at the array of law enforcers who had gathered. They had come screeching through the streets of Rome in armored vehicles with their sirens blaring. They leapt out of their tanks with a variety of assault weapons, ready to do battle. And seeing them come and pointing their weapons up at him, he remembered what Yikan had told him; that the destruction of London would not be enough to convince man to kneel; in fact, it would likely strengthen their resolve. And it had. With the armed forces below, and now, he hearing the roar of their fighter jets nearing, he understood the wisdom of Yikan's words about mortals; that they were God's most stubborn creation and would require every ounce of their hope to be extinguished. Now he understood what Yikan meant when he said that London was just the lightning of the match.

He looked back at the pontiff. "I have seen demons rise out of the abyss of Hell, Good Shepherd. I have seen them tear men in half like they were paper. But now, Aton has come to give the world hope, which it has never had with God. And...where is God to be found in your greatest hour of need?" Eric looked at him with utter curiosity. "Why have I not been struck down and you borne away upon the arms of an angel? Where is your God now?" His brow lowered. *"Who is your god now?"*

Eric looked at the storm he had created with the power of his own voice—the power of the chant. *I did that! I created that!* More exhilarating to him than the flush of pride he felt, was that he had snatched the pontiff right out of his bedchambers as he napped and stripped him bare for the entire world to see...and nothing had happened. God *did not* come and rescue the pontiff. No savior swooped in to save the old man. The power of The Holy Ghost—the living force of God—was nowhere to be felt.

"The answer is simple, pontiff," Eric told him. "Your all-powerful God, is not; but my god, Aton, is indeed. I defy gravity because of him. I have created a storm out of nothing but my voice, because he has anointed me as his lamb, as the son of a god." He gave the pontiff a sorrowful smile. "Your Christ will never return; that age is over; a new one has come; and it shall last forever and ever, amen." Eric called down to those below. "Mark this day, mortals. God, and every false god worshipped on earth, has died today. There is only one god. He is Aton. He is the sun—the giver of life. The Age of Aton has come."

Eric spread his arms, as though he were ready to be nailed to his cross. The pontiff fell. The throngs of onlookers screamed, as though they had all simultaneously gone mad.

The pontiff tumbled head over heel, and every foot he sped toward his grisly demise, was captured live and broadcast around the world. The soldiers began firing at Eric. With a sweep of his hand and a chant from his mouth, he turned their metal projectiles into sand, and then blew it back down upon them with a vicious gale, knocking them off their feet and sending them tumbling atop of one another.

Eric closed his eyes and began a new chant. The spinning storm clouds replied and darkened, and came to life with a belly full of lightning. He slowed the chant and began to sing, and then held a trembling note that echoed through the sky. The lighting rushed to the center of his storm, directly above where he hovered. Eric set his sights on the tan, slate roof of the Sistine Chapel—home of Michelangelo's famed fresco, *The Creation of Adam*—and released the gathered lightning upon it.

The roof exploded with a boom that shook the ground two miles away. The roof caved in as the lower level blew out in all directions, toppling the building; reducing it to rock and rubble, and setting it ablaze.

Black smoke began rising into the air. Eric called out a chant and took hold of the smoke. He changed it from sooty-black to a brilliant white, the color used by cardinals to signal the election of a new pontiff; a sign to the world that a new shepherd had come to replace the old one.

He chanted once again and called the winds to send him flying. He flew to the west, to Spain; to the gothic cathedral, Sagradra Família… and destroyed it as he did the Sistine Chapel, with lightning and fire. And then he flew to Notre Dame, and then to Germany's Cologne Cathedral, and on to Romania and Poland, toppling their greatest houses of worship and burying their priests and rabbis and Imams under them.

And now, he thought, it was America's turn. He chanted a wind current into life that swept him toward the ocean, and for many hours he glided above its surface, as warplanes crisscrossed overhead searching for him. And even if they could locate him—which he knew they couldn't— they would still be powerless to do anything to stop him. The mortals were made of flesh and their machines of metal, and both he could manipulate, alter, warp, and destroy with just a chant.

He soared across the eastern states to the Midwest, to the Salt Lake Temple in Utah, where he immolated its elders on the verdant green courtyard in front of it, just before demolishing their soaring, gray temple. He backtracked and flew to the Midwest, to Michigan's massive, America's Islamic Center, where he blew apart its gold dome and reduced the rest of America's largest mosque to dust and rubble.

He flew east and across America's seaboard, and once again set out to sea, where he transversed the Atlantic Ocean under the darkness of night. He had completed the tasks Yikan had given him. He had struck the great religions of the great nations in their hearts. He had humiliated and disposed of their religious leaders before the eyes of the world. Their houses of worship were now piles of smoldering rubble. Each church and basilica and mosque and temple that came tumbling down, and their leaders thereafter, was his proof given that God was indeed impotent.

Yikan had restored power to the electrical grids while he—the new *lamb* and *son*—had completed his task. But now that it was over…now that night had fallen, he looked down upon the world of mortals and watched as their lights began going out in swaths, as Yikan—he shutting the grids down once more—plunged the world back into darkness as a sign of the age of God having finally come to an end and the beginning of a new one set to begin.

The Age of Aton—the sun god of Egypt—had come.

CHAPTER 18

It was Umandi-lut—the setting of Wormwood in the west—when the Train of Souls came screaming around the bend. For the first time, Jared had a full-on view of the Westlands—that unholy realm of Astaroth that he had to pass through to get home. Though, too, looming off to his right, was the black dome of Phenóx; a nigh impenetrable shield fueled by the power of Lucifer himself and of the essence of the most vile of The Damned that had ever walked the earth. Bonfires lit the barren landscape for miles across, well past the horizon, which Wormwood was now nearing, swaying his arms and legs about in a dance of fire. There were hundreds of thousands of soldiers, it seemed to Jared. They looked like a slow moving swarm of bees. Their number seemed infinite...uncountable; *they were legion, for they were many.*

He felt Zim's body press against from behind. She moved her head next to his and gazed out the engine's window along with him.

"The Westlands were once a beauty to be seen," she remarked. "The land was green and lush. Many streams and rivers flowed through Astaroth's lands, that is, before he turned traitor."

She looked him in the eye and paused for a moment...just looking at him. She turned away, back to the sea of bonfires raging across the land. Between the screams of the train, the thudding of war drums could be heard in the distance, and was growing louder.

"Astaroth has destroyed his own realm to see Phenóx fall," she said. "Though I suppose in his mind, he has already conquered Phenóx, killed Lucifer, and taken the earth for himself. What need of a paltry realm in Hell then, hmm?"

"The cosmos maybe," Jared panned, and smiled.

"If he thought he had the slimmest chance of toppling The Father, I'm sure he would try," Zim said, and then returned a coy smile, but then her face became somber. Her brow grew heavy as she looked off to the horizon, where the sun-demon danced away. "When Wormwood leaves Hell and journeys to earth, the Heavenly Host and The Fallen will wage war for the last time. Your Christ will return to earth; The Father will damn the unrepentant sinners to Hell; and by the living force of The Father—The Holy Ghost—the earth will be made anew, that is, if good and evil are in balance on earth. If Astaroth is triumphant, all of that will be undone...forever."

"If he isn't?" Jared asked, looking off to the shimmering black dome. She didn't reply immediately, though began slowly moving her cheek against his.

"Damned if we do," she said.

"Damned if we don't." He leaned his head against hers.

"I cannot serve two masters, and neither can you."

"I know, Zim...I know. One of us would have to choose if...if this was ever going to be."

"I have chosen," she replied. "Eons ago, I did."

"A thousand years ago or two hundred thousand years, it doesn't matter, Zim," he said. "God always forgives. After I transformed and Heaven opened up, I felt him. I felt his love *and* his forgiveness. It's real, Zim." He bobbed his head slowly, staring into her eyes, praying she could see and hear the truth in his words. "All it takes is a bit of faith."

She moved her head away from his and gave him a curt smile. "And I have seen The Father with mine own eyes. There is far more than love and forgiveness that resides in him. The Father is a jealous god."

"He should be."

"That is a matter of opinion and of great debate, for here we are...Celestial Host and a Fallen one...side-by-side, saying things to one another that should never be said between us; and feeling such feelings, which should never be moved upon."

"Says who?"

"Says The Father," she replied.

"Who is forgiveness, for whatever you've done."

She scoffed. "I have lived for eons—through all of the ages of men—and have ruled them as goddess of the sky and earth for as long," she told him. "You don't know what I've done; what I have called for in sacrifice and received tenfold in blood and flesh for whatever I have asked for."

"It doesn't matter, Zim."

"Says who?" she asked, turning the tables on him.

"Says...." His lips remained parted, though no words came out.

He stared at her, searching her eyes. In that moment, Jared seized the chance he had been yearning for and leaned and kissed her pouty lips. She responded with equal vigor, and then some. They parted, though retreated no more than an inch from one another; and for a moment, they just looked into one another's eyes.

Jared looked down and nibbled at his lip. "Are we finally going to talk about this?"

"About what?" she asked, turning and walking over to the control panel. "You want me to betray my own kind?"

Jared was quick to nod. "Yes. For love."

"That's the mortal that you once were who is talking such nonsense."

He followed her and stood behind her. He put his hands on her shoulders. "No," he said softly, "its me...whether you want to call me Jared or Mizel, it doesn't matter. It doesn't change how I feel about you; how I felt about you the first time I saw you, when you were trying to kill me."

She grinned. "The feeling was mutual, though, I wasn't trying to kill you, just capture you."

"Lady Zim," a voice called from behind them.

Jared quickly backed away from Zim and turned around. Caym was standing at the door. And by the grim look Caym was giving him, Jared was sure he had already seen and had heard too much. Caym's dark, green eyes darted from him over to Zim, and then back again.

"We're nearing the station, my lady," he said, glaring at Jared all the while. "What's our play, now that Lord Flagon is dead and our illusions are no more? They will expect to see that traitorous, swamp lizard when the train arrives."

Zim's eyes narrowed. She glanced up and then down, and then looked over at the firebox's door, which glowed red-hot. "Hide the soldiers' armor in the firebox and then close the dampers," she told him.

"But that will cool the train and slow us," Caym said.

"Precisely," she said. "We'll wait until we're a few kilometers from port, and then we'll set the brakes."

"And then?" Caym asked.

"And then we hide," she said, glancing at the firebox. Caym and Jared looked over at the door as well.

Jared gawked. "The firebox?"

"They will not likely search there," she told him. "Once the soldiers board the train and realize something is amiss, trust that they will search it from end to end. Once the train's fires have cooled—if we start now, that is—we'll be able to withstand the fire for a time and hopefully long enough to hide in until they have searched and given up. It's our best course." She turned to Caym. "You and Thamuz will have to take care of the enchanters."

"The squids?" Caym bemoaned. "I've never liked those creatures anyway. Consider them ash."

"Once I hit the brakes, that's your cue to jump in," she told Caym.

"As you say," Caym said, with a genteel nod. He turned to Jared. "Come up and assist us, angel. Zim can handle things down here...*on her own*. I'll show you how to properly use that fine sword of yours." He smiled like a mischievous child. "Shall we go and dice ourselves some calamari?"

"Sure," Jared replied, smiling innocently at him.

Zim turned back to the control panel. "I'll be right behind you once I hit the brakes," she said.

Jared followed Caym out, and then up, though not before sneaking one last glance at Zim. She appeared engrossed with the controls of the train, though he knew it was only a ruse, just as much as his feigned in-difference toward leaving her was.

"Are you coming, angel?" Caym asked, leaning back and catching Jared with eyes still on Zim.

"I'm right behind you," Jared replied, following him into the corridor, and then over to the ladder leading up.

Caym grasped the rung and stopped, and then turned around. "Re-member why you're here in the first place. And you would do well to remember who she is, and who *you* are."

"If you want to say something, then say it."

Caym looked him up and down with a distasteful smirk. "The ob-vious doesn't need to be spoken. It's plain enough, indeed."

"Well," Jared paused, "you're wrong."

"Am I, angel?" Caym raised a brow. "Have the ages dimmed my eyes, so that now they deceive me? Or has time given me the wisdom to see that you play a very dangerous game? I would wager on the latter. You've a far better chance of returning to earth, than seeing your fantasies of what will never be coming true. If you were wise, you would mark my words carefully; desire has shown you a path to doom."

* * *

Jared stood on one side of the holding pen's doorway. Caym and Thamuz were on the other side and huddled close, speaking in their na-tive, demon tongue—soft and low—as they all awaited Zim setting the brake. They had dropped the rest of The Damned into the firebox, and then shut the dampers, smothering the raging fire below with bodies and depriving it of air. Next, they turned their attention to the enchanters, who having seen The Damned be dropped and no others herded in to replace them, began looking nervously at one another before suddenly, in a panic, they began whisking over to the corridor to escape. Thamuz bolted over to the doorway and conjured his sword, blocking their only exit. The half-humanoid, half-squid creatures went gliding back to the center of the room and crowded upon one another, jockeying for the middle of the huddle they had created.

Jared stood behind Caym with his sword conjured, ready to follow him and begin mimicking and learning his skill with the sword. He had struck Lord Flagon a mighty blow, but that had been luck—pure and simple—no matter how well balanced his sword was, or how powerful he was. Yikan had already showed him that pure power could be rendered powerless, which was, at least in his own case now, a good thing. Astaroth had the power of Hell behind him and legions of demon-soldiers eager to fight, and if need be, to die for him. He knew he needed every advantage he could get, even if it was from his sworn enemies, and one in particular, who was none too pleased with his familiarity with Zim.

Caym charged at the enchanters; Jared followed behind, becoming his shadow and copying his every move. Jared didn't engage the enchanters; Caym did, and was doing a fine job of cleaving their upper halves from their lowers, where their torsos met tentacles. Jared began to feel the rhythm of Caym's sway of his body and the deft, wind-whistling swings of his sword, and how he parried and then thrust with the same, smooth motion, taking arms from shoulders and heads from necks.

The enchanters were slow moving creatures, though they were far from benign. They cast their black, misty enchantments at Caym and Jared. Caym attacked the swirling black mist, slicing through the smoky enchantments, destroying the spells, and they dissipating before they could even draw near enough to strike. Jared saw that Caym never attacked the head of the mist—the tip of the enchantment—but always the body of it. And with the enchanters themselves, Caym seemed to anticipate their moves, even before the enchanters had even thought to move at all. It wasn't long before Caym had sent them all to the ether.

Caym turned around, having just sent the last of the enchanters on their way to nonexistence. "I hope you are a quick study, Miel-angel. Those were just enchanters. They're basically mindless, which is likely giving them too much credit at all. But they're not soldiers. Enchanters are meant to enchant, and soldiers to kill; and there will be many of them out there."

"I know. I've seen them."

"No-no, Miel," Thamuz said, walking over to them. "You've only seen what you could see. If tens and hundreds of thousands of soldiers you saw, then know that there are ten times as many that you have not yet seen."

"We are legion," Caym boasted.

"We are as numerous as the Celestial Host," Thamuz said.

"Or were," Caym panned. "Once Astaroth has finished us off by pitting us against one another, they'll be none of us left to fight come the last war."

"Be there a war at all," Thamuz said, with a reluctant bob of the head.

"We better get into position," Caym said to them.

They chose the pen at the far right of the train and went over and stood by its opening. Again, Caym and Thamuz stood on one side of the opening and Jared on the other. The Train of Souls screeched. The dropbell above the center of the room began ringing.

"Get ready," Thamuz called out, glancing up at the bell.

Jared shunted his lifeforce to his feet, making them become dense. Though still, he held onto the bars of the pen just in case. He was in Hell, and what could go wrong down here? he thought, chuckling at every thing that had gone wrong, from ending up in Hell in the first place, to now trying to find a way into Lucifer's unholy realm.

The brakes engaged and screamed nearly as loud as the train's whistle. The train flung them forward, though with their lifeforce anchoring them, they never lost their grip on the floor.

Zim came sprinting in. She dashed across the floor and stood next to Jared. "We're a kilometer from station," she said, calling over to Caym and Thamuz. "We'll wait until the last moment before jumping."

"Sounds delightful," Caym opined, with a look of disgust. "Why are we always, somehow, in the midst of those filthy, damned souls?"

"They've kept us alive and hidden with their multitudes thus far," Thamuz offered. "That's worth putting up with, if you ask me."

"Barely," Caym groaned.

Zim pointed to the lever across from them and moved her hand down with a sweeping motion. The lever moved down at her command and opened the trap door of the pen behind them. The Damned that were still burning released a torrent of screams. The oxygen-deprived flames of the firebox barely flared up to edge of the dropped floor and then died down.

Jared looked into the firebox. The red-glow of roasting, writhing souls shined upon his face. The heat, though far less intense than before, still pulled at his skin, drawing it taught, reminding him that it, too, with enough time, could turn him to ash.

"It's time," Zim told them.

Caym looked down on the screaming, thrashing souls and groaned, and then sighed and closed his eyes, and leapt in. Thamuz crossed the pen's threshold and did the same. Zim positioned herself in the doorway and looked at Jared.

"By the grace of The Morning Star, we will not be in here long," Zim said, glancing down into the firebox. "And then our most difficult path lies ahead."

"Phenóx," Jared said, and then cocked his head, "or did you mean you and me?"

"Damned if we do, damned if we don't," she remarked, giving him a bitter smile, and then leaping in.

Jared stepped up to the doorway and grasped both sides of the frame. He turned and looked at the room behind him, it was empty of soldiers, enchanters, and of the foul, swamp-demon, Flagon. He had made it this far and was still alive, which meant there was still a chance—a slim one; one that was barely nonexistent—, though still, the possibility of re-turning to earth remained. That was the plan and part of the pact he had forged with Chax, Beelzebub, and Agares—the lords of the infernal realm. Yet, the path where he and Zim could be together was nowhere near the one he had agreed to; in fact, it didn't exist; it wasn't supposed to. Jared turned around and jumped in.

His vision turned a glare red, yellow, and blue as he dropped into the flames. He crushed roasted souls beneath his feet and landed upon the metal bottom of the firebox; it was covered in a foot of ash and littered with armor and body parts of The Damned that were still burning like coals—black and cracked on the outside, and glowing red hot from within. After a few moments, his celestial vision adjusted to the flames and he could see Caym and Thamuz off to his right, and Zim just a few feet from them.

As the Train of Souls began to slow, the sound of voices and the pounding of drums grew louder, rising above the squeal of the brakes. The train came to a slow, grinding halt. Zim turned to each of them with a finger pressed to her lips, even as The Damned continued their shrieking and howling and crying and bemoaning. A squeal of grinding metal came from the right, from outside of the train. And then came a ground-shaking thud, which hopped them off their feet, as though a boulder had been dropped next to them. The sound of boots moving about and the muffled talk of soldiers began seeping through the firebox wall.

"Lord Flagon!" a voice called out. There was a pause, and then another call for the green lizard.

"Alusa-so, ollo Flagon?" one asked.

"Puat, monuh-et erok," a female replied.

"Check the holding pens," said a male, though a different one than before, and with a tone of strict authority.

The sound of footsteps rose and then faded. Moments after they faded away, the sound of their boots shuffling about came from above them. Jared and the others looked up. All above was suddenly quiet for a moment, and then they heard the soldiers retracing their steps, returning to the engineering room right outside the firebox.

"There's no one up top," a male reported.

"The souls?" a female asked.

"No one, Lady Moora."

There was silence for a moment. "Search the train," Moora said. "There's deceit afoot this *pass*. There is no Train of Souls without Lord Flagon, and he is not here. He is in the ether, as are his soldiers."

"Shall I dispatch a rider to Lady Lilith?" a female asked.

Again there was silence, though the blaring of a horn from far away abruptly interrupted it. Jared saw Zim, Thamuz, and Caym all stiffen at booming call of the horn. He knew it wasn't the mentioning of Lilith's name that had suddenly put them on edge; it was the rumble of the horn and what it meant; and though he had a good guess as to what it did mean, he wasn't sure he was ready to admit it, for that meant they may be too late if the March on Phenóx had already begun.

"No," Moora finally replied, and then confirmed Jared's fear. "The call to war has sounded. The assault begins. But this…Lord Flagon; this is the work of Chax, no doubt. Though, whatever move he has put into play has come too late." She called out the order. "Search the train and do it quickly! If there are souls in the rear freights, then herd them in. If you find the traitors amongst them, bring them to me. I'll see that they're smashed into vulags and hurled against the dome—that's all they're worth anyway. *Unload the train!*"

At Moora's command, the sound of boots spread out in all directions. Zim held up her hand to the others and moved toward wall. She turned her head and leaned in, listening to the soldiers as they carried out Moora's order and searched the train for them.

The remaining souls in the firebox had already turned to ash by the time the soldiers had given up and departed the train. Even then, out of fear that it was simply a ruse, none of them spoke or moved. Zim chanced it and leaned closer to the wall, nearly pressing her ear and horn against the hot metal.

"I believe they are gone," she said, though still spoke in a hush.

"We need to get out of here," Caym said. "You heard what Lady Moora said…you heard the horn. The war has begun."

Zim nodded at Thamuz and backed away from the wall. He trod through ash and armor, and came over to the wall and conjured his iridescent, black sword. He gripped it with both hands and brought it above his head.

Thamuz called out to Caym. "Enchant me, prince."

Caym raised his hands at Thamuz's sword and began swaying them slowly, moving them like they were snakes being charmed. He called out an enchantment in his demon tongue. Thamuz's blade burst into blue flames from tip to guard. He swung at the wall and cleaved it, breaking through to the other side. He yanked it out and swung at it again, this time splitting the metal all the way down to the floor. He hacked at each side of the tear he had created, and then dropped his sword, letting it vanish, and then began to cast a spell of his own. He brought his hands together and slowly began moving his arms out, as though he were pulling doors open on either side. The gash he had made followed his every move, and came screeching open, as though Thamuz had opened it with his actual hands.

With its seal broken, the firebox flared. It flashed a ball of fire out through the jagged opening. Zim brought her arm to her eyes and let the flare pass. She conjured her sword and took a step across the opening's threshold. She looked to either side of the room.

"It's all clear," Zim said, and then stepped through.

Jared conjured his sword, as did Caym and Thamuz, and then followed her out. He stepped into the engineering room. One of the walls was gone. Though, upon closer inspection, he saw that it wasn't just a wall, but a ramp, too; and it was unhinged and on the ground, and lay bare of what was the Westlands now...now that it was ready for war.

Jared sidestepped Zim and moved in front of her, and then looked out. He saw Wormwood just setting in the western horizon; and though it still glared bright white, the black dome around Phenóx pulled at its rays, taking it into itself and casting the Westlands in darkness, save for the bonfires that raged across the land. Thousands of Astaroth's soldiers teemed about on foot and horseback. Their catapults—three rows deep —were set in position by the bridge that led to Phenóx; and behind them, he saw thousands of The Damned lined-up, ready to be used as vulags—their bodies meshed together and set on fire, turning them into explosives of pure energy. Enchanters were floating up and down the rows next to The Damned, casting their inky-black spells upon them, distracting them from their impending fate with delusions of cold cups of water.

Thamuz laid a hand on Jared's shoulder and leaned in next to his face. "The point is not to be seen, angel."

Jared stepped back from the edge, just as the war horns bellowed across the staging field. *"Wahpun-na vulags!"* a distant voice cried out. The call was quickly followed by others yelling out the same and it spread across the field like a wave gathering strength before the crash.

"The vulags," Jared muttered, looking at Zim. "What about the vulags? What are they saying?"

"They're loading the catapults…see?" she said, pointing at the catapults lined up in front of the bridge. "They're going to launch the assault, which means that *now* is our time. We have to make it across the bridge, which is already heavily garrisoned."

"We cannot go out as we are," warned Thamuz. "Our illusions have faded. It would take a great amount of lifeforce to conjure them anew, which would leave us weakened when we need our strength the most."

"The armor," Zim said, darting her eyes to and fro. She nodded, as though concurring with herself. "Gather the armor you threw in the firebox."

Caym grinned. "Aye!"

"We'll mix in with Astaroth's soldiers and make our way across the bridge," she said.

"And then all we have to do—if we make it there at all—is dodge hundreds of vulags that will be coming our way," Caym jested.

"Hopefully, the dome will crack before we're crushed in a hail of them," Thamuz opined.

"First, let's pray to The Morning Star that we get there before Astaroth does," Zim said, stepping to the edge and peering out. "If we don't, then we've lost."

"And then you'll soon have a new place to call home, Miel-angel," Caym said, "be it here in Hell, or the ether the other."

∗ ∗ ∗

Dressed in the red and white armor of Astaroth's soldiers, Jared and the others crouched under the ramp until the soldiers, and the Damned that they herded, had marched off toward the staging arena. The war horns began sounding out again, though this time they came in a series, sometimes two in a row, other times three or four, one right after the other; and with each set of bellowing calls, the soldiers picked-up the pace of their tasks; whether it was herding The Damned quicker or lining up more catapults behind the three rows already in place. Zim poked her head out from under the ramp and held up a fist to the others, signaling them to hold their positions.

"One thing about us—the celestials of the cosmos, that is—is that there are so many of us," she said, speaking over her shoulder. "If we slip into their midst, we should be able to work our way to the bridge without them even knowing. They may not immediately recognize our faces, but they will know our names for sure...so do not use them at all."

Zim waited until the horns began sounding off anew, and then twirled her finger in the air, signaling them to go. They ran toward a group of soldiers marching a herd of The Damned off to the staging grounds. They stopped once and crouched as they neared within a hundred feet of them. At the blare of the next horn, they sprinted toward them again and caught up to the end of the herd, where three soldiers were keeping the souls at pace with strikes of their whips. Jared and the others conjured whips into their hands. Though then, one of the soldiers marching in front of them looked back at Jared and did a double-take, and then spun around and began walking backwards, facing them, giving them a queer look.

"Where did all of you come from?" she asked, speaking to Jared. "We were the last."

"*We...*" Jared began, but then hesitated, as he searched for lie. "We swept the train again on...on Lady Lilith's orders."

"We already did that," she said, raising her brow.

"And who are you?" Zim asked sharply.

"Brana-Le—servant of Lord Aka Mana—soldier of his grace, Duke Astaroth."

"And we serve the lady, Lilith, who has the ear of the duke; which means that you—Brana-Le," she said with a sneer, "are nothing to us. Mind your duty before I part your head from your neck."

Brana-Le bowed her head. "Yes, my lady." She turned around and swung her whip, smarting a slave on the back of the head. "Get on with you!" She aimed for another and struck. "Move it along, you vulags!"

The demons turned the herd of The Damned to the right, steering them into the midst of the amassed legions ready to march on Phenóx. The rock-strewn land—it drained of all of its force—was aglow in the light of dark orange and red flames from the bonfires. The further they traveled in, the more crowded it became. The Damned were lined up behind catapults, where enchanters were gliding up and down their rows, oozing their misty, black magic over them, keeping them docile until they could be mashed together and sent hurtling at the dome. Soldiers were still herding more of The Damned to the staging ground; others were on horseback, riding up and down the lines of soldiers in formation, shouting out orders and rallying their troops to give it their all...to see Phenóx fall, and Lucifer along with it; and to take both Hell and earth as their spoils of war; and to—once and for all—claim their rightful mantel of god and goddess.

Zim slowed down and let Thamuz move in front her. He broke off from the soldiers they were following and veered further right. He was easily a head taller than most of the other demons, and twice their bulk, which allowed him to barrel through the horde of them, creating a clear passage for them to follow.

The boom of a horn rang out from behind them and was followed by three more that came from the sides of them, and in front of them, where Phenóx lay, surrounded by a dome of pure energy—the darkest of black magic. The soldiers manning the catapults began casting spells, which spiraled out from their hands like mist. The soldiers next to them began moving The Damned up to the catapult's bucket. As The Damned were shoved in, trident-wielding demons on either side of the bucket jabbed at them, slicing their flesh, muscle, and bone into shreds, readying them to be merged with the next unlucky soul to follow. As the enchanted mist from the soldiers touched upon the mix-mash of body parts, it set them alight in a blaze of blue flames; and it was the same with the other catapults arrayed around them. The soldiers loaded their armament, turning all that could be seen of the Westlands into a sea of blue fire.

Thamuz picked up the pace. Jared sensed he was thinking the exact same thought he was...that the attack was imminent, and that they had yet to cross the bridge over to Phenóx; and that wasn't good...not good at all. It spelled failure. It meant doom for the earth, and as far as Zim, Caym, and Thamuz were concerned, for Hell as well. They all had something to lose, he understood. It didn't matter which side was right—the Celestial Host or the Fallen; The Father or Lucifer—, it was stopping Astaroth at all costs that mattered now.

Jared looked up at the dome. Wormwood was nearly above its apex. The dome pulled at Wormwood's glare-white light, curving the rays toward its sphere and taking it in, siphoning its energy. The dome seemed to grow larger with each jogging step he took. The legions of soldiers around them were still oblivious to their presence; they were far more preoccupied with chanting in time to the drums pounding the beat of war.

Their path suddenly became clear. They had passed through the front line; the bridge to Phenóx was right before them, though a black-haired, pale female on horseback blocked passage to the bridge with a cadre of soldiers behind her, who had swords drawn, as though they had been expecting them all along. The female moved her horse forward a few steps and looked down at Zim.

"You nearly had me," Lilith said to her. "When I caught word that Sheol was broken into and that the Train of Souls had arrived in port without its conductor and crew, I knew there was only one cunning enough—like me—who could have pulled it off." She placed a hand on her chest and looked at Zim with pride. "My dear sister, Zimarantha."

Jared looked at Zim with wide, unbelieving eyes. "*Sister?*"

"Absolutely, angel," Lilith said, turning and looking at him. The soldiers up close murmured to one another about an angel being in their midst. The news spread quickly. The legions buzzed like hornets whose nest had just been rattled. "We were brought from the ether together, as one, she and I. Though over the eons, we have grown apart. In my time, I have come to believe, and am willing to fight for a god worthy enough to rule Hell and earth; one who could stop the last Great War from ever coming about and save us all, giving us back dominion over what is rightfully ours. You, however, have fallen in league with Chax and his ragged band of lords, who are not even worthy of, or strong enough to defend their own lands."

"You cannot kill The Morning Star," Zim said.

"Cannot? Or should not? There is a difference," she said, and then looked above them and out across the field. "Either way, sister, it will be done, though not by my hands, but his."

Jared and the others turned around. Astaroth was approaching, though in grand style and flair, indeed, for he came upon a throne borne forth by a wave of body parts of The Damned, which rolled round and under each other, like a perverse conveyor belt. It set the duke down a few hundred feet from them. His throne was white, like his skin. His shendyt was dark red, as was his hair that swept down over his shoulders and onto his bare chest.

"At last we meet, Miel-angel," Astaroth called out from his throne. "I have waited thousands of years for your arrival, ever since the day The Lamb died upon the cross and bid the Egyptian, Tamen, to find you; to remake you into the Angel of Balance that you are now. It took some time to arrange it all; I assure you it was not an easy task. I, too, know what it is like to have any dealings with that Egyptian, Yikan. And I wager, we both feel the same way about him; that we despise him, though we have different reasons as to why, of course. But Yikan has been useful. You are in Hell, are you not?"

"I know you've been behind it all," Jared said.

Astaroth leaned forward. "You have the beauty of a god, the power of a god, and the wit of ant; not a good combination at all, Miel-angel. That you're just now realizing that, only because Chax has told you so, does not bode well for you, I'm afraid. None of you saw me coming, and I never stopped moving, not even once. I took Hell from the great lords before they even knew they had lost them. And now, it is I who stands in front of Phenóx and will slay its master in his sleep, with your assistance, Miel."

"Mine?" Jared grinned and shook his head. "You're getting nothing—"

"*I take what I please,*" Astaroth professed, sitting back and bone straight in his throne. "And I will have your lifeforce as well, just as I please. Look around you, Miel. I have Hell in my hands. Phenóx will fall and The Morning Star as well. You followed folly when you agreed to follow Chax, and Beelzebub, and Agares." He looked at Zim. "With a pretty face, they have beguiled you and led you to your doom."

"Don't believe him, Jared," Zim said.

"*Jared* is it, my dear?" he asked. "And I am the liar?"

"I'm not falling for it," Jared said.

"Oh, Miel," Astaroth bemoaned, "you already have."

Jared darted his eyes at Zim. She was looking at him. She had given her word—and a little more—and he trusted her. He lowered his arm and conjured his sword. He turned to Zim and nodded. She return the gesture by conjuring her sword as well; Thamuz and Caym conjured theirs right after and swiveled to the side, ready to defend their flanks.

Jared brought his sword up and in front of him, directing it at Astaroth. "You'll have to kill me to take my lifeforce, and I'm not going to make it easy. I don't care how many legions you have at your back, or how powerful you think you are. Your legions may eventually run us down, but who knows if *you'll* ever see it happen."

"I do, child," he professed, lolling his head to the side.

"Only if you're God," Jared said. "And you're not even fit to wash his feet."

Astaroth twiddled his fingers and looked at them with a pensive cock of the head. "If only I had the likes of you and Tamen allied with me, Chax would have given up a long time ago, instead of fighting a losing fight. You are brave, Miel. Even against such overwhelming odds as you face, you still have hope in The Father; you still persevere. You still desire to return home, when there is no returning home for you. Desire, Miel, has doomed many—celestial and mortal alike."

Jared heard a whirring sound, and then Zim, next to him, suddenly choke out a cry; the tail of a whip had been wrapped around her neck. She dropped her sword and grabbed at it, trying to pull the enchanted, leather bond from her neck. Jared spun around and saw that it was Lilith who had tethered Zim. With a yank, Lilith jerked Zim off her feet, sending her crashing backward to the rock-strewn ground.

Jared thrust his lifeforce into his sword and swung at the whip, severing it. Lilith cried out as her whip—that physical manifestation of her lifeforce—was severed, like the head of a snake being chopped off. Seizing upon her moment of shock, Thamuz darted in for the attack, though Lilith recovered enough to hold a hand up to him, and from it, a spell of red mist spiraled out and surrounded Thamuz, encasing him in a swirling tornado of it.

"*Love me*," she commanded of him. "Protect me."

The whole of Thamuz's eyes became white as the enchantment took hold of him. He turned and looked at Caym, and raised his sword at him.

"Break from her spell, you loof!" Caym blurted, raising his, too. Thamuz began walking toward him. "Thamuz...can you hear me?" Thamuz raised his sword higher and pulled back to strike.

Caym shook his head in disgust and reared back on his hunches, and then sprung at him. He met Thamuz's blade with his own, and then spun around him, and then kicked him square in the back, sending him flying forward and landing face down.

"Come on, Thamuz," Caym pleaded. "Break the enchantment. "

Thamuz lifted his head and looked at Caym with a blank expression, and eyes still white from end to end. Caym groaned and lifted his sword, and prepared to fight.

Jared pulled Zim to her feet. He stood facing Astaroth, and she, Lilith. Though then, Zimarantha moved around, pushing Jared to face Lilith.

"I will take Astaroth," Zim said. "You take care of her. Once she's gone, her enchantment over Thamuz will be broken."

"You are too late, my lady," Astaroth said, flicking his wrist forward and pointing at Phenóx.

The horns of war called out across the land at his signal; the order to attack had been given. The sky turned red as the fire-engulfed vulags were launched across it. They soared across the bridge and the moat it spanned, and struck the black sphere, exploding upon it in a burst of flames, and sent burning body parts of The Damned raining down. The black sphere rippled where the vulags had struck and sent concentric circles rippling out across its surface.

Lilith dismounted and extended her arm, conjuring a sword with a black blade. She began walking toward Jared.

"Prepared to go to the ether?" she asked, raising her brow and sword at him.

Jared raised his as well, as he recalled the movements Caym had showed him back on the train, and was ready to put his celestial lifeforce behind them. But then, the sky began rumbling, though it was not the vulags streaking across them that was causing it. It was a storm that was brewing—clouds appeared out of nowhere and quickly darkened. She was going to strike with lightning, he thought. Or was she going to strike with her blade? He wasn't sure. He prepared for both.

"Lightning will not save you," she said.

Jared cocked his head at her, and then glanced up. *My lightning? That's not my—*

He stopped in mid-thought as the hairs on his head began to rise. The air crackled all around them, sounding like fat sizzling in a hot pan. A bolt of lightning raced out of the storm cloud and arced halfway back up, before careening down.

Jared raised his sword to block the lightning, though missed it entirely, for it wasn't aimed at him, but at Lilith. She was enveloped in a bolt of pure, white energy. Within, he saw a shadow image of her; she had raised her sword and was blocking the bolt, though only where it touched her blade, and far from protecting the rest of her celestial skin, which roasted under the power of raw electromagnetism. She persevered until the bolt turned from bright white to dark blue, it now a mystical force far greater than nature could ever produce.

Lilith screamed and dropped her sword. She fell to her knees as the blue lightning cooked her from the inside out, and then abruptly shut off. White smoke rose from the ground. As it cleared, Jared could see the ashen image of Lilith—which was all that was left of her—still standing; she was on her haunches and her hands were raised to the air, as if begging for mercy. Though more importantly, behind her, he saw movement in the clearing smoke.

Farfal, Chax's lion-steed, broke through the smoke; and on top of his back, rode his master, the Duke of the Northlands. The rumble of Farfal's feet on the ground shook the ashen remains of Lilith apart. The great cat strode atop her ash as it approached Astaroth.

Zim and Jared retreated behind Chax. Caym, and now Thamuz—whose enchantment had been broken with Lilith's death—, came over and stood shoulder to shoulder with them. The legions facing them were silent. Astaroth stared at them with wide-eyes. He, too, for once, seemed speechless.

Astaroth rose from his throne and stepped down. The Damned immediately prostrated their bodies, offering up their backs for Astaroth to use as steps. Chax dismounted and walked forward, meeting him halfway in the small clearing that had been formed in front of the bridge.

Astaroth stared at Chax for a moment, and then cocked his head. "Why uncle, you've killed Lilith," he said nonchalantly, as though he was referring to a fly that had been swatted.

Chax smoothed the front of his silky, white shendyt, and then placed his hands on his hips. "I never did care much for her," he remarked. "I thought it was a mistake when The Father gave her to Adam."

"As did I."

"Not that Eve was any better," Chax said, and then sneered.

"Aye," Astaroth concurred heartily. "So we agree that The Father is fallible. And I'm sure we are also in agreement that mortals were one of his more egregious follies, too. Furthermore, that is, if we agree that mankind desperately craves our guidance, now more than ever, shouldn't we posit that it should be led by the greatest of us...*uncle?*"

The ground to Chax's right began to rumble, and then swelled like a boil coming to a head. It burst open and sent rocks and dust flying. The rocks rolled back to where they had come from, and then began gathering on themselves, rolling on top of one another, and then formed itself into the shape of a four-legged animal, complete with a rider upon its back. The rocks changed its consistency from hard to liquid—from gray to soot-black—reshaping itself into Beelzebub sitting atop a black panther with bright yellow eyes and fangs that hung past his jaw.

"You are far from being the greatest of us," Beelzebub remarked. He strode forward, positioning his panther next to Farfal, who greeted it with a growl, and it him, with a hiss. "Though once we are done with you, you will be the least amongst us; you will be nothing but ash."

Fire erupted from the ground to the left of Chax, and went soaring high into the sky, which was already ablaze with vulags streaking across it. The fire died down and formed into the shape of a figure, which, like

Beelzebub and Chax, sat upon a steed also. The fire turned fluid and congealed into the form of Agares, replete in a white skirt and criss-crossed fabric over her breasts. She strode forward upon an orange and black-stripped tigress and positioned herself on the opposite side of Farfal. She and Beelzebub dismounted, and walked over and stood on either side of Chax.

"Lady of the Eastlands," Astaroth said to her in greeting, his head held high in defiance and pride, "have you come to die also?"

"This *pass* will not mark my death," she replied, giving him a curt smile.

"Pride is what fell The Morning Star; remember?" he asked. "I am not him—I accept that. And, I do acknowledge that I am not the equal of The Father, either. Though a simple fact remains, my lords,…neither are you mine." The soldiers around him snapped to attention in unison. "The Lords of Hell will fall." The soldiers conjured their swords. "And Phenóx will fall." The soldiers took a step forward and grunted.

Astaroth raised his arms and called out with an echoing voice that flowed across the Westlands. His voice sent waves of energy flowing through the air, warping it like a reflection in a funhouse mirror. "Umaraku-de, susay a'tut!"

The Damned nearby them fell to ground and began to shiver and shake, and then began rolling toward each other, and then rolled on top of one another. Their bodies began meshing together, like they were melted wax and had been half-stirred into one another. Their clumped bodies formed a set of crude legs; and as other bodies rolled up and on top them, they too, began twisting and melding together to form the torso, and then the arms, and then the misshapen head composed of elbows, knees, backs, heads, and arms. Hundreds of the creatures made from the meshed bodies of The Damned began rising up, towering over the legions of soldiers below them. The creatures looked up to the vulag-streaked sky and howled like wolves ready for the kill.

Astaroth looked at Chax. "My lord, Chax…. Kneel, and then turn around and let us take Phenóx together. Let it be by my hand, and yours, that The Morning Star falls, and by his death, that he saves us all from the ether." He glanced at his lumbering, monstrous creatures formed out of The Damned. "You cannot stand against Hell, and I am it."

Chax took a step forward. "You may be Hell for now. Though always and forever, *I am Chax*." He flung his arms up. "Na-nufero kut va nufe-fero, amu ekra'ara zu koodun!"

Waves of black energy rippled out from around Chax and washed over scores of the legions. Farfal moved up next to Chax; the panther and ti-gress did as well, saddling up to their masters—Beelzebub and the panther on Chax's right, and Agares and the tigress on the left.

Chax, Beelzebub, and Agares conjured their swords. Chax turned his head to the side, where Jared and the others were. He nodded, and then turned back around.

"We must go," Zim said to Jared, pulling at his arm.

Jared didn't protest. He turned and ran with her to the bridge; Caym and Thamuz were right behind them. The gray, metal bridge seemed to go on forever, he thought, unable to see an end to it. Still, he ran—pushing his lifeforce into his legs to speed his already supernatural body—, knowing that at the end of that span, and then within the sphere it-self, there lay the possibility of returning home.

* * *

Chax turned back around. Zim and the others had fled across the bridge, and now, at least had a fighting chance, he thought. He looked at Astaroth, and then down at his lion-steed.

"You look famished, Farfal," he insisted.

Farfal took a step toward the soldiers, as did the other two great cats. They crouched on their front legs and raised their rear ones. They snarled at the soldiers, who, despite being armed with swords forged of their lifeforce, began to shuffle in their ranks, as the familiars of the Lords of Hell sized them up.

Chax aimed his sword at Astaroth. "Obey your master, Farfal. Send them all to the ether," he commanded.

Farfal, the panther, and the tiger leapt at the soldiers with teeth bared and claws extended. Astaroth darted and swung for Farfal. Chax was quicker, and thrust his sword between Astaroth's blade and Farfal's neck.

Farfal and the other cats crashed through the front lines of the troops, knocking them into the air; and then, with their trap-jaw mouths and bear-sized paws, they began mauling and striking at them, tearing through their breastplates and ripping their limbs from their bodies, treating them as though they were ragdolls they had been given to play with.

As the cats ripped through the scores of soldiers, Chax's enchantment he had cast earlier began to take effect. Those killed by Farfal and the other cats turned to ash, though did not stay as such; their bodies regenerated, though now, possessed of Chax's spell, their eyes were white, corner to corner. The white-eyed zombies rose from death and conjured swords, and began turning on their brethren. And as they killed their own, those who fell, too, began to rise from their ashes to fight alongside of them.

"*Necromancer!*" Astaroth seethed, seeing his troops fall, and then begin to rise and turn against him.

The death and rebirth of his troops began spreading and growing like a slow moving wave, and began rendering the catapults impotent, as the troops manning them fell under the sword of their enchanted comrades, and it now their turn to rise as lifeless, soldiers of Chax. Astaroth pushed his sword against Chax's, sliding him back.

"How great is the power of Hell, now that it has turned against itself, and upon you?" Chax asked, and then grinned mischievously.

"Spells will not save you," he replied. "The power you have drained from the angel will not change what will be. The power of Hell is far greater than the almighty, sky-god, Chax."

Astaroth swung at him. Chax blocked it with a swing up of the sword, and then thrust for Astaroth's neck. Astaroth was faster; he blocked it, and then attacked with a spell of black mist that jetted from his left palm, and a swing of his sword coming from the right.

Chax swung at the spell, though couldn't hold it at bay; tendrils of it were starting to seep past, and it was certain they brought death along with them. He retreated and swung again at the red tendrils, severing them, rendering them impotent, and they then dissipating in the air.

Chax looked to either side of him. Beelzebub and Agares were already gone...they were on the attack, adding their angel-fueled might to Farfal and the other great cats. He looked out and caught sight of the felines snatching up soldiers with their mouths and gnashing their teeth, ripping them apart. And with arms the length of a horse's leg, and claws sharp enough to rend metal, they fell soldiers in groups of two and three with just a swing.

Even Chax's spell of necromancy—a return of artificial life to the dead —had wrought awesome damage to Astaroth's legions. Though still, fresh troops were pouring in. For all of the dead that rose to fight for Chax, twice as many seemed to come flowing over the horizon to replace them. With an influx of new troops to man the catapults, the vulags again began flying overhead.

The Train of Souls's whistle screamed from afar. Astaroth and Chax looked off in its direction. Astaroth turned and looked at him, and then ran his sword along the ground between them. Where his blade touched the stony ground, it turned to powder, and caved in on itself.

"The Train of Souls will depart, and it will return and replace all of The Damned that I have used thus far, and more. And it will depart and return, and again, and again, until the dome is breached and your ashes are floating somewhere in the air of my Westlands." He looked Chax in the eye and held his gaze steady. "You choose, Chax. Me, your king, or the ether—nonexistence."

Chax grinned. "You have forgotten who I am."

"You are Chax!" Astaroth seethed, grudgingly. "You were Sky Father. You were king of the gods. But you are no more...I am now, and then some."

"You're toasting a victory you have yet to win," he said. "I live. Beelzebub and Agares still live." He raised his sword and widened his stance. "Only my death will give you the victory you seek. My death, dear nephew, will not come easy."

Astaroth shook his head. "Oh, uncle, it will. I promise."

* * *

Jared looked up at the dome. The sight of it looming over him made his lifeforce become thready with dread. They had passed the halfway mark across the grey, metal bridge, with its soaring towers and suspension cables. Below it, from what Jared could see, there was nothing there, just darkness, like the ether. They had ran the entire way, and all the while, vulags streaked overhead, coloring the sky with fire and smoke, exploding against the dome in grand bursts of flames, body parts, and raw energy released from The Damned.

Zim led the way down bridge; it was wide enough to march a row of soldiers through it, which was exactly what Astaroth had planned on doing. Jared, Caym, and Thamuz were just a step behind her. She stopped suddenly, bringing them to a halt. She turned around and looked back. Jared did as well.

"I can't see anything," he said, peering down the span of the bridge. "Can you?"

Zim shook her head no. "I see nothing…which may bode good or ill fortune; there's no way to tell. The vulags are still pounding the dome, which is a good thing, at least for you. But that also means that Astaroth is still in control."

"Not quite," Caym objected. "He hasn't sent his legions across the bridge."

"Perhaps because Duke Chax does not allow it," Thamuz opined.

"That is simply conjecture at this point," Zim said.

"Do not doubt my father," Caym said, speaking up quickly, and deeply, and commandingly, like the regal he was.

"I don't," Zim said. "Yet do not doubt Astaroth either."

"This is the last pass he will ever see," Caym vowed.

"Aye, my lord," Thamuz concurred.

They began running toward the dome again. The booming of the vulags exploding against it grew louder. Now closer, Jared could see the spray of flames coming from each impact for what they truly were— flaming heads and legs, arms and feet, torsos too, falling to the bridge like spent casings from a machine gun. As he looked toward the end of the bridge, amidst the flaming body parts raining down, he saw movement...figures; there were several of them standing where the bridge ended and the dome began.

"Zim?" Jared said.

"I see them."

"Who are they?"

"Ones I would rather not care to see."

She slowed to a walk and conjured her sword. Thamuz and Caym summoned their swords also, and set their sights on those at the end of the bridge, who were blocking the way into Phenóx.

They drew closer. Jared could see now that there were five of them. He conjured his sword.

"Do as you have done before," Zim said to him. "Let your sword be an extension of your arm, and channel as much of your lifeforce through it when you strike. You found the strength to shatter Flagon's blade. Find it again. We need it now."

"*The lady, Zimarantha, is correct*," Aka Mana said, calling out to them as they approached. The ram-headed count cocked his head at them, looking at them with all three of his eyes—two of them as they should be, and one in the middle of his forehead. "You will need all the power The Father has given you—*and more*—if you seek to pass us, angel."

King Purson, the lion-faced ruler of Sheol, was to the right of Aka Mana; and next to him was Count Morax, the black, fur-covered demon with the head of a bull. The fair-skinned, dark-haired King Moloch, and the archer, the Marquis Leraje—his opposite in color—were to Aka Mana's left. They were spread out in a line across the bridge, just feet in front of Phenóx's doorstep. Purson, Morax, and Moloch wielded swords; Aka Mana held on to a gray, metal staff that was more than a foot taller than he was. Leraje had his bow at his cheek, with an arrow cocked and ready to fly.

"I want Zimarantha," Purson said, stepping forward, breaking the line.

Jared bristled at Purson's words. He moved closer to Zim and gripped his sword tighter, ready to defend her.

"It seems you'll have to slay Zimarantha's suitor first," Morax remarked, looking at Jared with a wry raise of his brow.

"It would be my pleasure to kill the angel," Purson said. "He has yet to atone for his sins against me and my realm…all of them, to be exact." His feline, amber eyes roved across Jared and the others. "You've killed Lord Flagon and his crew. That, too, requires recompense; and I demand that debt be made whole with their ashes."

"They are traitors," Leraje professed, holding his bow steady at the cheek. "That's reason enough to see them to the ether."

"I need no reason not to see them all to the ether," Moloch said. "Though, they are all a bit old for my taste, save the angel. I could make do with him."

"Patience and persistence, brother," Aka Mana advised, with a glance Moloch's way. "The earth will be opened to us once more, and the mortals will sacrifice their offspring to you in droves, *as they once did*. Your temple will flow with blood, and they will blacken the sky with the burn of their young for your pleasure; that is, once we have sent these traitors to the ether."

"You see victory, my lord, Aka Mana?" Caym poised.

A volley of vulags crashed into the dome right above them and sent ripples emanating across the surface of it. The dome began shuddering where the vulags had pounded it. It screeched as though it were alive, sounding like fork tines being dragged across metal. Flaming parts of The Damned rained down on the bridge, and more vulags were on their way.

Aka Mana looked up at the dome and smiled. "Aye, prince," he said to Caym. "You will fall, and so will Phenóx, along with the lord of the realm."

"You won't talk so boldly once The Morning Star awakens and discovers your betrayal," Caym said, grabbing his flaming sword with both hands. He swung it around and aimed it at the ground. He looked at Aka Mana and the others standing with him, and smiled. "But then again, by that time, you'll all be ash anyway."

Caym slammed his sword down, burying half of it into the metal bridge. The red flames around his blade turned dark green. The ground began rumbling. Vines as thick as arms burst through the bridge at Aka Mana and the other's feet, snaking up their legs and circling around them. Leraje released his arrow just before the vines reached his arms and bound them to his sides. The arrow was for Jared; it went whistling through the air, speeding right for his head.

Jared raised his sword to block it, though Zim got there first. She swung her sword around in a circle and knocked the arrow away, with just inches to spare before it struck.

Jared sighed in relief. "Thanks!"

"Don't mention it," she said, bringing her sword around and up.

Caym's vines wound around Leraje's limbs and encircled his mouth, preventing him from calling out in spell. The snaking vines also caught Moloch and Morax off their guard, wrapping around their arms and knocking their swords from their hands. Their swords disappeared in a puff of smoke before they even hit the ground.

Aka Mana pointed his staff at the vines entangling Moloch and Morax. His grey staff glowed red; the vines went still and began to wither, and then turned to dust.

He turned and brought the staff up by his shoulder, cocked it like a javelin, and slung it at the vines where they grew at Leraje's feet; he was nearly mummified, except for his bulging, panic-stricken eyes. The glowing staff pierced the tangle of vines, negating the spell that had brought them into being. They shriveled and released Leraje, who fell face first to the ground. Aka Mana's staff disappeared like wind-blown smoke and rematerialized back in his hands.

Jared stepped away from Zim, positioning himself on Aka Mana's right. Caym took Jared's cue and charged at Moloch, drawing him away from Aka Mana, and Leraje, who was lying motionless on the ground. Caym pressed the attack, forcing Moloch back toward the side of the bridge, and then spun around and dashed back for Leraje with his sword held high and ready strike.

Aka Mana lunged at Caym. However, Jared was already on the way, and just in time. He thrust his blade as Aka Mana's glowing, red staff swung down and blocked it with just inches to spare, freeing Caym to strike, which he did—straight through the middle of Leraje's back and into the ground. Aka Mana yelled out as Leraje burst into flames, like he had been doused with gasoline and lit. He turned to ash in moments.

"You're going to regret that, angel," Aka Mana said, glaring at him, and then in a blur, proceeding to swing at him.

Jared bent backward at the waist as the staff came zooming across. It passed just over his face, nearly nicking his nose. Zim moved in and lunged at Aka Mana, and attacked with sword and spell. Jared spun around and moved to Aka Mana's backside, and thrust at him. Aka Mana blocked both of their attacks with his staff and a spell of his own, and still he found enough quarter to sneak in an attack on both of them; a black, spiraling spell for Jared and a flurry of strikes aimed for Zim's head. Zim managed to block them all, though the last strike sent her sliding back on her feet.

Aka Mana looked at Jared. The misty, black spell was still headed Jared's way. "Chax has given your comrades the power of his realm to fight with it. Well…so too has His Grace, Astaroth…only, my lord commands all of Hell, and he has far more to give."

Aka Mana held out his hand and spread his fingers. A black, misty spell spread out from them and surrounded Jared. Now, instead of one enchanted tendril to sever, there were ten of them; and they whispered to him as they moved in. *Madness! Kill yourself. Do it now! Fall on your blade. Drive it through your chest. Curse The Father. Curse The Ghost!* Do it!

The spell-bound mist attacked Jared from every angle. Some of it circled around on itself and appeared to dart one way, only to go another, while other tendrils of it wove between each other before moving in for the strike. Jared back up as he slashed right and left in front of his body, trying to keep the foul mist at bay. The more he swung, the lighter the sword seemed to become. He began feeling the sword as part of himself, as though his sense extended all the way out to its tip.

He took out a tendril to his right, and then on his left with one swift swing. He felt his courage rising, and his confidence in himself burgeoning as well. He had tapped a fraction of the power of the ether once, and he believed he could do it again. He knew he had to.

His arm and sword began to blur and leave ghost-trails as he cut tendril after tendril, right and left, above and below, until only one remained. It reared back like a cobra ready to strike, and then dove at him. Jared turned to the side and swung his blade down and up, and cut the tip off. The mist dissipated away.

To his right, Purson and Morax were still posturing at Thamuz, and he at them; they all waiting to see who would make the first move...the lion, the bull, or Thamuz—the hulking beast who stood a foot taller than either one of them. Purson crouched and lunged at Thamuz from the left; Morax came swinging on the right. Thamuz blocked both blows with a swift swing to either side, and then pulled his blade back, preparing to thrust and skewer Purson through the gut; however, he did not see Purson's claw coming up from below. Purson's claw tore into Thamuz's breastplate and ripped the metal apart.

Thamuz yelled as the claws tore into him, though never lost his flow or step. He grabbed one side of the split breastplate and tore it off as he spun around, and then swung it at Morax, who had stepped in and was just about to strike. He smashed it against Morax's face, knocking him back and into Purson. Thamuz backed away from them and glance at his chest. His flesh had been flayed in four, vertical rows.

Thamuz began speaking in his demon tongue and began to radiate from within, making his skin glow dark purple. His body began to grow, adding mass that pushed his height two feet taller, and his width, another foot across. The armor plates on his shins, thighs, and arms expanded; and stretched to their limits, they popped off and clang on the bridge. The black sword he held elongated and widened. Once again, he had tapped into the power of Orsha-Na that Chax had given him.

Purson and Morax came back at him. They rushed at him from either side. Morax aimed low; Purson swung high. Thamuz slammed his foot on the ground as they neared. The force of his stomp heaved the bridge and sent Purson and Morax off their feet; and using their own momentum against them, they came hurtling—ungracefully—toward Thamuz.

Thamuz leaned left and thrust his sword, just as Purson came sailing toward him. His blade pierced Purson's chest and slid through and out the other side. Purson roared in agony. He swung at Thamuz, trying to take him to the ether along with him. Thamuz yelled out and raised his sword, bringing Purson up in the air along with it and out of striking distance. Purson wasn't dissuaded and kept swinging for him, though it was all for naught; he was already turning black, and quickly becoming gray. He slid down Thamuz's blade and turned to ash before he touched the hilt.

Jared had only just recovered from fending off the mist, and had reengaged Aka Mana from behind, when the bridge—by Thamuz's mighty stomp—heaved and flung him up and back, and into the dome. His breastplate, which had blunted his impact and was resting against the dome, began to freeze, crusting over with ice. He pushed off the ground, moving away from the dome. He ripped the breastplate off and tossed it. It turned white all over and cracked, and broke apart into thumb-sized pieces.

The rocking of the bridge had thrown Zim and Aka Mana off their stances as well. They stumbled...he toward her and she toward the bridge's span, though both soon recovered their footing and were back at it, trading blows with staff and sword and spell.

On his left, Caym had backed Moloch against the side of the bridge and pressed the attack with a flurry of strikes of his flaming sword. Caym stopped and retreated a step, and then cast his sword away; it turned to mist and disappeared. He stretched his arms out toward the ground and spread his finger, and called out in spell. Moloch dashed in to attack while he was unarmed.

Moloch swung. Caym didn't move.

Moloch's blade was inches shy of slicing Caym's head in half—diagonally—when vines shot forth over his shoulder and grasped it, and encircled it twice and thrice, and yanked it out of his hands. More of Caym's vines came up from behind and bound his leg, his chest, his arms, spreading him out by the limbs until he resembled and X. It bound his mouth, smothering any spell he might dare try to cast, and pulled him off of his feet, and ensnared him in a cocoon of vines. Caym casually walked over to him and reformed his sword; it came to life in a burst of flames. He crouched down in front of Moloch and cocked his head.

"What say Moloch, now?" Caym asked. "You have betrayed us...betrayed my father. My mother and I have come to seek his revenge."

The vines began piercing Moloch, boring into him like worms tunneling into dirt, only faster, and draining him of lifeforce. Moloch's pale skin wrinkled, and then shriveled. His eyes sank into his skull, and then just as quickly, out of the holes that were left, vines sprouted out from them. The vines crawled in and out of his body, like needles and thread through cloth. He turned to ash and fell apart. Caym joined Jared and Zim in their assault on Aka Mana.

Though even with three attacking Aka Mana—Zim from the front, Jared from the rear, and now Caym to the side of him—he kept them at bay with darting black spells and swings of his enchanted, glowing staff; and by the power of Hell given to him by Astaroth, he wielded them both simultaneously. Though soon after Caym joined the fray, Thamuz did, too; he came running at Aka Mana's flank with Morax's head in his hand, and flung it at him. Aka Mana turned and swung his staff at it, splitting the decapitated head in half, which turned to ash in midair.

Still—*now*—they had Aka Mana surrounded on all fronts. Jared and the others paused and glanced at each other. As though by agreement and a silent countdown, they charged Aka Mana as one. Aka Mana brought his staff straight up and in line with his body, and then slammed it on the ground.

A blue wave of energy burst out in a circle from all around Aka Mana. The wave hit Jared, Zim, and the others, knocking them from their feet and sliding them across the ground. Aka Mana turned around in a circle, looking upon all of them, even as vulags crashed into the dome and the flaming body parts that they were, continued raining down around them.

"You've struck down kings and noblemen," Aka Mana said, turning round as he spoke. "I, too, am a king, and a god, and imbued with the power of Hell. Strike us down, and many more will take our place."

Aka Mana began casting a spell. Black smoke oozed from his palms and swirled around his glowing staff. He brought it up, and then slammed it on the ground again. And as though he were never solid to begin with, he turned into black smoke and separated into four swirling clouds, which spread out and rushed toward Jared and the others. The smoke swirled around and refashioned into four likenesses of Aka Mana, each with a staff in hand and a scowl on each of their goat faces.

"From the moment you set off from Orsha-Na," the doppelgangers said in unison, "you should have known you were going to fail." The doppelgangers cocked their staff and lunged at each one of them.

Jared parried Aka Mana's thrust with a swift raise of his sword, and then thrust for his chest; Aka Mana blocked the strike with a mist-borne spell. Jared swung at the spiraling mist and managed to disarm it, and just in time; Aka Mana's staff was already coming his way from the other side. Jared pivoted on his heels and met the staff with his sword, though did not see Aka Mana's fist coming at him from the other side in time. The fist slammed into his jaw, popping it and turning his vision bright white, and sent him tumbling head-over-heel.

Jared scrambled to his feet. Aka Mana was already rushing in for the attack, with his staff raised and a black spell twirling from his other hand, and yet, another spell—a white one—came darting under Aka Mana's raised arms. Jared attacked both spells, and then tumble-rolled under Aka Mana's swing of his staff. He looked over at the doppelganger that was battering Thamuz with a series of staff strikes, and saw the tail end of the white spell that he had just come for him. Thamuz's doppelganger looked over at him and smiled, and then sent another white, twisting spell his way, just as the Aka Mana he had been fighting came rushing back in on him.

The other doppelgangers were doing the same thing; attacking the foe in front of them, while aiding one another in their fight with spells sent across and diagonally at Jared and the others. The doppelgangers attack was throwing them off balance, keeping them confused. And it was working marvelously. Caym's doppelganger had backed him up to the side of the bridge; Zim and Thamuz were falling further and further back with each blow from theirs. And if it was working, Jared thought, then it wasn't such a bad idea after all. He decided to give Aka Mana a taste of his own tactic.

He retreated out of Aka Mana's reach and cocked his sword like a spear, and then threw it. Aka Mana quickly turned his body to the side.

Jared's sword went zooming past him, passing through the ghostly trails he left behind. Aka Mana straightened up and smiled at him.

Aka Mana sneered. "You missed, angel."

Jared cocked his head. "No...I was dead on."

A cry called out from behind them. Jared's doppelganger spun around and looked. The doppelganger that was battling Zim had Jared's sword squarely in his back, buried to the hilt, and was trying to reach behind himself to extract it. Zim sprung at him and swung high, and lopped his head from his neck with one clean strike. The headless creature fell to its knees and turned to ash.

Jared's doppelganger spun back around. Its cold, gray eyes became red and began to glow. It raised its staff and its other hand—it glowing with a spell just waiting to be released—and moved to strike. Jared sent his lifeforce streaming into his hands, bidding it to refashion his sword, and quickly, though he was too late. The hilt of his sword was just forming as Aka Mana's spell and staff came within striking distance; he could feel the burn of power from each on his skin.

With but a moment to spare before staff and spell struck him down, sending him to the ether, a sword came jutting through Aka Man's neck; its point stopped mere inches from Jared's face. Aka Mana choked out a screech and flung his arms up, dropping his staff and loosing his spell. Zim moved out from behind Aka Mana and looked up at him. Her hands still gripped the sword sticking through his neck.

"Obviously," she said to him, "you didn't know it was *you* who was going to fall this pass." She twisted the sword around in his neck. Aka Mana screeched again and turned to ash. She grabbed Jared by the shoulder. "Well played, Jared. Now come on." She pulled at him, moving him toward Thamuz and Caym, who were being battered by their doppelgangers. "I know this spell. Once one is killed, the other takes on its strength. We get Thamuz first, and then Caym; with his mother's strength with him, he'll have a better chance than, Thamuz, but not much. *Hurry!*"

Jared attacked Thamuz's doppelganger from the side, knowing that the creature would sense him coming and would strike; and the creature did. It swung for him, just as he predicted, and he was ready for it.

He let go of his sword—it vanished—and he thrust that lifeforce into his muscles instead. He tucked and rolled on the ground, and out of the way the doppelganger's staff that came swooshing through the air for him. He gathered his lifeforce and pushed it out through his palm, conjuring his sword back, and swung for the creature's arm as he rolled up to his feet. He gashed the creature's arm, though not deep enough to stop him. Though it was enough to get a howl out of him, and throw him off rhythm for a moment. And a moment was all that was needed.

Zim came around the creature from the other side and swung low. Jared pulled his back and swung high. Thamuz had already claimed the moment and had leapt at the creature, sword gripped in both hands and aimed for its chest.

As one, they struck.

Zim took its leg clean off…Jared, its arm at the shoulder; Thamuz brought his sword straight down and through the creature, and landed on top of him. Thamuz pulled his sword out and swung it across the creature's neck, taking its head off. Both head and body turned gray; they became ash.

As the ashes vanished, Jared and the others turned their attention to the lone creature, now Aka Mana back whole and undiminished in power, and overpowering Caym at the moment. Though as they rushed in for the attack, Aka Mana kicked Caym in the gut, flinging him back against the side of the bride, and then spun around and sent a spell of black mist spiraling from his palm at them. The mist stopped and re-shaped itself into a wall of black thickets with thorns as thick as wrists. The thickets moved toward them, walking on their thorns like they were feet. The thickets began encircling them, and jabbing their thorns at them, trying to stab any part of them that they could.

Jared swung high and low in a flurry of crisscrossing strikes. Though the more dagger-thorns he sliced away, the more they seemed to come. He had no choice but to retreat, just as Zim and Thamuz were, the thickets pushing them further and further away from Caym, who was now in desperate need of their help.

Through the thickets he hacked away, and before they could grow back, he saw Aka Mana battering Caym relentlessly. Caym was but moments from being turned into ash; and the thickets were growing even quicker and had formed a circle around Jared and the others.

The sound of thunder boomed from above and shook the bridge. Jared glanced up. Black, roiling clouds had formed. Lighting arched through it in every direction. A voice called down from the clouds. *"Get away from my son!"*

Lightning careened out of the cloud and struck Aka Mana, encasing him in a vortex of lightning that swayed out to the side, like a bowing tornado. The lightning shut off as quickly as it had come. Where Aka Mana had once stood, there was now just a red-hot crater in the midst of the bridge. Even his ash had been incinerated.

Aka Mana was no more. His spell of crawling thickets followed him into oblivion. They stopped in mid-motion and turned back into mist and smoke, and then dispersed into the air.

Thunder boomed from the cloud. Another bolt of lightning came down and struck in front of them. This one, however, was not meant to kill, but to deliver. The lightning disappeared, leaving Chax in its place.

Jared never thought he would be glad to see a demon, though proved himself wrong and sighed in relief at the sight of the wood-skinned demon. He nodded at Chax, thanking him, which again, he never envisioned ever doing. He remembered how different the world was now. He felt as though he was finally, truly, accepting that as fact for the first time…all of it…Zim included.

"I wasn't going to let Aka Mana kill my beloved son," Chax said. He took a step and fell to a knee. Caym ran and knelt beside him, holding him steady at the shoulder. He looked at Caym. "What is it like to see a god on his knee?" He smiled and managed a chuckle.

"You are spent, father," Caym said harshly, unmoved by the attempted levity.

"I am Chax," his father replied proudly, and pushed up from his knee and stood, and wobbled. He looked down the bridge's span. "Astaroth will be here soon. We could not stop him."

A swarm of flies came swooping up from under the bridge. It gathered itself next to Chax and changed into flesh, forming Lord Beelzebub. "We have weakened him," said he, as his mouth formed from flies to flesh, "but so, too, are we."

Flames shot up from the bridge on the other side of Chax and took form and shape of the Duchess Agares. "He has sent much of his power overhead," she said, looking to the skies filled with streaking vulags. "But the Train of Souls will return soon to replenish what he has lost. The soldiers will march across the bridge, and Astaroth will lead them."

A heavy barrage of vulags came streaking overhead. They smashed against the dome as one and exploded, casting them all in an orange glow of fire. A cracking noise, like glass slowly being stepped upon, could be heard from where the vulags had hit.

Chax looked down at Jared. "The dome will fall, but Astaroth will be here well before then, and we will not be able to stop him. I have kept my end of the pact to the best of my ability."

"As have I," Beelzebub said.

"And I, too," Agares added.

"Though we may fall, think about it, angel," Chax said, "it was worth a try, was it not? We, who are each other's enemy, have come and fought, and will die fighting together."

Jared looked at the dome. Another round of vulags were crashing against it. The sound of it cracking was getting louder. Though, as he looked down the span of the bridge, he saw that Chax was right; Astaroth was coming, approaching on horseback at full gallop with his sword raised and his silky-red hair flowing out behind him; *and behind him*, legions of soldiers charging forward. And again, Chax was right... the dome wasn't going to crack in time.

"Give the power back," Jared said to Zim, Caym, and Thamuz, turning to them, and then looking at all of them. "Chax is the only one who can stop Astaroth, or at least slow him down until the dome cracks. We all know it. *I* know it."

"'Tis' true," said Beelzebub.

Caym laid his hand on his father's shoulder. Green mist began spiraling out from his skin. "Take it, father."

Chax leaned his head back. Caym's mist flowed away from his body and was pulled in to Chax's. Zim and Thamuz approached him as well, and released their mist and hold over the lands of Orsha-Na that Chax had given them.

The returned lifeforce renewed Chax's body. His eyes once again sparkled like jewels. His wood grain skin glistened with power. He turned and faced the bridge. Astaroth was a few hundred yards off, though his army was now far behind him and struggling to keep up with his air blurring speed.

Beelzebub and Agares moved in on either side of Chax. They conjured their swords, ready to attack or defend. Astaroth came within feet and sprung off of his horse, rocketing himself toward them and was already swinging for them. All four of their swords connected, and at their meeting—the power of the four Lords of Hell came together—that focal point exploded, releasing raw power, which knocked Chax, Agares, and Beelzebub to the ground, though left the one lord who controlled the power of Hell still standing.

"Once again, the mighty Chax and his band of bereft lords have fallen," Astaroth said, grinning with pride. He approached Chax, who was on his back and defensively holding his sword up and across his body. Astaroth raised his sword. "This pass marks the end of the great and almighty Chax, once and for all."

Jared dashed toward them with his sword aimed straight out. The dome was cracking and was nearly apart near the foot of the bridge, but it still wasn't enough. He needed Chax, and gave it no thought to rushing in, even as Zim yell for him not to.

With both hands, he stuck his sword between Chax and Astaroth. Astaroth's blade came flying down upon Jared's and was stopped cold. In a pause, as their swords lay upon the other—neither giving and neither retreating—they looked at one another...Jared with determination, and Astaroth, with indignation at his challenge.

Jared channeled all of his lifeforce and strength into his sword and yelled out, and pushed off with it, knocking Astaroth nearly ten feet back. He grabbed Chax's arm and pulled him to his feet.

Chax half-grinned. "Who says angels are not brave?"

"Jared! Watch out!" Zim cried from behind.

Jared turned to Astaroth. Astaroth's hand was glowing red and aimed at him. As the glow of his hand brightened, his soldiers charging toward them began to fall to the ground, crumbling to ash, as their lifeforce was taken from them and funneled into his body. He released the energy upon Jared.

The crimson blast of energy hit Jared before he could even think to raise his sword and block it. And even if he had, it would not have made a difference, for the beam of energy was as wide as his chest, which was where it hit. It batted him like a ball, sending him flying against the dome and pinning him there. Jared's skin began to roast like meat over an open flame.

Chax thrust his sword between the ray of pure, red lifeforce and deflected it up and at the dome, adding its fiery concussive power to that of the vulags, which had nearly cracked the dome apart where the bridge met it. Jared fell to the ground. He smoked all over…burnt by fire on the front, and by ice on his back, where he was pinned against the dome. Zim rushed over and knelt beside him. She pulled him to his feet and bore his weight on her shoulders.

He was injured, though it was not all for naught. With Astaroth's deflected power added to the assault of vulags, the cracks in the dome spread out, screeching like a wounded animal. A few of those cracks descended to the foot of the bridge, where the dome was already fractured and weak, and shattered it.

Astaroth cried out and shut off his flow of power. His pale skin had become gray, and his green eyes, once bright like emeralds, were the color of mud. He was weakened—yes—; though the passage to Phenóx, which was ever his goal, was now open. Astaroth smiled, and then looked through the cleft into that land of bitter, burning ice.

"Subterfuge, dear angel. It is all about subterfuge," Chax said, turning to Jared, who was leaning against Zim.

Jared bristled at Chax's words. He had been tricked, he thought. Fear began squeezing him like a vise.

He had helped the demons break into Phenóx, which was what they had wanted all along, he thought suddenly. And now that they had, their ruse was up; their trick was revealed; their deception was brought into the light.

"You gave your word, Chax!"

Chax smiled at him. "And so I did."

"As did I," said Beelzebub.

"And I, too," Agares said.

Chax raised his arms at Jared. Jared cried out; it was the only defense he had now. Though instead of being hit and incinerated by another blast of pure lifeforce, he felt his body suddenly grow light and rise in the air, and Zim's along with him. He looked at Caym and Thamuz; Chax was bringing them aloft in the air as well.

Chax flicked his hand forward, and they all—he, Zim, Thamuz, and Caym—went flying through the breach of the dome, and fell into the land of Phenóx. They scrambled to their feet and looked back through the fissure they had been slung through. Chax was looking at them. The dome was already sealing itself back up.

"Subterfuge," Chax called out to them, as the opening continued sealing. "I am far from spent, angel. Though it is Astaroth who is now weakened. And we shall kill him." He conjured his sword. "And then, our pact shall be honored. I am Chax, after all."

Chax turned and faced Astaroth as the dome sealed itself back up, sealing Jared and the others in the realm of the greatest and the foulest creature ever created by God.

He was in Phenóx at last; at the end of the road that led home.

CHAPTER 19

Henrì had little room to pace in the limestone cellar—it a hidden room behind the shelf in the pantry off the kitchen, meant for hiding from Union soldiers during the war, and now, meant for hiding from immortals trying to kill them. Henrì stopped at the wall and wiped at the dust-covered cobwebs. There was a coat of webs on every wall and across the slat wood ceiling, which hung just a few inches above his head. Thaddeus sat on the dirt floor with his knees pulled up and spread wide, with his hands clasped between them.

"I don't like it," Henrì grumbled.

Thaddeus looked up. "Say what, son?"

"I don't like this!" Henrì pointed to the wood-slat door. "We're here, and they're out there, Thaddeus. That's our family out there, and we're doing what? Sitting here? Waiting until—"

"Don't say it, son," Thaddeus urged.

"I don't have to," Henrì said, and then leaned his back against wall. "I can't stop thinking it's all going to go wrong. I know you're thinking the same." He looked down, and then over at the door. "We just fed them to the lions. You know that, right?"

Thaddeus huffed. "And so was brother, Daniel."

Henrì glared at him and sighed. "If God wants to send an angel down to take care of our lions, like Daniel's, then he's more than welcome to.

But seeing that he's not, you'll forgive me, deacon, if my faith in him is a little shaky at the moment."

"Seems to me like that shaky faith is all you got right now." Thaddeus chuckled. "I wouldn't go throwin' it away just yet."

"The minute they start chanting, Yikan's going to come running for them."

"And we got two, tough ol' birds out there fighting for us," he said. "And we got Chris, too. And he's already been up against Yikan and lived to tell it."

"That was luck."

"He made it out."

"Jared didn't," Henrì panned.

Thaddeus bit his lip and looked down. Henrì knew he had taken it too far. He kicked at the dirt and grumbled. "Yikan wants blood—our blood. That's the only way he secures his future as a god. And knowing he'll do anything to have it, and kill anyone, too, makes me sick that I can't even help." Henrì sat and looked at him. He shook his head and sighed. "So, I need more faith, huh?"

"A prayer ain't gonna hurt either."

Henrì shrugged. He lowered his head and clasped his hands. "Well... go on then, deacon."

Thaddeus lowered his head and began the Lord's Prayer. Henrì joined him midway through it, though neither of them finished it.

Thaddeus's eyes began to close. His head lolled to the side, as the rest of his body went limp. Henrì knew Thaddeus wasn't really sleeping, but was in an illusion created to hide his conscious mind; for when Yikan came for them, he would sense out anything alive and kill it. But he couldn't kill what he couldn't sense—that was Chris's idea, who only a few years ago couldn't grasp basic math facts, yet now, he had come up with a plot to trick a creature that was thousands of years old.

The light from the dangling bulb in the center of the room began to dim. Henrì felt his muscles suddenly grow heavy; and then the darkness took him, and from that nothingness of blackness came light. He opened his eyes to rolling hills of honey-wheat just ripe for the harvest. The sun was at its apex. Behind him, on the hilltop where he stood, was a sky-soaring oak tree, thick of branch and covered in dark, green leaves. And beside the mighty oak was Thaddeus, turning about and taking in the golden field of summertime dreams.

Henrì walked over to him. They both turned and looked off toward the horizon, where blue skies met gold wheat. "And now we wait," Henrì said.

"And pray."

They both went to their knees and folded their hands.

"Our Father, who art in heaven, hallowed be thy name...."

This time they finished it. And then began it again; and then again; and then again.

* * *

Chris looked up at Dorthea and Olivia, who were crouched on the floor opposite of him. Between them was the golden tome, which was opened three-quarters of the way through. He looked over at Phineas, who standing by the door.

"They're inside the illusion," Chris said. "I guess we're ready to start."

The three of them joined hands. They closed their eyes, though only for a moment. Dorthea and Olivia proceeded to stand, and then began walking over to the door.

Phineas stepped in their way. "Whoa...where ya'll goin'?"

The two women looked at one another. Olivia turned and smiled at him. "We're going to give Jared the help he needs to get home. That's what we're doing."

Phineas shook his head. "By doing what? Getting' yourselves killed? Ya'll 'spose to be helping the boy chant, and ya'll think ya'll goin' where? I know Henrì and Thaddeus don't know about this."

"They know all they need to know," Olivia told him.

"This is how it's going be, Phineas," Dorthea said.

"If you want Jared back, I would listen to them," Chris said, looking at the tome, not bothering to glance up.

"But...."

"But what, Phineas?" Dorthea asked, giving him a steely glare. Moments passed with no reply from him. "You protect Chris—that's what you do. All right? And pray to God that killer comes with them, 'cause that's our baby's way back home—that's his only way. So if I gotta give my life—"

"And mine, too," Olivia said, jumping in.

"Me three," Chris added.

Dorthea raised her head proud. "If we have to die to give Jared even a little bit of a chance, then that's what we're going to do. What are you ready to do?"

Phineas fixed his eyes dead on hers and nodded. "The same."

"Then protect Chris," Dorthea said, "and let's get our son back home."

* * *

"Hey, Eric," Blain called. Eric was standing just a few feet behind him, looking out the palace entrance. "I think we have more incoming."

Blain had been watching as Yikan transmuted sand into stone blocks, and then stacking them one on top of the other, completing a wall to his desert, godly palace, when suddenly, he just stopped. The winds Yikan had conjured to raise the sand into the air had ceased; the grains of sand sprinkled to ground.

Eric turned and looked up at Yikan, who was sitting on his throne, and was, at the moment, absolutely still and blankly staring forward. He walked over to the dais.

"What's happening?" Blain asked Eric, following and catching up to him. "Just grab the missiles and return to sender, like last time. But go bigger—that's what I would do if I were you two. Taking out their priests and rabbis, and turning London into a parking lot didn't drive the lesson home. So if you really want to get them on their knees," Eric kept walking, ignoring him, "I'd take it to America. Take out D.C. and New York; set Paris and Berlin on fire, too, and they'll sing a whole new tune for you."

Eric waved him off with a flick of the hand. "It's not that, mortal."

"Then what is it?"

"The chant!" Yikan answered, with a voice that echoed throughout the palace. His liquid, blue eyes raced round and round. "They call upon the sacred chant!"

"They're using the tome," Blain muttered, as though not believing it.

"To no end," Eric said.

"To their deaths," Yikan added.

"You said they would, and they did," Blain said. "I didn't think they would be stupid enough to do it, but they are. And you knew they would."

"He is Aton," Eric said proudly, looking up at Yikan with eyes wide with veneration.

"We can end this now," said Blain, looking from one to the other. "Ever since I found out about that creature in me, I've been trying to find a way to escape going to the other side."

"You'll burn there," Eric assured him.

"Forever and ever," Yikan said.

"You said you could help me, if I help you...and I am; and I will. If you can save me from going down there," he looked at the floor, though all knew what he meant, "then I'll kill anything you want me to. I'll even get on my knees." And he did. "Save me from the fire, Aton...my god. Who do you want me to kill? Tell me?

Yikan looked down at him. The spin of his blue eyes slowed to a crawl. *Kill them all!*"

CHAPTER 20

Jared's body was repairing what Astaroth had scorched and battered, though slowly, far slower than even after he had fallen into Hell. The difference? He was in Phenóx now—where all within the dome, which had sealed the chasm Chax had flung them through, belonged to The Morning Star. Though his skin was slowly changing from fire-cooked black to brown, white mist—his lifeforce—was seeping from his skin, like steam escaping an iron.

It was the same with Zim, Thamuz, and Caym, he saw, looking upon them. Their lifeforce was being pulled from them as well, flowing down their bodies and along the bridge. In the distance, he saw where it was headed.

A sparkling, silver palace gleamed within the gloom of Phenóx. The palace-city lay open like a *Jack in the Pulpit*, with low, square towers in the front that rose up and around, soaring high into the sky and coming to point. And at its top, it glowed bright white, like a beacon leading sailors safely to port, though for them, most likely leading them to their doom, Jared thought.

He was in the realm of the greatest celestial of them all; the first of them who had fallen from grace; the one who was most perfect of all of God's creations. And even in slumber, he proved his power awesome, for he and the others were already loosing their force to him, making him stronger and them weaker.

"Can you run, Jared?" Zim asked.

"Not really, but I will," Jared replied. "I don't have a choice."

Caym looked at him. Mist was oozing away from his face; the glow of his dark green eyes was fading. "No you don't, and neither do we."

They took off running, each step drawing them closer to Lucifer's palace…his lair…the home of The Morning Star.

CHAPTER 21

"I haven't played hide and seek in years," Eric called out, as he walked into the seemingly empty mansion hidden away in the depths of the bayou.

It was dark inside, save the stray beam of moonlight peeking past the cloud-streaked, night sky. Blain Hopps was standing next to him, just a step inside the foyer. He was dressed casual, in khakis, with a white button-up shirt, like another day at the office all done and over with. However, Eric—Yikan's symbolic lamb—was dressed in a stark white, flowing robe and stood like a regal, with his head high, as though self-assured of his god-given birthright. They walked to the hallway, which led left or right. There was no sound or movement from either end.

"Perhaps we should think of this as more of a cat and mouse game," Eric said, calling out to the right. "That is…Blain and I being the cats, and all of you, the mice." He looked the other way. "And like mice, if there's one, there's a nest of them."

"Which way do you want?" Blain asked. He raised the cimeter and looked at it; the knife was crescent shaped and razor-sharp, a butcher's tool of choice for cutting flesh clean from the bone, leaving only the bone, no bits or pieces ever wasted.

Eric said nothing, though turned and went right. His immortal eyes pierced the gloom of the hallway and searched for movement. There were doors off to his right, and where the hall ended, it turned left. He stopped at the first door. "Christopher...was that you we heard chanting? Or have you found someone else who can?" He turned the handle. It was locked. He sought out the locking mechanism with his mind and turned the gears inside. It clicked and opened.

He came into a gentlemen's room, one of comfort and leisure with puffy leather chairs and a wall of bookcases, and not an empty space to be seen on them. In front of the bookcases there was an ornate desk, with letters and papers neatly arranged on them. He went over to it and shuffled through the papers and letters.

"*Henrì, Henrì,*" he muttered. His brow furrowed; he didn't recognize the name. He picked up the picture frame on the desk and looked at it. He ignored the black woman sitting on the white man's knee, focusing on the man alone.

Henrì's face was familiar to him, where the name had not been. It was in the Egyptian desert he had seen him, Eric remembered; that night that Shazadeh and Tamen met their end. Amidst all of the death and fire, and demons rising and the Heavenly Host revealing themselves in the sky, he had seen the man, if only a glimpse of him. He was with Tamen and the boy, Jared, who was no longer just a boy anymore. And now....

"Henrì Bedeau!" Eric called, as he walked out of the room and continued down the hall. "I remember you now. You were in the midst of it all. Have you always been? Oh, but you are now." He ran his hand along the walls and walked along leisurely and assuredly. "You survived that night...many did not. You were fortunate. The only thing is, you didn't know that your days had then become numbered—you've only delayed the inevitable. Aton was always going to rise, no matter what happened that night. He was destined to be what he is, as was I. And now, no force —not even God—can stop us."

He paused at the next door, opened the lock by thought, and then walked in. It was a parlor. The furniture was light in color; the drapes and valances were embroidered in a swirling baroque pattern. Though like the room before, there was no one there. He walked out and down the hall, and then turned left; there were more doors off the hallway and another set straight ahead.

"Chant again if you dare. Maybe this time you'll stumble on the right spell and maybe have a chance of...*of doing what exactly?*" He paused and smiled. "You think there is hope where there is none. There is no escape either. This manor will either be your mausoleum or that place where you shall always remember that you turned to the one true faith and saved yourselves. So show yourselves, and I will be merciful. Bring me Metatron's tome and I will spare your lives."

Eric began unlocking the door to his right, when he heard a chant being called out. He turned his head to the side and listened closer. It was faint. It had no echo. It was coming from outside the house, he sensed.

He went back to the foyer. Just as he was about to step outside, he heard someone chant again, though this time, it had come from inside the mansion...upstairs. As he debated which one to follow, he heard yet another chant, and this one from down the hall where Blain had gone.

"Mice, mice, everywhere," Eric whispered. "Do not fear mortals. The cats have come to play. And we are starved for company."

* * *

"We know you're here," Blain cried out.

He was standing in the main living room. He looked around, and then turned toward the patio doors. He walked over and looked out, forming his hands into blinders against the glass; the cimeter was right next to his face. Nothing moved among the shrubs as far as he could see. He turned around.

"I don't want to do this, you know. But it doesn't bother me either." He shrugged. He crossed the room and headed out. "I like choosing who I kill. I follow them for a while and get to know them; that's what makes it so good. You see, you may think of me as just a killer, but there's more to me than just that. I'm not heartless. I appreciate what I kill. I understand that each life I take was once one full of hopes and dreams. And they understand, that once I have them, that it's all over; I like that look in their eyes when they finally realize that. You just gotta see it to appreciate it."

He walked out and turned right, heading for the kitchen. "Hell is all too real," he said, opening the doors and walking in. "Do I deserve it?" He paused a moment, as though it were actually up for debate. "I *do*. I'm what people call pure evil." He walked into the panty. "I don't have anything against you folks personally, but you want to bring Jesus back so he can dole out judgment to folks like me and save good ol' folks like you. But if he comes, that means I'll be keeping company with demons. And they'll be real happy to see me coming. Yikan said I'd probably end up in Phenóx, where the worst of the worst of The Damned go—that's where Lucifer lives. And we all know he ain't such a nice guy." He went to the next shelf, placed his ear next to it and listened. He waited a moment. He heard nothing.

"You see why I need to kill you now?" he asked. "Or you could come out from wherever you are and do that one thing that will end all of this…bow to him." Blain looked around and waited, as though possibly, there might come a reply. "I know Yikan isn't your God, but he's god now." He implored them. "Save yourselves. Yikan and Eric are going to control earth. Basically, *they already do.* If you give him the tome, you'll live. If you don't, then I'll find you eventually, or Eric will, and you'll wish you'd just given it to us, because sooner or later, we're going to get it; just like we're going to get all of you."

He went to the next set of shelves. He ran his fingers along the edge of it where cans of peaches, corn, and beans were arranged neatly in a row. The board was cool to the touch. He ran the back of his hand across the cans. They were cool just like the shelf, despite the room being warm and humid. He grabbed the shelf with both hands and began pulling back on it.

"Mr. Hopps," Eric called from behind.

Blain turned around. "I've checked the big room down the hall," he said, and shook his head. "Nothing."

"They're here," Eric assured him. "Inside or out, they're nearby. I've heard them chant again already…three times." He around the pantry, and then walked out. Blain followed after.

"Can't you listen for their thoughts?"

"They're blocking me. All I hear is static."

"How can they do that?"

"They've unlocked some of the chant. I assume with Chris's assistance," Eric said, pausing as he reached the hallway. "With the tome—the power within—all is possible. In capable hands, it can unravel the fabric of reality."

"Yours, you mean?"

"No."

"Yikan's?"

"*Yes*...once we have killed them and taken it," Eric said, with a tone of certainty. He headed back to the foyer. "I'll search the grounds. If you find them, kill them; they've had chance enough to surrender." He called out, amplifying his voice tenfold. "No more bargaining! Do you hear me, mortals?"

Eric went out the main doors. Blain walked back down the hall and took the stairs against the far wall, across from the foyer. He twirled the cimeter in his hand as he walked up the stairs.

He began reciting a rhyme. It was one of his own making that he had cobbled together over the years, when he first began cutting, and then killing, and then torturing before killing.

"There once was a little sheep.

"Pretty white—pretty sweet.

"Butcher's got a knife for you.

"So tell me now.

"What do I do?

"What would you like me to do for you?

"With all of the pieces I cut from you.

"Fix lamb chop pie, or lamb chop stew?"

CHAPTER 22

The bridge Jared and the others traveled lay just atop the frozen waters, which rose up level with the bridge. At first, there was only the frozen lake that stretched out to either side of them, but as they ran on, they came upon the first of many bodies frozen on it. Their numbers quickly multiplied, and then seemed to grow exponentially, blanketing the lake with their bodies.

Each face of The Damned was frozen in the midst of their agony. Arms were frozen in mid-flail and mouths captured wide in mid-scream. Though they struck various poses of anguish, what they had in common was that they were all oozing mist, which rolled onto the bridge, slowly making its wispy way toward the palace...toward Lucifer, The Morning Star.

The leeching of force was no different for them, Jared thought, he feeling weaker the closer he drew to the palace. He looked at Caym, who was running next to him. Mist was oozing from his face and arms and hands, and out from under his breastplate.

Zim brought them to a halt. Thamuz squatted on his haunches. Caym put his hands on his hips and bent over at the waist; though it wasn't air he or Thamuz needed, for they required none; it was lifeforce their bodies craved, and they were loosing more and more of it with each passing moment.

"We must get going soon," Zim said to them, staring at her hand and watching the lifeforce ooze off of it.

"You think they can keep Astaroth out of here?" Jared asked.

"He's not here now," Caym said, replying in her stead. "Astaroth is weakened. He's used a great deal of Hell's might to open up the dome, but was denied entrance—"

"By your efforts, Jared," Zim quickly acknowledged. "You saved Chax's life, and ours as well. What I do know for certain is that we must make haste to the palace. At the top of it," she pointed to the white glow coming from the top of the tallest tower, "that is where we will find The Morning Star and the three who sit in watch—the gods of Phenóx."

They all looked at the gleaming, silver palace, it glowing in the gloom of Phenóx like a candle in the dark. Jared started ahead with a jog and quickly turned it into a full on sprint. The others caught up to him.

"You may believe we are not gods," Zim said, matching him stride for stride, "but The Morning Star is not like us—any of us. He is the meaning of the word ancient. He and time and space were brought to life all at once. Only The Father, The Lamb, and The Ghost know of a time, before time began.

"They say he is nigh omnipotent," Caym added.

"But he's asleep, right?" Jared asked. "God put him to sleep until the end of days."

"Aye," Caym replied. "But how sleeps a god?"

"Zim?" Jared asked, looking at her, hoping for a slightly less dire opinion. She pursed her lips; that was her reply. Jared looked at Caym.

"I guess we're going to find out pretty soon."

"Aye," Caym said. "That we shall."

* * *

They had run for miles and were now just past halfway to the palace. They slowed to a jog as more and more of their lifeforce wisped away, leaving them weaker with each step. The frigid cold of Phenóx only made matters worse. They shucked the rest of their armor, which had become crusted with ice and began to weigh them down.

"We must pause," Caym said, stopping abruptly. His body quivered. Mist oozed from his face.

Jared and the others came to stop just steps ahead of him. They gave no argument for the respite.

"He's going to have us drained before we even get there," Jared bemoaned, feeling as though his body was made of lead, and it growing denser by the moment. Even keeping his head upright was starting to become a struggle.

"That is not an option, Miel-angel," Caym retorted. "But it's getting back through the dome I'm most worried about. If the Lords of Hell cannot kill Astaroth, or even subdue him, they will not regain their former strength; and they must have it all if they're going to breach the dome to let us out. We'll be in the same position as you if they cannot, I fear." He looked out at The Damned on the lake. Their combined mist obscured the pathway; the bridge's towers seemed to rise out of the mist from nowhere. He walked over to the side of the bridge and beckoned for Jared.

Jared went over and looked across lake. He felt empathy for The Damned, though too, they repulsed him all the same for what they had done to be damned to this place.

"There's so many of them," Jared remarked, staring at them all, marveling at how they seemed to just go on and on, soul after soul for endless miles on both sides.

Zim walked up next to him. "Mankind has reproduced over one hundred and eight billion times—this we know, for the oldest of us were there to see it. Evil has always existed. Man has always devolved to his worst instinct...to dominate and control what is around him. Man is not like us, Jared. Man sees us as gods, and will bow to obtain his heart's desire; but deep down, man wants to be god, too. So he dominates others with the spear, the sword, the bullet, and now the atom, and has brought his kind nearly to ruin." She nodded at the souls on the lake. "Just look at what The Father has wrought upon the innocent."

Caym reached out to a soul, and put his finger by a twirling tendril of mist oozing from the white man's face. It coiled around his finger like a snake. He presented it to Jared.

"*Touch it*." Caym said, with a wicked smile. "See why The Father has damned him for eternity."

Jared moved his finger to the mist. It unfurled from Caym's and wrapped around his. In his mind's eye, he saw the man Caym had taken the mist from, though now, the man was alive—talking and moving about—not frozen in time clawing at his face and his mouth twisted in a scream.

His name was Jonathan Procter Bates, Jared discovered, as pieces of the man's life began flashing before his mind's eye, showing him the people the man knew; the places he went; *and oh*, the abominable things he had done.

Jonathan was an American slaver—an overseer—when he was mortal. He had branded slaves, raped them, and hacked their limbs off, and those were the least of his cruel sins, Jared saw. He was known for making examples of a few slaves to subdue the many, and it worked beautifully; he prided himself on it…quartering, that is…in front of the entire plantation, for all to bear witness what disobedience brings.

With ropes tied to each limb of the biggest, darkest male slave on the plantation, and each rope tethered to a horse, he would have the horses whipped until they pulled and yanked, and yanked and pulled, and ran free with whatever part they had ripped from the slave. How Jonathan laughed at the wrenched torsos and heads left lying in the dirt. It only took once or—

"…if they were that ignorant sort of niggah; that stubborn type," Jonathan would say to potential clients—slave owners, that is. "Hard headed and nappy headed. You gotta do it…and like it. Tear that niggah apart! And let'em see that you like it. And I damn well guarantee you this—and I'll make wager on everythin' I got—not only will you never have a problem with your niggahs runnin' away, but for generations to come—*and you mark my words, suh*—we will subdue the entire race of them for generation after generation, after generation. You'll never have to raise another whip at'em again," which he is where he would always chuckled when giving his pitch, letting them know they were a stone-cold fool if they doubted him on this one, "those niggahs will claw each other to get that whip and do it for ya." He spoke in a high screech. "Yes suh, massah suh. How hard you want me to knock this niggah for ya?" Jonathan would then lower his head and peer up at them from under his heavy brow. "You just mark my words. And if you're knowin' what I'm sayin' is the God's honest gospel, then I, good suh, can get started with all due haste."

Though, as more of Jonathan's past came flashing by, Jared saw that it was only the tip of his many great sins against the slaves—against humanity. Next came the lynching rope for them, and then the tar and feathering and lighting on fire, and the slow roasting of human flesh over a spit for days, and the eye blinding with red-hot irons, and the cutting out of tongues, an....

Jared shook his hand, shucking the tendril from his finger. It curled in the air and fell to the ground, and mixed in with the rest of the mist flowing along.

"He's...." Jared began, though could not find the words to finish it.

"Vile?" Caym helped.

"Worse!" Jared argued, looking at Jonathan Procter Bates with utter disgust. Any glimmer of empathy he had Jonathan and the rest of The Damned completely evaporated in that moment. With just a taste of evil from one of them, he was glad for the predicament of all of them, though wished it were harsher. And it was.

Just then, a spear of ice came jutting up in front of Jonathan from the lake and pierced the veneer of ice covering his face. It went through his head and clean out the other side. From behind him came another spear, though this one was aimed for his chest. Jared looked at the other Damned that were nearby. They, too, were being impaled from all angles, and unable to move...unable to even scream their agony.

"To the depths of their souls, mortals—for the most part—are just vile creatures," Zim said.

"Aye," Thamuz grumbled. " And these are not even the worst; those are kept in the palace. The Morning Star keeps the darkest souls closest to him. Their punishment, let us say, is unique."

"The ether isn't looking so bad after all," Jared muttered, backing away from the edge. "I'd just rather not exist."

"I'm sure each of these poor bastards feel the same," Caym opined.

An explosion rang out from behind them. Ripples emanated from the end of the bridge all across the surface of the dome, shaking it, making it seem as though it were about to crack all over and come crashing down.

Jared began walking backwards toward the palace. He knew that he knew what he knew to be true; and it was making his celestial bones ache. He had no doubt about what he was sensing.

"Astaroth's here," Jared said, as he continued walking backwards with his sight set on the dome. "He's in Phenóx."

"We don't know that," Caym was quick to say. He straightened up and clenched his jaw, and stood ready, as though his second wind had finally come. His dull eyes, however, spoke to the contrary.

Zim looked at Caym. "I haven't forgotten who my duke is. He is Chax—Sky Father."

"He *is* Chax," Thamuz concurred, giving Caym's shoulder a reassuring squeeze.

"He is Chax," Caym said firmly, agreeing wholeheartedly with a stiff nod of the head.

Jared walked up to him and grinned. "Your dad's a bad ass!" Caym chuckled and shook his head at Jared. "If there's a way to stop Astaroth, Chax will find it—we all know that."

"Aye!" cried Zim.

"Aye!" Thamuz concurred.

"Whether Astaroth is in Phenóx or not, we better get going," Zim said.

"Yeah," Jared muttered, raising his hands and watching the mist rise off of them. "We better, before there's nothing left of us."

* * *

They took rest twice more before reaching the dual, two story tall palace doors. All the while, the non-stop explosions that had been rattling the dome had ceased. All was silent again in the frigid world of Phenóx.

Jared looked up at the silver-colored palace. It glowed from the white light cast down on it from on top, where Lucifer was.

"It's all metal," Jared said, as he laid his hand flat against the door.

"Platinum actually," Zim told him. "But unlike Earth's, its pure, through and through, unadulterated, just like The Morning Star."

"That's debatable."

Caym approached the palace doors and stood next to Jared and Zim. "There is no debate about it, Miel-angel. It's an immutable fact."

"He was made to be perfect in every way, by the word of The Father —your God," Zim curtly reminded him.

"How about we find a way inside instead of squabbling," Thamuz said, as he looked up at the smooth, metal doors that had no handles.

Thamuz approached them and began pushing on the right door. It didn't budge an inch. He turned and shook his head. "I don't have the strength, especially now that I've returned the power of Orsha-Na back to the duke. Even if I still had it, I don't think it would be enough."

"There's has to be another way in," Jared said, looking at the inscription on either door. There were four stars arranged in the shape of a diamond; a large one at the top, and three smaller ones; two were on either side and one was at the bottom…The Father, The Lamb, The Ghost, and The Morning Star.

"There doesn't have to be another way in," Zim argued.

"Aye," Caym said. "This is the home of a god. It's not meant to be entered by any other."

Just as Caym spoke, the doors of the palace began to swing in. The white light inside shot out and pushed the gloom away from them. A figure from within the light approached them.

"I thought myself mad," the figure said in relief, "when I heard the fall of footsteps in the realm. Nothing stirs in Phenóx. Sometimes the guardians up above do, when they are summoned, but that is all. Though now, I see that I am not mad at all."

Caym put his hand on his chest and bowed his head. "Good Passing, Lord Xaphan—Keeper of the Ice!"

"My lord," Zim and Thamuz said, bowing their heads.

"Good Passing, Orsha-Narians," Xaphan replied, sliding closer and looking down on them, standing well over a foot taller than even Thamuz.

Xaphan was a creature of ice, like a living glacier whose face had broke off. He was jagged and razor-sharp in some parts, and smooth as glass in others. From the waist down he was a solid chunk of ice, which he used to slide across the mist-covered ground.

Xaphan looked at Jared. "What is an angel of The Father doing in Phenóx?"

"I'm trying to get back to earth," Jared said, making it simple.

"Return the same way you arrived, hmm?"

"It's the only way," Jared said.

"True…true," Xaphan said, nodding his head, breaking off pieces of ice from his neck. "There is no other way out of Hell. Though, too, it is a fool's quest."

"Will you let us enter?" Jared asked, undeterred.

"I am the Keeper of the Ice," he said. "I am a guardian of Hell. I have bent my knee before The Morning Star and given him my vow to keep the realm in eternal ice—that is my only duty. That is my charge. Enter if you will. Though know if you do, you will never pass through these doors again. Either the earth will have you, or The Morning Star shall."

A thunderous boom came from the other side of the bridge. The dome of Phenóx shook. Xaphan glanced up. Ripples ran across the top of the dome. The echo of the explosion soon faded. Silence returned to Phenóx.

"What is this?" Xaphan said, as his snow-white eyes grew large. "Someone else is here. I sense a powerful force moving this way. It is full of pride and hate."

"Astaroth," Jared said, looking to the bridge.

"Is it him?" Zim asked.

Xaphan's neck crackled and snapped as he nodded. "He travels with haste."

"You must do something, my lord," Caym implored.

"He's coming to kill Lucifer," Jared added. "You vowed to protect Hell. So isn't protecting Lucifer protecting Hell, too?"

Xaphan chuckled, though it sounded more like chunks of ice crashing to the ground. "You think to outwit me, angel? I gave the cold throb of deceit to men when they were first formed. *Freeze the waters of Phenóx and The Damned upon them'...* that was the last command The Morning Star gave me, before he was cast into sleep by The Father; and that is what I must do—keep the waters frozen. Whether The Morning Star lives or dies, I will see that these waters never thaw. If they do, know that it is only because I have been sent to the ether."

"Astaroth will doom all of us," Caym argued. "Even you."

"I will not abandon my duty."

Jared saw Caym was on to something, though he hadn't fully realized it yet. Jared did and he pounced on it.

"This will all be slush. If Astaroth takes over Hell, he'll control Phenóx, too," Jared warned. "He wants the souls on the lake and the ones inside here, too. He wants to punch a hole from Hell to earth and march his legions through it, and that's going to take a whole lotta power. He won't have time to waste feeding on their mist," Jared shook his head side to side, "Uh uh. He'll need their force right now! And that means thawing the lake."

"Over my cold corpse," Xaphan swore.

"Then it will be, my lord," Thamuz said, giving Jared a laud-laden nod. "The angel is correct."

"False!" Xaphan charged.

"No," Zim said, "tis' true, my lord."

Xaphan swiveled his stump around and faced the bridge. "There are two ways to the top—The Morning Star's throne room," Xaphan said to them, though his focus was forward. "A staircase lies on either side of the castle; both lead to the top; and there you will find The Morning Star and the other gods of Phenóx." He paused a moment. "And I will stay here and wait for Duke Astaroth to arrive, for now, he I have a matter to discuss, though I think it will not be with words."

Jared and the others entered the palace, leaving Lord Xaphan staring out and waiting for Astaroth to arrive. The Damned inside the welcoming hall were placed about like statues on exhibit. Their combined mist covered the platinum floor and rolled away, separating left and right.

Caym came over and stood next to Jared. "Your choice, Miel-angel," he said. "Right or the left."

Jared looked to Zim for guidance. She shrugged.

"Neither way is better or worse," she said. "Both paths lead to our final destination, or possibly…."

"I know," Jared said, watching as her lifeforce oozed away from her.

She was weak, though he was too, as was Thamuz and Caym. Once they reached Lucifer's chamber, their duty of getting him there would be done; the pact would be fulfilled, and they would be free to leave, though he would remain, alone and waiting. For how long he could survive being leeched on he didn't know and didn't want to, though he did know it would not be for long. Still, it was his only chance—his only option.

He chose left.

The others followed.

* * *

"Good pass to you, Lord Xaphan," Astaroth said, as he came upon the end of the bridge leading to the palace.

"Is it, my lord?" Xaphan asked. He was standing off to the side of the palace doors with a suspicious look upon his jagged face of ice.

"Surely it is, for I have come."

"You should not be here."

"Yet I am."

"And what of their graces, Chax, Beelzebub, Agares? What ill fortune have you brought them?"

"I have given them over to the ether. They are no more. I have flung their ashen carcasses to the wind."

"Oh, my lord," Xaphan groaned. "What have thou wrought?"

"A new age, guardian," Astaroth answered promptly.

"Nearly so…though not yet," Xaphan said.

"The master inside," Astaroth said, "'s that whom you speak of? He lives for now, that is, until I pierce his chest with my blade."

"Do not enter his abode," Xaphan warned.

"Or what, my lord?"

"The ice must be kept—that is my duty," he replied. "I will not see it thawed."

Astaroth conjured his sword. "You will soon take orders from a new master, old one."

"The current lord of the realm is not yet dead."

"*Not yet.*"

"No, my lord," Xaphan said, turning toward the doors, "not quite yet." Ice began forming across the door's threshold. In moments, the ice was feet thick and bulged from the doorway like blister. Astaroth gave Xaphan a foul glare. "It is my duty to keep the ice... *my lord.*"

Astaroth turned to the ice and conjured his sword. He raised it, and then looked back at Xaphan. "You'll call me god before this *pass* is over," he vowed.

"If ever I do see you again, perhaps I will."

Astaroth's sword began to glow red as he funneled his lifeforce into it. He swung at the ice; huge chunks of it went flying. "There is no *perhaps*, my lord; just certainty."

CHAPTER 23

Dorthea realized her prayers of thanks of not being discovered had been premature. One of the men had come into Henrì's room and had stood just on the other side of the bookcase, which she was hidden behind, in another of the mansion's secret recesses. She masked her thoughts, just as Chris had shown her and Olivia to do. And it worked. The man stayed for a few moments rifling through Henrì's papers and things on his desk, and then left; and she had sighed in relief and gave praise to God for it. Though, shortly after was when she heard the mansion doors slamming against the walls, and then next, Olivia screaming.

Their plan had fallen apart, she thought, as panic over what to do next made her heart start racing. Having each of them hiding in different places and chanting—just a little—to confuse the men looking for them, was the best plan than could think of, and had settled on, and had agreed was their only chance of getting Jared back home. Olivia would hide in the thick of the bayou and she would hide in Henrì's study, in the cellar behind the bookcase. However, their ploy to confuse the men, while Chris performed The Chant of Changing, had not worked. They had Olivia now, and were using her as bait to draw them out. Or…was it trick? she wondered and grew anxious. Were they just using their foul magic to mimic Olivia's voice?

"You don't have long to decide!" she heard one of the men call out, and then right after, Olivia yelp. "We found her in the swamp, if you're wondering. I was going to cut her throat, but had a better idea. I mean…she seems like a nice woman and all. I know she thinks what she's doing is right."

The sound of the man's voice grew louder. He was coming closer. It sounded as though he was right outside the room's door.

"But when you look at things from my side, she's the enemy," the man said. "And when you meet your enemy, you kill'em, right? And see, I have her now. She's the enemy. You already know what I need to do if you don't come out."

Dorthea pressed her ear against the door. The man was still talking, but it was becoming mumbled. He was walking away.

She thought about chanting again, though knew if Olivia really was captured, the men could easily follow it back to her. Though, if she didn't come out like they demanded, they would kill Olivia, and then come looking for her anyway. With time, they would find her eventually; and if Chris chanted, they would find him, too. And time was exactly what Chris needed more of.

She backed away from the door and felt for the wall behind her. It was completely dark in the room. However, suddenly, she realized she wasn't alone in the dark. She began hearing whispers off to the side of her, and then above her, and then from below.

The shadows of the mansion had snuck into the cellar with her. But why? she wondered. Why now? The shadows were all whispering at the same time, she couldn't make out what any of them were saying.

From the other side of the door, she heard voices. Two of them were unfamiliar, though one was not. It was Phineas she could hear talking… arguing. She recognized his deep, southern drawl right away, even if it was muffled. And if he was out of hiding, she thought, then that meant that Yikan's killer was likely in the mansion; and Phineas, the only one who could stop him, was standing up to him. Though, too, she thought, the killer was Jared's only way home.

Her heart began racing at the thought of Jared escaping Hell, though also, him not being able to. Yet, hiding in a cellar was not going to help him. She opened the door and pushed against the bookcase. It slid away on the smooth, polished floor with barely a squeak.

She paused at the threshold and listened, while her eyes adjusted to the gloomy, moonlit room. There was no one there, but soon there was; the shadows oozed out of the cellar and up the walls and onto the ceiling.

She looked up. A large shadow broke off from the rest and moved toward the door, and ran down it, and across the floor, stopping in front of her. It rose straight up and took shape, and began forming itself into the image of a man—a middle-aged black man.

Dorthea gasped. "*Jacks*—"

The shadow, Jackson Lovell, put his finger to his lips. He pointed at the door behind him and swayed his head side-to-side, again bidding her not to make a sound.

She nodded.

He smiled, though his expression quickly turned grim; his brow furrowed; he curled his black, bottom lip in and held it snug with his teeth. Jackson's illusion of a dark skinned man—and his clothes—began to blur and reshape. He began shrinking and reforming anew, taking on an entirely different façade. He pointed at the door and nodded.

Though he hadn't spoke, Dorthea understood what he was conveying in both his gesture and the new form he had assumed. She went to the door, opened it, and walked out into the hallway.

The shadow, Jackson Lovell, followed.

* * *

We've lost. Jared's lost. He ain't ever coming back now, Phineas thought, as Dorthea entered the living room, and Chris, he following right behind her. She was supposed to be hiding. And Chris, who he had just left upstairs in a hidden room behind a closet, was supposed to chanting and transforming into an immortal to give them a chance. Though they were both here now, which meant, he knew, that their plan had failed miserably.

Dorthea and Chris walked over and stood next to him. Dorthea was in the middle; Chris was on her other side. Chris looked at Phineas and bowed his head. Phineas shook his at him and turned back to the matter at hand; that is, Eric and Blain who were standing in front of them, and

Blain having Olivia positioned in front of him with his knife pressed against her neck.

"I'm glad you good folks decided to listen to reason," Blain said, looking at all of them. He held Olivia at the waist with one arm, and with the other, kept the knife steady at her throat. "This is more like it, huh?" His eyebrows arched. He smiled and looked at Olivia. Tears were rolling off her cheek. "Now no one has to die, unless you give us a reason. *But,*" Blain said, and paused, as he took her left hand and raised it up for them to see. Her palm had been stabbed repeatedly and was dripping blood on the floor, creating a puddle of it. "I couldn't help myself." He turned his head and looked at Olivia from the side. His eyes roved up and down her face. "*She's so beautiful.* They say the demons in Hell are unimaginably beautiful. They're obsessed with that whole idea of perfection, you know. And she," he appraised Olivia again, "puts me in the mind of what they might look like. Her skin…perfect. Her eyes… perfect! Her lips…*mmm.* But for demons to keep their perfection, they have to feed off The Damned by torturing them day and night til' kingdom come. That's how they do it." His tone went from whimsical to indignant. "That's not going to be me. I'm going to bow to Yikan… *Aton*…whatever he wants to call himself. If you had any sense, you would get on your knees, too."

"I can't do that," Dorthea said. "I have only one God."

"Lady," Blain scolded, "I thought we were making headway. What part of *'you can't win'* don't you get?"

"You wanted us to come out and we did," she argued. "So now, you can let our friend go."

"We shall," Eric promised, "when you give us the tome."

Dorthea shook her head side to side. "*No-no-no!* You let her go first, and then we'll talk about the tome going here or there." She pointed at Olivia. "But you let her go first."

Eric was silent for a moment, and then looked at Blain and nodded. "Give her to them."

Blain cocked his brow. "You sure?"

"Yes," Eric said, slowly turning back to Dorthea and the others. "How far can they get before I run them down?"

"You got a point," Blain replied.

Blain leaned over and whispered in Olivia's ear. Her eyes grew wide. Her lips trembled.

Blain moved the blade away from her neck and spread his arms. Olivia took a hesitant step forward, as though, at any moment, she expected Blain to renege and swoop in slice her neck. She took a few more steps and looked back. Blain cocked his head and smiled at her. She turned and ran to Phineas, who then ran to her and wrapped her in his arms. He hustled her back next to Dorthea.

Blain wagged his knife at Phineas. "Careful, minister. We don't want to get too close and have those guardians of ours making an appearance, do we? That would get really, really messy."

"I don't have no problem with mine," Phineas bragged. "I'm not running away from my judgment, like you. There's gonna come a time when you ain't gonna have that demon to protect you. And when it's done letting you run around killing folks, it's gonna eat you alive...bit by bit."

Blain pointed the knife at Phineas like it was a finger. "That's where you're wrong, old man." He then aimed it at Chris. "Yikan is going to do the same with me, as he did with him, you see? He's been rewiring my brain and teaching me how to chant, too. So, when my guardian decides to up and move on to the next evil sonofabitch, I'm gonna become like this guy, here." He looked at Eric. "I'll be immortal just like him. And when Yikan stops the End of Days by becoming a demon himself and throwing off God's holy balance, I won't have to worry about going to Hell and having my guts pulled out and set on fire." He gave a smug grin. "In fact, I'll be a god—or god-like—just like Eric. That's an offer I can't turn down. It's a win-win for me, but not so much for all of you, if you don't give us that goddamn tome."

"Where is it?" Eric demanded.

"It's here," Dorthea said.

Eric scowled at her. "Obviously, woman." He looked at Chris. "*Christopher!* You could have had everything. You could have been a god amongst men, but your love for your friend, Jared, and his family has altered your judgment. The angel Miel is dead."

"That's a lie!" Dorthea blurted, her voice cracking.

"No, woman…it is not," Eric replied, his voice chock full of irritation. "Your son was dead the moment Lady Muchenlay took him. There's no coming back from that. So you see, Christopher,…there's no fight to be won here for you. There is only Aton. There will ever only be Aton. Accept that. Bow before it. Now…*give me the tome.*"

Chris didn't say a word, but instead, shook his head side to side.

Eric looked at Blain, and then over at Dorthea. "Her…" he said, "cut her throat. I'm sure they'll be ready to sing like angels when her head is lying on the floor."

Blain slowly began walking toward Dorthea. "Don't make this hard," he pleaded, with a wry grin, as though hoping she would. Chris stepped in front of Dorthea and the others, and spread his arms, blocking Blain's way. "*Ahhhhh*…come on, kid. Don't do this. Get out of the way."

Chris shook his head and smiled. Suddenly, his body began to blur and turn black, and became like floating mist. In the very next moment, it reshaped into the form of a black man. As he did—as Jackson Lovell revealed his true, shadowy form—the other shadows came rushing into the room from under the door and from the edges of the ceiling, and through the seams of walls, they all howling and wailing and bemoaning. They swept toward the middle of the room and formed a collective, and then separated into two. One group rushed at Eric, and the other for Blain, and then began swirling around them like tornados.

Blain swung at the wailing shadows, though his knife went harmlessly through them. The shadows swept around him faster and faster with each pass, obscuring his sight. They encased Eric in the same manner, and moved where he moved, keeping his vision obscured.

"*Run!*" Phineas yelled at Dorthea, as he pulled Olivia along with him toward the door.

Dorthea ran out of the room and went to the right. Phineas had gotten Olivia to the doorway and was about to go left, when he heard Eric chanting. He turned around just as a gale arose from still air upon Eric's mystical command. The gusts lifted books and lamps and vases and pictures, and flung them around them around the room. Though also, it began to separate the shadows from one another, breaking apart their tornadic cocoons. Eric chanted again; the windstorm howled and doubled in strength and began dispersing the shadows.

Phineas grabbed Olivia's hand and ran. He glanced back down the hallway. There was no sign of Dorthea. She was gone, and hopefully well hid already, he hoped. He pulled Olivia the other way.

"Come on, woman!" he said to Olivia, hustling her toward the kitchen. "Ain't no exit back here, is there?" She shook her head no. "Well, it's all we got now. As long as you stay behind me, they ain't gonna touch you—hear me?" She nodded. "We'll...we'll draw them away from Dorthea." He turned the corner and stopped, and stuck his head back around and looked down the hall they had come from. The doors to the living room were being flung open and closed by the magic-borne winds inside.

Phineas pulled her into the kitchen and closed the doors. He moved his body in front of Olivia's and began walking backwards. He kept watch on the doors as he skirted the kitchen island, backing them into the corner of the room.

"Now chant," he told Olivia. "Bring them to us so we can give Chris more time."

Suddenly, just as Phineas spoke, the floor began shuddering. The pots and pans hanging from the baker's rack above the kitchen island began dancing up and down, and swaying, threatening to jump off their hooks. Olivia grabbed Phineas's shoulders and looked around the quaking room.

"He might not need anymore time," she said.

CHAPTER 24

The further they ascended the stairs of the palace, the colder it became. The bitter freeze had settled into Jared's bones, causing them to shake and shiver, despite the illusion of warmth from the white glow coming from The Morning Star high above them, which grew brighter and brighter the closer they drew to him.

They had just passed the frozen body of Hirohito, the once emperor of Japan, he dressed in his ribbon and medal heavy, military regalia. In his right hand he grasped the hilt of his sword; his other was straight down at his side; he was postured as though he was still standing in front of his people during that time of war, when he commanded that they torture and kill thousands of innocents—which they did—; they followed their emperor's commands and raped, and disemboweled, and gouged out eyes, and castrated, and beheaded, and hacked off limbs of their enemies and their own people.

The emperor wore his punishment for his sins on his face, or what was left of it. His face looked like taffy that had been twisted. His right eye socket—there was no eye in it, just a black, gaping hole—was swirled up and in the midst of his forehead. His left eye was down by his cheek. The corners of his lips were sliced all the way up to each ear, giving him a wicked smile.

Jared had looked closer at the emperor and saw that his face was still on the move; it was still slowly swirling around. And from the ice covering his body in a sheath, finger long daggers of ice bore into him from every angle—his legs, his gut, his groin, and chest, his face and neck, too.

The thought of freezing to death started to become a real possibility to Jared, as ice began forming on his skin. The ice cracked and fell away as he trudged up the steps, however, the further they went, the thicker the ice became, and it no longer cracked easily, and began sticking to his flesh and was starting to burn. They came to the next landing; and to the left, there was another set of stairs; and next to it, at the threshold, was another of the frozen Damned—a woman. Zim stopped in front of the woman and peered through her shell of ice.

"Please tell me it's someone possessed of the most wretched soul there is," Caym implored. "I thought back at Heinrich and Maximilien, that we had neared the aerie; and then we passed Caligula, and I just knew we had made it to the top. And…and I forgot all about that plague of a king, Leopold, back there." He nodded toward the stairs leading down, where the Belgium king was, who, under his rule, had tortured and murdered millions of the Congolese, casting a dark shadow of death over the African nation that still remains, even now. "How does one even forget Leopold?" He rebuked himself. "The Morning Star has drained my strength, and now my senses as well."

Jared moved up next to Zim and looked at the woman in the ice. "Do you recognize her?"

"Aye," she replied, nodding at the woman. The woman's mouth was open; her tongue was nowhere to be seen, though a spear of ice was working its way from under her chin and had gone through her mouth, and was in the process of digging into her skull. "Tis' Elizabeth Bathory —the Hungarian countess."

"Blessed is The Morning Star!" Caym exclaimed. He walked over and stood behind Jared and Zim, and looked upon the countess with gladness and relief. "We must be close to the top if we have come up to this wicked wench."

"She's the one who drank blood, right?" Jared asked.

"Drank it…bathe in it…ate the flesh of children when she was bored," Caym said offhandedly. "And look how innocent she seems, with that pale skin and those pink cheeks, and those large doe eyes of hers. Who would have thought *her* a monster?"

Zim proceeded up the next flight of spiraling stairs. The others, weakened by the loss of their lifeforce, trudged behind her.

"Good Passing to you, Ghengis," Thamuz muttered, as they passed by the Mongol emperor. His limbs—his head, too—had been torn away from his torso, and he held together and upright only by the ice surrounding him. Thamuz scoffed at him and kept walking. "Who do you think we should find at the very top, my lady?"

"I think we shall soon see," she said, cresting another landing.

Jared followed behind her as she walked across the landing, which was different from the others, for on the opposite end of it, he saw the other set of stairs of the palace. In the center of the landing, there was as stairway that led up, though in front of it was a set of souls, four of them —a wicked menagerie of them bound together in ice.

"So these are the vilest mortals humanity has offered to The Morning Star," Caym said, walking over to the souls with the rest of them, and nodding approvingly at the selection that had been made. "Hitler I expected. And of course Vlad is here—there was never any doubt in my mind about the Impaler."

"Nor mine," Zim readily agreed, looking over the souls.

Jared walked around the souls. There were four of them bound together at the waist; they shared one set of legs. Their upper bodies were spread out like flower petals, each facing a different direction. Hitler was in front...its centerpiece. He was dressed in his khaki, Nazi regalia, with his right arm extended out in salute and his left at his side and bearing a red patch, with a black swastika.

Fire raged beneath the fuhrer's coat of ice, burning away his skin down to the bone. And as the waves of rolling fire roasted his flesh and bone, his body repaired what had been burnt, only to have it assaulted again by a new wave of fire rolling over it, scorching it, cooking it, and turning it to ash. The fuhrer's eyes bulged from his skull. His mouth was askew and frozen in mid-scream. He burned alive, just like the millions upon millions of Jews that had under his command. Though he, unlike

them, could not flail and wail about in agony, but was frozen on the outside as he roasted on the inside.

To his right was Vlad—The Impaler, who Jared recognized, though
not by his face, but by the spear-long icicles that transversed his body
from every angle, making him look as though he was a human pincushion, with very large needles, indeed. The ice-spears had pierced his
eyes, mouth, ears, and nose, and were moving through each at a glacial
pace.

Jared walked around and looked at the soul directly behind Hitler,
who had a ring of hair around his baldhead. Strips of skin had been
ripped from his face and neck, exposing the muscle below.

"A friar?" Jared said, gawking at the man, and then turning to the
others.

"Of course," Caym said, rather smugly, coming around and standing
next to him. "The good friar, Torquemada, gives this piece of art a lovely
touch."

"He is the Grand Inquisitor of Spain," Zim explained to Jared.

"*Was*," Caym opined flippantly.

Jared looked at the Inquisitor's face again, and just in time to see a
strip of skin ripping away from his forehead, and then it flapping down
on his bloody, bulbous nose. And then came another strip being pulled
from the friar's cheek. And then, a strip from the side of his head, above
his ear began to tear off. Jared heard the skin tearing; it sounded like wet
fabric being ripped; and then he saw the flap of skin, with the ear at-
tached, flop down on his neck.

"He was known for skinning, as though you couldn't tell," Thamuz
said. "The friar was my mortal. He wanted power, so I gave him power
through the idea of the Inquisition, though it was he who brought it
alive and spread it across Europe. They say it is best to be careful what
you wish for." Thamuz walked up to the last soul conjoined with the
rest. "It looks as though comrade Stalin has fared no better in his
choices."

Jared moved over and looked at Joseph Stalin, the Russian dictator,
who, along with torturing millions of his own people, had murdered
sixty million of them as well. To Stalin, there was no infant that was too

young or woman too old to be shot in the face, or raped, or hacked apart, or beheaded, or fed to their own family; for such was the monster that he was, and such was his everlasting punishment Jared saw, as he looked at the dictator's neck. A blade of ice was slowly making its way across and through Stalin's neck, severing it from his body, even as the side of it that was already cut was coming back together and becoming whole again; and right behind it, another blade of ice was on the move, ready to slice his neck anew.

Caym came around and looked at Stalin's neck. He looked at it with disgust. "*Ewwwww*," he uttered. "Which is worse, Miel-angel? Roasting alive and cannot move, impalement, being skinned, or repeatedly being beheaded?"

"None," Jared muttered. "But I can't say they don't deserve it."

Thamuz looked at him as though he had grown a third eye. "You? You, an angel of The Father, is saying they deserve their fate? *Now* you see the wretchedness of humanity?"

"They're not all like that."

"Though so many are," Caym objected.

"Well these four are, and they are The Morning Star's to do with as his godly conscious dictates," Zim said. "But we need to go up. And once we are there," she looked at Jared with wide, sorrowful eyes, "then our duty is done."

Jared felt as though his lifeforce had been drained away again. In his mind's eye, he saw every fantasy of being with her suddenly turn to mist, like that which was at his feet, and that which was oozing from their skins...all of it, which was slowly creeping up the last stairway to its final destination.

"No one, but the Guardians of Hell, have been in the presence of The Morning Star since he was put in sleep," Zim remarked, and then became silent, as suddenly, a disturbance of sounds began echoing up from both stairways.

Caym walked over to the edge of the landing and turned his ear toward it. "There's movement below."

"It can only be Astaroth," Zim remarked.

"From the sounds of it, he is already on the rise."

Zim looked at Jared. "I guess this means that once we reach The Morning Star's chamber, our duty is not quite finished."

"Aye," Thamuz concurred. "No harm may come to The Morning Star."

"Then it's up to us to stop him. All of us," Caym said, turning and looking at Jared with a raised brow.

Jared began walking up the stairs. "If I get back to earth," he said over his shoulder, "I'm going to have a hard time explaining why I had to protect God's greatest adversary."

"Right now," Zim said, as more sounds echoed up from below, "getting back to earth is the least of your worries."

* * *

It was a room of pure, white light, Jared thought, as he stepped into the circular room. The walls, which were adorned with arcane, celestial symbols from top to bottom, reflected the glow coming from the center of the room a thousand times over.

"Here we are," said Caym, looking about in wide-mouth awe.

"And there they are." Zim pointed to the dais across from them.

There were two levels to the dais. On the lower one, there were three white marble thrones with demons encased in ice sitting upon each. On the upper dais was another throne, though this one was of platinum, like the rest of the palace.

Jared spied Lady Muchenlay on the left throne, the demon that had been responsible for abducting him to Hell. The demon in the center—a male with black skin—seemed hardly even there at all. His form faded in and out of view beneath the ice, as though he were there, and not there at the same time. On the right was a female; her skin was milk white, though her hair was coal-black and swept down across her shoulders, curtaining her bare breasts. In her right hand she held a spear with four heads stacked through it, each face portraying a moment of horror frozen in time.

Caym stumbled as he walked up and stood next to Jared and Zim. Jared looked at him. The gleam of his dark green eyes, and shimmer of his skin, was all but gone. Even his feet, which before were as swift as the wind, had begun to betray him.

Caym pointed at Lady Muchenlay. "She is the Plague, and he," Caym said, moving on to the center demon, "is Earl Creon-Pa. You know him best by his mortal-given moniker…the Shadow of Death. And here is Fatina Morunna, goddess of Enmity—forever war, never peace."

The sound of rumbling echoed up from the stairway. "He's getting closer," Thamuz warned. He began walking toward the brilliant light in the center of the room.

Jared and the others followed him over. As they grew closer, they began to see the light for what it—*he*—truly was. It was Lucifer, The Morning Star—the former Prince of Heaven lying upon a slab of pure platinum, a godly resting spot for a would-be-god. He was the great, pure light that illuminated the dark of Phenóx. His hair was blond, nearly white, like his skin. His eyes were oval and delicate like a woman's, though his jaw was strong, square, and pronounced—all male. His lips were full and pink; his cheeks high and round. He was, as Zim and the others had so often said, perfect in every way, Jared thought. Though, too, Jared could not forget that despite Lucifer's veneer of seemingly, utter perfection, he was the source of all that was evil in the world.

Jared looked at the mist floating away from them. It floated straight away to Lucifer, whose body absorbed it—fed off of it. The thick, white mist on the floor from The Damned crept up the platinum slab, supplying The Morning Star with an endless well of power.

Zim, Caym, and Thamuz knelt and folded their hands in prayer. "Morning Star, be merciful," Thamuz implored. "A great force moves your way and seeks to end your existence. We have come to stop him. Bless us, my lord."

"Though you drain life from us," Zim continued, "give us the strength to protect you from your enemy."

"Strengthen our hands and our spells," Caym added. "Help us vanquish this usurper and return Hell to its rightful rulers."

A deep cry sounded out from the stairway. Jared turned toward it. "Hey everybody," he called. His eyes never left the stairway. "I don't think Lucifer can help us now."

"Nor The Father either," Caym retorted. He grunted as he pushed off the floor and stood.

"It doesn't matter either way," Zim said, as she rose and looked over at the stairs, and then turned to Jared. "Whether The Morning Star intercedes or not, we must all protect him. He cannot be allowed to die, for all our sakes."

"I'll do what I have to do," Jared said, "whether I like it or not. I always have."

"Thy resolve is commendable, Miel-angel," a voice called out. It seemed to come from all over, up and down, too.

Jared and the others turned round, trying to track the voice. Jared stopped and looked down at Lucifer. Lucifer's eyes were still closed. He still appeared to be resting comfortably in his eternal sleep.

"This ground is holy. It is forbidden to come into my domain uninvited."

The mist stopped flowing up the slab and began gathering behind it, growing tall, and taking on the shape of a male. Jared nudged Zim. *"Look!"*

"I see it," she said in a hush.

The mist thickened and took on the appearance of flesh. A slender nose and ocean blue eyes, pouty lips and ears protruded out of the mist; and from the head and about the shoulders, the mist turned into long, wavy blond hair. The rest of the white mist swirled around his body and transformed into a pristine white, flowing gown, the same color as he who wore it. Zim, Caym, and Thamuz dropped to their knees as the visage of their Morning Star coalesced completely.

"My body may sleep, Miel—Angel of Balance," said Lucifer. "Yet, my mind never has. It cannot. I am always aware, and am always watching, and listening. There is nothing I do not see. There is no trespass hidden from me, nor any deed of goodness. I can hear the stars moving if I wish." Lucifer cocked his head. "Though, I must admit, to see an angel of The Most High in my hall is such a thing that I never imagined would ever come to pass, and observe...*it has!*"

"I'm not here to fight you," Jared told him, as though that was even a possibility.

"I know this."

"I just want to go home."

"I know that."

"The covenant…your covenant between you and God has been destroyed," Jared said. "We're enemies. *I get that.* But right now—"

"You've come to save me." Lucifer's body transformed back into mist and sunk to the floor. The mist swooped around the platinum slab and reformed back into Lucifer in front of Jared, standing nearly two feet above him. "How noble of you," Lucifer said, as his face formed back again. "I know who ascends my staircase one laborious step at a time, and he is well spent after having torn the veil to my realm asunder, not once, *but twice.* He will soon march up those stairs to commit a deed he thinks righteous, to claim Hell and Earth for himself. However, I am compelled to state the obvious, which is, that, neither Hell nor Earth is my home, Miel-angel. *Heaven is.*"

"I know you think it is."

"Think?" Lucifer smiled. "So says the one who does not desire to reside in Heaven. I have yet to glimpse the yearn for the glory of Heaven in your mind. Your desire is for the earth and the mortals upon it. You care for them far too much. They were the cause of your downfall before and will be again, if you choose unwisely, that is."

"Choose what?"

"Aye, Miel," Lucifer said. "'Tis' rare indeed that one is made a celestial. You are unique, Mizel…*as am I.* We were both given life for a purpose; me to give this cosmos form and beauty, and you, to counter the imbalance wrought by Astaroth's machinations. He has always desired my throne—and my light. Though still, no matter how mighty he thinks he has become, he is not fit to wield the power given to me by The Father —*no creature in this cosmos is.* Yet, he perseveres in the belief that he is worthy to wield the power of one who sits below The Father, as a god, as first born, as creation personified.

"*In the beginning there was The Father, The Lamb, and The Ghost—and darkness.* And The Ghost—the living will of The Father—moved about the formless void, and The Father said, '*Let there be light!*'; and thus was I born—a living creature brought forth from nothing!"

A clatter of metal came echoing from the stairs again. Lucifer looked peaceful, utterly unperturbed by it. However, Zim, Caym, and Thamuz were. They struggled to their feet and turned around, facing the stairway, ready to do battle to protect their god.

"Death approaches," Lucifer said, looking at Jared, with his lips just barely parted, waiting with proverbial bated breath for him to respond in some manner. "But, it need not be this way, Mizel-angel."

Jared's brow furrowed. "What do you mean?"

"I say that, you need not die."

"How?" Jared asked, looking him over, searching for the trick at play.

"Both of our lives are in grave danger," Lucifer explained. "If you fall, the earth falls. Though—*yet*—if I fall, again, the earth will also. Would it not be wise to strike a pact between us, Miel-angel? Your precious earth teeters on the brink of damnation. So too does your mother and step-father, and your father and your friend, Henrì Bedeau, and his wife. And I cannot forget your dear, beloved friend, Christopher, the brother of your heart."

"I've already done that with Chax," Jared told him, suspect of the demon's words from start to finish...beginning to end...*alpha to omega.*

"My Chax...*Sky Father*," Lucifer gushed. "He is noble, indeed."

"We needed each other, so I made the deal with him. But I got lucky," Jared said, with a crooked grin. "I'm not going to double down on that. I know where I am and I know who you are."

"You know nothing," Lucifer said, scolding him gently. "My body may lie in sleep, though my mind is unbound, and with it, *my power.*"

Jared shook his head. He already knew where Lucifer was going and was having no part of it. "*No!*"

"I may inhabit another if they are willing."

"I said no!"

"I can save both our worlds."

"Not happening!"

Lucifer leaned in, placing his perfect, plump lips just a pucker from Jared's. He spoke softly—secretly. "If thou say yes, I will sate thy hunger for desire."

"Zim," Jared whispered, half afraid to even say her name.

Lucifer grinned.

"Jared," Caym called over his shoulder, "perhaps you should consider—"

"There's nothing *to* consider," Jared said, staring into Lucifer's crystal blue eyes; their depth seemed endless. Those eyes pledge honesty and truthfulness. They said trust them; trust Lucifer. However, Jared knew better; literally fighting through Hell had been a crash course he never, ever wanted to take again. But he'd learned its lesson well, and spoke like he did. "We all better get it settled in our heads that we're going to the ether, because, Lucifer…you possessing me will never happen. So if we're all going to die anyway, then we might as well give Astaroth the fight of his life before we do."

"You will die, Miel-angel," Lucifer told him, with a voice as bitter cold as his realm. "I may have beguiled the woman, Eve, though you, I shall not. Do nothing, and you *will* fall. She," he nodded at Zim, "will fall, too. And Astaroth will plunge a blade into my chest, steal my power, and be on to your world, where all those you love will assuredly die." He nodded at the stairway, where Zim and the others were standing guard. "The Duke of the Westlands nears."

"If I let you possess me and you stopped Astaroth, what's to stop you from using me to get to earth? You know I can't do what you're asking."

"Then you doom us all," Thamuz accused.

"Even if it was a trick," Caym said, "still, there will be nothing and no one to save Lucifer from if Astaroth kills him. If Lucifer dies, then we all die, and Astaroth wins. And if you die, you can't help those you claim to love so very much."

"Jared…." Zim began, turning and looking at him.

He looked at her and shook his head. "Don't Zim."

"I…."

"There's no choice for me to make. I'm of the Heavenly Host. I'm God's balance on—"

"Do what you know to be right," she blurted, before he could say another word.

Jared gasped and grinned, and gasped again out of utter disbelief. Zim had just gone against her own kind to side with the right thing to do, or better yet, what not to do. He knew at that moment that atonement and redemption, no matter what she had done or how many times she had done it, could be hers. It was a possibility. It was hopefulness. For a moment, it made him grow warm with desire for her against the cold of Phenóx.

Thamuz and Caym looked at Zim with mixed expressions of sorrow, anger, and betrayal, and a huge dose of disbelief. "Zim?" Caym uttered.

She looked forward and raised her chin proudly. "I will always do what is right, and Jared is right. He has fought along side of us and has saved us a few times, if truth be told. We cannot ask him to do this." She turned and gave Caym a cold stare. "I will not ask him to do it."

"Because you love him," Caym sneered.

"Because it is right," Zim argued.

"It is love, my lady," Thamuz insisted. "But, too, she is right, and so is Mizel."

"Thamuz!" Caym cried. "You speak like a traitor. Lucifer's possession of Mizel is our only hope, and you speak against it? Are you smitten with the dashing angel, too?"

"You would not go against The Morning Star, would you?" Zim posed.

"Of course not," Caym said quickly.

"Then do not ask Jared to go against his God," she said.

"You speak with a lover's tongue, not a warrior's."

Zim turned around and looked at Jared for a moment. She turned back. "It is love," she admitted. "But it has not influenced my decision one way or the other; and if he feels the same, then I know it hasn't swayed his either."

Jared was still looking at Lucifer, though had caught every one of Zim's words. He gave Lucifer a cocky, crooked smile. "You're losing your touch, Old Scratch."

Lucifer smiled, and then with a start, he lunged at Jared and turned into a cloud of mist just as he reached him. "And you will lose your head," Lucifer whispered from within the white, billowing mist.

The mist gathered upon itself and swept over to the dais, and then floated up to the platinum throne. The mist reformed back into the image of Lucifer, with him now sitting on the throne and looking down on them.

Lucifer leaned forward. "He has come."

"Father!" The call came from the stairwell.

Lucifer sat back in his throne and looked just above where Jared, Zim, and the others waited a few feet from the edge of the stairs. "Welcome, Duke of the Westlands."

Jared pushed what traces of lifeforce he could must into his palm and conjured his sword. It flickered—disappearing and reappearing—before finally becoming solid. He looked at Zim. She nodded in solidarity and smiled lovingly, and then conjured her sword. Thamuz and Caym followed her lead and conjured theirs as well.

"*I have*…have come for thee, father," Astaroth said, as his head crested the top of the stairs. "I desire thy light and power."

Astaroth's glowing white skin was no more; it was dull and wrinkled, and now gray, like an aged white man nearing the end of his life. His cheeks were sunk in. His green eyes were dark, muddy-brown. His fire-red hair had lost its sheen and lay limp over his shoulders. Astaroth moved up the stairs, dragging his sword behind him like it was an anchor. Mist oozed from every inch of his body.

He was greatly weakened, Jared though, though too, so were they. He glanced down at his body, and then looked over at Zim and the others. They were seeping as much misty lifeforce as Astaroth was, and looked just as ragged as he did, if not more.

Astaroth stopped. He grasped his sword with both hands and grunted as he lifted it. He looked at Jared. "I told you I will have my prize, Miel-angel, and I have moved all of Hell to get it."

Jared raised his sword. The sword was still utterly balanced, though now weighed in his hands like lead. "You still haven't won. We're still alive and ready to fight."

"Quite right you are," Astaroth replied, with a genial, concurring nod of the head. He looked at Lucifer's apparition on the throne. "You'll pardon me for delaying your demise." He looked back at Jared and the others and began approaching them. He cocked his sword over his shoulder. "But do not fear, my lord. I shant be long."

CHAPTER 25

Phineas and Olivia stood at the doors to the kitchen. The mansion had stopped rumbling and silence had returned. Though, for Phineas, it was disconcerting.

"Maybe it was Chris," Olivia whispered, standing behind him.

"And maybe it wasn't," Phineas said. He grabbed the handle and pressed his ear to the door and listened. He heard nothing. "I don't know. But if it was Chris, and he did do it, he still can't fight both of them by himself."

"Then we have to go back."

"I know," he replied. He took her hand and slowly turned the handle. He whispered. "No matter what, stay behind me."

Olivia nodded. She squeezed his hand as they walked out into the hallway and began retracing their steps to the living room. They stayed close to the wall. They cringed and paused every time their foot hit an errant floorboard, making it squeak and squeal.

They reached the room. The door closest to them was shut; the other hanging only by its top hinge. He pointed at her, and then at the floor, telling her to stay put. She nodded. He moved to walk in, but suddenly, she grabbed his hand and squeezed it hard, and closed her eyes for a moment; and he was glad for it. He needed all the strength and prayers that he could get, he thought. He took a breath and stepped away from her, moving into the half-opened doorway.

"Here we all are once again," Eric said, as Phineas showed himself.

The shadows were gone. But a new sight—a welcome one—was there, in their place. Chris was standing just a few feet in front of him.

Chris turned and glanced at him. His pale green eyes were now black from corner to corner. His eyelashes, brows, and hair were all gone, leaving him with just smooth, milk-white skin all over.

"You've all surprised me, and disappointed me," Eric panned, and then looked at Chris. "Especially you. You've finally become what Aton has offered to you many times over, but you've chosen the wrong side, Christopher. There is no future with these mortals or any mortals, for that matter." He raised his arms. "This is the age of Aton! The old religions are gone—destroyed! And Astaroth, for all of his scheming and plotting over the ages, will never step foot into our world. Yikan will become a celestial and will stop The Christ from ever returning. That is how it will be, you foolish boy!"

Chris began walking toward the fireplace. He pointed at Phineas, though kept his eyes on Eric. "If Blain comes for me, you get in his way."

Phineas locked eyes with the murderer. Blain raised his knife in reply. "Your knife can't hurt me, boy," Phineas said.

"Christopher...*Christopher*," Eric bemoaned, lolling his head to the side. "Do not do this. Do not sacrifice your life for these mortals. You feel that great, godly power surging through you, don't you? You feel invincible. You may be half human and half celestial, but you feel that sense of humanity slipping from you—I know you do. You see age making its mark across their fragile skin, while yours has been arrested, forever. You are immortal now. You can live forever in an age of Aton. Mortals are clumsy and foolish, whereas now, you are graceful and wise. And if you peer into their thoughts, you may see all of their sinful weaknesses, their vices, and depths of their animalistic nature, and know you have evolved into something far greater than they will ever comprehend."

"I'm not a god," Christopher insisted. "I've seen real angels up close, and I'm *wise* enough to know that I'm nothing like them. I'm a perversion of them, and so are you...so is Yikan. But I became one because there just one thing I need to do, and that's getting my friend back."

"Amen!" Phineas said.

"Your son is dead!" Eric cried out, with a voice that shook the room like a quake.

"Liar!" Chris yelled back. And on that same breath, he began to chant. "Norraka-sum—thevo—sha'arum-dexa."

The warm, moist air of the room suddenly turned bitter cold. Phineas's breath froze and became mist as it left his mouth. Ice formed around Chris's hands and at his feet, and then spread across the floor, moving at Eric like a wave.

"You could have been a god!" Eric admonished. He chanted at the wave of ice rolling toward him.

Crimson fire spewed from Eric's hands in the form of a winding vortex, and struck the cresting wave of ice, producing an explosion of fire, ice, and mist as the opposites met. As mystical fire and ice waged war, Phineas darted left, where Blain was. He had to touch him; that was the only way to summon Blain's demon from Hell, and hopefully, he prayed, Jared along with it.

Eric raised the cry of his chant. His tornadic flames instantly doubled in size and began pushing back against Chris's wave ice. Chris replied with a rise of his own chant, spiraling his voice skyward, and thickening his wall of ice, moving Eric's fire back. The elements raged upon one another; neither giving; neither retreating. And then, as though sensing the stalemate between them, Eric and Chris ceased their attack upon one another, leaving the room thick with warm mist

"You'll not prevail, Christopher," Blain promised. "You may know some of the secrets of the chant, for you stand transformed before us, but...you are just newly born. You have no skill in the art of magic. You have no idea of its true power. But I do. I have been taught by one far wiser than both of us, yet you still believe you can kill me."

"You're weak," Chris accused. "You were a nobody before Yikan got a hold of you, and you still are. You sold your soul to Yikan, but you might as well have sold it to Astaroth. Because if I lose, he wins—not you and Yikan."

"Say what you will, *Christopher Knopfitter,*" Eric mocked. "No matter how this plays out, you will die tonight."

Chris smiled and shrugged. His white skin began to glow like a light. "I already know that, but that's not the point; it's never been the point," he told him, and then without warning, he ran and leapt at Blain with his arms outstretched.

Chris moved so fast that his body blurred. In one fleeting moment he was by the fireplace, and in the next, he had crossed the room in a flash and was just inches from touching Blain...barely a second away from unleashing Blain's demon from Hell. Though as quick as Chris was, he wasn't fast enough. Eric—he too possessed of supernatural speed—blocked Chris's path and caught hold of his arms. He pulled Chris in close, positioning them face-to-face.

"You want the demon to come out? *Why?*" Eric demanded.

Though Eric had figured what they wanted from Blain, he didn't know why, Phineas thought. Which meant, he had to get to Blain before Eric eventually did, and he would if he waited any longer. And so he ran for Blain. He slipped on the floor, it wet from Chris and Eric's war of ice and fire. He lost his balance and almost fell on the end table. He caught the corner of it with his hand instead and using it to his advantage, pushed off against it, giving himself a boost.

"Don't let them touch you!" Eric yelled at Blain.

Blain darted toward Eric, seeking safety behind him. Though Chris didn't let Eric's moment of distraction pass by. He was already casting a chant. His pallid skin turned gray as stone. He snatched his hands from Eric's grip and flipped his hands around, taking hold of him instead. He swung him around, trading places with him, and sending Eric scurrying away from him, right back to Phineas.

Blain slid to a halt and held up his hands. "Are all of you crazy? You're trying to get that demon to come?" He stopped and stared at Phineas. And then suddenly, his face drooped as his eyes widened. He spoke in a nervous hush. "*You want it to come.*"

Phineas said nothing. He hadn't time for it. All of his focus was on where Blain was going to run to now, or what he was going to try, and how could he could outwit and touch, and bring his beast from Hell to earth.

He wanted his son back. The yearn for his son gave his heart—a father's heart—a deeper beat. It pushed a wave of adrenalin through him. He felt the burn in his gut and tightening of his chest. He pushed off from his arthritic knees and ran for Blain. He had no plan of being denied.

* * *

Lady Muchenlay began to shake. Jared turned and looked, though turned back and raised his sword to block just as Astaroth's sword came bearing down on him. He blocked it just in time, though already he was on the defense again from a red, mist-borne spell spun from Astaroth's hands.

Caym was on his right, and too, had gone into defense mode against a spiraling red spell sent his way, too. Zim and Thamuz were on his left, and faring no better at pressing the attack against Astaroth.

They were all weakened, though Astaroth not as much as they were, for he had the power of Hell to bolster his power. And though he had used much of his power to burst through the dome for the second time, and what he had left Lucifer was steadily draining from him, he was still blazingly fast. He spun spells, two at a time. And with his sword, he battered them from the left, as well as from the right, hopping the sword from one hand to the other as he spun spells and struck, and struck and spun. And bearing witness to it all from his throne was Lucifer—The Morning Star of the heavens.

The red, misty spell danced around Jared. "*Death*" it whispered, as though it were alive, as it darted low and high, and twirled, and then jabbed for him. He swung for the heads of the tendrils of mist, knowing that if he severed them from their body, it would neutralize the spell. Though, Astaroth's spells were no ordinary spells. They were swifter. They seemed to anticipate where he was going to swing next and dodged his strike, and in turn, attacked.

He and Caym retreated as the red mist advanced on them. Jared dared a glance over at Zim and Thamuz. His lifeforce went still at the sight of seeing Zim suddenly brought aloft in mid-air, ensnared at the arms and legs by a spell of red mist. Her sword was gone. And Thamuz, who was next to her, was faltering under Astaroth's unrelenting blows. Thamuz fell to a knee, and swung up wildly with his sword, as though now just hoping to get lucky and block a deathblow that was sure to come at any moment.

"Get away from her!" Jared cried, turning back to the advancing mist. The lifeforce in his chest surged suddenly, giving him a second wind.

Though his sword weighed heavily in his hands, Jared began swinging it as though it weighed nothing. He swung for the spell-borne mist, though this time, focusing on anticipating *its* moves. And it began to work.

This time, when he aimed for the head of the tendrils of mist, he struck true, instead of just narrowly missing as before. The first tendril fell, and then the second and the third. And from there, he had the upper hand and pressed forward against it, until their were only three left—two above his head and one winding round like a corkscrew, aiming for his chest.

Jared brought his sword in front of him. The three tendrils of mist reared back. And then they came for him, all three at once.

Jared swung his sword up and around in a circle, cutting the heads off of the two at the top, and coming around the bottom and then swinging up, severing the tendril that was just moments from striking his chest. The tendrils of death dissipated like smoke.

He had no sooner cut the tendrils than he was off rushing over to Zim, who was now yelling out in agony. Her dark skin was turning gray even as he ran for her with his sword poised high, ready to strike. In his mind, he ran back to the blackness—that place where nothing was *everything* solely by the word of God himself. He reached for a touch of that infinite power. The white vein of his sword began to glow. The black blade surrounding it shimmered and whistled a pure, high pitch note as he swung it and sliced the air, almost seeming to rip the fabric of matter that it was.

His blade hit the tendril of mist where it branched out into four to bind Zim's arms and legs. The impact released a throbbing boom that echoed through the room. Jared's blade continued on through the tendril and dug into the platinum floor, carving a foot long gash in it. The spell dissipated. Zim fell to the floor. And Jared, not done yet, charged at Astaroth.

Jared swung, knowing Astaroth was going to block his blow, yet he didn't care. He would go right through it if he could…if he believed he could…if he had faith enough to trust in God and what God had given him. He poured his love for God, and for the earth, and for life; and for Zim into the blow. And as he predicted, Astaroth blocked it, though soon regretted it.

He knocked Astaroth back and off his feet, sending him sliding on front, face included. Astaroth looked up with eyes black from corner-to-corner.

"I'm going to pull the bones from your body," he seethed. He rose and raised his sword.

"You'll not get the chance this pass," a voice called from the stairs below.

"Or any other pass, for that matter," another said, from the stairwell.

"Your victory is denied!" a female called out.

Astaroth spun around, facing the stairs. He raised his sword and backed away as the Lords of Hell—Beelzebub, Agares, and Chax—ascended them. "Impossible!" Astaroth cried.

"No, my lord," Chax said, as he stepped up on the landing, "not impossible."

Beelzebub and Agares moved up and stood on either side of Chax. Beelzebub's glorious black body was now just a horde of buzzing flies and maggots shakily binding him together. Agares's milk-white skin was covered in fist-sized, angry red boils. Chax's wood-skin veneer had become black and green—full of rot. His legs seemed ready to buckle. He barely held his head up.

Chax looked at Astaroth. "You…you've forgotten who I am," he admonished. "I am still Chax!"

"Father!" Caym cried out, even as he continued battling the enchanted, twirling red mist around him.

Chax raised his hand toward the mist and spoke. "Nusafah amarak!"

The mist stopped in mid-twirl at the command of Chax's spell upon it. Caym leapt at the mist that was now frozen in time. He cut the heads off of the tendrils. The red mist turned black and dissipated. Caym dropped to the ground in exhaustion, though with a smile on his face at the sight of his father.

Chax, Beelzebub, and Agares began advancing on Astaroth. Jared ran back and slid on the floor next to Zim, and took her up in his arms. She was unconscious. Her skin was still gray, nearly ash. Lady Muchenlay's body began rumbling even harder, cracking the ice veneer over her body, and it falling to the floor in chunks and breaking apart like glass. The demon was being summoned and would soon depart, he knew. Only moments remained before she would leave, taking his one-way trip back to earth along with her and trapping him in Hell, where he knew he would not long survive.

He gathered her legs in his other arm and stood, bringing her aloft. Her head lolled onto his chest. "I've got you, Zim. I'm not going to let you die."

Caym and Thamuz had turned their attention to Astaroth and had joined the Lords of Hell in surrounding him. Caym, however, looked back at Jared, and seeing Zim in his arms, cried out. "What are you doing?"

Jared held Zim even tighter and began trudging up the steps of the dais. He looked back at Caym and shook his head. He didn't care that she was a demon or what she had done. He cared that there was a God, and a Son, and a Ghost, who through them, there was always a way. And he was going to find it for her.

"You thought us dead and gone to the ether," Chax said, positioning himself in front of Astaroth, while the others—Agares and Beelzebub on his right, and Caym and Thamuz on his left—surrounded him, and slowly advanced upon, forcing him back to retreat to the far end of the dais.

"I turned you to ash!" Astaroth swore.

"You turned a doppelganger to ash," Chax replied.

"Three of them, as a matter of fact," Agares said.

"You thought we would face you in the flesh?" Beelzebub asked, cocking his head of flies to side.

"We are now," Agares said, "though were not before."

Chax raised his sword. The other's followed his lead. "It took great magic to conjure doppelgangers that would fool you. Though, as we all see now, it was well worth the cost. My lady has given all her lands to see it be done. And I have made a promise that I will rebuild Varencia twice…three times as great as it was before. And I, Chax, keep my word —it is holy."

"You are nothing, Chax!" Astaroth shouted, walking the stairs backwards, heading for Fatina Morunna. Caym and Thamuz came around and cut him off. "You are weakened. Look at you!"

"Aye," Chax agreed readily. "Though so are you, my lord. Breaching the dome for the second time has cost you dearly, and in your hubris— thinking us dead—you allowed us entry. Yet now, there are five of us and only one of you." He held up his hand and looked at his lifeforce floating away. "How much lifeforce do you have left to give?"

Astaroth stopped and postured at them. "More than enough to see all of you to the ether…for good!"

Astaroth swung his sword to the left and crossed his other hand under it, and cast a spell right; and it worked for a moment. By the power of Hell, he was still faster than they were, though not by much. Breaching the dome twice, and his battle with the doppelgangers, as well as with Lord Xaphan, had exhausted nearly all of his stolen force. Still, it was enough to push Caym and Thamuz back with hammering blows upon each of their swords, and to send a wall of enchanted mist at Beelzebub and Agares, blocking them, while he pulled back to block Chax's on-coming swing of the sword.

Jared made it to the top of the dais where Lady Muchenlay rumbled and trembled, shaking off sheets of ice that came crashing down and breaking on the floor. He knelt at Lady Muchenlay's knee and wrapped his arm around it, and then pulled Zim in close to him with the other. He looked at her lips. They were grey and beginning to crumble. He looked at his arm. The ash from Zim's body had covered it in a sprinkling of ash. He had stopped Astaroth's spell, though the damage had already been done. She was dying—turning to ash —on her way to the ether.

He looked over at Chax and the others battling Astaroth by the guardian, Fatina Morunna. Beelzebub had dispersed his flies and sent them in for the attack. Agares had cut through Astaroth's enchanted mist and had rejoined Chax, Thamuz, and Caym in attacking him from every angle they could. Astaroth held them at bay, though Jared began to see him lose his rhythm, and his momentum. He began retreating from the onslaught of four, and the mass of flies making it five.

Lady Muchenlay's leg grew warm, and then suddenly turned hot. Jared looked up at her. Her eyes opened. Her fingers began to twitch. Her mouth began to move.

Jared looked at Zim's lips once more. This time, he bent down and kissed them gently—they felt like powder. He closed his eyes and sought out her mind—what was left of it. He yelled for her. She whimpered from somewhere in the darkness. She was barely there at all.

Jared pushed the traces of his lifeforce from his chest to his lips, and then opened his mouth wide. He gave her half of the lifeforce he had left.

He opened his eyes and looked at her lips again; they began to turn brown, and then turned black. Like ink on a sheet, her black hue spread out from her lips, over her face, and down across her body. He saw her eyes moving behind her eyelids and sighed in relief. Though then, her skin began to lose color once more. He looked at his hands; the same was happening to him, too. He had given too much of himself and was dying; and he had given her too little, and she too, again, was on her way to the ether.

"Take my hand, Miel," Lucifer said, looking down upon them—two dying lovers in embrace. "You and Zimarantha will die before the lady Muchenlay departs. Give yourself to me. It is the only way."

Jared looked over at the mêlée. They had Astaroth cornered against the wall, though still, he fought on. He looked down at Zim. The gray of ash was spreading across her body, and his as well.

He looked at Lucifer. Lucifer smiled and leaned forward. He extended his hand to Jared.

CHAPTER 26

It was never about beating Eric, Chris thought. It was always and only ever about getting Jared back. He looked down at his immortal body; it now scorched and bruised all over. Eric had pummeled him with his fists and then scorched him with lightning conjured from his hands, all in the protection of Blain.

Chris was by the patio doors. In the midst of their fight, the doors had been blown off their hinges and flung somewhere out into the garden, along with most of the frame. The ceiling had been ripped apart and beams from the floorboards above hung down from what was left of it like rigid streamers. Eric and Blain were in middle of the room surrounded by a pile of broken furniture and glass from the chandelier that had come crashing down. Phineas stood on the opposite side of them. And now they played a game of cat and mouse, with Eric facing Chris, and Blain standing off against Phineas, and they all taking turns as cats and mice.

"You are not strong enough, Christopher," Eric said. "You'll only get yourself killed at this point."

"I don't mind dying," Chris retorted, wobbling on his feet, struggling to stand upright.

"You should," Eric said. "The mortals go to Heaven or Hell, and the celestials, fallen or not, go to the ether; they return to the nothingness that they were. And who knows where we, hybrids of both, will go. I doubt Heaven is an option for us."

Chris clenched his hands into fists and stepped forward. "I'll let you know when I get there."

"Please do!" Eric taunted, and then chanted and flung his arms out at Chris. Fire—blue fire this time—erupted from his hands.

Chris didn't chant to block it, even though he could have. It was time for sacrifice and he had made up his mind to be the willing lamb. The blue fire struck him and enveloped him in a sphere of it. Unlike the red flames Eric had scorched him with previously, the blue flames charred his skin in moments.

Phineas ran for Blain.

"Stop preacher," Eric yelled. "I'll kill the boy!"

Phineas never paused. He veered to the right, and then pushed off to the left, as Blain tried to outwit him with false moves and starts. Though as Blain pushed off with his foot, again trying to dart to the right, he slipped on the glass that was littered across the floor and fell. He scrambled to stand back up.

Phineas was only a few feet away him. And Blain was nearly on his feet again. As though knowing he wouldn't make it in time, he cried out and leapt at him with outstretched arms.

* * *

Lady Muchenlay awoke and stood with a start.

Jared tightened his grip on the demon's leg and around Zim's waist with equal ferocity. He was determined to go back home, that is, if he wasn't ash by that time. And if he returned, he was taking Zim with him. There, one earth, she would be exposed to the dark energy of the cosmos. There he could save her life.

"Zim no!" Jared heard Caym cry out from across the way.

He looked over at Caym, who with his father and the others, had weakened Astaroth to point where they were now able to dodge his blows, and strike and wound the surrounded duke. Though now, Caym's attention was divided between the fight and them.

"*Get away from her!*" Caym yelled. He backed away from the fight. "Let her go!"

"Caym!" Chax cried, as he swung at a spiraling tendril Astaroth hastily weaved his way. He readily beheaded it. "Leave her!"

"No!" Caym cried and ran for her. "He'll not take her!"

Lady Muchenlay's body grew hot. Jared felt his arm beginning to burn and his sight begin to dim. The sound of clashing swords grew muffled. And in the haze, before the darkness had him completely, he saw Caym running for them, reaching for them; and behind Caym, where the others fought, he glimpsed a great flash of light, though only briefly, for now, the darkness had him.

He was gone...no longer there or anywhere for that matter. He was where space and time intersected, where every possibility was possible, and deeper within, those unfathomable possibilities constantly repeating over and again unending.

* * *

And then there was light. He saw the glow of blue fire streaming from a man's hand against another, surrounding his captive in a raging ball of it. Jared looked down. Zim was unconscious...unaware of what he had done. Though, grasped on her leg was Caym, a prince of Hell, who was looking at him and well aware of what had just transpired. Behind them was the hoofed demon, Muchenlay, and in front of them, the three-face Order, Oriziel, Nigiel, and Palis.

Eric shut-off his stream of fire and backed away from both celestials. Jared looked over at the person Eric had been roasting alive. Even through the crusted black skin that covered him from top to bottom, Jared immediately sensed who it was—he could feel him, as though he were a part of him. Chris fell to the ground face forward. Jared held Zim tight and pulled them across the floor toward Chris. Caym followed them, though with a scowl at Jared the entire way.

"Trickery once more!" Muchenlay decried, looking down at Jared and the others. "Here I see mongrels who should not exist, an angel who should be in Hell, and yet, those who should be in Hell though are not. The balance has been altered. The Covenant is defiled! The Lamb will never stand triumphant as king of kings. The Host has lost. Earth is damned!"

"Or perhaps it is saved," Palis suggested; she the female face of the Order. She looked at Jared, and then over at Zim, where her eyes lingered.

"The all of everything was but a moment from ruin, until now," said Oriziel, the center face.

"Earth has been given another chance for salvation," said Nigiel on the left.

Muchenlay smiled and looked at Zim; her double-rowed, razor sharp teeth sliced into her black lips, shredding the flesh. She nodded at Zim, directing the Order's attention to her. "'Tis' Lady Zimarantha—the center rod of Duke Chax's forces." She looked up at Nigiel. "Love is fickle, my lord. Trust not in it. And never trust *what is*, for *what is*, is never what it ever seems to be. It's always far, far worse."

"I believe," a voice called out from behind Muchenlay, "the lady is referring to me."

"*No!*" Jared uttered, as he saw the Duke of the Westlands step out from behind Muchenlay. Jared pulled Zim close to Chris, and then stood and conjured his sword.

"No-no my lord, Miel," Astaroth said, stumbling forward and nearly falling. His skin was the color of ash, though there were spots on his face that were starting to lighten. "This day will not be the day that I am sent to the ether. Chax and the other lords may have denied me The Morning Star's power and light...*he is Chax after all*...yet, I still stand. I suppose I'll have to content myself with this world—for now; now that the balance is no more."

"It will be in a second," Jared said, raising his sword.

Astaroth came up and stood next to Muchenlay. He looked up at her, and then over at Jared and shook his head.

"Do not test irony," he advised. "Lady Muchenlay might perceive the swing of your sword at me as a threat to her ward. How awful it would be for you to have fought through Hell and return home, only to be torn asunder by the one who absconded with you there in the first place. You must admit it would make for a wonderful tragedy."

"You're not getting out of here," Jared replied, refusing to lower his weapon, even though he knew Astaroth was right.

Astaroth smiled. "Yes, my lord…I will." He looked up at Muchenlay. "I will see that no harm comes to thy ward. Return and take my head if I break my vow."

Muchenlay looked down at him. "Be assured that I shall."

"Then return to Phenóx, my lady," Astaroth told her. " Perhaps you will find the cold ashes of Chax, and Beelzebub, and Agares upon your return, for they may have denied me what I sought, though at the grave cost of their own lives. The Morning Star will have what remains of them."

Lady Muchenlay's body inverted—falling in upon itself; and returned to Phenóx, leaving Blain nude and unconscious, and falling backwards. Astaroth caught him; and in the same motion, he swooped down with his other arm and brought Blain's legs aloft, and held him like a child snuggled in a father's protective embrace.

"And you," Astaroth said, turning his attention to Eric. "I am Ishtar, and Inanna, and Astarte…*I am Astaroth*, god of this earth. My offer will only be given once, never twice." He paused and then said. "Stand behind me."

Eric looked at Jared and the others, and then up at the three faces of the Order. He walked over and stood behind, and off to the side of Astaroth. He lowered his head. "My lord."

"I shall recover, though so shall you, Miel," Astaroth said. "And you will seek to end me, for there is no salvation for man with demons upon the earth…three of us and only one of you. There is no balance. I have won. And I am god."

Astaroth turned and walked out the patio doors with Blain in his arms, and with Eric following close behind them. They rose in the air and began floating off toward the sky, and disappearing into the darkness. Their destination was unknown, though their ultimate objective was plainly clear.

Nigiel, Palis, and Oriziel turned its collective head and cast their eyes down at Jared and the others. "Do not listen to the duke," they said as one, as their body began reverting back to that of Phineas. "Balance can be brought back to the covenant. Though even if it is, still, Astaroth is here, and all should fear what is to come, for what has already been wrought upon the earth by the Egyptian, shall pale to what the duke shall bring."

CHAPTER 27

"Hello Henrì…Thaddeus," Jared said, as the two men entered the ravaged living room.

Jared was crouched on the floor next to Zim and Chris, and across from them, on his haunches was Caym, who stood when the men entered. Henrì and Thaddeus both scuttled back at the sight of the dark green demon.

"What the hell's that?" Henrì cried, pointing at Caym as though he were a thing, not a living creature. He looked down at Zim. *"And that?"*

Olivia came running over to him and hugged him. Still, he was fixated on Caym; he seemed to barely notice her or Dorthea and Phineas who were on the other side of the room, she kneeling next to him and trying to wake him.

"Jared," Henrì said, his mouth hanging open. "Why…why are there demons here? And why aren't they trying to kill us?"

"I am not a demon, mortal man," Caym said, turning and taking Henrì's measure from head to toe. "I am a prince; the son of Duke Chax and Lady Pnemoxsis, and heir to the Northlands of Hell."

Henrì stared at Caym as though he had just assured him the moon was indeed made out of cheese—*Limburger,* to be precise. He slowly turned back to Jared and shook his head in bewilderment. "Explain?"

"They are The Fallen," Jared said. He looked up at Caym. The glow was coming back to his green skin now that he was exposed to the dark energy of the cosmos. "The male's name is Prince Caym. And she," he looked at Zim; her plump lips were moving against one another, "is Lady Zimarantha."

Henrì moved Olivia behind him. "He's not a prince, and she's certainly no lady."

"A sharp tongue this one has," Caym said, sneering at him.

"I'm not the one who's green," Henrì replied, looking at him in disgust.

"No, you are not, mortal," Caym said, readily and happily agreeing. "Nor do you have beauty, or skill, or power, or magnificence, or—"

"Caym!" Jared called out.

"You brought me to this miserable world," Caym said.

"I brought Zim, not you."

"That you brought any of them is the problem, Jared!" Henrì cried out, like a crazy man who had lost his invisible radio yet again.

Jared turned and spoke to everyone. "Look…the only reason I'm not still in Hell is because of them. They've helped me from beginning to end. They saved my life…*more than once*."

"And now they're here," Henrì panned. "Is it just now occurring to you that this is what they wanted all along?"

"I assure you it is not," Caym answered. "But this is what Astaroth has achieved for all of his grandiose scheming."

"What do you mean?" Henrì asked, turning from Caym to Jared, and then back again.

"Astaroth is here," Caym said, "and gone into the night with some mongrel hybrid and a mortal protected by the lady, Muchenlay."

"Is that…true?" Henrì asked, looking at Jared.

Jared nodded. "It is. He's here and on the loose."

Olivia gasped and covered her mouth. "Oh my God," she muttered.

"Astaroth's here along with these two demons," Henrì said, matter of fact. He looked up at hole of a ceiling that was left and around the ravaged room. "Our plan was to get you back to make things better, not worse."

"We're all lucky to be alive," Jared said, as he laid his hand on Chris's charred body and began pulling in the dark energy around him, funneling it into Chris. Chris's eyes opened, cracking the char that had sealed them shut. His eyes locked on Jared. "Hey buddy. You're going to be all right." Chris blinked at him. Jared smiled.

"No," Henrì muttered. "*No-no-no-no-no....* He's not going to be all right, or fine, or Ok, or anything. Now that Astaroth's here, he's going to suffer the same way we're going to. We're all going to suffer, and then he's going to kill us all." He looked at Zim and Caym. "If they don't kill us first."

CHAPTER 28

Orsha-Na—the Northlands—the realm of Duke Chax was never so flush with the souls of The Damned as it was now. The cities teemed with them. The towns overflowed with them. The cages that house The Damned were refilled as quickly as they were emptied by the long starved demons of Orsha-Na. Though now, with The Damned flowing back into the land, there was much damage to be undone.

Chax stood in the midst of the road leading to the forest of his lady. He wore a stark-white robe edged in gold over his magnificent wood-grain skin, it now renewed back to its illustrious glory after draining the essence of a few hundred of The Damned. Though, it would not all be as such if it were not for his mate, the Lady Pnemoxsis, who claimed the power of Hell once Astaroth relinquished it by escaping to earth. She arrived in the Westlands upon The Train of Souls with its cargo bays teeming with The Damned. And with The Damned, she launched vulag after vulag at the dome, breaching it, and allowing him and the others lords to escape the realm just in time; The Morning Star had nearly drained them completely, and he, Agares, and Beelzebub were nearly all ash when they came stumbling through the breach.

Chax turned his attention to the forest, which was now a barren landscape of rocks and dirt. Beside him was Farfal, who looked up at his master with ever-watchful eyes. And behind the great lion were rows and rows of The Damned who had been corralled by soldiers, and lulled into submission by the floating enchanters to be used in the restoration of the forest.

He closed his eyes and drew in the force of The Damned. The first five rows of them burst into flames and turned to ash; and as they did, trees burst out of the rocky landscape in front of him and went soaring high into the sky. Dark green grass began sprouting at the base of their trunks and spread out across the ground. The more of The Damned Chax burned, the more trees and shrubs and plants and grasses and streams and ponds came into being. The green wonderland of Varencia was returning.

Though then...a gloom came across the sky when it should not have. There was never gloom upon Hell's skies, though now—Chax opened his eyes—there was.

Chax felt his lifeforce become thready as he looked from dark horizon to dark horizon, and Wormwood nowhere to be seen. He looked straight up. Far off in the distance, barely even perceptible to his celestial eyes, he saw a glimmer of Wormwood racing off. Chax knew where the sun-demon was headed and what that meant. Wormwood's departure was an omen, both for Hell and for earth, bearing good tidings for neither.

Chax walked back and mounted Farfal. The great lion rose and turned around, facing Palace Adoja. He kicked at Farfal's flanks and sent them riding off to the palace. The horns of war were about to sound out again. Though this time, he thought, it would not be a civil war amongst The Fallen, but one against their celestial brethren, the Celestial Host and The Lamb, who would lead them into battle; for if Wormwood was gone from Hell, that meant The Lamb was on his way to earth, and bearing a sword in his right hand for the wicked, and in his left, redemption for the repentant. Though, Chax thought, that also might mean doom for The Fallen.

How, he wondered, as he entered the city walls, could there be balance upon the earth when Astaroth, Caym, and Zim were upon it; and they were all fallen; and of the Celestial Host, there was only one there, Miel? As quick as the question came to him, the answer to his riddle revealed itself with the face of Lady Zimarantha coming to his mind's eye.

"Love," he whispered. *It cannot be*, he thought, even though he knew it to be true. Wormwood's absence from Hell was his living proof.

Hell was weak. The civil war had decimated the legions. And legions upon legions were what they needed if they were to have chance of defeating the Celestial Host. Now, he thought, he had to be wiser, for there was no way they could defeat, let alone mount a defense against them.

There was a new enemy to be dealt with, and his name was Miel, Chax thought. And though they were realms away and separated by space and time, he did not worry about being able to reach him, for he, in a sense, was already there...and his name was Caym—Prince of Orsha-Na, son of Chax.

"You are the son of the Sky Father," he spoke, as though Caym were next to him "...and of Adroa, and of Odin, and of Zeus, and of Atum-Ra...do not fail your lord, god.

"Love," Chax muttered, as he thought of Zim and Jared together. "I will see you both in the ether before I let love fall me. I am Chax, after all."

CHAPTER 29

Love, Lucifer thought, and then smiled.

"Indeed, my lord, Chax…tis' love that has now wrought this upon us all," Lucifer said, through the ghostly apparition of himself seated upon his platinum throne.

"Fare thee well, Wormwood," Lucifer called out. "Fly on to earth and let it be known to all that live, that their days are now measured, and I— The Morning Star of Heaven—shall soon awake and rise, and claim the glory of my rightful place beside The Father, The Lamb, and The Ghost.

"Go thee on, Wormwood, and proclaim to all that I am Lucifer.

"I am firstborn.

"I am life.

"I am death.

"I am god!

"And it shall be so."

"This I say in the name of The Father, The Lamb, The Ghost… and myself!

"Amen."

CHAPTER 30
EPILOGUE

The place seemed like tranquility served on a platter, Jared thought, as he looked out from the back porch of an abandoned home set deep in the country they had found. They were not far from Nuxta, where his family first encountered the Egyptian, Tamen. Who knew then, he wondered, that they would now be at this moment, where the world and beyond, all the way to the end of the cosmos, was set to fall into ruin?

He rested his arms on the railing and leaned on it. He was dressed in jeans and a white t-shirt, looking more the part of a country boy hanging out after chores, than a celestial who had just come face-to-face with Astaroth and Lucifer, and had survived to tell the tale. Though the tale, he thought, was far from over.

He needed the serenity of the farm right now. He needed Zim to be right where she was, which was just a hundred steps in front of him standing in the unkempt, waist high grasses, facing the orange-red sunset, knowing she was looking beyond that...she seeing the heavens and feeling the dark energy that had been denied her in Hell now flowing through her. This world must be strange to her, he thought, she having lived for thousands of years under the perverted white light of the mad, arm-waving Wormwood who never set.

Dorthea had wanted to go home. Though there, or anywhere that was familiar, was to be avoided. And where they were was a good move for now, he thought. The cities were in utter mayhem. Yikan had not been heard from in days, though neither had they heard anything from Astaroth. Still, Jared had no doubt Astaroth would strike, and soon.

"I didn't think I could sneak up on you," Henrì said, moving up next to him. He looked out at Zim, and then turned back to Jared. "You can't do this. You can't, Jared."

"She's not our enemy."

He huffed and laughed. He turned and leaned his waist against railing's post. "Yes...she is."

Jared turned to him. "She helped me, Henrì—way more than you know."

"Ok and so what? You don't fall in love with her because of it. What are you thinking?"

"It's not like that."

"You're really going to try and rationalize this?" he said, through a crooked grin. "What story do you expect me to be OK with where you and her," he pointed at Zim, "is supposed to make any sense at all?"

"She's changed Henrì."

Henrì shook his head. "She's playing you. And the one on the roof is too."

"His name is Caym."

Henrì scoffed. "I don't care. I don't want him keeping watch over us, and I don't want her near us."

"She wants to atone. I can feel it. I know her."

"You don't know her, Jared," he said. "But she knows you and your weakness for her."

"Low, Henrì," Jared said, turning away. "Really low."

"It's true."

"It's a lie," Jared insisted. "Our enemy is her enemy, and that's Astaroth. We all want him taken down; and I tell you what, Henrì, we're going to need them to do it."

"So you've got it all figured out, like the last time," Henrì muttered. "I distinctly recall me telling you it's a trap and you saying you want to spring it."

"Now we're back at that?"

Henrì looked at Zim and sighed. "No...now we're at this."

Jared was about to reply, though turned around instead and looked out past Zim. He felt something moving toward them.

"Wha? What is it Jared?" Henrì asked, turning and looking out toward the field.

Jared saw it—saw him—though didn't want to say, for at the moment, he didn't quite believe who he was seeing running across the field at such an inhuman pace. From behind him, Jared felt a whoosh of air, and felt Chris come up next to him. Even Chris had sensed who was coming, Jared thought.

"Chris, don't!" Jared said, holding his arm in front of his friend, whose body had finally healed and been remade. "I want to hear what he says."

"I don't," Chris said. "I want to kill him."

Caym slid off the roof like he was riding a wave and landed just in front of them on the grass. "Not if I get to him first," Caym said, walking out toward Zim and conjuring his flaming sword. Zim conjured hers as well. He walked over and stood next to her.

"Who…who is it? Astaroth?" Henrì asked, his eyes becoming wide.

"No, not Astaroth," Jared said.

"Someone just as bad," Chris muttered.

"Who?" Henrì asked.

"Yikan," Jared answered.

"Yikan? Here?" Henrì asked, just as Yikan slowed and stopped in front of Zim and Caym, and then held his arms up in surrender. "Jared, kill that sonofabitch!"

Zim and Caym marched him over to them by the point of their swords aimed at his neck on either side. Dorthea, Thaddeus, Olivia, and Phineas came out the back and stared at Yikan with open mouths and wide, unbelieving eyes.

"So this is Astaroth's lap dog," Caym said. He brought Yikan to a halt with a move of his flaming sword just under his neck.

"I wouldn't say we were ever that close," Yikan replied, moving his head back as far from the flames as he could.

"You weren't saying that when he was promising to put the earth at your feet," Jared said. "You know you're not leaving here alive, right?"

"I've come to not expect much of anything anymore."

"Good philosophy," Henrì said with a sneer.

"Why are you here, mongrel?" Zim questioned. "Speak before you die."

"I have been betrayed."

"Good," Henrì crowed.

"Eric and Blain have traded allegiance," Yikan said. "They tried to kill me the same night they tried to kill all of you. Astaroth has yet to regain his full strength, and Eric was never my equal, obviously." He shrugged. "Still, I was lucky to have escaped. I went to that abode of yours in the swamps," he looked at Henrì, "and have been following all of your ever since."

"Why?" Jared asked. "Because now you're being hunted again? You put the entire planet in jeopardy, murdered scores of innocent people, all because you're an egomaniac; and now you've followed us here because why? What the hell do you expect from us?"

"Tis' a good question, dog," Caym added. "There is no one here who doesn't want to see you turned into sludge. I'm quite eager to do it myself."

"You may all want that, and may have prayed for it many a night," Yikan told them, "but my death may not serve you well. In fact, it may just doom you all."

"Bullshit!" Henrì seethed. "Just kill him, Jared. We've got bigger problems to worry about than going round and round with this psychopath."

"You can't kill him!" Yikan cried out.

"Astaroth?" Jared asked, and then shook his head. "Demons die...I've seen it. They just turn to ash; and Astaroth's no different."

"That's not what I mean," Yikan said. "I'm saying...you can't kill him without me."

"That's a lie!" Zim said.

"It's the truth," Yikan replied. "Part of the truth."

"See?" Henrì crowed. "Lies and more lies."

"You can't kill him," Yikan said, "but we can send him back to Hell."

"Because you know how?" Henrì asked, with a sneering grin.

"Yes!" Yikan answered stoutly. "Once I had enough mortals to feed upon, and with a spell from the tome, I was going to part the veil between earth and Hell long enough for him to transform me into a celestial. I was never going to allow him to pass through."

"No surprise there," Jared opined. "You wanted it all."

"The point being, Miel," he said, "is that if we can part the veil but a little, or perhaps, even a great deal, we may be able to send the demon back to where he came from."

"And what's in it for you?" Jared asked.

"It's another trick, Jared," Henrì warned.

"Not this time, mortal," Yikan said. "I heard what you said back at the mansion, Jared. 'There's God's side, Lucifer's side, and then Astaroth's—a God and two would-be gods; it's time for me to pick one, instead of trying to be one.'"

Chris moved up in front of Yikan. "We'll do fine on our—" He stopped abruptly. He looked up at Jared; his brows furrowed. "I just felt something strange. Did you?" Jared nodded.

"I felt it, too!" Caym said.

"As did I," Zim added.

Jared looked toward the northern sky; it now dark and the light of stars light years away were twinkling upon it, except for one. One of them shone brighter than the others, and with his celestial vision, he could see that it was coming closer by the moment.

"It cannot be!" Caym muttered, staring off at it.

"Jared-baby, what is it?" Dorthea asked. "What are you all looking at?"

Jared turned around slowly and faced them all. His face was as grim as the voice that came from his mouth. "It's Wormwood, Hell's sun-demon," he said. "He's come to proclaim the End of Days."

GOD OF GODS

THE GODS SAGA III: ALPHA AND OMEGA

Thanks to Sara Stinkski for lending me two of
the best books on writing that I have ever read.

Stephen King's "On Writing"

and

White and Strunks' "Elements of Style"

The flawless and bewitching dance of the
Rise and Fall by the Countess Asani

is dedicated to

Misty Copeland – America's first black
Principal Dancer for the American Ballet Theater

To my family, friends, and fans who have
been so patient with me through this process…

Thank you!

God of Gods - The Gods Saga III – Alpha and Omega

Coming soon!